GW01036303

Magicom

The Arcannen Chronicles

Magicom

Adam Joseph

Independently published.

For my mum.

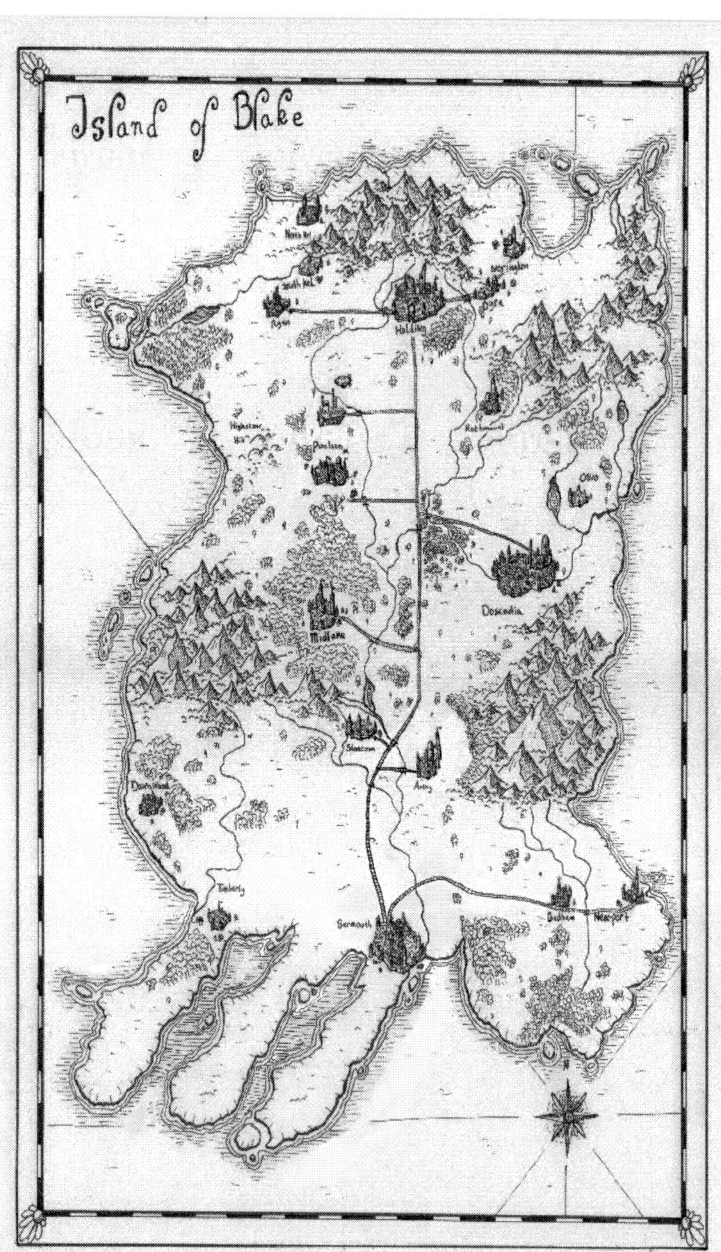
Island of Blake
Halding
Poulson
Olio
Doscadia
Midfane
Timberly
Sermouth
Nearport

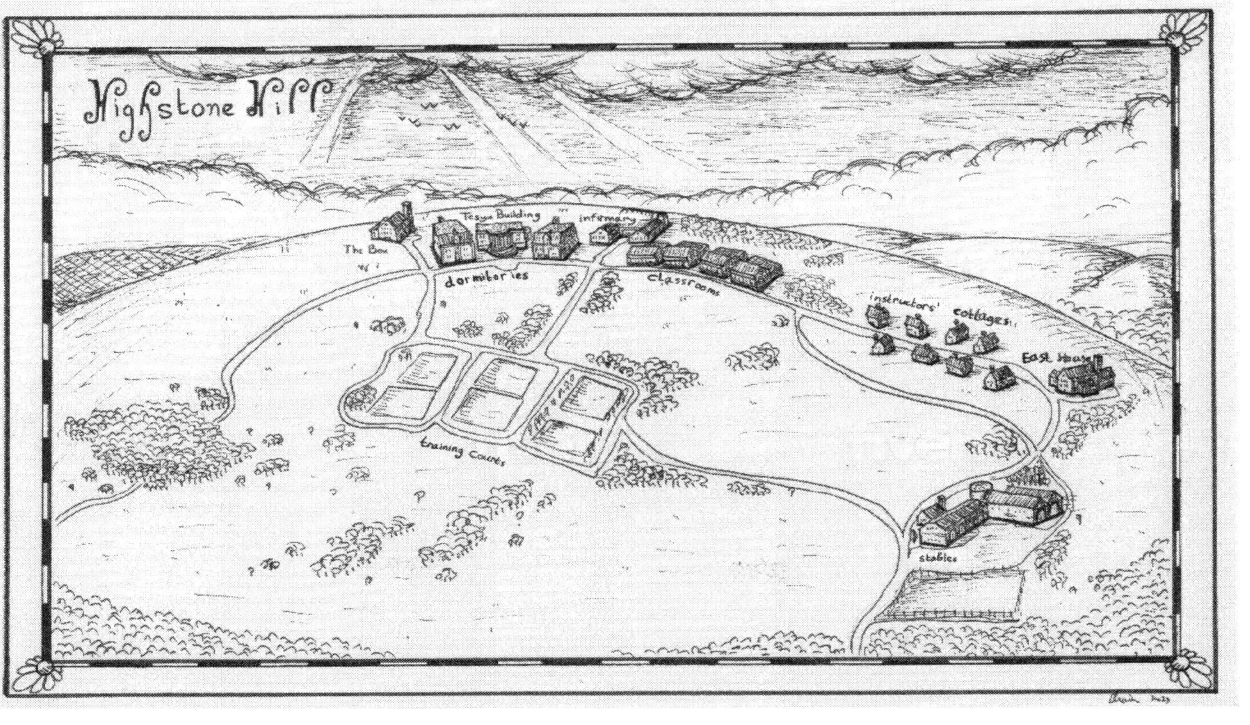

Highstone Hill
The Box
Tesyn Building
infirmary
dormitories
classrooms
instructors' cottages
East House
training courts
stables

PROLOGUE

Holding Castle was not the structure of old. Its grounds had long since been replaced by barracks, an outer wall separating the soldiers' lodgings from the rest of the city. An inner wall enclosed a keep and a bailey, where several blimps were stationed, 'Magicom' painted on their surfaces in large, red letters.

Rox Salvamal, general of Magicom's private army, strode atop the ramparts with purpose. He cared nothing for the relic from a long time past, aside from the strategic and symbolic nature of using a castle as his base of operations. Once, it would have catered to a monarchy ruling over the city and, indeed, the whole of the Island of Blake; now, it only served to demonstrate Magicom's position of power.

The brass hilt of Salvamal's sword, attached at his hip, reflected the nearby torchlight while the soft thud of his boots filled the air. As he neared the wooden doors leading into the keep, two soldiers wearing the same grey uniform as their general came into view. They saluted.

"Good evening, sir," one said. "He is waiting for you inside."

Salvamal took a moment to steel himself before pushing open the doors.

Darkness shrouded the room he found himself in, the only light coming from a fire that crackled and spat from its hearth in the stone wall. A polished, oaken table dominated the room's centre, at the head of which sat Linus Atkins, a government official dressed in a smartly tailored suit with amber skin and hair as grey as Salvamal's own. He wore a self-satisfied smile as he watched Salvamal approach.

Salvamal conjured a fireball in the palm of his hand, a swirling mass of heat and flame, and that smile soon vanished. Masking his own amusement, Salvamal moved to a bracket on one side of the wall, cupping his hand to light the torch within before extinguishing the flame and turning back to face the official.

"Was that really necessary, General?" Atkins asked, his voice tinged with irritation.

"Apologies. There wasn't a lot of light to see by."

"Why have you called me here? Other than to show off your magic, I mean?"

Salvamal met his gaze. Atkins was a hero of the Spirit Mage Wars and had a right arm made from bronze, currently resting against the table's surface, to prove it. Not one to let personal injury get in the way of ambition, Atkins had used his status to become the single most powerful figure on the Governmental Council. Not a lot went through without his say-so.

Making this meeting a tiresome but necessary one.

"I have discovered the identity of Ashes' leader," Salvamal said at last.

If Atkins was surprised by this information, he didn't show it. "You are sure of this?"

"Certain. His name is August Silvershield; my informants report he's in Holding right now, recruiting." Salvamal took an exaggerated breath before continuing. "My proposal is this: the government issues a warrant for his arrest and we close the gates of the city until my soldiers can detain him."

Atkins drummed the fingers of his flesh-and-bone hand against the table. "Ashes are little more than thieves – they steal arcannen potions from your company's clinics because they don't like to pay for their magic like everybody else. Do you not worry, General, that issuing an arrest warrant for this man will show they pose a problem for Magicom? Would it not be easier to simply … make him disappear?"

Salvamal stepped closer to the official. "You speak as if Ashes are exclusively a Magicom problem. *Your* government puts forward the laws, including the one that states only Magicom can distribute arcannen. By stealing arcannen, Ashes are going against the government, and the people of Blake need to be shown this cannot be tolerated. *That* is why we must move against Ashes' leader – publicly – to ensure all know the consequences. Of course, if we are not aligned in this, I could always speak to my board."

Atkins' eyes narrowed, but this time Salvamal knew there would be no more questions. His barely concealed threat would have seen to that. *This whole meeting is a farce anyway. One day soon, none of this will be necessary.*

"Very well, General. I will inform the council. Bring Silvershield in."

"Matters will be put into motion immediately." Salvamal glanced away from Atkins, already dismissing him. "I assume the soldiers outside were sent by Lieutenant Rookevelt to show you in? I will ask them to escort you back to your carriage."

"Lieutenant Rookevelt accompanied me to the keep himself. There were no other soldiers."

The government official and Salvamal looked at one another for a moment, a look that lasted long enough for

Salvamal to realise something was wrong. *It's nothing. Rookevelt probably sent them so we wouldn't be disturbed.* He moved to the door and tried the handle.

It was locked.

"What is it, General?" Atkins demanded as Salvamal cursed. "Those were your soldiers, were they not?"

Before Salvamal had a chance to respond, a series of explosions reverberated from outside, an almighty staccato that made it feel as if the whole keep was shaking. He froze in place. *No … they wouldn't dare …* Atkins was out of his chair at once, looking at Salvamal in horror.

"Wait here," said Salvamal before the man could speak. There was another door on the opposite side of the room, one that led into the rest of the keep. Salvamal marched to it. Once outside, he sprinted through the corridor and up a spiral stone staircase built into one of the towers. Finally, he found what he was looking for – a slit looking out into the bailey.

Men and women were in the courtyard below, fireballs streaking upwards as they tore holes in the remaining airborne blimps. The others had already fallen. No longer able to retain their shape without the helium within their envelopes, they now lay flat and deflated on the ground alongside the smashed metal of their gondolas. Even from where he was, the smell of burning rubber reached Salvamal's nostrils while shouting and cheering filled the air. Salvamal didn't know where his soldiers were, but he had no doubt Ashes had barricaded them outside the inner wall like they'd barricaded him in the keep.

And he knew that August Silvershield was somewhere below, his supposed recruitment in the city a ruse that Salvamal's useless informants had swallowed. Somehow, he'd made his way into the heart of Magicom's defences and declared war.

Rage filled Rox Salvamal, a tempest of emotion that internally screamed his frustration. He pushed his fingertips against the tower wall so hard he could feel the grains of stone crumble beneath. The pressure did not dispel his anger, but it did focus his mind, allowing him to make a promise to himself.

Wherever Silvershield went, wherever he tried to hide, Salvamal would find him.

And end him.

CHAPTER ONE

"Young man, you are filthy!"

Roeden Mason managed to look suitably guilty under his mother's stern stare as he halted in the hallway of the guesthouse, his boots, trousers and shirt caked in mud. His face was smeared in it too, but he couldn't help but laugh as Axe, the long-legged terrier, bounded over and stood on his hind legs, licking Roeden's face.

"What am I going to do with you?" she said, pushing Axe away and wiping his cheek with a napkin. Roeden screwed up his face as the rough fabric rubbed against it. "Have you been playing that fighting game again?"

"It's not a *fighting* game," he told his mother, rolling his eyes. "It's a *war* game." The children of Bodham's favourite game was to pretend they were in Ashes, acting out magical battles or duelling with wooden swords given to them by the town's amused carpenter. From the crooked, cobblestoned streets to the labyrinth of alleyways, their town was their battlefield. The adults left them to it. After all, better they were playing within Bodham's high stone walls than out in the wilderness.

"And the difference is?" sighed his mother with a shake of her head. "Don't bother answering. It's all beyond my understanding, I'm sure. Well, the boiler's on. You'd better have a bath while I prepare your supper.

Phantex will probably be wanting one as well."

"Phantex's coming home?" Roeden beamed. It'd been weeks since he'd last seen his brother.

"To help with the move tomorrow," she said, smiling at his reaction, although he didn't miss the anxious look in her eyes. It seemed to appear every time they discussed their relocation to Sermouth. "A letter arrived by bird earlier."

Roeden washed himself with haste after that, slowed down only by the time it took to dry his thick, curly hair and wishing, not for the first time, that his mother would let him have it braided like Phantex's. Ten years old, she had argued, was too young, something he could not see the logic in *at all*. He dressed himself in another shirt and trousers from his bedroom on the top floor and, on his descent back to the hallway, found his brother had arrived and was talking to their mother near the front door.

"Roe," acknowledged Phantex, spotting him at the bottom of the stairs, his quiet voice, as always, seeming to belie his height and strength. Despite his brother being fifteen years Roeden's senior, their shared copper skin, narrow faces and quick, brown eyes hinted at their kinship – if not the braided hair. Roeden bounded the rest of the way and ran into an embrace as Phantex, who was wearing riding leathers, laughed and said, "I hear you and your friends have been having all sorts of adventures."

Roeden grinned as he looked up. "Well, we can't fight for real – like you. Have you been hunting manabeasts, Phantex? Is that why you've been away so much lately? Mother won't tell me."

Phantex opened his mouth to reply but seemed to hesitate – a mistake, Roeden thought, because it gave their mother a chance to jump in.

"Don't speak so flippantly about manabeasts, Roeden!

You've no idea how dangerous the wilderness is. Thank the Trinity we have your brother to protect us on the road tomorrow."

"I'll take an arcannen potion before we leave," said Phantex, turning his eyes to their mother. "I have plenty spare at the moment." Roeden noticed this comment seemed to make his mother purse her lips. He didn't understand – surely that was the sensible thing to do. Phantex wouldn't be able to use magic without one.

"Do you think we'll see any … of them?" he asked Phantex, thinking his question might go down better if he didn't name the creatures. He was wrong.

"No," their mother replied. "We'll travel by day and stick to the Southern Road – the hunters keep it relatively safe. Now, it's getting late. I'll prepare your supper, then I want you to make your way up to your bedroom and stay there, understood? I have a few people to see before we leave tomorrow and both of you need to rest. You'll have plenty of time to speak to Phantex on the road."

Plenty of time to speak to him while you're there monitoring, thought Roeden, but his mother's tone suggested arguing wouldn't be an option, so he put on his meekest look and nodded his assent before heading up the stairs, already planning to speak with Phantex as soon as she left.

The box room he occupied held a small bed on which Axe lay dozing, facing a slanted window built above an alcove in the wall. The window was ajar, as his mother had wanted him to 'air his room' before their departure, whatever that meant. A stack of boxes filled with his clothes and books sat in one corner, ready to load into the wagon his mother had hired. Roeden dug in one of these until he found a particularly large leather-bound tome titled *Jarian the Dragon Hunter*. He dropped onto his bed, snuggling into the warmth of Axe's fur as he read.

Jarian was a hero from the Ancient Days who travelled the Six Isles with his friend, Felix, vanquishing dragons and saving villages. By the time his mother arrived with a baked potato and butter, Roeden was already engrossed in the story of Jarian felling the Chaos Dragon from atop a black tower. He finished as he ate and was still in the process of deciding which to read next when he heard muffled voices from below. He briefly hesitated but then jumped off his bed and moved onto the window ledge inside the alcove to listen.

"You needn't worry so, Mother," came Phantex's soft voice, apparently continuing a conversation that had started inside. "This is a precaution, nothing more, but a necessary one. August and I worry Magicom might make the connection. He's already gone to great pains to protect his own family."

Roeden had never gone so still in his life. *August? Magicom?*

"You don't understand how it's been recently," replied their mother. "Magicom soldiers swarming the town, looking for any sign of August Silvershield and Ashes. Word is it's the same everywhere after what happened at Holding Castle last month. Speaking of which, please tell me you weren't involved."

"Ashes needed to make a statement; the people of Blake need to see Magicom aren't untouchable."

"Are those August's words or yours? No, save your retort – I don't want to argue, Phantex. I'm proud of you for fighting Magicom, as would your father have been. But please, reconsider your decision to fight with Ashes. Stay in Sermouth with us. You're trained in magic and you're intelligent; it would be easy for you to find work there. Please consider it … for the sake of our family."

There was a pause. "I will," Roeden heard his brother

say eventually.

As the back door shut softly, Roeden lowered himself to the floor, stunned. It all made sense. The sudden moving, Phantex's disappearances, his mother's fears. Phantex was in Ashes! Which meant, Roeden reasoned as his mind started whirring, that Phantex knew August Silvershield! Roeden thought about the man whose face was plastered on wanted posters throughout Bodham, the young man with long hair and dangerous eyes.

Roeden thought then about the warning his mother had given Phantex. She was wrong to try to talk Phantex into leaving Ashes, he decided. Going against Magicom was dangerous, Roeden understood that, but Ashes were heroes just like Jarian the Dragon Hunter. Normal people might avoid danger, but heroes do not. As for their father, he had died when Roeden was still a baby, so Roeden didn't think it mattered what he would have thought.

Assuming his mother had now departed the guesthouse, Roeden made his way back downstairs and spotted Phantex through the open door of the dining room, the nearest room to the bottom of the stairs. His brother was standing by the front window, clearly deep in thought, but seemed to sense Roeden's approach and drew the curtains, turning with a smile. Candles burned on the rectangular table to complement the oil lamps attached to the walls, but the fireplace was empty, and the room felt cold for it. Aside from the chairs around the table, and the carpeted floor, the room was bare, everything else already packed away.

"Roe," Phantex said, shaking his head now. "It's been barely a minute since Mother left."

"I'm too excited to sleep," replied Roeden, his excuses ready. "I can't wait to see Sermouth. Is it true they have steam trains?"

"Tracks connect the Three Big Cities," said Phantex, pulling out a chair and sitting, which Roeden took as his cue to do the same, cross-legged. "They also have buildings taller than you can imagine and a library half the size of Bodham." Roeden's jaw dropped and Phantex chuckled. "You'll have more than just *Jarian the Dragon Hunter* to read, Roe. But you'll also have to make sure you're helpful to Mother – she taught you your letters and numbers for a reason. Most children in this town will grow up to be miners or farmers, but a young man who can read and write could go a long way in a city."

"Why didn't you stay at Wing, Phantex?"

Phantex seemed surprised at the question. "Wing? I thought we were talking about Sermouth. Why do you want to know about my time at Wing?"

Because I'd rather train as a mage than bookkeep at a guesthouse.

Roeden felt it best not to air his thoughts aloud, though. Phantex might try to discourage him like their mother often did. Instead, he tried to sound unconcerned. "I was just curious."

Phantex's look was appraising, but it didn't stop him from answering. "I left because I finished my four years there. That's how it works – Wing trains young men and women for a year to use and control magic, granting them mage status. Mages repay Wing with three years of service. Wing, in turn, makes its coin and papers from those who hire their mages." He looked at Roeden closely. "Just because anyone can train to use magic doesn't mean everyone does. It can be a hard life."

Roeden chose his next words carefully. "They say August Silvershield's a powerful mage. Did he train at Wing at the same time as you, Phantex? I've seen those posters – he looks about the same age. Ashes must be full of mages. Do you … do you think he'd let someone related to one of his followers join?"

Phantex stared at him for a moment. "You know," his brother said at last. "How?"

Any thoughts of deceit evaporated under Phantex's stare. "I heard you and Mother talking just now."

Phantex shook his head again, although there was something different in his expression this time. "Of course, your room's right above the back door. Poor Mother – she's been so careful about keeping this from you, and then one lapse and you find out! Then again, it probably never occurred to her you might be eavesdropping from above."

"It wasn't on purpose! Mother left my window open earlier. Are we moving because of him, Phantex? Because of August?"

Phantex's smile was tinged with bitterness. "I think you already know the answer to that question. I'm sorry to do this to you and to Mother, but we're no longer safe in a town so close to Holding. One day Magicom could find out who I am, like they have August, and come looking for me. It'll be easier to stay hidden in Sermouth – it's a big city, and although they have clinics like everywhere else, Magicom's presence and influence are minimal. Besides, Mother will do well with her new guesthouse there. Away from people who know of her connection to me."

They were silent for a moment, Roeden processing everything Phantex had told him. "I can't wait until I'm old enough to train at Wing."

Phantex opened his mouth to respond, but three loud bangs on the front door cut him off. He turned his head and frowned. "Was Mother expecting anyone?"

Roeden shook his head. Phantex walked to the

window and pulled aside one of the curtains, peering through the uncovered part of the glass pane. Roeden heard a sudden intake of breath from his brother. Phantex turned back, his face serious. "Roe, we need to leave out of the back. Now. No arguments."

Roeden slowly got to his feet. "You sound like Mother. What …"

But before Roeden could finish, Phantex had gripped him by the shoulders, turned him around and was marching him through the length of the hallway to where the kitchen was located.

Roeden's heartbeat quickened as he realised something was terribly wrong.

The kitchen was a large open space with a counter in the middle. Usually, there would've been pots, pans and utensils hanging from all sides, but because of their move, these were all contained in boxes that sat on the wooden worktops. They reached the back door, and Phantex turned the knob, opening it to the alleyway beyond.

Where half a dozen Magicom soldiers waited.

Roeden felt a lurch in his stomach. There was no mistaking that uniform – all grey with a red "M" stitched on the breast. He'd seen it on the soldiers posted outside the town's clinic often enough. He felt a protective arm across his chest as Phantex backed them both to the centre of the kitchen. Roeden's heart was now thumping. *Are they … are they here for Phantex? Do they know he's in Ashes?* The soldiers moved in, stone-faced, two blocking the exit while another walked through the kitchen and into the hallway. The others surrounded them, their hands behind their backs, silent.

Phantex knelt before him, placing a hand on his shoulder, drawing Roeden's eyes away from the soldiers' sheathed blades. "When I give you the opportunity, you must run," Phantex whispered.

"But …"

"Please, Roeden." Phantex's eyes were wide and pleading, his grip on Roeden's shoulder strong. In the background, Roeden could hear the front door unlocking. "Find Mother. Get out of here. I'll be taken, but August will find me. Promise me, Roeden – you … you must be smart about this."

Phantex squeezed his shoulder until he nodded, yet Roeden was still having difficulty processing everything. One moment he and Phantex had been discussing Wing and Ashes, the next, Magicom soldiers were invading their home. Phantex frowned, a look of concern in his eyes. Not wanting his brother to worry, Roeden nodded again, this time more firmly. Phantex fixed him with a grim smile.

"Going somewhere, Mr Mason?" A new soldier strode in from the hallway, his eyes moving over the boxes and chests stacked around the kitchen. He had a young, pale face and a shock of blond hair, yet his demeanour, and the fact he was the only soldier with a red stripe around his arm, suggested he was in charge. Phantex didn't answer as he rose, but the soldier wasn't deterred. "Ah, you're waiting to see how much I know, aren't you? Well, how's this? Your full name's Phantex Mason, you're twenty-five, and you were born in the town of Bodham. You attended Wing between your sixteenth and twentieth years, where you met and befriended August Silvershield."

Phantex shrugged. "What point are you trying to make? I haven't seen August Silvershield in years."

"Oh, haven't you? That's a shame." The man ran his finger along the surface of the counter before examining one of the boxes. Roeden watched him with apprehension. The man spun to face Phantex. "You never said where it was you were going."

"My family and I are moving to Doscadia," said Phantex. "My mother wants my brother to grow up in one of the Three Big Cities to give him a better chance at life. She's been planning it for years."

"This is your brother?" The man moved closer. He placed his hands behind his back and peered down at Roeden. "Nice to meet you, young man. My name's Commander Remi Maynard. Doscadia is a far nicer place to live in than this dump of a town, I'll admit." He raised his eyes. "Well, if you haven't seen August Silvershield in years, Mr Mason, then we've nothing more to discuss." The man turned to leave. Roeden let out a sigh of relief and made to move from behind Phantex's back, but Phantex kept him there with a shift of his arms. That was when Roeden noticed the other soldiers hadn't moved.

"But you have to admit, your attempt to slip out of the back just now looks rather suspicious," said Maynard, spinning back around. "As does your family's relocation so soon after the Holding Castle incident. Some might make the assumption you're trying to hide them because of your connection to Silvershield." The commander crossed his arms. "If that was your plan, you're too late, Mr Mason. As soon as General Salvamal discovered Silvershield trained at Wing, he made a point of finding everyone Silvershield was known to be friendly with. Right now, up and down Blake, all Silvershield's former colleagues are having similar visits. You'll have to come with us for questioning."

"Like I said, I haven't seen August Silvershield in years, but I will of course cooperate and answer any questions Magicom have," said Phantex. Roeden shot him a look. His brother spoke in a pleasant tone as if the whole thing was a simple misunderstanding. "Roeden, you stay here and let Mother know what's happened, and tell her to go ahead to Doscadia for me. You'll do that, won't you, Roeden?" Phantex's look said everything: *be smart*. Roeden nodded. There seemed no other way out of the situation.

"Oh, no, Mr Mason," said Maynard with a little laugh. "Your brother and mother will be coming along too. We shall need them if you need any persuasion to … tell the truth."

Phantex moved so quickly Roeden actually yelled out in alarm. His brother swung an arm out and a fireball shot towards the back of the kitchen, exploding the back door off its hinges with a bang and throwing the soldiers standing there sideways. He shot another towards Maynard, but the commander was too quick, deflecting the fireball with a wave of his arm, so it exploded to the side, a look of triumph on his face as he drew his sword. Roeden stared. *He redirected it? Was that … wind magic?*

"Roeden, go!" yelled Phantex, pushing him towards the back door. Roeden coughed as smoke filled the kitchen, the Magicom soldiers disappearing in the haze, but the sound of unsheathing swords was unmistakable. "Remember what you promised!" Roeden stood there, frozen in place. Phantex gave him another push. "I need you to do this! To warn Mother! Go!"

The word 'need' had an effect on Roeden. He ran through the remains of the back door as more bangs resounded and more of the kitchen exploded in dust and smoke. Looking back, he saw Phantex guarding the exit with his arms out. He felt an instinctual need to stay and help his brother, but he'd promised, and that, more than anything else, forced him to retreat.

He ran through the alleyway and into the nearest street. The streetlamps were lit, illuminating the brick walls and slate roofs of the houses, as well as the cobblestones beneath. He stopped, hesitating. He knew he should do as Phantex asked, but fear for his brother consumed him and leaving him felt like a betrayal.

He was still hesitating when someone grabbed him from behind. He swivelled to find a sallow-skinned, middle-aged man holding his arm. The man wore a suit that seemed to hang from him, making Roeden think of a scarecrow.

"What happened?" the man demanded. "Where's Phantex? I saw you coming from his guesthouse …"

"Get off me!" shouted Roeden, shrugging him off. Was this man with Magicom? He didn't look like it – but how could Roeden tell?

"They found him," muttered the man as he looked towards where the back of the guesthouse could be seen, smoke billowing into the air. When he looked back at Roeden, his expression was more discerning. "You're his brother, aren't you? You must come with me."

"I have to find my mother!"

"Your mother?" The man shook his head. "No, we don't have time. I saw how many came through the gate. As soon as they have Phantex detained, they'll seal off the town so you and your mother can't do the same. Come – I have a horse. We'll leave while the gate's unguarded and your brother's occupying them, but we must be quick." The man tried to push him forward, but Roeden stood his ground, causing the man to let out a breath of impatience. "This is your only chance!"

"I said *no*!" shouted Roeden, turning to run in the opposite direction. Whether this man was with Magicom or a friend of Phantex's, he didn't care. He would find and warn their mother – he'd promised. But as soon as he looked away, something clipped him over the back of his head, and the world fell into darkness.

CHAPTER TWO

The manabeast's yellow eyes locked onto Pink. A wolf-type, matted grey fur covered its mangy body, and drool dripped from its muzzle as it bared its teeth, a low growl emanating from its throat. Pink tried to ready herself in a battle stance, knowing there were only seconds before the door to its cage opened, but all she could imagine was what those teeth could do to her flesh.

"Sara Arrancove, you have one minute," came Gabriel's soft voice from the other side of the fence, where he sat at a wooden table with Victorian. The assistant master of Wing did not have to speak loudly to be heard.

"Good luck, Pink!" called Victorian.

Something about those words helped Pink to master her fear. Sara Arrancove was the frightened girl who'd arrived at Wing untrained and unconfident. Pink wasn't just the nickname given to her on account of her unnatural hair colour; it was the confident trainee she'd become. She could do this. *Just follow your training.*

Instructor May, who'd been standing behind the cage, unclasped its door from the side, swung it open and moved backwards. The manabeast came for Pink at once, its streamlined body crossing the training court in a matter of seconds, a cerulean-blue sphere of energy forming from its mouth even as it ran. She threw herself to one side just in time, coming up into a roll as its magic came close enough for her to feel the heat whooshing by her face.

Landing on one knee, she pushed her arms out, so her palms were facing the beast. It stopped and hunched low, taking a few steps back.

It knows, thought Pink. *I'm not the first it's gone against today. It's learnt that when opponents extend their arms, there's going to be pain.*

Keeping her arms outstretched, she rose to her feet and side-stepped across the court. The manabeast remained low and watched her. She focused – bringing her right arm down with her palm facing up, simultaneously activating the arcannen in her blood. She could sense it like a living thing, desperate to be used as it shot through her body, allowing her to *feel* the elements. She summoned air to the palm of her hand before sparking to life a fireball that swirled above her skin, the heat dulled by the added protection. Pink threw it in the direction of the beast, striking the tarmac before it in an explosion of noise. She ran to close the distance as the air filled with smoke, already creating another. *I'll strike it at close range; I won't even need the full minute!* But before she could follow through, a blue light appeared from within the dusty cloud. She tried to roll out of the way, but this time she was struck on her side, the force causing her to lose her footing, sending her skidding along the hard ground.

She was on her feet at once. There was pain, as if someone had poured boiling water on her skin, but her uniform's syntaxicite material, although shredded at the waist, had done its job and absorbed much of the damage.

The dissipating smoke ahead revealed the outline of her opponent. She muttered a curse. *Just because I couldn't see it didn't mean it couldn't see me.* Her mind worked quickly. *It'll expect another fireball, so I'll blast it with wind – it won't see that coming as easily.* She shot out her arms, but the manabeast didn't retreat this time. Instead, it charged as if trying to reach her before she could summon her magic.

Suddenly, she realised there was no time.

The thought had barely completed when the manabeast was lifted in the air with a yelp and suspended high above the ground, scarcely five feet from her. A scuffle of boots drew Pink's attention to the fact Victorian had entered the training court and was using her own magic to levitate it. It didn't resist – again, it must have learned it was useless to do so – but Pink was close enough to see the feral look in its eyes.

She forced back a shudder.

"The minute is up," said Gabriel from his position outside of the fence. "Well done, Sara."

Dragging her eyes away, Pink made her way to the side of the court as Victorian and Instructor May dealt with returning the manabeast to its cage, trying not to think about what, given another couple of seconds, might've happened, but instead assessing her performance as she caught her breath. *I got hit by its magic! Will that count against me? But I lasted the whole minute without Instructor May having to intervene – that was the criteria we were given. Surely that means I passed?* She clenched her fists. *By the Trinity, I hope so. I couldn't bear waiting for another assessment.*

She opened the gate at the side of the fence and walked along the adjacent path until she stood in front of Gabriel James, a middle-aged man with straight jet-black hair and a lithe build. He was dressed, like her, in the forest-green trousers and long-sleeved top that made up their Wing uniform. The only difference (aside from the damage to hers) was the black felt bird's wing sewn to his breast. The assistant master had a steel nib in his hand and was scratching notes on a piece of paper, dipping the tip into a bottle of ink every now and then. She waited, hands clasped behind her back, trying not to show the nerves fluttering inside nor stare with longing at the miniature wooden chests arranged in rows at the end of the table. After a moment, Instructor May and Victorian returned. The latter smiled at Pink as she and Instructor May sat down either side of Gabriel. Pink smiled back, warmth filling her cheeks.

Victorian Dex was her hero. She was young for an instructor, somewhere in her mid-to-late twenties, but as skilled as any. Her bright orange hair, held back by a brown band, fell to her shoulders, and creases around her eyes, embedded into her pale skin, suggested she spent much of her time laughing. She was the opposite of Instructor May, whose weathered face often held a frown, as it did now.

"Well, let's not keep Ms Arrancove waiting any longer," said Gabriel as he finished his notes. He looked up at Pink. She found that gaze unnerving but held it anyway. "Sara Arrancove, seventeen years old, arrived at Wing one year ago this month and has already passed the theory test. All correct?"

"Yes, Assistant Master."

"Good. Instructor May, Instructor Dex … what did you think?"

"She held her own for the whole minute," said Victorian, keeping her eyes on Pink. "She was very impressive."

"She barely held her own," scoffed Instructor May, dampening the pride Pink felt at Victorian's words. "If she wasn't wearing syntaxicite, that energy blast would have done considerable damage."

"But she *was* wearing syntaxicite. She was tactical in keeping her distance, and she used her magic effectively even if it didn't strike its target."

Gabriel twirled the nib between his fingers. "Personally, I felt she met the criteria for passing. I can already tell you think so as well, Instructor Dex. What about you, Instructor May?"

Pink inclined her head before turning to the bad-tempered instructor. He locked eyes with her as if trying to test her mettle. She forced herself not to look away. *I need three passes. Please …*

"A pass," acknowledged Instructor May with a sigh and a bow of his head. *Yes!* thought Pink, at the same time fighting to keep the joy from her face. *I'm an official mage now. I must show discipline.*

But she was unable to prevent the smile that appeared.

"Congratulations, Sara," said Gabriel, allowing her a small one of his own. "Wing is honoured to have your service for the next three years. The mentor listings will be placed in the Tesyn Building tomorrow morning, and contracts will be assigned to you in due course." He picked up and held out one of the chests. She took it, unhooked the attached bronze lever and opened the lid – nestled inside was a piece of black felt in the shape of a bird's wing. Pink's smile broadened. "You may depart. Instructor Dex, if you wouldn't mind collecting the next trainee?"

As she made to leave, Pink couldn't help but glance once more towards the cage. She couldn't see the manabeast – the angles, fence and bars of the cage all saw to that – but she felt as if it could still see *her*.

A gentle hand on her back made her jump. "You get used to them," said Victorian, understanding in her voice. "Come, let's set off."

Ignoring the dull pain in her side and ensuring the shredded part of the uniform was facing away from Victorian, Pink followed after the instructor. The path they trod ran adjacent to the training courts and led, in a winding sort of way, up Highstone Hill, its grassy patches scattered with colourful flowers. Ahead, the buildings of Wing stood at the top of the rise, a regiment of bricks and mortar towering over the high metal fences of the courtyards.

Pink thought desperately for something interesting or insightful to say, but every time she rehearsed something in her head, it sounded foolish. In the end, it was Victorian who broke the silence. "I asked to be your mentor if you passed," she said, looking at Pink sideways. "Gabriel has as good as confirmed it, so it looks like we'll be spending a lot of time together soon."

"You asked for *me*?" said Pink, incredulous. "It's a good thing I didn't fail then."

Victorian sighed. "Despite Instructor May's … attitude, the purpose of these assessments is only to filter out those who are not yet ready to use their magic in real-life battle situations. The training you've undertaken over the past year gives a much better indication of your ability, and yours has been outstanding, Pink. You have focus and a natural affinity with magic. Tell me, had you any practice before you came to Highstone Hill? Did your family teach you?"

The pride Pink felt at Victorian's compliments deflated a little. *My family … do I have to lie to Victorian?* "I was brought up by my uncle and auntie. My uncle showed me a bit." *There you are, not a lie, just not the entire truth.*

"Well, they're going to be very proud. You should send a bird – let them know."

"I'll do that," said Pink. They had reached the doors

of the Box, a name given to Highstone Hill's canteen due to its square brick walls. "Thank you, Instructor Dex. I look forward to working together."

The instructor laughed as she opened the doors, allowing the sound of chatter to escape. "No need to be so formal! You can call me Victorian, Pink. Everyone else does. By the way, you're not hiding that injury as well as you think. I would see the healer about getting a liniment."

Pink nodded sheepishly. They entered, the building quietening a little as Victorian called for the next trainee. A mass of syntaxicite-clad individuals swarmed inside, filling the rows of wooden benches and tables or hovering around the more open area in the centre. The smell of baked bread wafted from the attached kitchen, and sunlight streamed in through tall windows. Pink said goodbye to Victorian and trailed between the tables until she found the person she was looking for, a boy with a thin, pale face and straggly blond hair. He'd been chatting amicably with some of the others, but now he turned to face her, a grin sprouting on his features.

"I can already tell you've passed. You've got it written all over your face," he said as she squeezed in beside him.

"Is it that obvious, Jase?" she said with a smirk, placing the wooden chest down on the table. A few others sitting nearby offered congratulations, and she thanked them in turn but made sure to keep her responses minimal enough for the interactions to trail away. She wasn't close to anyone aside from Jase, and that was how things needed to stay. Pink couldn't risk anyone else finding out who she was. They soon lost interest – all but one, anyway. She noticed Lena Valentine watching her from a couple of places away, a stony look on her features.

"I'm surprised the manabeast even left a mark on you," said Jase, noting where she'd been struck, his grin still in evidence. "How does it feel to be a recognised mage?"

"It feels good, but even better to know I'll be spending less time trapped on Highstone Hill," Pink said, ignoring Lena. "We just need you to pass now."

Jase's expression changed so quickly it would have been comical on anyone else, but she knew how much he had been dreading their assessments. "Not much chance of that," he muttered. "I don't have enough control of my magic yet to fight a manabeast. My fireballs are never on target."

"Fire magic isn't as effective as you think – at least, it wasn't for me." Out of the corner of her eye, she noticed Bale Fallbrook, another trainee, leaning against the nearby wall with his arms crossed look over. Jase looked down at the ground, so Pink grabbed his arm until he met her eyes. "Use wind, keep your distance, waste time. The minute will be over before you know it."

Jase grunted but didn't give her a proper reply. She decided not to seek the healer – bringing further attention to the injury would only serve to make Jase more nervous. Instead, she tried to engage him in other conversations. As the time passed, however, she found him more and more withdrawn, his attention fixated on the entrance, where Victorian would periodically appear to collect the next trainee.

"Bale was the last to go, and he hasn't come back," he said at one point. "If he didn't pass … I mean, he was the best trainee after you and Lena."

"Bale is even less sociable than I am. Pass or fail, what reason would he have to come back?"

Jase ignored this. "And he's older."

"By what, a year? He arrived at Wing about the same time we did."

Jase went back to staring at the door. Finally, Victorian returned with the previous trainee and called Jase's name. He trudged out of the Box, head down, already looking defeated. *I wish they hadn't left him until last. He's had too much time to think about it.* Pink picked up her chest and took Bale's place against the wall, seeing no further need to sit on the benches now Jase had left. She waited, using the hard surface as support, thinking of words of consolation as she rotated the chest in her hands. After a while, however, Lena's voice interrupted her thoughts.

"… won't last ten seconds, never mind a minute. Jasen Vine doesn't have a chance of passing …"

Pink's eyes drifted towards the girl, who was talking animatedly and loudly from her seat at the table. Between the curtains of Lena's raven-black hair, her eyes darted to Pink, and a smirk appeared on her porcelain features. *She wants me to hear.*

"… some people just aren't cut out to be mages."

"And some people need to mind their manners," Pink said loud enough for Lena to hear before she could help herself.

Lena feigned surprise as many of the others looked uncomfortable. "Oh, *Pink*. I didn't think you liked talking to us."

Pink smiled pleasantly. "I'm unsurprised with your admission you don't think. It would explain all the random noise that comes out of your mouth."

Lena's dark eyes narrowed. "Are you upset because I don't think Jase will pass his assessment? It's the truth. Even you must know it."

"I know nothing of the sort," replied Pink, feeling guilty that she'd been thinking just that, "but even if that were true, I wouldn't talk about it in public. By the way, congratulations on passing your own assessment earlier.

I'm sure that's why you feel the need to pass judgement on those who haven't. I just hope the result of our last training session wasn't too much of a hindrance."

Lena stood up and took a step towards her. Pink pushed herself off the wall, feeling the arcannen circulating inside, tensing her body and readying it for action. The silence from Lena's table spread quickly, and before she knew it, the whole of the Box was quiet, everyone staring at the two newly qualified mages standing face to face. Pink knew both she and Lena were thinking the same thing – yesterday, during training, Pink's wind magic had launched Lena halfway across one of the courtyards. *It's her own fault. She's always desperate to prove she's better than me.*

Lena scrunched up her face as if Pink was something disgusting she'd stepped in. "Despite your pitiful attempts to sound clever, you're not clever enough to mind what you say to me. This isn't some training ground exercise. You don't have your precious Victorian here to guide you. Do you really think you could beat me one-on-one if it was for real?"

Pink met her gaze, thought of her reply for a moment, and then said, "You have really bad breath."

Lena's hand whipped down, and her fingers extended as if to summon her magic. Pink did the same. *Come on, Lena, try it.*

At that same moment, the door to the Box swung open, the rushing air filling the silence. Victorian entered, looked around and caught sight of Pink and Lena standing toe to toe. "What's going on in here?" she demanded, brow furrowed.

Before anyone had a chance to reply, Jase bounced in from behind the instructor, a beaming smile on his face. He moved straight towards Pink, not even seeming to notice the hush, waving a small wooden chest at her. "Pink – I did it! I passed!"

Several others in the canteen cheered, and then a round of applause started up. Pink, completely forgetting about Lena, laughed and gave him a hug. *He deserves that,* she thought as he faced his audience with a placating hand, seemingly bemused by the attention. Lena, who, like Pink, had apparently thought better of fighting in front of an instructor, made her way back to the table with a snort. Pink didn't even spare her a glance, but she did feel a sudden knot in the pit of her stomach. *I've just become a mage, and I was about to use magic to fight another member of Wing. I have to be more disciplined. I can't act like …*

"What's wrong, Pink?" asked Jase as the noise levels in the Box picked up again, the show evidently over.

"Nothing," replied Pink with a forced smile. "What could be wrong? We're both now official mages, Victorian's going to be my mentor, and you just made Lena look foolish in front of everyone. This is probably the best day of my life."

"Instructor!" The voice was loud enough to silence the Box again. One of their fellow mages had barrelled into the building, his face flushed. Victorian, who'd been talking to a group of trainees nearby, turned towards the newcomer. "Rodric! You look like you've run a mile. Whatever's the matter?"

"Gabriel … he needs you … at once," replied Rodric through ragged breaths.

Victorian placed a hand on his arm. She was obviously trying to be discreet, but Pink had no doubt every ear in the building was straining to hear what was being said.

"Why?" Victorian asked.

"It's Magicom, Instructor. They're here! Magicom are at Wing!"

CHAPTER THREE

What followed was a mass exodus from the Box. The majority of its inhabitants headed for the exit, a chorus of loud chatter filling the air. Pink hung back for a moment, trepidation building in her mind. *Could it be Magicom are here … for me?* She exchanged a look with Jase, who, by his expression, seemed to know exactly what she was thinking before they followed the few remaining occupants to the exit.

Outside, the crowd had frozen on the path and looking around the bodies, Pink could see why. A dozen or so soldiers were marching up the hill, their grey syntaxicite a stark contrast to Wing's green.

I wonder how Master Wing feels about Magicom using the material he developed for Wing mages.

"I asked for Instructor Dex, Rodric, not half of Highstone Hill," said Gabriel from a little ahead, a dry edge in his tone as his eyes found the flushed messenger. Rodric muttered something incomprehensible in reply. Victorian made her way to the side of the assistant master as the Magicom soldiers drew closer.

"What's this, a welcoming committee?" demanded one of the soldiers. He was an older man and the only one with a strip of red on his sleeve.

"What can we do for you?" asked Gabriel, calm as

ever. Pink sensed a collective holding of breath from the crowd.

The soldier responded by holding out a scroll. Gabriel took it, looking down at the roll of paper as if it might explode at any moment. He unravelled it and read what was inside, his reaction unreadable. A small crease appeared on Victorian's brow as she leaned over his shoulder to read. Pink's heartbeat quickened – what if her name was on that scroll? She felt a touch on her arm and looked up to meet Jase's eyes. *It's probably not what you think,* they seemed to say.

"We'd best discuss this in my cottage," said Gabriel at last.

"I don't think so, *Assistant Master.* That's just the sort of thing someone giving August Silvershield shelter might say in order for him to escape. Not that it would matter. We have units surrounding this whole area. We'll start our search with the buildings. I suggest you join us so I can question you as we go."

"Can I remind you this is a privately-owned military facility?" said Gabriel. "Have you written permission from Articulas Wing to enter his property?"

The soldier's expression was nothing short of a snarl. "The government have charged Magicom with the apprehension of August Silvershield. That gives us license to go where we want, privately-owned or not. Are you sure you want to make this more difficult than it needs to be?"

The assistant master inclined his head and swung out a hand towards the buildings, a sardonic look on his features. As Gabriel and Victorian followed the departing soldiers, nearly the entire crowd started to talk at once. Pink, though, breathed a sigh of relief and shared a shaky laugh with Jase. The soldiers weren't at Wing for her, nor would they find August.

After all, she'd know if her brother was at Highstone Hill.

***

Where was August Silvershield? Was he really at Wing, sheltered by Gabriel and the other instructors? That was all anyone could talk about for the rest of the afternoon, the Box full of excited chatter as the possibilities were discussed. Normally, the newly qualified mages would be more concerned about whom their mentors might be, but this new development had overshadowed even that.

Pink, keen to avoid the Magicom soldiers, whiled away the time with Jase playing Elementals, a strategy board game popular at Wing. Jase, who often lost to Pink, was having even less success paying attention to his painted wooden discs than usual. Every time he heard someone talking about Magicom, he would insert himself into that conversation.

"I suppose he's disguised himself as a patient," he proclaimed sarcastically on hearing the soldiers were searching the infirmary, "or maybe Healer Perola has actually been the leader of Ashes this entire time."

Jase did, at least, have the good sense to remain quiet when the soldiers appeared to search the Box, head down and suddenly more interested in the game.

Pink was well on her way to beating him for the fourth time when Rodric, who was beginning to be seen as an authority on the subject, wandered into the building and announced that Magicom were about to depart. This caused a second emptying of the Box in a day. This time the crowd (including Pink and Jase) followed Rodric along the path to the eastern slope of the hill, which looked over the plains of the wilderness. Several armoured steam vans were stationed on the flatter land below, their metal reflecting the setting sunlight. There, Gabriel was speaking with the commanding soldier while the others were boarding the vehicles from the rear doors.

"They've been searching Wing for hours," said Jase, nodding his head knowingly. "They've been in the dormitories, the stables and every single building in between. Obviously, they haven't found August Silvershield."

He turned to Pink and gave her a short nod as if to say, *you're welcome.* She managed to restrain her eyes from rolling. She appreciated what he was trying to do, but as far as she was concerned, the less they mentioned August, the less chance anyone would have of connecting him to her.

"I'd love to look inside one of those steam vans – see how the engine works, where they store the coal," she said, changing the subject.

Jase grunted, obviously less interested. "Pretty much the same way the trains work, I imagine. They've got that same funnelly thing at the top." He raised an eyebrow at her. "I see you're still in a good mood."

Pink laughed. "What's there to be upset about? Magicom are leaving." *And they obviously have no idea where August is, or they wouldn't be here.* "By the way, you haven't told me how your assessment went," she said as they turned to leave. "All you've been talking about is Magicom."

Jase shrugged. "I did as you said. I didn't try to use fire magic, stuck to wind and kept my distance. The manabeast seemed wary – I think it'd spent the entire morning having magic thrown at it. Instructor May said he would have to pass me on the basis there was no reason *not* to pass me."

Jase grinned at the memory as if it was the best compliment anyone could've paid him.

***

Pink stitched her felt wing to the breast of a new top the following morning, feeling a surge of satisfaction at seeing the physical confirmation of her mage status. She threw the old, ruined uniform away. As smooth and durable as leather (but with more elasticity), syntaxicite offered some protection against magical assaults but could only do so much.

After they'd eaten breakfast and Pink had helped Jase with his own sewing, she took him to the Tesyn Building to look at the mentor listings. She sensed his reluctance all the way. Her friend could talk until the sun came down, but his confidence with magic just didn't come as naturally. Although their formal training was at an end, their mentors would expect them to continue practising the elements on a one-to-one basis, and that likely worried him. Still, the sooner he improved his magical skill, the better. And if she happened to give him a little nudge in the meantime, well, that was all for his own good, wasn't it?

The Tesyn Building was two storeys tall, standing near the hill's summit, nestled between the boys' and girls' dormitories. The smell of mahogany wood greeted them as they pushed through its double doors and stepped into the auditorium, where a stone statue was centrally placed to make the most of the light streaming through the many windows. It depicted a curly-haired woman wearing spectacles, a golden plaque at its base, which read:

TETTE TESYN

CREATOR OF THE ARCANNEN POTION

They bypassed the statue and made their way to the back of the auditorium. Pinned there, they found a piece of parchment that ran down the wall with the names of newly qualified mages scribbled underneath their respective instructors.

"Here you are, Jase," she said, spotting 'Jasen Vine' near the top of the list. "Gabriel's your mentor. That's brilliant!"

She knew she needn't look herself, but the thought of seeing Victorian confirmed as her mentor was too satisfying to ignore. She searched the listings until she found 'Instructor Dex' and read the names underneath.

Hers wasn't there.

Pink felt the smile she'd been wearing falter. Surely there'd been some kind of mistake. Had they forgotten to include her? Or was it because Victorian had already told her verbally? But as her eyes ran under the other listed instructors, she found, to her dismay, 'Sara Arrancove' right at the bottom, written underneath another name. One she didn't recognise. She ran a finger along the scratchy surface as if that would make it more real.

Instructor Texeria.

"Pink …" Jase had seen it as well. "I thought Victorian said she was going to be your mentor? Who's Instructor Tex … ear … ia? I've never heard that name before."

"Looks like all that fawning didn't pay off after all," another voice said. Pink didn't need to turn to know who it belonged to; she could hear the barely concealed glee in it. "What a shame," continued Lena as Pink closed her eyes and breathed through her nose. "Now you'll have to start from the beginning with a new instructor."

Pink spun and took a step towards Lena, but Jase grabbed her arm, shaking his head. The smirk Lena wore faltered for a moment, but she recovered well enough to scoff as Pink stormed from the building, pushing past her on the way.

Outside, Pink inhaled deeply, taking in the fresh air, trying to calm herself. Lena wasn't her priority right now; Victorian was. *Why have I changed mentors?* She searched her mind frantically for a reason. Was it because of that incident in the Box? She could hardly be sanctioned for that, could she? And why was it that every instructor was mentoring several mages, and this Instructor Texeria only had one – her?

She needed answers.

"I'm going to East House," she told Jase, coming to a decision.

"No, wait! Pink! The instructors won't like that … you can't just …"

Jase hurried to catch up as she marched down the pathway east, trying to convince her to wait, to think things through, to see what happened. But she didn't slow – her disappointment wouldn't allow for it. Eventually, the cottages belonging to the instructors came into sight, along with East House, a larger two-storey building that acted as the instructors' communal area, a bit like their version of the Box. As they neared, the sounds of loud voices could be heard from behind the building, as if people were at work there. Once she'd stepped off the pathway to approach the wooden door, Pink let out a long breath and knocked while Jase stood to one side, shuffling his feet, looking like he'd rather be anywhere but there.

Instructor May answered, his scruffy greying hair and permanent scowl in evidence. "What do you want?" he demanded, eyes darting between them.

"We want to see Instructor Texeria," she replied, forcing herself to meet his gaze.

"Do you now, *Sara?* And do you have an appointment?"

"No, but as he's my mentor—"

"You need an appointment to—"

"Henning, is that Pink? Let her in."

Pink's heart leapt in her chest. *Victorian's voice!* May's eyes narrowed, but he stood to one side.

They found themselves in a room with an open doorway, a fireplace carved into the wall and a polished wooden table that stood underneath a gasolier, black smudges stained on the ceiling above. Victorian lounged in an armchair, facing a sofa filled with three other instructors. Pink found her resolve dropping under their questioning stares, but when Victorian pushed herself to her feet, she stopped caring.

"I know why you're here," said Victorian, placing a hand on her shoulder. The other instructors continued whatever conversation they'd been having – Pink heard the words 'Gabriel' and 'Magicom' in hushed tones – while Instructor May stormed outside, slamming the door behind. "I'm sorry, Pink. I know I told you I'd be the one mentoring you."

Pink tried to form words in response, but all she could manage was, "Why aren't you?"

"I … don't know. Until today, I thought I would be. Gabriel put together the listings, and as you can imagine, he's been rather busy over the last couple of days. I don't feel like now is the right time to mention it."

"What do you know about Pink's new instructor?" asked Jase as Pink continued to struggle for words. She felt a surge of gratitude for her friend. It was the right sort of question to ask, and she was too off-keel to ask it.

Victorian appeared to hesitate but answered all the same. "Keat Texeria. He arrived this morning. He was serving his three years as a mage here around the same time as I, although I don't pretend to remember him well. I do know that, until recently, he's been working as an illusionist in Holding."

That did surprise Pink. "An illusionist?"

"Men and women who perform on stage, trying to impress the audience with visual tricks and such. You sometimes see them at Holding Theatre. I'm surprised he's now an instructor at Wing. Makes you wonder why the sudden change." Victorian stopped short as if realising she'd said too much. "But I'm sure he's a worthy mentor for you. Did you say you were looking for him? There's a storage area at the end of that corridor. Last room on the left. He's taken it as his … quarters."

"Thank you, Instructor Dex," said Pink, making sure she kept to the formalities, at which Victorian smiled sadly. Now Pink knew the change was not Victorian's decision, she wanted to say something about how much the instructor's teaching and support over the last year had meant to her. But the words got stuck in her throat, and all she could do was smile stupidly as Victorian squeezed her shoulder before returning to her place in the armchair, joining back in with the instructors' conversation, leaving Pink feeling foolish.

"Come on, Pink," said Jase, gently putting his hand on her back. "Let's find this mentor of yours."

She allowed herself to be led through the doorway and into the corridor, still reeling from her lack of composure.

The storage room was a welcome distraction. It was more spacious than Pink had imagined, with a concrete floor – taken up mostly by piles of wooden crates – a high ceiling and small rectangular windows through which very little light crept. It felt airier than the other room, yet somehow still retained a musty smell. As they made their way further into the space, Pink could hear, from around one of the piles of crates, a voice giving orders and metal clanging. She and Jase exchanged a glance before they peered around the corner.

A man with a mop of black curls stood with his back to them. His cotton shirt and woollen trousers were a similar forest green to their uniforms, and he was directing several men and women while they unloaded wooden crates from two wagons that stood outside of a rear metal shutter. Pink made to speak to the man, but a glass cage near the centre of the room caught her attention. Inside, there were small creatures scurrying in and around mounds of straw and sticks, making quiet crunching sounds as they moved.

"What *are* they?" whispered Pink in awe, coming for a closer look. She knelt down so she was at eye level with the creatures. Up close, they looked like rodents, but with hard shells on their back and long scaly tails. *It's like they're wearing armour!*

"They look like rats with turtle shells," observed Jase as he stood alongside her and peered over the edge, which had an open top.

The man with the curls turned to face them. He looked to be about the same age as Victorian. Dark circles under his eyes stood out against his chalky skin and he had stubble on his face and chin. "Hmm? Oh, hello there! Those? If they were animals, you would call them *armadillos*, but as they're infused with their own magic, technically, they're a type of manabeast." And with that, he went back to his directing, ignoring the fact that Pink and Jase had jumped back from the glass in shock.

Pink made her way to the man – or to the man's back – and said in disbelief, "Are you allowed to bring manabeasts in here?"

"It was my understanding instructors can use manabeasts for training purposes," he said without turning. "Besides, unlike many species of manabeasts, these are harmless. They rely on magic for defence rather than attack. You've nothing to fear."

Pink looked back at the creatures. They moved quickly inside the cage, using their little claws every now and then to scratch at the concrete where they could reach it as if they were used to digging, but they certainly didn't look violent. Even if they were, their small size wouldn't make them much of a threat. Pink actually thought they were kind of cute. *I wonder what their magic does.* She looked back at the man. *Did he imply they were for training purposes?*

"Instructor Texeria," she said, quite certain now as to whom she was addressing. "My name's Pink and this is Jase. I acquired mage status yesterday, and from what I understand, you're to mentor me."

Keat Texeria did turn this time. His features retained their jovial countenance, but Pink had the feeling this was the first time he was properly paying attention to them. He cocked his head and said, "I must say, you have very unusual hair."

"I hear that a lot," Pink said. He continued to stare at her until she felt she had to add something. "They say sometimes magic can affect unborns in the womb, change their appearance … hair colour, eye colour, that sort of thing."

"Fascinating stuff," he said.

"I don't mean to sound rude," said Pink, more to fill the awkward silence than anything – she could sense Jase trying not to snigger at her side – "but I was told Victorian … Instructor Dex … would be my mentor. Why are you now mentoring me?"

Texeria shrugged. "As a new instructor, I needed a charge. You were recommended. I arrived quite last minute, so I guess Gabriel had to change his plans." He gave her a lopsided smile. "And we're going to be busy – we already have a contract to fulfil!"

The retort she'd been about to make died in Pink's throat. *Already? Newly qualified mages never get contracts so early! I was expecting to wait at least a month.* She'd been looking forward to her first contract – a chance to show she could be the best mage at Highstone Hill like she'd been the best trainee. "Where from?" she asked, trying to keep her face neutral.

Something akin to amusement flashed in Texeria's eyes, but all he said was, "Are you both familiar with the town of Poulsen?"

Pink and Jase exchanged a glance. "Of course," replied Pink. "It's the nearest town to Wing. Trainees are allowed to visit there – only during the day, that is."

Texeria nodded. "Why not at night?"

So we're playing this game, are we? "Manabeasts," replied Pink at once. "When you've reached mage status, you're deemed able to protect yourself in the event you come across a wolf-type."

"A wolf-type?"

"Yes. They're the native manabeast in this area. That's why they're used in our assessments."

"And they're dangerous, correct? They've killed people in the time you've been at Wing?"

"Rarely," said Pink, unsure what he was getting at.

"Instructors keep them from getting too close to Highstone Hill. That's part of their job. I've heard sometimes people travelling to and from Poulsen have been attacked. A few have died if I remember correctly."

"And their bodies?"

"I'm sorry, Instructor Texeria. Why are we having this conversation?"

Keat Texeria rubbed his hands. "These wolf-type manabeasts attack and kill humans because that's what their instincts tell them to do. But there's always a body. They don't drag them off somewhere, even if they feed on them for sustenance. However, no one's seen wolf-types in this area for weeks now."

"My assessment …"

"Was with a wolf-type. But one taken from elsewhere. Wing had real trouble getting them in for this year's assessments, I hear." He paused. "Pink, Jase, the strange thing is this." He came closer to them and placed a hand on each of their shoulders, hazel eyes darting from one to the other as he spoke. "The contract comes from the Mayor of Poulsen. Some of his residents have gone missing in recent weeks. Naturally, manabeasts are suspected, but there have been no bodies. They've just simply … vanished. So not only have the wolf-types disappeared from the Poulsen area, but many of its people have as well. Why might that be?"

Pink simply stared at the instructor, at a loss for what to say. *Why does he look so excited?*

"He's asked for a meeting tomorrow evening," continued Texeria, apparently oblivious to her unease as he grabbed a metal bar and started to pry open one of the crates. "We'll need to collect horses from the stables, then ride to Poulsen to see what he has to say. Jase, would you care to join us? And perhaps you two could find one or two others? The more protection we have out in the wilderness, the better."

Pink looked to Jase to see what he thought, but he was simply staring at Keat Texeria, eyebrows raised.

"We'll be there, Instructor," said Pink, at which he froze mid-pry. *Is it because I called him Instructor?* "By the way," she said, looking around the storage room – she guessed it was now fully loaded by the way Texeria's help was waiting by the rear exit, most with their arms crossed – "what's all this equipment for?"

He seemed to consider the question before saying, "Magic."

And with that, he headed away from them towards his workers, leaving Pink and Jase to look at one another in bewilderment.

CHAPTER FOUR

A raindrop splashed against the nape of Roeden's neck, awakening him from dreams that were as fragmented as they were disturbing.

The dreams had involved Phantex and Magicom soldiers, but Roeden remembered little else. He kept his eyes closed, the sound of galloping hooves reaching his ears as his head bumped against a hard, scratchy surface, and the liquid trickled down the back of his shirt, cold and uncomfortable. The first time he'd awoken like this, he hadn't known where he was or why it'd felt like he was moving. Now it seemed he was used to it.

He opened his eyes as he felt further droplets on his skin. It was past dusk, the moonlight revealing the cloaked figure of the man who called himself Chadwick, sitting ahead of Roeden on the horse they were riding. Roeden was tied in place by a long piece of rope to the stirrups on either side. His wrists felt sore, but then every part of his body felt sore. Even his eyelids were heavy and painful.

When he'd woken the first time, he'd been at the front of the saddle. Chadwick hadn't said much, only reiterated he was Phantex's friend and was taking Roeden someplace safe. Roeden had demanded to be let go. Phantex had surely defeated those Magicom soldiers by now and was probably wondering where he was. His mother would be worried too. But Chadwick had insisted it was too dangerous, and he would have to stay for his own good.

Roeden could hardly drop off a moving horse, so he'd waited until that night to escape, planning to somehow return to Bodham through the wilderness. But he'd been caught, and after many tears and tantrums – of which he was now slightly ashamed – he'd found himself first tied to a tree, then to the horse once they'd set out the next day. Whether Chadwick truly was Phantex's friend or not, Roeden would never forgive him for the humiliation he'd suffered.

But he'd calmed down sufficiently to realise he needed information.

"Where are you taking me?" he called at last to Chadwick's back. The droplets had now become a drizzle, making Roeden wish he wore a cloak. He knew Chadwick had a spare one in the leather pack attached to the saddle – he'd wrapped it around Roeden on the first night – but Roeden refused to ask his captor for anything.

Chadwick slowed his horse to a trot. "Being civil now, are we?" The touch of amusement in Chadwick's voice made Roeden hate him even more. "I told you this before, but maybe you'll listen this time. I'm taking you somewhere safe, where Magicom cannot find you."

"I did listen last time," said Roeden through gritted teeth. "It's just not for you to decide what's safe for me, and besides, 'somewhere safe' is not telling me where we're going."

The man chuckled. "You're nothing like Phantex, do you know that?"

Roeden could have screamed. "Are you with Ashes?" he asked instead, trying to keep his voice even.

The reply took longer than Roeden expected, and when it came, it was quiet, so quiet he barely heard it over the trotting hooves and drizzling rain.

"I … I am."

There was something in the way he said these words that made Roeden wonder. It was almost as if they were mingled with … what? Fear? Uncertainty? He frowned. A member of Ashes should sound confident and certain, not … however this man sounded. Then again, Chadwick hadn't helped Phantex fight off Magicom, so he probably wasn't a real part of their group. Maybe he was some kind of messenger – hadn't he said he'd come to Bodham to warn Phantex? It made Roeden feel better to think Chadwick had failed in his mission.

"I could untie you," Chadwick said suddenly, "if you promise not to try to run off again. That way, you could sit at the front of the saddle and have a blanket, and I wouldn't have to worry about losing it in the wilderness if it fell off. It would be pointless to run anyway – if the manabeasts didn't get you, a fever would. You'd catch your death in this weather on foot."

"I promise," said Roeden straight away. He wasn't foolish – he could see the sense in that. He would escape *after* they'd reached whatever town or village they were going to.

Chadwick reined in the horse and jumped down. "You know I didn't want to do this, but worrying about you and manabeasts is too much," he said as he unfastened the rope from the stirrups on one side. "I didn't sleep a wink last night, keeping watch."

"I heard you snoring."

"Okay, well, maybe I did drift off for a bit, which isn't wise in the wilderness without having someone on watch. But I've been travelling for days now. I'm exhausted."

Roeden looked across at this ridiculous man. He had a few days of stubble growth on his pale cheeks, bloodshot eyes and his chestnut-brown hair stuck up at the ends. Still, tiredness was hardly something a hero should complain about – Chadwick was definitely not Ashes material. He didn't even dress like a hero, with that suit he wore beneath his cloak. Roeden would have to talk to Phantex about it.

Chadwick finished untying Roeden's right hand and went around to do his left. When both were free, Roeden rubbed his wrists, sighing with relief, the red marks around them already starting to fade. He looked at his surroundings but could still see nothing but plains shrouded in darkness, illuminated only by the moon and stars above. Chadwick gave him a little stale bread from his pack and a sip of something disgusting from a metal container that burned his throat, despite Chadwick sighing with satisfaction after his own mouthful. He proceeded to pass Roeden a blanket, which Roeden wrapped around himself, trying not to show any relief as the warm fabric enclosed him.

It wasn't long before they arrived at Chadwick's 'somewhere safe', but, to Roeden's confusion, no high stone wall appeared, only a wooden fence that seemed to stretch on into the darkness, its pickets pointing upwards like hundreds of wooden swords. Chadwick brought his horse to a halt as they neared a gate set inside the fence. He jumped off, unhooked the metal lock, pushed the gate open and climbed back on.

As he waited, Roeden, now back at the front of the horse, huddled further into his cloak, feeling disappointed. His whole plan had relied on someone taking him back to Bodham, perhaps a merchant with a horse and cart whom he could promise payment to on arrival, but he could see no roofs on the other side of the fence, nor a gatekeeper, nor any other sign of a town or village. Where were they then? Were they even at a settlement? He thought about asking Chadwick but quickly decided against it. *That will just cause him to be suspicious.*

As they trotted their way inside, Roeden saw they were on a path that wound through a field. On either side, metal fences separated the land. Wooden shelters sat inside, and there was a very specific smell of animals in the air. *A farm,* he thought to himself, annoyed it'd taken him so long to work it out. *We're at a farm.*

It took no longer than a few minutes for the path to lead to a stone house with a thatched roof and a light glowing from its ground-floor window. As they neared, Roeden saw someone standing outside the front door, watching them approach. He was a man a little older than Chadwick, although just as skinny, dressed in a waistcoat and woollen trousers, with the sleeves of his white shirt pulled up. He also carried a rifle, which hung at his side.

"We've come to visit Dwight Taurus," Chadwick called to the man as he reined in their mount again. He hesitated before adding, "Tell him Chadwick Penworth is here."

The man grunted. "He did say he was expecting someone, but he said they'd be on their own. Who's the little lad?"

"An unexpected bounty," said Chadwick, chuckling as Roeden decided whether he should be more insulted by 'little lad' or 'bounty'. *No, there's no competition. 'Little lad' is worse.*

The front door swung open and a figure blocked the light: a large, imposing man with a beard as black as his hair, wearing dark woollen trousers, heavy-looking boots and a white vest displaying his considerable inked arms.

"Is that you, Chadwick?" the big man called in a gruff

voice, clear despite the sound of the rain. "How did you find out where I lived?"

"I asked the right people," called back Chadwick. "Can we talk inside?"

The man called Taurus remained stationary. "Who's the boy?" he asked with a nod of his head.

"Someone who's going to get very ill if I have to keep answering that question."

Taurus grunted in annoyance before turning to the skinny man. "Samuel, could you take our visitor's bay to the stable?" He turned back to them as a still suspicious-looking Samuel came forward to handle the reins. Taurus' eyes narrowed. "You'd better have a good explanation for being here."

As he allowed Chadwick to help him off the horse and Dwight Taurus disappeared back into the cottage, Roeden caught the look on his captor's face. *I thought these people were his friends. Why does he look so worried?*

Roeden was too eager to get out of the rain to care much about the apparent unfriendliness of the big man. Wordlessly, he passed his cloak to Chadwick and hurried to the cottage's entrance, immediate warmth hitting him as he crossed the threshold and found himself in a room with a fire crackling invitingly from its hearth. The room was simply decorated, with a couch and table in one area and a kitchen in another. A counter separated the two, behind which Dwight Taurus was now clanging about, half-hidden by hanging pots and pans. To one side, a spiral staircase rose to another level, and the wooden floorboards were bare. Roeden headed straight for the fire, spreading his hands in front of him, breathing a sigh of relief as the heat warmed his numb fingers.

Roeden stayed that way until he heard a chuckle. Cranking his neck sideways (and up), he saw Dwight

Taurus standing over him, holding a pewter mug, the light seeming to dance in his black beetle eyes. A smile appeared underneath his beard, and up close, Roeden realised he was older than he'd first thought, his face craggier and lined in the light. The smile became a frown as he turned to Chadwick, who had deposited himself on a couch.

"Get off there, Chadwick, you idiot! You're dripping wet. At least the boy has the sense to stand." He turned back to Roeden. "I've made you some warm milk – here."

Roeden took the mug with a word of thanks and drank the liquid in one go, uncaring about the gurgling sounds he made.

"That's amazing!" he said to Taurus, who was continuing to watch him. "It's so … sweet."

"I put sugar in it, lad. I suppose you're probably not used to that."

Chuckling to himself again, Taurus moved back to the kitchen and returned with another couple of mugs, liquid foaming at the top. He passed one to Chadwick, who drank deep, making a noise akin to when he'd drunk from his flask.

"Why are you here, Chadwick?" asked Taurus after taking a sip himself.

"I'll get right to the point," replied Chadwick, wiping his mouth. "Phantex has been taken by Magicom."

Taurus threw his mug on the floor so suddenly that Roeden jumped in spite of himself. The metal clanged off the wooden floorboards, and amber liquid flew in all directions. Taurus seemed unconcerned about the mess, his face a mask of disbelief. Chadwick's eyes widened, but Roeden approved of the big man's reaction.

"He thought this might happen," Taurus muttered, looking at the spilt liquid as if unsure how it'd got there.

"He was trying to warn all his old Wing friends. But wasn't Phantex taking his family to Sermouth?"

Chadwick opened his mouth to reply, but Roeden spoke first. "They came before we could leave. And you don't have to say 'he'. I know you mean August Silvershield."

Taurus guffawed at that. He looked at Roeden again, more closely than before. "You're Phantex's brother," he said. It was more of a statement than a question, but Roeden nodded anyway. The big man turned to Chadwick in amazement. "How is it he's with you?"

"I managed to get him out of Bodham." A smug look appeared on Chadwick's features. "Not an easy job, I assure you. The boy was not interested in accompanying me."

Roeden blushed. "Yet you forced me to anyway."

"How did you know what Magicom were about?" Taurus asked Chadwick, ignoring the glares they were shooting one another. "How did you know they were coming for Phantex?"

"Same way. I knew where you lived, Taurus. I'm good at finding things out. I have contacts in Holding. I've told you and August this before. If he would only use my skills …"

"All right, all right," said Taurus with a wave of his hand. "The important thing now is finding some way to get Phantex back."

Roeden found he liked this man. He was older than Roeden had envisioned a member of Ashes would be, but he clearly had the right attitude. "What about my mother?" Roeden asked.

"She was taken too?" Taurus asked Chadwick.

The other man nodded. "There's no doubt about that. Magicom planned to take Phantex's entire family. That way, they could …"

"That's enough for now," said Taurus sharply. He looked displeased with Chadwick again. "You need to rest, lad," Taurus said to Roeden before he could work out why. He placed a hand on Roeden's shoulder, heavy but comforting. "By the sounds of it, you've been through a lot. I've got a room upstairs you can use – I assume you've been sleeping in the wilderness, and I can only imagine how scary that must have been. But you'll be safe here tonight."

"I wasn't scared, and I'm not tired. I want to know how you're going to help Phantex and Mother."

Taurus patted his shoulder. "These things take time – we won't be able to come up with a plan on the spot."

"Will you tell August Silvershield what happened?"

A wry smile appeared on Taurus' face. "He'll know sooner than you think, I promise."

Not completely satisfied but not wanting Taurus to think him fussy, Roeden allowed himself to be led up the spiral staircase and into a small hallway with two doors. Taurus took him into the one to their left. Inside was a small room with a slanted ceiling and the same wooden floorboards as the rest of the house. Taurus struck a match from a box he'd taken from his trouser pocket and lit a few candles on a small bedside table. It was colder at the top of the farmhouse, but animal skins were piled on the bed.

Taurus was right. Compared to sleeping in the wilderness, this was paradise.

Roeden walked to the bed and ran a hand across the skins, feeling the fluffy texture underneath his fingers, before turning back to Taurus. "Is this your room? Or the skinny man's? What was his name again? Are you both in Ashes?"

Taurus smiled and shook his head. "One question at a time, Roeden. I'll try my best to answer them all; then you try your best to get some sleep – agreed?" He waited for a nod before he continued. "No, this is not my room or Samuel's. Mine is across the hall, and he has one on the ground floor. You have to go around the side of the house to get to it, beyond the sty. Samuel is my business partner. We invested in this place together. He's not in Ashes, but I am." The big man looked suddenly uncomfortable. "But we try to keep information like that secret, okay?"

Roeden nodded. "So Magicom don't find out."

"They would lock us all up and throw away the key if they could, all aside from August, whose head they'd prefer to have on a stake. Ashes' advantage is through secrecy. There's not many of us."

"How come everyone knows who August is then?"

"He took on that sacrifice. He believed Ashes needed a figurehead for the people of Blake to believe in. It was only a matter of time before Magicom found out who he was anyway – not that it would do them any good. August is … the ultimate strategist."

Roeden nodded, looking back around the room. "So if this room's not yours, and it's not Samuel's, who does it belong to?"

A strange look came over Taurus' face. "My son," he said. "He's dead before you can ask your next question."

Roeden cursed himself for his lack of tact. "I'm sorry," he said.

"Nothing to be sorry about. It was an honest question."

"How did he die?"

Taurus walked to the window, looking out at the rain as it pattered against the pane. *Did I go too far?* "Magicom," Taurus said, at last, not looking away. Taurus looked as if he might say more but then shook his head ruefully before moving to the door and looking over his shoulder. "We'll talk more in the morning. Good night, Roeden."

"Good night," replied Roeden quietly. But the big man had already gone.

***

Roeden woke a few hours later. He knew not much time had passed because the candles were not yet at the end of their wicks. Assuming the pattering rain had disturbed him, he turned on his side, snuggling deeper into the skins as he attempted to get back to sleep. It was only then that he realised he could hear the sound of angry, muffled voices coming from outside.

He opened his eyes, listening hard. Were Taurus and Chadwick arguing again? He pushed himself out of the bed and hurried to the window to find out.

His heart sank.

Below, there were half a dozen Magicom soldiers, lit up by the flames two held in their palms. They were all on horseback aside from one woman with short, dark hair who stood at the front, facing Samuel, her mount's reins held by one of the others. Roeden noted Samuel carried his rifle again. As gently as he could, Roeden lifted the bottom of the window. Splashes of rain struck his fingertips as he felt the cold air come in, but he could now hear what was being said.

"… not going to invade my privacy," Samuel was shouting over the rain. "This is my home – you cannot come here and make demands."

"We can and we have," came the reply. She spoke in a bored voice. Roeden noticed she was the only one with a red stripe around the sleeve of her uniform. "We need to search inside. If the boy we're looking for is not present, we'll be on our way."

"You won't be coming inside," yelled Samuel, louder than he needed to be, Roeden thought.

"It sounds like you're trying to hide something, farmer," replied the soldier, placing a hand on the hilt of her sword. "This is your last chance to put down that gun. It would be completely ineffective against us anyway – bullets can't travel through a good air shield."

"Commander!" yelled one of the soldiers on horseback. "Up at the window – look!"

Roeden gasped. The soldier was pointing right at him! The commander looked up just as Samuel raised his rifle. There was a huge bang, and, unable to look away, Roeden saw Samuel tossed like a rag doll against the stone walls of the cottage, the sickening thud audible even over the sound of the rain.

"Idiot!" the commander bellowed, rounding on the soldier who'd thrown the magic. "Didn't you see that *solid* wall behind him? He's clearly dead. Wonderful, now we can't question him."

"He raised his gun," said the soldier weakly.

But the commander ignored him, instead looking up to where Roeden was watching.

Roeden took a step back.

The door of the room burst open, and Taurus appeared in its frame.

"Put your boots on and come with me," he said. Roeden quickly obliged, feeling tears sting his eyes. He made sure to turn away as he tied his laces, although he didn't miss Taurus making a movement as if swigging something. Moments later, they were charging down the stairs, finding Chadwick rising from the couch, suit crumpled and hair askew. "Taurus … what's going on?"

he asked.

"Magicom," said Taurus. Chadwick moaned. "Samuel's distracting them – we have to leave now."

"Taurus," Roeden said in a shaky voice. "I think they … killed him." Taurus turned sharply, looking at Roeden in disbelief. "And … and I think they're here for me. One of them said they were looking for a boy."

Taurus cursed. "I didn't think they'd be searching this far from Bodham." He turned back to Chadwick. "Go out of the back, grab a horse and leave. If they're focused on me, they might not spot you." Chadwick stood there, gaping at Taurus. "What are you waiting for?" Taurus yelled, grabbing Chadwick's arm and hurling him roughly in the direction of the back door. "Go – now!"

The movement seemed to galvanise Chadwick into action. He took hold of Roeden's arm in turn, grabbed their cloaks from a stand and dragged him towards the back of the house.

"Wait," started Roeden, turning back to look at Taurus.

Chadwick knelt down and pushed one of the cloaks into Roeden's chest. "We need to move," he implored. "Now." Roeden wanted to argue, the image of Samuel blasted with magic at the forefront of his mind, but Taurus was already at the front door. Roeden reluctantly nodded, throwing on the cloak. Chadwick did the same before leading them through a back door and into an open yard.

By the light of the moon, Roeden could see a small stable opposite. They raced towards it. Once through the entrance, Chadwick jumped into the nearest stall, working on saddling the horse within – the same bay they'd made the journey with. He was finishing up when an explosion reverberated from the front of the cottage, causing panicked neighs and stomping hooves. Gripping the reins tightly, Chadwick tried to soothe the horse with soft words before kicking open the stall's gate and lifting Roeden atop the animal before he could protest. More explosions filled the air as Chadwick mounted up behind him. The horse snorted and tried to spin, but Chadwick held it under control before riding to the side of the cottage and back towards the front.

Devastation greeted them. The wooden front door had been completely blasted from its hinges, and the soldiers were raining fireballs towards the opening. The thatched roof was aflame, and so much smoke billowed in their direction that Roeden had to cover his eyes with his arm. As Chadwick continued towards the pathway on the opposite side, Roeden managed to catch a glimpse of Taurus throwing his own fireball from the blasted entrance. The big man disappeared back behind the stone wall as returning magic came his way. Roeden could see what they were trying to do. Eventually, the whole building would be in flames, and Taurus would be forced into the open.

"Taurus' attack has likely caught them off guard," said Chadwick, turning his head, "but it's just a matter of time before one of them thinks to watch for others escaping from the back, like at your guesthouse. We have to keep moving."

Thanks to the smoke and noise of the battle, they rode unnoticed until they got back on the narrow confines of the pathway. It was here where Chadwick reined in and turned back, indecision on his features.

"We have to go," he said. "We can't wait for Taurus. If he wins, he'll find us. If he loses, well … what would be the point in staying?"

"We have to wait," whispered Roeden, watching the

scene. Even he could tell it was not looking good for the big man. The six soldiers were unhurt, and flames now licked inside the cottage as well as out. "They'll kill him like they did Samuel."

Chadwick waited a moment more, then blew out his cheeks. "There's nothing more we can do," he said, the decision clear in his voice.

Chadwick turned the horse. Roeden was about to protest further when something caught his attention. He cried out in alarm – riding up the pathway was a cloaked figure, almost on top of them! The sound of the battle and rain must have disguised its coming.

"What's happening?" the rider demanded in a man's voice, giving them no time to recover. Aside from his pale skin and a flicker of wet hair sticking out from under the hood, Roeden couldn't see his features well. *Is he a neighbour? Maybe from a nearby farm?*

"Taurus …" was all Chadwick seemed able to say, pointing in the direction of the cottage. The appearance of the rider seemed to have taken him aback.

"Hold my reins," the man said, passing them to Chadwick, who took them wordlessly. "Better I'm on my feet for this."

The man dismounted and, without any sign of hesitation, strode towards the soldiers.

A suspicion rose in Roeden's mind as he remembered something Taurus had said earlier. *He'll know sooner than you think.* "Chadwick …" said Roeden slowly. He turned to look up. "Is that …?"

Chadwick returned his gaze, slack-jawed. "It's August."

Roeden looked in the direction of the battle just in time to see the ground explode near to where most of the soldiers were clustered. Horses panicked and reared on their hind legs, causing three of the five riders to be instantly thrown from their mounts, while the one holding the commander's reins went the same way moments later, trying in vain to keep hold of the fleeing animal. Roeden gasped. *That was earth magic!* The commander and the only soldier still mounted spun as the other horses bolted in all directions. August Silvershield, whose arms were outstretched, formed a fireball and shot it at the latter, sending him to the ground in a heap. Snarling, the commander shot her own fireball at August, but the Ashes leader seemed to jump *over* it as he twisted in the air. He landed on his feet, returned another fireball, and the commander struck the wall of the cottage, just as Samuel had earlier.

And just like that, it was over.

With a shaky laugh, Roeden shared a look with Chadwick, who let out an audible sigh of relief, his shoulders sagging. Squinting through the rain, Roeden could see Taurus, now outside the cottage, clasping August's hand before kneeling down where Samuel's body lay. *Samuel's body … they killed him …* The sudden excitement of what he'd witnessed vanished, and nausea filled Roeden – it was all he could do not to throw up right there and then.

August placed a hand on the big man's shoulder and said something to him. Whatever it was, Taurus nodded in response, and together he and August headed back to where they were, August's eyes on the feebly stirring soldiers all the way.

August's hood had fallen down, and Roeden now recognised him from the wanted posters around Bodham: a man about the same age and height as his brother, although August's dark hair hung loosely at his shoulders. His hood was attached to a long cloak, but underneath, there was the clear gleam of black syntaxicite. "We will grieve for Samuel," August was saying as they approached, his deep voice clear over the rain and the crackling of the flames, "but we need to leave *now*."

Taurus shook his head, and although his eyes held a haunted look, his voice was as strong and steady as ever. "The situation's changed, August, but you don't need to change your plans. Go to Doscadia, and take Chadwick and the boy with you. I'll grab a horse and take Samuel's body away from here so I can bury it properly. Once I'm done, I'll stop by one of the nearby farms and see if someone can take care of the animals, although the government will likely take control of the holdings now." He took a deep breath. "Then I'll need to go to Bodham. Assuming she's not been taken to Alsing with Phantex, Esta Mason is likely being held there by Magicom." Taurus turned to Roeden. "I will get your mother out if I can."

"Roeden?" August turned his head, recognition in his voice.

Roeden shrank away from the dangerous glint in his dark eyes.

"Chadwick will have to explain what's going on," said Taurus, dragging them back to him. "You're right – we need to get moving. Those soldiers aren't moving any time soon, but they could still cause trouble. And more will come looking for us."

"Taurus, I'm so sorry," croaked Roeden, close to tears again. Those soldiers had been looking for *him*. "Your son's room … Samuel …"

Taurus stepped close to their horse, which amazingly still put him at about level with Roeden, and held out his hand, which Roeden took in his own. The big man put his second hand over it and smiled warmly under his black beard. "Don't worry about the room, Roeden. You just get yourself somewhere safe." He looked back at the soldiers. All but one were still on the ground, and the one who'd risen could only make it to his knees. "As for Samuel, I will make them pay for his death; don't you worry about that." Taurus' gentle tone evaporated at those words, and Roeden was suddenly glad they were leaving.

"Let's be off then," said August abruptly. He and Taurus clasped hands again before August returned to his horse. Roeden stared at him. Had he really just taken all those soldiers out all by himself? Roeden suddenly felt a surge of hope for Phantex. August patted his horse's neck before looking back to the big man. "You know where to meet us when you're done?"

Taurus nodded and immediately began hurrying in the other direction. August looked sideways at them and said, "You're travelling with me now. Be on your guard. Nearly everyone in Blake knows my name and likeness, and many will be after the reward for my capture." He paused and turned to look at them directly. The flames from the cottage danced in his eyes. "Once we get moving, I want to know exactly how Phantex was taken."

CHAPTER FIVE

Finding 'one or two' others to join them on the Poulsen contract proved to be trickier than Pink envisioned. Jase had suggestions, but she turned them all down. The person or people she chose would need to help support the fulfilment of their contract, nothing more – she wasn't interested in making new friends, something she suspected Jase was trying to instigate. Finally, the perfect individual came to her as they were eating breakfast in the Box on the morning of their departure.

"Bale," she said suddenly, looking over at their now-fellow mage sitting alone on one of the benches, his usual messy brown hair and serious expression in attendance.

It took Jase, on the opposite side of their table, a moment to realise what she meant. "Bale!" he exclaimed before choking on the food he was eating.

"Thanks," he said as a passing Rodric patted him on the back. "Bale!" he exclaimed again, causing a girl sitting nearby to jump and spill half the contents of her mug. She fixed him with a glare. Jase seemed unaware – all he could do was stare at Pink like she'd gone mad. "By the Trinity, why would you want him to come with us?"

"Come on, Jase, he's not so bad. He may be rather … sullen, but he was a very good trainee."

Jase did not answer. He merely continued to meet

Pink's gaze, doubt evident in his clear blue eyes. "You know, you could sit this one out," she said after a moment.

"What, and leave you at the mercy of Keat Texeria and Bale?" Jase scoffed. "I would never do that. We're sticking together. If you want Bale as our third, then I doubt there's anything I can say to change your mind."

She gave him a wry smile. "Just like always. Sometimes I think you must regret making friends with me on that first day."

Jase did look away this time. "I don't abandon my friends," he muttered, "even if their magical prowess is beyond my own."

"Jase." She put her hand on his. "It's confidence in your own ability you're lacking, not *prowess*."

Jase seemed unable to reply, so he turned his attention to Bale. A smile crept onto his face. "Bale isn't too dissimilar from you, you know. He's very serious about his magic, and his training, and himself …"

"I get the idea," she said, ignoring his sniggering as she rose. They made their way over to Bale, the smell of food more prominent as they passed the central table, where baskets of hot bread sat alongside jams and butter. "Hello, Bale," Pink said, sitting opposite him. Slowly, Bale looked up, the light from the window creating patterns of different shades on his olive skin. Jase joined them with what he obviously fancied a respectful nod, but Pink thought more of a twitch.

"Pink," replied Bale, putting down the mug he'd been holding but making no further effort to engage in conversation. Nevertheless, she thought she saw some curiosity in his expression.

"We have a proposition for you. Listen …"

***

Several hours later, Pink, Jase and Bale were collecting their horses from the stables on the eastern slope of the hill. They wore black, woollen cloaks over their uniforms and had attached packs to the horses' saddles, which contained waterskins and a few medical supplies.

While the three geldings grazed on the grass under their hooves, Pink spared Bale a glance as he stared out into the wilderness. He'd been easy to convince once she said they were working a contract. As Wing mages, they were expected to fulfil a number of these over their three years. There wasn't a set amount, as contracts could vary in length, but the time they had spent would be reviewed each year by their mentor. Instructor Texeria might be running the Poulsen contract, but it would count towards Jase's and Bale's quotas as well as her own.

A tuneless whistling stole into her thoughts. Keat Texeria was bouncing his way down the slope, hands in the pockets of a grey leather coat that reached down to his black boots, a sack slung over one shoulder. He was not alone. A boy of about their age followed alongside, carrying a rolled piece of paper, his stiff movements at odds with Texeria's gait. The boy wore his dark hair short, and from the way it was styled, Pink imagined some effort had gone into ensuring not a single strand would fall out of place. She'd seen him around Wing a few times over the last year but never during training. *Which means he acquired mage status before us.*

"Pink," whispered Jase at her side. "That's Sol!"

She looked at him sideways. "And?"

Jase's eyes were wide with alarm. "*And* … he's part of that group who want to join Magicom!"

"A good afternoon to you all," said her mentor brightly, preventing her from having to think of a reply. He made a show of looking at the sky. "The weather seems to have turned. A shame ... Ah, this is Sol Draeon. I don't know if any of you've met. The charming Instructor May insisted he join us on our expedition."

Sol's tone was all business as he spoke to them. "The paperwork I have here," – he tried to pass the rolled paper to Pink – "is a directive from Instructor May giving me permission to join this contract. Can you read? His signature is at the bottom to show its authenticity."

"Of course I can read," replied Pink, irritated at the question and ignoring the offered paper. "I can write too. Would you like me to write you something? Then I can ask you to read it. I wouldn't want you to feel left out of the stupid question game."

Jase snorted as the boy's lightly tanned cheeks blushed. "I wasn't trying to offend you," Sol snapped. "Not all mages are educated in letters and numbers."

Maybe I was a little harsh. I think Jase got into my head with that Magicom comment. I need to stay away from all that. She opened her mouth to apologise, but Texeria cut in. "Well done, Pink. Together, we've put together a little party. I feel much safer going into the wilderness now."

As Sol shot a disbelieving look Texeria's way, the instructor rummaged in his sack and brought out four vials of black liquid, which he passed to them in turn. "This should be enough arcannen for our journey," he said before moving to speak with the approaching stable master, a small man called Ored with wild, white hair, who gave them all dark looks as he muttered under his breath.

"Nice to see Ored's as unfriendly with mages as he is with trainees," Jase commented cheerfully as he pulled out the stopper and downed his potion.

Pink laughed and did the same in a single swift gulp. It was best not to think too much about the harsh metallic taste of the liquid. The payoff was worth it, though.

Almost at once, her fingers tingled and she felt alive to the elements.

They did not have to suffer the stable master for long. After introducing himself to Bale, Texeria collected their empty vials, mounted his own gelding (much more gracefully than Pink would've imagined), and, after they'd done the same, took them on the road that ran downhill, its meandering route visible for miles through green and yellow fields.

As they trotted along the countryside, the tingling in Pink's fingers subsided, her body growing more accustomed to the dose. It wouldn't go away completely, of course – that attuned feeling to the elements would be there for at least another twenty-four hours – but unless she used her magic, it would remain dulled.

There wasn't much talk at first, the tweeting birds the only sound accompanying their progress. Eventually, however, Sol rode his horse alongside Pink's.

"What's your plan after we meet this mayor?" he asked, for some reason thinking she was the one to direct that question to. "How are we going to find out what happened to these missing people?"

Pink shot him a look. "That will depend on what he says."

"Despite the missing wolf-types, I can't see this being anything other than manabeast-related," said Sol, looking over the plains. "Who else in the town do you think will be able to help us with this contract?"

"I don't know." Why did he think she had all the answers? His comments made something else occur to her, though. "Jase's mother has a farm there, isn't that right, Jase? Do you think she knows anything?"

"Not that she's told me," muttered Jase, who was riding on her other side. He shot her a look that clearly said, *Don't tell him anything else about me.*

"Farmers?" Sol glanced at Jase. "I assume you have something else in mind for when you finish your three years?"

Pink groaned. *Does this boy actually think before he speaks?* A quick glance at Jase showed his cheeks had, unsurprisingly, turned a shade of red.

"When I'm finished at Wing, farming is how I plan to spend my life."

"You want to be a farmer when you leave Wing?" Sol seemed incredulous. "But you're a trained mage!"

"Farming is a peaceful occupation, as long as you take proper precautions against manabeasts. You can live off the land and give back to it. Not everyone wants to be a soldier … or hunter, or security, or whatever."

"It seems pointless to attend a military facility like Wing and become a farmer." Sol lifted his chin up. "I plan to join Magicom's army myself."

"So you have aspirations to kidnap, steal and murder?"

The look Sol shot Jase was contemptuous. "Is that really what you believe Magicom does?"

Jase did not respond, but a small smile formed on his lips. Pink sighed. *That's his retaliation for the farming comment.*

"What about the peace Magicom brought at the end of the Spirit Mage Wars? Does that not fit into your little list?" demanded Sol.

"If by peace you mean using the Spirit Mage Wars to control the government and, by extension, the rest of Blake, then sure, you can include it."

"They helped the government to survive, you fool! The Spirit Mage Wars are the perfect example of why magic should be regulated! The Spirit Mage and his followers came close to enslaving the whole of Blake. By only allowing Magicom to control arcannen, the Mage

Charter ensures that will never happen again. On top of that, the government often *employs* Magicom's army to enforce its laws – so instead of saying 'kidnap and murder', you should actually be saying 'arrest and sentence.' As for stealing, Ashes are the only organisation responsible for that. Magicom are the ones who *own* the arcannen mines."

Pink shifted uneasily in her saddle, but Jase was not deterred. "Ashes argue that magic shouldn't be exclusively controlled by Magicom, who sell it at a price beyond the reach of most. Many support Ashes because of that and because they're the only ones who will stand up to Magicom's *enforcement.* Magicom soldiers abuse their power. Only a fool couldn't see *that.*"

"Ashes aren't as noble as they make out." Sol's voice, which had risen in volume as he and Jase argued, now took on a quieter quality. Pink could see he was gripping his reins tightly. "Your mother is a farmer; mine works at a Magicom clinic. Or did. I come from Rynn, near Holding. A couple of months ago, Ashes decided to raid the town's clinic. My mother tried to fight them off, took a fireball at point-blank range without syntaxicite, and, well, let's just say she's been bedridden ever since." There was anger in Sol's eyes now. He looked from Pink to Jase as if daring them to contradict him. "Don't speak to me of Ashes' heroics. Whatever morals they spout, they're nothing but criminals."

He rode ahead before they could answer. Pink exchanged an uneasy glance with Jase.

"You know what I'm going to say, don't you?" she murmured so only he could hear.

Jase nodded.

Sol Draeon could never find out she was August's sister.

***

It was nearing nightfall by the time Poulsen came into view. The town was enclosed by spiked wooden walls, behind which stone watchtowers rose, fires alight on their highest platforms. Pink's horse nickered as if it knew it would soon be in a stable, warm and resting for the night. She patted its neck, thinking she'd be happy for the rest and warmth as well – the air was chilly, and a light drizzle had started to fall.

They'd travelled the distance without incident, passing several farmyards on the way. The animals from the farms would be locked up for the night by now, Jase had told them, away from the threat of manabeast attacks. Pink was glad his own family farm was on the other side of the town – it lessened the chances of another interaction between Sol and Jase. She hadn't liked how the previous one had led to the topic of Ashes.

Making their way through the town's open gate, they received a nod from the gatekeeper before passing by the stone watchtowers and onto a road with terraced houses on either side, the brick walls and slate roofs a common feature of Poulsen. The street lamps had been lit and illuminated the road as their horses clip-clopped on the cobblestones beneath. On a grassy patch just before the houses, two steam vans were parked. Pink pursed her lips – were they the same ones that had recently been parked at the foot of Highstone Hill?

Eventually, the group arrived at a street corner where a tavern stood. Lights shone through its diamond-framed windows, and a sign hung from above, with a painting of an upside-down swine underneath the words 'The Salted

Pig'. The tavern's wooden door creaked open, and two men wandered out wearing black-smudged trousers and shirts rolled to their elbows.

Before they reached the tavern, Texeria reined in his horse at a stone archway built in between two buildings. Pink smelled before she saw the stables at the end of a small alley, where a few horses stood grazing in box stalls.

Casually dismounting, Texeria waited until Sol and Bale had joined them before holding out the reins. "We'll be meeting the mayor at this tavern. Would you two mind dealing with our horses while we sort out accommodation for the night? It seems an unnecessary risk to travel back before morning, and besides, I have a feeling we'll need to follow up on any information we receive."

Pink and Jase dismounted (more carefully than Texeria had) and handed their reins to Sol, who gave them a look of disgust as if it was their idea the instructor had given him a job he obviously felt beneath him. Pink decided not to say anything and grabbed Jase's arm before he could, following her mentor through the tavern's entrance.

The first thing Pink noticed was the group of Magicom soldiers hunched together at a table in the corner. *My suspicions were right then.* They were talking in low voices, lit candles illuminating serious faces. She recognised the commanding officer who'd handed the search warrant to Gabriel among them. There was a low level of chatter coming from several patrons dotted around the other oaken tables, either on the main floor or in booths. Some glanced in their direction, their eyes lingering a little longer on Pink, probably on account of her hair. The room was warm thanks to a fire burning heartily from a hearth near the entrance, and the smell of cooked food filled the air – Pink could almost taste it in her mouth, and Jase looked all but ready to drool.

"You want rooms for the night, sir?" A broad-shouldered, middle-aged man, whom Pink assumed was the innkeeper, approached them. He'd done a quick once-over of the three and decided Texeria was the one to talk to.

Texeria nodded curtly. "There are five of us, plus our mounts."

"If the other two are Wing mages, I have a room all four of them can share at a cheap price and a smaller one for yourself," he said, to which Texeria nodded again. "The washroom is across the hall from both rooms, and supper is beef and seasonal vegetables, with a tomato soup, ready in thirty minutes." He indicated to one corner of the room, where a dusty old longcase clock was ticking.

He turned to go but stopped and hesitated as if he was deciding something. He glanced around and added in a low voice, "Take care in the common room, all right?"

Texeria followed the innkeeper's gaze to the soldiers. "Ah," was all he said.

The innkeeper grunted. "The sooner they leave, the better. Not good for business."

Once the innkeeper had gone, Texeria went to check on Sol and Bale while Pink and Jase found a booth to sit in. "Why do you think those soldiers are here?" asked Jase, leaning over the table as soon as they'd sat. "Do they think August might be at Poulsen?"

"I'm not sure. But they could just be stopping on their way back to Holding." Pink glanced around the common room but froze as she spotted a familiar face, or the profile of one anyway, printed on a large sheet of paper pinned to a noticeboard, overlapping many of the others. She stared at it for a moment more, horrified. Ignoring Jase's questions and the arrival of Sol and Bale through the entrance, she wandered over, avoiding a rather intoxicated blond-haired man en route. She read the writing beneath.

WANTED

AUGUST SILVERSHIELD

LEADER OF THE UNLAWFUL ORGANISATION KNOWN AS ASHES. WANTED FOR THEFT, CRIMINAL DAMAGE, ARSON AND ASSAULT OF MAGICOM SOLDIERS.

DECREED BY BLAKIAN GOVERNMENT.

GENEROUS OFFER OF 100 PHOENIXES FOR CAPTURE OR INFORMATION LEADING TO ARREST. PLEASE SPEAK TO AN OFFICER IN UNIFORM OR VISIT A CLINIC TO MAKE A CLAIM.

The tears in Pink's eyes surprised her. She brushed them aside roughly, angry with herself. What had she expected? She'd known he was being hunted by Magicom; she could've guessed wanted posters would have gone up around Blake. They'd come to Wing looking for him, after all. But something about seeing it here, now, unexpectedly, was too much. She kept her eyes on the board, not wanting the others to take note of her reaction, then took a deep breath and made sure her face was a mask of indifference before returning to the booth.

"I heard those posters had been put up," said Sol as she rejoined them, his lip curling. "They're probably in every tavern and clinic in Blake. There's nowhere for August Silvershield to hide now."

With some effort, Pink kept her mask in place.

"Where's Instructor Texeria?"

Sol shrugged. "He said he was going for a walk. I hope he gets here before this mayor does. It doesn't look good otherwise. I have to say, I couldn't imagine Instructor May wandering off before a meeting."

"Maybe you should go look for him," suggested Jase bluntly.

Sol's response was to glare at Jase before turning to look out of the window, his back to them. Bale, who didn't seem to notice the exchange, merely stared down at his lap. Thankfully the awkward silence didn't last for long, as moments later, a rush of air signalled the arrival of a portly man in the doorway, his tailored suit immaculate but his mop of blond hair windswept and dampened. He looked around, noticed them, and made for their booth.

"You're the Wing mages," he said, a little breathless. He looked around the common room. "I thought there'd be an instructor with you."

"He should be along soon," replied Pink, surprised she was in agreement with Sol. *It's not very professional of Instructor Texeria. Where is he?* "Perhaps you'd like to wait?"

"No time for that," murmured the man, eyeing the Magicom soldiers in the corner before frowning at the intoxicated man Pink had avoided. He sat down, motioning Sol and Bale to shift on their side of the booth. As he lowered himself, Pink got an eyeful of the golden buttons on his waistcoat.

"I don't want to be here longer than necessary," the mayor said. "My name's Spencer Sharp. As you've probably worked out, I'm the Mayor of Poulsen, so it falls to me to deal with this … unfortunate scenario we find ourselves in." Spencer Sharp scratched his chin, looking around at them. "You'll want to know the details, I suppose. Well, it's like this: three weeks ago, a jeweller named Declan Mint went missing. He owns a shop in Poulsen but undertakes a lot of his trading in Holding. He was on his way back from one of these visits when he disappeared. *Before* dusk, I should add. He was last seen at Poulsen Station, so whatever happened to him must have happened on the road from there to here. Many of us went out looking the next day. We didn't say so to his family, but we were looking for a body – manabeast attacks are rare during daylight hours, but they do happen. Nothing, however, was found."

The mayor crossed his arms and leaned back. "I should add I never thought it was a manabeast attack myself. I knew Declan had accumulated debts and was struggling to pay them off. I assumed he'd missed payments with unsavoury clients, and debt collectors had chosen to exact … repayment on the road, where there were no witnesses. The lack of a body seemed to confirm this. My guess was that they had hidden the evidence – that way, no one could say it was *not* a manabeast attack.

"Then, about a week later, a whole group of coal miners went missing. Seven of them! We searched the mines, but there were no bodies. We thought it must have been a pack, and I started to wonder if Declan *had* been killed by the same manabeasts. Aside from those closest to the miners, many of the other townsfolk were not eager to be involved in the search – we don't have many mages or soldiers here, you see. We did, however, have Divella Bane. She's our town hunter, skilled and trained in magic. Don't misunderstand me, she was not assigned the task of eliminating a whole pack of manabeasts by herself, but I thought she could look for signs and tell us something of what happened. Well, I'm sure you've worked out the pattern in this story. She went looking and hasn't been seen since. I was struggling with what to do next, but a couple of weeks passed and there were no more attacks. People became less wary, although no less upset, of course. Trips that had been put off were being made again. But then, a couple of days ago, someone else went missing. Tell me, how much do you know about dukesbane?"

Pink shrugged. "It's a plant with an orange flower and … white spots?" She looked to Jase and Sol, but both seemed confused by the question.

Bale, however, nodded and said, "They always grow near rocks that contain the arcannen mineral."

"Exactly. There's an exhausted arcannen mine just east of Poulsen, where a company from Holding cultivate these plants. They have some plan to use them for a new type of potion. Probably one of those so-called health elixirs – the city is full of them. However, it was a great benefit to us when this company arrived, as they employed people from Poulsen to help pick the plants. One of these workers, a man named Corey Leathers, is the latest person to have gone missing."

The mayor paused, looking around, before bending close. "There's something else as well. Another of their workers – Cylan Wight, a friend of my son's – went to the site last night to retrieve something he'd left behind. Pretty foolish to be out in the wilderness after dusk, especially in the same area where Leathers went missing, but my son doesn't have the smartest of friends, and Wight probably thought he'd be safe on horseback. He returned, of course, but told my son he'd seen a manabeast prowling the area. Not a wolf-type, but something … else. He's kept his story relatively quiet – Scottie, my son, told me he thinks no one will believe what he saw."

"This manabeast," said Sol, who, like the others, had

been paying rapt attention. "What did it look like?"

"I think you'll need to ask him that. I haven't put anyone else onto it – no one wants to be trekking across the wilderness around here at the moment. But you're all trained mages, and I hear Wing are second to none. I think you're my best chance at finding out what's going on."

Pink winced at the not-so-subtle flattery, but it certainly seemed to go down well with Jase and Sol, who both wore pleased expressions. That was until they caught each other's eyes. "We'll have to speak to Instructor Texeria, of course," said Pink, resisting the temptation to roll her eyes as they looked away from each other in disgust, "but I gather he'll want us to investigate."

The sudden sound of smashing glass made her jump. She swivelled to locate its source and found a scene that filled her with instant trepidation. The intoxicated blond man was pointing the remains of a glass mug at the Magicom soldiers, who were on their feet, looking angry. The rest of the glass was on the table, and blood dripped from the man's right hand where he held the jagged edge. The common room went deathly silent, and a few people even got out of their seats to head for the exit. The mayor groaned.

"… think you … own Blake. This is … our town … I'm not afraid of you!"

He's going to get himself killed, the idiot.

"Sit down," hissed Sol as she rose from her seat. "This isn't anything to do with us."

Ignoring him, she moved over as the commander drew his sword and, in one swift movement, slashed the man's arm. The man yelled in pain, dropping the jagged glass and clutching at the wound before another soldier moved around the side of the table and threw him bodily to the ground. Several stomping boots followed.

"Stop!" she shouted as she hurried over. The soldiers looked up in surprise at her arrival. "Can't you see he's not able to defend himself?"

"Don't get involved, girl," one of them said.

"Wing," said the commander, eyeing her uniform as if that explained it. He glanced over her shoulder at Jase and Bale, who'd both followed. Jase looked like he'd rather be anywhere else in the world, and even Bale wore a wary expression. Sol and the mayor hadn't moved.

"He's clearly had too much to drink," Pink said. "Let me take him home where he can't be a bother to anyone else."

"It's too late for that," replied the commander as Pink knelt down to put a hand on the man's back. "He doesn't get to threaten us. Now move aside!"

Pink continued to stare up at him, unmoving. The commander's eyes flashed, and he stepped forward and backhanded her hard across the face, causing her to tumble back, her ears ringing. She clutched her face, shooting daggers at him.

"Commander Riccard, isn't it? Perhaps I can be of assistance?"

"There's nothing you can assist with, *Mayor*," spat the commander as Spencer Sharp arrived, placing a hand on Pink's shoulder.

"Perhaps you should reconsider. You see, that was my son you were attacking."

This seemed to amuse some of the soldiers, and as Jase and Bale helped her to her feet, Pink noticed a look of anger on the mayor's face, which was quickly hidden.

"Quite," he said, chortling along. "But you *should* allow me to take him home, Commander. You could take him to Holding, of course, but why bother with all that effort over someone who's had a bit too much to drink? Besides,

I don't think your superiors would be amused by my constant appeals."

"How dare …" said one of the soldiers, stepping forward, but Riccard held out an arm, looking at Spencer Sharp with his lip curled.

"Actions have consequences. It would be wise to remind your son of that, Sharp." The commander spat on the ground and inclined his head for the mayor to take his son. They seemed to have forgotten about Pink, which suited her fine.

"Let's get you home, Scottie," the mayor said as he helped his son rise, placing one of his arms over his shoulder. His son mumbled something incoherent but allowed himself to be led away.

CHAPTER SIX

Pink was woken by the strong light of the sun. It beamed through the tavern's ground-floor window, barely hindered by the drawn, yellow curtains. She threw off the blankets covering her and looked around the room, taking in three empty beds. *I've slept late. But at least that means I can wash and dress more easily.*

She headed to the adjacent washroom, where a bathtub sat beneath a circular metallic plate. Bronze pipes connected the plate to a pump and handle and to a boiler on the far side of the room. She undressed, stepped into the tub and pumped the handle so it sprayed hot water, running two fingers over her cheek as the liquid ran down her body. Her skin still felt tender. That soldier, Commander Riccard, had hit her hard, but what could she do? The highest authority in the town, the mayor, had seen it happen and had been unwilling or unable to do anything other than defuse the situation. Certainly, there would be no repercussions for the commander – nobody in their right mind would go against Magicom for something like that.

Anger rose up in her at the unfairness of it all, but she controlled it. Just. August was the one who fought Magicom; she had other priorities. She focused instead on the mission ahead as she redressed and descended the stairs to the common room where the others were seated.

"Come and have some breakfast, Pink," said Jase, shifting to make space for her in the booth. "I asked the innkeeper to leave you some – look!" On the centre of the table was a china plate covered by another. Jase pushed it towards her, lifting off the covering plate, revealing eggs, bacon and fried tomatoes underneath. He beamed at her. She couldn't help but be amused – it was clear Jase was trying to make her feel better about the previous evening. And she had to admit the food smelled amazing.

Sol, who sat on the opposite side of the booth with Bale, wouldn't make eye contact with her at all. She thought she knew why – he'd done nothing to help the previous evening. Bale merely looked bored.

"I concur with Master Vine." Instructor Texeria strolled over, a saucer of tea in his hands, steam rising from the liquid. "A good breakfast is an important start to the day." He had found them in their room the previous evening after they'd made a quick exit from the common room and the Magicom soldiers. They'd passed on everything the mayor had told them, but, as of yet, he hadn't told them what he was planning on doing with that information, nor what he'd been doing himself.

"How long did I sleep for?" asked Pink, resisting the temptation to roll her eyes at the pair of them as she accepted a knife and fork from Jase and started to tackle her food.

"Sunrise was a few hours ago," replied Texeria. "Now, I've been thinking about what you told me last night, and I think you should visit the dukesbane site to conduct some interviews, primarily with Cylan Wight, the man who witnessed this strange manabeast. Our contract is to find out what happened to these missing townsfolk, and since the latest disappearance – Corey Leathers –

happened to be one of their workers, there may be some connection. This should help." He reached into his grey coat and pulled out a rolled piece of paper that he passed to Pink. Raising an eyebrow, she put down her cutlery and took it. She unrolled the paper and, with Jase leaning over her shoulder, found a map of western Blake – Wing and Poulsen clearly marked, as well as the old arcannen mine. She also spotted the coal mines about ten miles south of Wing.

"We can do that," she replied, looking around at the others to receive their nods of agreement. She frowned. Something about that seemed to have amused Texeria. *He wore that same look when I first asked him about the contract.*

"The way you say that makes it sounds like you're not going to be there," said Sol before Pink could ask him what was so funny.

Texeria gave them a lopsided smile. "Something's come up. I can't go with you today. I leave it all in Pink's capable hands and look forward to hearing the outcome."

Sol, who'd leaned over the table to take a closer look at the map, looked up at the instructor. "Where will you be?"

"That's private, I'm afraid, Master Draeon."

Sol crossed his arms, a hard look coming into his eyes. "You're the instructor in charge of fulfilling this contract, yet when we find a lead, you won't join us, nor will you tell us what you're doing instead."

There was an awkward silence at the table. Pink shot Sol an irritated look. Keat Texeria was *her* mentor. What right did Sol have to speak to him that way? She doubted he would dare to speak to Instructor May in the same manner.

Texeria, unsurprisingly, didn't rise to the bait. "These contracts are yours to fulfil," he replied curtly, "in repayment for the training Wing provided you with."

Looking mutinous but perhaps realising he'd overstepped his bounds, Sol chose not to respond.

Once Pink had finished her breakfast, they were back outside of the tavern, the air chilly but dry. Only a few puddles gave any indication it'd been raining the previous night. Texeria said his goodbyes and walked in the direction of the western gate, whistling as his boots scraped along the road. Pink watched him go. Although she accepted his decision not to tell them, she did wonder what he was up to.

They retrieved their horses and trotted in the opposite direction. At the end of the street, the road widened and led into a loud and busy market area. The sound of merchants advertising their wares pierced through the noise while the smells of cooked meat and spices filled their nostrils. Once they'd manoeuvred their way through the marketplace, the road continued on through another residential street. On the first corner stood a Magicom clinic, its white marble walls standing out against the nearby brickwork. Posters of August covered much of its large, glass window, and two grey-clad soldiers stood guard outside. Pink determinedly kept her eyes ahead.

The eastern gate soon came into sight, a small archway built into the wall with a guardhouse to one side. Seeing that Bale had ridden a little ahead, Pink decided to trot her horse alongside his.

"Thank you for last night," she said. He looked over, the briefest hint of puzzlement in his brown eyes. "For your support with that … *incident*," she clarified. "You didn't have to come over with Jase. But you did."

"We're both part of Wing," he said as if that explained everything.

Pink's response died on her lips as he trotted ahead

again. She watched his back, feeling a small smile forming.

He was the right person for this contract, after all.

The sun shone brightly as they rode northeast from Poulsen, the warmth in the air a stark contrast to the previous day. After an hour or so, the terrain began to change. Grass and fields gave way to reddish-brown rock, and shrubbery became more sporadic, while great caverns appeared from mounds in the earth with smoother and flatter land before them, evidence of moved rocks and soil. Above these mounds, the land rose and fell, greener again, and Pink could see patchy arcas where plants with orange flowers grew. *Dukesbane.*

They trotted their horses around these mounds until they found a large building made out of brick with high windows – many of which were broken – and a slanted slate roof. Pink might've thought it deserted had it not been for the two Magicom soldiers standing guard outside the main entrance, eyes watchful. Plainly dressed men and women sat on the grass nearby, sleeves rolled up and muddy boots to one side, eating sandwiches and drinking from flasks. They looked over curiously.

"What business do you have here?" the nearest soldier asked once they'd reined up near the building, distrust obvious in his features.

"We're Wing mages," Pink replied, wondering the same thing.

"We can see that," said the same soldier. "What do you want?"

"We were hoping to speak to … whoever's in charge," Pink said, trying to keep her voice even. This was not a good start. "It's regarding Corey Leathers."

The two soldiers looked at one another. The first one looked back and said, "Be on your way."

"But …"

The soldier's eyes narrowed. "I won't say it again. You've no business here, sticking your noses into—"

At that point, the door to the building creaked open, and a middle-aged woman stepped out. With neatly brushed auburn hair cut at the shoulders and dressed in a stylish black suit and white shirt, Pink guessed she wasn't at the site to forage.

"I thought I heard something." The woman studied them, managing to smile while looking politely puzzled. "You're from Wing. My, that syntaxicite looks spectacular. How it shines! Articulas Wing's a genius, isn't he? My name is Miriam Shawgrave – I'm the manager here. Can I help you?"

"We're undertaking a contract to investigate the disappearance of Corey Leathers," replied Pink as the soldiers shuffled about, looking annoyed – *she's less confrontational, at least* – "and other missing people from Poulsen."

Miriam's eyes narrowed. "You were hired by someone *from* Poulsen?"

Pink hesitated. Contracts were supposed to be confidential unless specified otherwise. "Yes – you'll understand that I can't say whom."

The look Miriam gave Pink suggested withholding this information wouldn't be an option.

"Articulas Wing would be grateful," said Bale unexpectedly.

Miriam turned to Bale, cocking her head. "Very well," she said, "although I don't think I can tell you anything you don't already know. There's a picket around that side of the building." She pointed. "You can tie up your horses there."

"Madam Shawgrave …" began one of the soldiers.

"Excuse me, who's in charge here?" she shot back.

The soldier looked furious. Pink gave a word of thanks and dismounted with the others, then led her horse around the side quickly. If there was going to be an argument, she didn't want to be in the middle of it.

"Thanks again," Pink said to Bale as they tied their horses to the picket. "Part of Wing, right?"

She was sure he almost smiled that time.

Miriam was waiting for them on their return, holding the doors open so they could pass into the building. Pink ignored the glowers of the soldiers.

Crates upon crates of dukesbane flowers, like regiments of orange petals, sat on the concrete ground inside, their aromatic scent thick in the air, brightened by the natural light streaming into the building. The rest of the space was bare aside from a metal stairway that led to a walkway above.

"There are so many," gasped Pink. The others murmured agreement at her side.

Miriam seemed pleased by this reaction. "This area is a hotspot for the plant," she explained. "Something about its proximity to the arcannen mineral helps it to thrive. Magicom discovered the connection first – that was how they found the areas where arcannen could be mined, not long after Tette Tesyn created the first arcannen potion. They no longer use the mines here, but they own the surrounding lands, so you could say we're renting it from them. They insisted we use their soldiers as part of the deal."

"You're using the plant to make a health elixir?" Sol asked, repeating what the mayor had said.

Miriam looked at him open-mouthed. "What those quacks sell in Holding? Mrs Madsen's All-Remedy Cure and the like? By the Trinity, no. Nothing like that." She swung her hand over to the boxes. "We're trying to create something very unique back in Holding – a sedative, essentially. One that puts the user in a lucid state, useful for surgery, childbirth and injuries. The flower of the dukesbane plant is known to hold these properties, but it can be dangerous, even toxic. However, my people in the city have been doing good work using its ground-up petals to synthesize a compound that negates the harmful effects and promotes the useful ones."

"Those people outside collected all these flowers?" asked Jase, amazement in his voice.

Miriam's lopsided smile made Pink think of Keat Texeria. "This is almost a week's worth of collection. After it's cultivated, it's taken to Poulsen Station by wagon and then goes on the trade train to Holding."

"This is all very interesting," said Pink, "but what about Corey Leathers? Can you tell us anything about what happened to him?"

"You're straight to the point, aren't you?" said Miriam, her eyes shining. "I can see why you're the team leader. And that hair … magnificent."

Pink shifted awkwardly but refused to look at any of the others. It was her mentor who'd taken on the contract, but they were all mages; they all had equal standing.

"Please don't feel embarrassed," said Miriam, smiling. "I only say what I see – and I am a scientist at heart, so naturally, your hair is interesting to me. But I won't digress. Let's see … Corey Leathers …" Her expression changed then – the smile dropped, and her lips drew into a thin line. "I assume whoever sent you knows as much as I. Corey went missing earlier this week. I'd warned my workers to stick together and not work too close to dusk – he obviously chose to ignore both those instructions. I don't want to sound unsympathetic, but I cannot keep my workers safe if they act foolishly. Those abandoned mines make the perfect den for manabeasts. My guess is he got too close to one of the openings and something attacked him from within."

"I told you these disappearances were nothing but manabeast attacks," muttered Sol from one side.

Pink turned to him. "That wouldn't explain what happened to the bodies."

"That may be something you don't want to think too much about," said Miriam, drawing her attention back. "I too am aware others have gone missing from the wilderness around Poulsen. Manabeasts are the very reason why we're so strict here about our rules."

"The information we've received suggests manabeasts haven't been seen in the area for some time."

Miriam pursed her lips. "I find that … difficult to believe. Manabeasts don't just disappear. My best bet is there is a wolf-type pack living within the mines here and another in the coal mines nearer to Highstone Hill, where I heard several miners were attacked."

Pink nodded but didn't feel convinced. *There's no evidence to show those miners were attacked. Like Corey Leathers, they just … vanished.* It seemed bizarre that so many had gone missing, and no one had seen the manabeasts responsible. Well, almost no one. "Is there somebody who works here named Cylan Wight?" she asked.

A flicker of surprise crossed Miriam's face. "Why, yes, he's outside with the others."

"Would you mind if we spoke to him?"

Miriam took a moment to consider. "May I ask why?"

"It would be good to speak to one of your workers, and he was a name given by the person who contracted us," said Pink, choosing her words carefully. If Miriam was as strict about the rules as she made out, Pink didn't want this man to lose his job because of their involvement. "It could be he was the only person our client knew."

"So, with that in mind, it doesn't matter who you talk to?"

"We were told he was trustworthy," said Sol, unexpectedly coming to her aid, "so we'd rather speak to someone whose character is vouched for."

"Not that we think you're not," added Pink hastily.

Miriam sighed. "Very well. But don't talk to him for too long, if you wouldn't mind. With the rainfall we've had, many new dukesbane plants are ripe for picking. I need my workers out there."

They left with assurances they would be quick and made their way from the building. *She was helpful,* thought Pink as they moved towards the group having their lunch, *but she seemed uncomfortable about us speaking to her workers. Does she believe we're going to make them think twice about the safety of their job? Or is it something else?*

"Which one of you is Cylan Wight?" Sol asked, his words coming out a little too quickly as if he wanted to be seen as the one in charge. Pink scratched her nose, using her hand to hide an amused smile.

A spindly middle-aged man with scruffy brown hair and, from the look of it, several missing teeth raised his hand slowly, looking on guard. "Excuse us," said Pink, giving him a smile she hoped was more reassuring than the look Sol wore. "We wondered if we could have a quick word with you?"

When they had led him away from the others, Pink asked, "We heard you saw something unusual around here. A type of manabeast?"

The man looked positively alarmed now. "I don't know what you mean."

Pink told him about the mayor's son.

"Scottie," spat the man. "I knew I shouldn't drink with him. Can't trust a politician's son. Okay, maybe I did see something, but I shouldn't say. I could get in trouble."

He looked towards the building, where Miriam was outside, speaking to the Magicom soldiers. Pink followed his gaze and then looked back at him. "We won't say anything," she assured him.

The man hesitated.

"You can trust us," added Pink. "We've already heard the story. We just want to hear it from your point of view."

"Well, if you already know, I won't deny it." The man took a last look at Miriam and the soldiers before continuing. "Sometimes, we have a little card game before we return to town. We usually play for coin. Not much – just a few wyrms. On the day you mentioned, Miriam was trying to clear us out pretty quick, and I … er … left my bag of winnings by the old building." He shook his head as if he still couldn't believe it'd happened. "We're not allowed to be on site after dusk, but I had to come back; I couldn't bear knowing my coins were lying around, waiting for someone else to pick them up. It was foolish, I know, but I took my sword just in case. Anyway, although it was dark by the time I got here, I found my coins, only," – he stopped, biting his bottom lip – "I saw something."

"A manabeast?" asked Pink.

"A wolf-type?" asked Sol.

Cylan wrung his hands. "I don't know what I saw, to be honest. It didn't have the look of a wolf … it was more like … a shadow crawling on four legs." He looked at them as if expecting laughter. When none came, he continued. "The only thing I saw clearly was its yellow eyes before it shot its magic at me. It missed its mark, but the energy blast was enough to convince me my sword would be useless. I was on my horse and away in seconds."

"Is it possible this manabeast shelters in the mines?" Pink asked him, thinking about what Miriam had said. The manager did not know Cylan had seen this creature, but his words supported her assumption.

Cylan rubbed his chin. "I suppose that would make sense." He glanced in the direction of the mines as if suddenly worried about their proximity.

"We can take this back to Instructor Texeria," said Pink, looking around at the others. "Thank you," she said to Cylan. "You've been very helpful."

"You will keep your word? I don't want to lose my job."

"We won't say a thing to your manager," said Pink, glancing at the building. Miriam had gone, but Pink was sure she would have her own questions for Cylan once they'd left.

***

Once they'd returned their horses to the Salted Pig's stables, Pink practically bounced into the tavern, eager to find Instructor Texeria and tell him all they'd discovered. Inside, however, she saw only the innkeeper and Magicom soldiers. Disappointed, she approached the counter.

"Have you seen our instructor?" she asked.

The innkeeper gave her a look that could've meant anything and then nodded his head towards the soldiers. It was then that Pink noticed what she hadn't before – Instructor Texeria sitting in their midst, passing something to one of them. Her mouth fell open.

One of the soldiers passed him something back,

something that looked small and metallic. Texeria pocketed it in his grey coat and, looking up and spotting them, said something to the soldiers before moving over.

"Hello, gang!" he said. If he noticed their surprise, he didn't show it. "How did it go?"

Pink, thrown off guard, quickly recounted what Miriam Shawgrave and Cylan Wight had told them. "What should we do now?" she asked when she'd finished.

Texeria, who'd looked as if he'd only been half-listening, shrugged his shoulders. "I suppose I'll give it some thought. Well, there's no need to stay here any longer. Let's be on our way."

Pink, who'd been hoping for a better response than this, frowned at his back as he departed the tavern. There was a larger issue at hand, though. Sol and Bale didn't seem concerned as they followed Instructor Texeria outside, but Pink could read the unasked question in Jase's eyes.

What had Instructor Texeria been trading with Magicom soldiers?

CHAPTER SEVEN

Rox Salvamal raised a silk handkerchief to his nose, as he always did when visiting the rancid prisons of Alsing. Men and women pleaded at him as he and his lieutenant, Rael Rookevelt, made their way through the dank corridor. He ignored them all. These people had committed crimes – they deserved to spend their days down in the cold, unforgiving cells. Soon, Salvamal would fill these cells with all those who allied themselves with August Silvershield and Ashes.

He'd already made a start.

"Has the prisoner yielded *anything* useful?" asked Salvamal, speaking to Rookevelt for the first time that evening.

On his arrival to Alsing, Rookevelt had told him that the prisoner had claimed not to know Silvershield's location. Salvamal had been hoping for more and had remained silent as a means of showing his displeasure.

"I'm afraid not."

Another officer might have issued a grovelling apology following these words, but Rookevelt, a middle-aged man with short, silver hair, showed no sign of acknowledging his failure. *Doubtless, the infallible Rael Rookevelt's too proud for that.* Although usually reliable, the lieutenant did lack imagination in certain areas, and this was a perfect example of that.

"And the family?" asked Salvamal.

"The mother remains under house arrest. There has been no sign of the younger brother since he escaped the farmhouse. Mason remains unaware of their fates."

Interesting. Salvamal stored that bit of information for future reference. "You tried every form of persuasion with Mason, just in case he was lying?"

"We were very persuasive." Rookevelt's tone suggested he found such tactics distasteful. *A great weakness*, Salvamal thought. A good soldier should be willing to do anything for his side's victory. Especially considering they had a license to do as they pleased in Alsing. While prisoners' crimes were ultimately judged by the government, the prison was a Magicom-owned building.

"Well, perhaps I should ask him myself."

They'd stopped at a cell where the door built into the bars was wide open, the man inside chained to the ceiling. Rookevelt hadn't understated the level of persuasion Phantex Mason had endured – his bare chest was covered in angry red cuts, while his face was dominated by welts and bruises. Despite all this, when Mason looked up and met his eyes, Salvamal didn't like the defiance he still saw.

"Good evening, Mr Mason." Salvamal came closer, the prisoner's eyes following him. "I assume you've lost track of time down here, but if you're at all curious, it's been four days since your capture." Salvamal moved to the side, where a bowl of water stood waiting on a wooden stool. He picked it up and lifted it to the cracked lips of the hanging man. It wasn't refused.

"Do you know who I am?" Salvamal asked as he returned the bowl.

The prisoner breathed deeply, a sigh escaping his lips

as the water trickled down. His voice was hoarse as he spoke. "Rox Salvamal. General of Magicom's military forces."

Salvamal smiled. "Good. I see you're a direct man who doesn't play games. In that case, I shall be direct with you – I want to offer you a deal." Mason said nothing but continued to meet Salvamal's eyes. Rookevelt stayed to one side, hands behind his back. Salvamal continued. "Tell me how to find your friend Silvershield, and I'll set you free – all charges dropped. I'll put it in writing and have it signed by government officials, so you can be assured it is binding."

Mason briefly closed his eyes. "General," he croaked. "Do you really believe that if I knew where August was, he wouldn't just change his plans and go elsewhere? It's been four days, you say. He'll know I've been captured by now."

"That has occurred to me, but I asked you to tell me how to find him, not where he is now. You must know some of his hideaways or what his next plan is. Anything that will lead to his capture, even indirectly, will lead to your release."

Mason looked away in apparent disgust, but Salvamal pursued his point. "You're known to us now, Phantex Mason, just as Silvershield is. No longer can you hide away as an unknown member of Ashes like the others. We know who you are, who your family are and where you're from. Even if you weren't in Alsing, with that information, there would be no escape for you or the ones you love. There is only one way out of this for you now. Why fight when you've already lost? Just give me what I want."

Mason met his eyes. "I will never help you find August."

Salvamal tsked his annoyance. *He believes I'll kill him, yet he's prepared to meet that end in order to ensure Silvershield's safety.*

It was time for a different tactic. "Lieutenant," he said without removing his gaze from Mason. Rookevelt came forward. "You said we had Esta Mason and the younger brother, whom we found hiding at a farmhouse, in custody, did you not?" He didn't wait for an answer. Seeing Mason's eyes widen was enough. "Bring them both to Alsing. Let's see how much longer Mr Mason wants to keep his friend's secrets while they're being *questioned* in front of him."

Phantex Mason let out a roar and tried to pull the chains from the ceiling, all restraint evaporating. He did no more than crumble a bit of stone but did not let up. *It's strange how prisoners always do that when they're angry. They must know they'll never break out of those chains.* Salvamal watched him struggle for a little longer, a small smile playing on his lips, before turning on his heel and marching out of the cell, Mason's shouted threats ignored.

"Let him mull that over for a while," said Salvamal once they were ascending the concrete stairs again. "I won't trust anything he says until his mother is in there with him anyway, and the brother if we can find him. When they are, we'll have everything he knows about August Silvershield – I guarantee it."

CHAPTER EIGHT

If someone had told him a few days ago that Roeden would be journeying the wilderness with August Silvershield, he wouldn't have believed them. Yet not even this exciting development was enough to quell the anxiety building over his brother's and mother's safety. It was constant, like a ball of fear in the pit of his stomach, and every time he thought about what had happened to Samuel, it grew worse.

We will rescue them, he kept telling himself. *Taurus is on his way to free Mother, and August will do the same for Phantex.*

Following their departure from the farmhouse, Chadwick had relayed to August the finer details of Phantex's capture. August's initial response had been silence. It was only after they'd put many leagues behind them, and August had suggested they take a few hours rest before dawn, that he'd spoken about it.

"Phantex will be taken to Alsing, Magicom's prison complex in Holding," he'd said. "Breaking him out will be no easy task and near-impossible without arcannen, which I'm running low on." August had looked grim at these words. "I'd planned to stock up in Doscadia. As much as it pains me to delay, we must stick to that plan."

Two days had passed since then, and although Roeden understood August's reasoning for not saving Phantex right away, the delay gnawed at him, especially as he'd had too much time to think about it. Travelling was boring, the wilderness not as interesting as he'd imagined, the roads, woodlands and fields all very much the same. He found he missed the scenery of Bodham – the little alleyways, the abandoned buildings, the places none of the adults knew how to get to. He didn't enjoy sleeping out in the open either, and that wasn't just because he was having nightmares about Phantex being blasted with magic in the same way Samuel had been.

Although the rain had cleared up, the ground was still damp and the nights cold. Even wrapped in his blanket, he failed to gain any great level of comfort, not to mention the soreness in his limbs when he awoke. It made him pine for his bed with its feather mattress and pillows.

They saw no manabeasts, but Roeden didn't mind *that* so much – he'd been told how dangerous they were his entire life, and that fear was deeply embedded.

August Silvershield was another issue entirely. When the Ashes leader had first appeared at the farmhouse, he'd been incredible, taking out half a dozen Magicom soldiers by himself – in seconds! Roeden hadn't forgotten how August had flipped in the air to avoid an incoming fireball and had rehearsed many times in his mind how he'd recount that particular feat to his friends back in Bodham. Since then, however, August hadn't met Roeden's expectations. He didn't ride with them and, since he'd briefly shared his plans on that first night, had barely spared them a word.

He did, however, always conjure a flame whenever they needed a fire. Thanks to Phantex, Roeden knew a bit about magic, and one of the things he knew was that magic from an arcannen potion lasted for about twenty-four hours. So when August continued to use magic twenty-four hours *after* the farmhouse incident, Roeden realised the Ashes leader was taking extra. This surprised him – surely August should only take a potion when needed?

The only time August did show any interest was when they were camped at night. Roeden would catch August staring at him and Chadwick, dark eyes appraising as if they were a puzzle he couldn't work out. Roeden wished Taurus was with them – he'd liked the big man. Still, if anyone (aside from August) had to be sent to rescue his mother, Roeden was thankful it was him. Even without magic, Taurus looked like a force to be reckoned with.

It was nearing sunset on the second day when August called them to a halt. As they reined in, Roeden looked beyond Chadwick to see the road dipping towards two merging tributaries below, a huge body of water flowing eastwards, a forest dominating both sides of its banks. On the south of this merging was a hub of wooden buildings and people. Voices, mixed with the calls of various river birds, carried up towards them.

Despite the splendour of the river, Roeden only had eyes for one thing. In the V-shape where the two tributaries met, a magnificent-looking glass structure had been built, inside which a stationary steam locomotive chugged next to a concrete platform. His eyes bulged with excitement. He'd never seen a train before! The tracks exiting the structure ran west and east, the former joining another in the distance that ran north and south.

"It's a crossroads," said Chadwick, glancing over his shoulder at Roeden. "The tracks run to the Three Big Cities: Holding, Sermouth and Doscadia."

Roeden's eyes followed each track until it disappeared into the horizon. "Which one runs to Doscadia?" he asked.

"The eastern one, alongside the river."

They continued to trot their horses down the slope, the sound of the people below drawing ever nearer. When they were about halfway to the hub, August reined in, pulled up the hood of his cloak and chucked Chadwick a brown leather purse, which jingled with the unmistakable sound of coins.

"It would be unwise for me to get any nearer," he explained to Roeden, who was looking over curiously. "There are posters of me everywhere, which means plenty will be on the lookout – especially with the reward on offer. There are bound to be Magicom soldiers around too. You two will need to gather supplies for the journey ahead. I'll meet you within the forest on this side of the bank, below the main road."

"August, I've been meaning to ask you something," Chadwick said. August looked over and waited as Chadwick shuffled on his horse. "I understand why you have … come out in the open now. But where have you been hiding all this time?"

August gave Chadwick a look, one Roeden would have found difficult to meet had those dark eyes been on him. "Verity Ravenscar's been sheltering me," August said after a moment.

"The Minister for Agriculture?" Chadwick seemed amazed. "Is she … on our side?"

"For all intents and purposes. Many in the government don't care for Magicom, but having the support of someone of her stature will have a huge impact. And if she could bring more to the cause …" August looked up into the air as if deep in thought. "She's still wary though and would deny any involvement at this point. There's no way to prove she's affiliated with us, and it would be foolish for anyone to try. Her family are very powerful."

Roeden thought that an odd comment, but perhaps this was what Taurus had meant about August. He was always planning ahead. Chadwick made an impressed *hmm* noise before asking, "Is she anything to do with your going to Doscadia?"

August's eyes fell back on Chadwick. Instead of answering, he asked, "How did you find out about the threat to Phantex?"

"You know I'm good with my ear to the ground, and I'm good at drinking in taverns. Even ones frequented by Magicom soldiers. You learn things. Unfortunately, I learned about the unit heading to Bodham a little too late."

For the first time, Roeden felt something shift in regard to his feelings towards Chadwick. He *had* tried to save Roeden's brother, and leaving Roeden's mother there had turned out to be the right thing to do. Taurus was much better equipped to rescue her than Chadwick and Roeden were. "Perhaps when we're in Doscadia, I'll tell you the plan," August said at last. "With Taurus gone and you two in his place, I need to rethink things a bit." He jumped off his horse and passed the reins to Chadwick, who raised his eyebrows in surprise. "Try to get a good price for them," August said.

"We're selling the horses?" Chadwick was evidently confused. "What if you're recognised on the road? We may need them to outrun any pursuers."

"We're not taking the Doscadian Road." August looked over to where the trees met the river banks. "We're taking the River Road."

Chadwick's hands tightened on the reins and when he spoke, the pitch of his voice seemed higher than usual. "The River Road is dangerous!"

August looked back over his shoulder. "No more

dangerous than taking the Doscadian Road where anyone could see us, where patrolling Magicom soldiers will be questioning every man of my age. Being on foot will take longer, but it cannot be helped. I won't be much use to Phantex if I get myself captured at the first opportunity. Besides, even if we did outrun any pursuers, Magicom would know where we were heading."

"And what about the rumours about what *lives* in that river? How many travellers and hunters have *Severity News* reported missing over the past year? No one goes that way anymore."

August's look was hard. "Exactly."

Chadwick threw up his hands in exasperation. "There must be another way, August. What makes you think we'll fare any better than those who have gone before?"

August seemed to think for a moment before he said, "Because you're with me."

Turning his back, August hitched up his sack and moved down the slope in the direction of the forest. Chadwick wore a look of disbelief as he watched him go. After a moment, he shook his head and muttered to himself before climbing off the horse and holding out his arms for Roeden to do likewise. He handed the reins of August's horse to Roeden, who understood they were now to walk their horses towards the hub. Roeden could see that Chadwick was agitated and knew it was best not to speak.

"What lives in that river?" he asked, finding he could not help himself.

Chadwick turned to look at him; his brow furrowed as if he'd forgotten Roeden was there. "Nobody knows," he said moodily, turning back. "*Severity News* believes it to be some species of manabeast, but no one has ever reported seeing it. All those who've hunted it have disappeared.

August is mad to take us that way, MAD."

"What's *Severity News*?"

"It's a publication. The only one worth reading. They hire reporters to write news stories," he added, looking back and spotting Roeden's confused face. "Of course, Magicom lean on it heavily, affecting what it publishes in order to show themselves in a positive manner. Since the trains have expanded over the wilderness, many people outside of Holding can now read it on the same day it's printed."

Roeden thought the only news stories *he'd* be interested in reading would be the ones about Ashes but did not say anything because it seemed, from Chadwick's tone, that he thought highly of the publication, and Roeden did not want him to stop answering questions.

"Why aren't we taking the train to Doscadia?" was his next one, though Roeden wondered if he was asking too much.

Chadwick obviously thought so because he tittered irritably. "You do want to know about everything, don't you? Your brother is far less talkative than you are." He sighed. "We cannot get the train because the station – both here and in Doscadia – will be teeming with Magicom soldiers, and probably so will the trains themselves. Besides, who knows when the next passenger one is? Look, we're here, so you can stop asking questions."

They had reached the first hut. Other travellers – garbed in similar cloaks as them – were steadily moving in and out of its wooden door, a bell above jingling every time they did so.

"Stay outside with the horses," muttered Chadwick as he handed Roeden his own reins before pushing his way inside. The horses seemed quite content to graze on the grass, so Roeden watched a group of swans that had wandered over from the bank, pecking at the ground. It was a few moments before he noticed August's profile staring out at him from the familiar posters stuck to the side of the hut. It was a strange feeling to see August there when the real one had been with them only moments before.

Chadwick soon returned with his pack bulging. As he took back his reins, Roeden could smell the unmistakable aroma of freshly cooked bread. If the food they'd had on their journey so far was any comparison, he guessed that Chadwick had also bought cheese and dried meat. Roeden's stomach rumbled at the thought of the meal – their last bite of bread had been stale, but all this travelling was a hungry business, and they'd not eaten since noon.

"We need to sell the horses next," said Chadwick as they walked through the throng of people. His tone suggested he was still feeling bitter about it. Chadwick led them past a couple more huts and a tavern until they reached a stable near the bank. Inside, Chadwick spoke to the stable master while Roeden tried not to gag from the smell. Eventually, their horses were bought, and Chadwick received a jingling bag, not unlike the one August had given him.

"Selling for your train ticket, friend?"

Roeden glanced towards the entrance to see two men in long woollen overcoats, with satchels slung over their shoulders, blocking some of the light from outside. The one at the back was large and wore a cap over his brown hair; the other, the one who'd spoken, had long, dank hair and a scar reminiscent of an anchor running down one side of his face. Roeden didn't like the way he was eyeing the new purse Chadwick was holding in his hand and, from Chadwick's frown, neither did he.

"Nothing like that," he replied curtly. "Come on, Roeden."

Roeden followed Chadwick from the stables. The two men, who reeked of smoke and sweat, parted – barely – so they could pass through, but when they were outside, the one who'd spoken called out to them.

"Be safe out there. There are dangerous manabeasts around these parts, even on the Doscadian Road."

"We're taking the River Road," said Roeden, turning back. He didn't like this man's manner, as if he thought they couldn't fend for themselves. Perhaps if he heard they were taking this seemingly perilous road, he might be more suitably impressed.

"The River Road?" The man frowned. For some reason, Chadwick shot Roeden an annoyed look. The man spoke to Chadwick. "No one goes that way – you can't seriously be considering taking a child there?"

"My nephew and I need to get to Doscadia quickly," said Chadwick, speaking as if weighing each word, "to meet the boy's father, who works as a city guard."

Before the man could say another word, Chadwick put an arm around Roeden's shoulders and led him away. Roeden felt their eyes on his back all the way.

"Mind what you say to strangers," Chadwick told Roeden as they followed the river outside towards the woods. They were the only ones walking in this direction and so were alone now, aside from the duck and geese that ambled across their path. "Now those men know exactly where we're going."

"Why shouldn't they?" asked Roeden.

"Don't be naive. Why do you think they took an interest in us? They saw the purse of coins the stable master gave us for the horses. There are all sorts of people in the wild, and not all are as honourable as August

Silvershield. Those men could have been bandits."

"I did notice the interest they took in the coins," snapped Roeden, angered at being called naive.

Chadwick grunted but didn't reply. They walked the rest of the way in silence, stepping on the stony path that ran adjacent to the river – the noise from the hub becoming a distant murmur and the trickle of the water getting louder as it became shallower over the rocks and stones. Eventually, they reached an old wooden sign that had the words 'River Road' carved into it, standing before the woodland.

"No August yet," Chadwick murmured, peering around the trunks as they made their way under the branches.

"Chadwick, I've been wondering something," said Roeden, realising he was mimicking Chadwick's words to August from earlier.

Chadwick's mouth grew smaller, but Roeden had the feeling he was trying not to smile. "Oh, yes?" he said, coming to a stop and sitting on a fallen trunk, the interest in his voice sounding just a little feigned.

"Why does August not speak with us unless he has to? Is he usually like this?"

Chadwick nodded his head and looked more enthusiastic as if he thought the question was a good one. "No – he's usually a bit more … charismatic. I think Phantex being caught has shaken him. Not that it's unexpected. The game has changed since Holding Castle – now Magicom know his identity, they are coming after him with their considerable resources. He always knew the danger would increase the more risks he took, but knowing and experiencing are two separate things. On top of that, he was close to Phantex – those two are *like* brothers. I think he's worried about Magicom taking someone away from him again."

"Again?"

Chadwick glanced at him. "Have you ever wondered about the name 'Ashes'?"

Roeden shook his head.

"August was almost married once. Her name was Ashe. She was one of those casualties that seem to crop up whenever Magicom are involved. He doesn't talk about it much, but revenge is as important to August as freeing Blake from Magicom's influence."

Roeden tried to imagine August getting married and found he could not, but Chadwick's last statement reminded him of what Taurus had said about his son. "Why are you in Ashes?" he asked Chadwick, thinking perhaps there was more to the man than Roeden gave him credit for.

Chadwick looked away. "I have my reasons."

Roeden thought that a frustratingly ambiguous answer, but Chadwick seemed disinclined to say more, so they waited in silence, disturbed only by the tweeting birds and occasional hoot of an owl. Beneath their feet and through the forest, the road was still visible despite being overrun by plants and nettles, making Roeden appreciate how it would be impossible for the horses to make it through. Now the sun had almost completely set, the air felt chilly and damp under the canopy of leaves, and the darkness enveloped them like a blanket, taking even the comfort of light away. Chadwick continued to look around while Roeden stepped into a clearing to have a closer look at the river, watching it wind and flow in the distance. Eventually, the crack of twigs and the rustling of disturbed bushes told him August had arrived. He spun around but froze when he saw it was not August at all but the two men from the stables.

The men had a look around as they neared. Chadwick, who had backed away into the clearing towards Roeden, created a ball of fire in his hand. The fact Chadwick could use magic was a surprise to Roeden; he had never shown any evidence of it before, nor had Roeden ever seen him in possession of arcannen. Whether Chadwick had conjured the flame to help him see in the gathering darkness or as protection, Roeden didn't know. From the way they slowed, it seemed the men did not either.

"We never introduced ourselves earlier," said the man with the scar pleasantly, conjuring a ball of fire in his own hand. His ball was considerably larger, and the flames seemed to almost lick his face while the light danced in his eyes. Memories flooded back to Roeden of the kitchen in the guesthouse, and suddenly, despite the open space, he felt trapped. The second man didn't, or couldn't, conjure his own magic, but a shift of his cloak revealed a shabby-looking leather holster attached to his midsection, the bronzed curved handle of a pistol visible. "I'm Raff, and this is Baton. We've discussed your journey and feel that, as honest travellers, we cannot leave you to wander the River Road without protection, especially with a child. We're here to offer our services to take you safely to Doscadia." The two men exchanged grins. "Our fee would be modest."

"Thank you, but no," replied Chadwick.

"Are you sure, friend?" The man called Raff moved closer, and once again, Roeden could smell the smoke and sweat on him. Roeden took a step back. "You'd be much safer with us – it'd be a shame if something happened to you. No one would know." Raff glanced behind him as if he wanted to check how far into the woods they were.

"I told you no," said Chadwick, but this time his voice seemed to betray fear. Raff smiled in a way that was not pleasant at all.

"There is no one else to protect you," he said. "I must insist." Roeden's heart skipped a beat as he realised they were not going to take no for an answer. The problem was, if Chadwick accepted, they would be further into the woods and away from any form of protection.

"As it happens, there is," said a voice from behind them. The two men swung around, and Roeden looked past them to see August step into the clearing, hood still up and pack slung over his shoulder. Roeden had been so focused on Raff and Baton that he hadn't seen the Ashes leader approach.

"Who are *you*?" said the man called Baton in a wheezy voice. Roeden noticed his hand moving to the handle of his pistol. Raff said nothing but watched August draw nearer with narrowed eyes.

"These people have already hired me to take them where they need to go. That's why they're refusing your services, no doubt."

Raff didn't look back at Chadwick to see if that was true but moved his hand slightly so the fire lit more of August. "You don't seem very old to have much experience of the wilderness, friend," he said. "These good people would be better protected by us."

"I assure you I'm all the protection anyone needs."

Raff seemed to hesitate. He did not seem to know quite what to make of August. "Have we met before?" he said. "You have a familiar look about you. What's your name?"

August took another step closer. Roeden couldn't see the two men's faces as they faced August but imagined the uncertainty in their eyes. "We must be off," said August, ignoring the question. "I'm sure you gentlemen have other things to be doing as well."

August and Raff stood facing each other for a moment, but eventually, Raff extinguished his flame and signalled to Baton. The two men walked away past August. "Well, if they're in someone else's care, I don't feel so bad about leaving them," said Raff over his shoulder. "Good luck to you all." As they withdrew, Roeden could hear them arguing in hushed, angry voices.

August's eyes followed them all the way.

CHAPTER NINE

August led Chadwick and Roeden east through the forest. Above, the white orb of the moon and the sprinkle of stars fought to shine their light through the canopy of leaves, but it was the flame suspended above August's right palm, moving like a bobbing lantern, that gave them the illumination they needed to navigate the many twists and turns of the path. Roeden took frequent glances behind to see if Raff and Baton were following, but all he could see was darkness and all he could hear – aside from the crunching of the leaves underneath their boots – was the gurgling of the fast-flowing Doscadian River to their left.

He'd been sure at first that the two men would return and attack while their backs were turned – he was in no doubt now what their business was about. As the time passed, however, and the air took on a bite that left his eyes sore and fingers numb, Roeden's thoughts drifted to his warm bed back home and the hearth where the fire crackled in the lounge and Axe's soft fur, and his mother's cooking …

Roeden stumbled, snapping up his drooping head. August glanced in his direction.

"We'll rest here," the Ashes leader said a few minutes later, pointing to a clearing off the path. Roeden and Chadwick were quick to unpack their blankets and wrap the warm wool around their shoulders while August went about finding twigs and fallen branches, stacking them in a specific way that Roeden watched with interest before setting them on fire with a lazy wave of his hand. Once August settled down in front of the crackling flames, he and Chadwick began to discuss a timetable for keeping watch.

"I want to help," said Roeden.

"No," replied August at once. "You need your rest. You're dead on your feet, Roeden."

"I can stay awake," Roeden replied, but he was already wrapped inside his blanket, his head resting against a nearby stump, and he could feel his eyes growing heavy even as he said it …

When he opened his eyes again, the fire seemed to be burning on its last embers. It must still have been night, as all was dark. Roeden could just make out the back of August sitting where the clearing opened, wrapped in his blanket, the hood of his cloak back up. He had a swirling ball of water rotating above his hand and seemed to be concentrating on it. Roeden fell back asleep, still wondering what August was doing.

He was woken by Chadwick at daybreak. Feeling more rested than he had in days and much warmer than the previous night, he untangled himself from his blanket and stood up, watching August kicking aside the burnt sticks from the previous night's fire before covering it with as many leaves as he could.

"In case anyone comes this way," he said in response to Roeden's curious look.

"They might find us anyway," said Chadwick.

August smiled, but there was nothing friendly about it. "Bad luck to them if they do."

The going was much easier in daylight. The adjacent

river had become shallower – they could now see the rocks that protruded above the surface, causing, Roeden was sure, the gurgling sound it was making. His thoughts drifted to the rumours Chadwick had spoken about the previous day. *No manabeast could live in water that shallow,* he thought to himself. *Nothing dangerous, anyway.*

But as they trudged on, the water got quieter, wider and unmistakably deeper. Forced to rethink this assumption, Roeden kept one eye on the river, wondering what had caused so many travellers and hunters to disappear. Roeden always felt relieved when the meandering path took them away from the river.

"See that up there?" Chadwick said to him during one of these times, pointing through the narrow, thin trees on their right to where the ground rose in a steep climb. "At the top is the Doscadian Road, running in the same direction as us, yet straighter and smoother."

"Yet no less dangerous," called August from ahead.

At midday, the three stopped for their lunch of bread and cheese by an apple tree. Excited to pick the fruit, Roeden, with the aid of Chadwick, filled up his pack. When they stopped to find a place to rest that evening, in a spot where the trees were much less dense, Roeden collapsed at once, exhausted from the walking. The evening meal was much the same, but with dried meat. Breakfast the next morning was the same as their lunch the previous day, and Roeden began to wish there was something else to eat. He didn't complain, but his thoughts drifted once again to his mother's cooking: roasted slabs of beef, honey-glazed parsnips, golden crispy potatoes …

As the second day in the woods wore on, Roeden continued to notice the lack of interest August had in communicating with him, or with Chadwick for that matter. Often, he marched a little ahead, rarely speaking aside from offering them some of the food or talking to Chadwick about the watch. Strategizing a plan for Phantex was, perhaps, at the forefront of his mind, yet if that was the case, Roeden wished he'd share his thoughts. While August was still an enigma, Chadwick would talk a great deal. Perhaps it'd been discomfort at the dangers they'd faced when fleeing Magicom that'd left him so surly before, but now he seemed grateful to have such a willing audience in Roeden.

As Roeden had never seen a city, Chadwick told him all about the people of Holding: the affluent hosting social events and meeting for afternoon teas; the marketplaces brimming with traders; the theatres and troupes of street-corner entertainers; and Magicom soldiers everywhere, overseeing the laws as the city guard.

"What about Doscadia?" Roeden asked. "Is that like Holding?"

"It's of a similar size, being one of the Three Big Cities. It's divided into districts, much like Holding, and each district is as large as your little town. It's true – you'll see for yourself!" he added with a laugh, catching sight of Roeden's expression. "Outside the walls, you have the farms – there are thousands living in the city, and so nearby agriculture is a necessity. Just inside the walls of the city, you have the Outskirts – many of the poorer citizens live there. Further in, to the south and the north, are their Working Districts. Near the centre, they have what is called the Scholastic District – as you may have guessed, that's where the scholars live, alongside government officials and other well-off and important people."

"The government live outside Holding?"

"Largely, they live and govern inside Holding, but

Doscadia has less of a Magicom presence than Holding. For example, Doscaida's city guard are not comprised of Magicom soldiers. They work directly under the government. You'll still find clinics, though, and the city guard would never overrule a Magicom decision."

"Why, though?" asked Roeden. "Why doesn't the city revolt and remove them?"

Chadwick laughed. "Arcannen," he said simply. "Magicom control and distribute it, so all it would have to do is stop the supply arriving from the trains each day, and Doscadia would have a magic drought. If you had two sides, one with magic and one without – well, there would only be one winner."

"August used earth magic at Taurus' farm, didn't he?" Roeden asked, thinking back. "Phantex once told me that earth magic is the most dangerous of the elements, and mages rarely use it. Why is that?"

"They're all dangerous to use. That's why institutions like Wing exist. But the answer to your question is about *where* the elements go once you've manipulated them. When you use wind magic, the element returns to the air. Water will dissipate and fireballs will extinguish, as long as there aren't any flammable materials nearby – which is the reason why it's against the law to use fire magic in settlements. When you use earth, however, you're manipulating a solid mass from one place to another. Losing control of where that earth goes can be dangerous. On top of that, it's hard to displace the correct amount. Very few mages risk it." He looked sideways at Roeden. "Magic has many dangers. Arcannen, for example, is toxic in high amounts. That's why you'd never see a mage drink more than one vial at a time."

Roeden chewed on this for a moment before nodding ahead at the Ashes leader and asking, "Why won't August tell you what he's doing in Doscadia? Aren't you friends?"

"By the Trinity, you flit through subjects more than anyone I've ever met!" Chadwick chuckled and shook his head but soon grew serious again. "I suppose a good leader doesn't get too close to his subordinates. The men and women in Ashes love August, and August is generally respectful and friendly to his followers. But he is a general, much in the same way Rox Salvamal is."

"He's nothing like him!" said Roeden, appalled that Chadwick could even suggest such a thing.

"Do you know Magicom's general personally?" asked Chadwick. Roeden found he had no response to that, so he screwed up his face instead. "Anyway, I didn't say he was *like* Salvamal. The point I was trying to make was their positions are similar. It's true, August's charisma may well have won him followers – but it's not friendship with August that has so many rebelling against Magicom. It's the idea of a world where everyone can have access to arcannen, so they don't have to cower behind their town walls out of fear of manabeasts, where Magicom soldiers can't do what they like with the people they claim to be protecting. And you've never seen real poverty, Roeden. You don't have much, I know, but your mother does have a business, a source of income. You'll see it in the cities, though, people who have nothing and live on the streets. I suppose it was only a matter of time before an organisation like Ashes emerged."

"Emerged?" Roeden repeated the word slowly, having never heard it before.

"It means to appear … but appear stealthily, I suppose. Like it was always there, only now it's in plain sight."

"I quite like it." Roeden thought for a moment. "You don't sound much like someone in Ashes, Chadwick. The way you talk is more like someone from the outside looking in. Someone like, well, like me, I suppose."

Chadwick smiled, but this time he had nothing to say.

That night, something woke Roeden. At first, he wasn't sure what, but as the grogginess of sleep faded, he realised there had been a loud splashing sound from the river as if something heavy had fallen in.

Sitting up in alarm, Roeden looked beyond the spindly trees they'd camped behind. There was little light emanating from the fire but enough to see August standing on the bank, looking intently at the water.

Did he throw something in there? Roeden thought to himself as he untangled his body from his blankets. *No, the noise that woke me was much louder than that.* Ignoring the night's cutting chill, he removed the last warmth of his covering, got to his feet and tiptoed around the heap of blankets that was Chadwick, who grunted as Roeden neared but appeared fast asleep by the sound of his snoring. *He was drinking quite a lot out of that silver flask when we camped for the night … I don't think it was water either.* Roeden made his way from the leafy patch where they had settled and came alongside August.

August's head turned slightly at his arrival, but for once, Roeden didn't have eyes for him. He could only stare at the river, where ripples and foam were the only evidence that something had happened. "What was that?" he whispered at last.

August turned back towards the river's edge. "Our manabeast, I think," he said quietly.

Roeden took an involuntary step back. August looked back at him, eyes glinting from the hood that never seemed to come down. "Perhaps you're right. Let's make our way back to the fire."

As they returned to camp, August picked up some firewood he'd piled earlier, placing a few logs at certain angles in the flames. Apparently satisfied, he perched on a thick trunk and began conjuring water in the palm of his hand, making the liquid swirl in a ball.

"Didn't you say you were running low on arcannen?" asked Roeden, still whispering as he sat cross-legged opposite August. Without his blankets, the warmth of the fire felt pleasant on his skin.

"I did," replied August, not taking his eyes off the watery globe, "but I always take a potion on the road. If we were attacked, by manabeast or human, the seconds it would take to uncork a vial and drink its contents could be enough to incapacitate me. Chadwick is doing the same. Besides, it's important that I practise."

"What *was* that thing?"

August seemed to know straight away what Roeden meant. "I didn't see it, just heard it, like you. Whatever it is, it seems we've entered into its territory. Be on your guard near the river's edge from now on, Roeden."

Despite the warmth, Roeden shivered and hugged himself. "Is it really that dangerous?"

"Extremely, but we're not in danger from it – to think that way would be to fall into the trap of sensationalism." This time August did look up as if he could sense the confusion that'd appeared on Roeden's face. "People like Chadwick," he explained, "think that because our manabeast has killed those who have tried to hunt it, coming this way equates to certain death. If we disturb the water, we've something to fear. But we will not. We will quietly make our way through this woodland and stay clear of the water's edge. The stories from *Severity News* have worked in our favour, at least. We're unlikely to see anyone else."

Roeden wasn't convinced, and he wasn't sure Chadwick would be either. "Why did it … emerge …

where we camped?" he asked, liking the sound of the new word on his tongue.

"Probably an unlucky bird that settled on the river." August hesitated. "Possibly, it was nearby and could sense my magic. Some manabeasts can do that, having their own kind of unique magic – but do not fear, I doubt it can get to us this far out of the water, and I wouldn't be foolish enough to do this any closer. Anyway, you should be careful whom you listen to, Roeden. Or trust, for that matter." August did not speak further but looked over to the sleeping form of their travelling companion. *What is this strange relationship that August and Chadwick have? If August doesn't trust Chadwick, why does he allow him to travel with us?*

Roeden watched August in silence for a few moments, guessing the Ashes leader would not want to talk further on that particular matter but not wanting to break the longest conversation they'd had so far. August appeared to be concentrating on his ball of swirling water, and suddenly, Roeden noticed something was happening to it.

"It's freezing," he gasped. "It's turning to ice!"

He'd barely finished speaking when the ball in August's hand had become completely solid, levitating for a few minutes longer before August let it drop to the ground, shattering.

"How did you do that?" asked Roeden, leaning forward to look at the remains of August's magic. He'd not seen much magic in his life – his mother was no mage, and Phantex did not often have arcannen in his blood when within the walls of Bodham. Yet from what Roeden knew, only water, earth, fire and wind could be summoned. He'd never heard of ice being summoned before.

"With great concentration," replied August, meeting

Roeden's eyes. "Drawing water from the air is drawing water from its gas form – vapour – and transferring it to a liquid. It's just another step to freeze the liquid into its final state of matter – ice."

"So it's hard?"

"Very. I don't mean this to sound harsh, but it's tricky to explain to someone who's never taken an arcannen potion. Someone once explained magic to me as having an extra set of four limbs. You can move your arms and legs because when your brain tells your body to move, it does. It's the same when you have arcannen in your blood. It's like having another limb for each element, and using them feels just as natural. Willing the water from the air into the palm of your hand, willing the air to levitate it there …"

"You were using wind magic at the same time?"

"Of course. Think about it, how would mages hold fireballs without wind magic? What would stop the flames from burning their skin? It's the same with water. If wind magic didn't hold the liquid in place, it would just splash everywhere as soon as it's formed. Willing that water to freeze, on the other hand, is more like … balancing on one leg. It takes a bit more skill and concentration."

"I like that description," said Roeden with a smile, which August returned. "Who told you that?"

The smile faded. "Someone at Wing, a long time ago." Once again, strangely, August took a quick glance at the sleeping Chadwick before continuing. "She was called Ashe. She used to have a lot of funny analogies and sayings." The smile returned. "I used to tease her mercilessly for it."

"She was the one who you were going to marry? The one Ashes is named after?"

August's smile became sardonic. "I see our mutual

friend has been sharing."

"Sorry," said Roeden quickly, realising he might have asked too much.

But although a sorrowful expression had appeared on August's face, he didn't look put out. "You don't have to be sorry, Roeden. We should talk about those who have passed; that way, they're not forgotten. We keep their memory alive by speaking about them."

"Can I ask … how she died?"

August didn't answer immediately. In fact, as the seconds dragged on, Roeden began to wonder if he was going to answer at all. When he did finally speak, he didn't look up but spoke into the dancing flames. "It happened during her final Wing contract. There'd been reports about remnants of Spirit Mage followers forming a faction in Sermouth. Wing were contracted to find and expose them. However, Magicom had received the same reports and sent their own soldiers to Sermouth. Their whole philosophy is built on the idea that there must be an organisation to control the distribution of arcannen, and if the Spirit Mage was ever freed from his prison – as the faction planned – he would try to take that role from them. Magicom arrived in Sermouth at the same time as Wing and didn't differentiate between them and the enemy. Everyone was killed."

Roeden was horrified. "How did they get away with it?"

When August spoke, his voice was ridden with barely concealed bitterness. "They're Magicom." The fire's glow reflected in his eyes as they met Roeden's. "The story goes that when Tette Tesyn first discovered what arcannen could do, there was a mass race to locate and mine the ore that contains it. The Spirit Mage and his followers managed to use this knowledge to take control of

Contrata over the sea and eventually tried to do the same in Blake. They failed. After the wars ended, the government gave Magicom the means to monitor and control the flow of arcannen, and with it, they were meant to protect the people of Blake. That was the whole point of the Mage Charter. But over the course of time, Magicom's vast wealth gave them too much power, and with it, they lost accountability for their actions. Now they have an army large enough to crush the government if they wanted to. They know it; the government knows it. It's only a matter of time before they take over Blake entirely. When that happens, not only will arcannen be restricted even further – they've made their wealth now, after all – but there'll be no opposition to the things they do. That's why Ashes. Someone needs to stop them before it's too late. Disrupting their arcannen supply is only the first step. We need to collect allies and put together a force strong enough to fight them head-on."

The passion in August's voice had become more prominent as his speech went on, so much so that Roeden had begun to feel swept up in it. Now more than ever, Roeden wanted to be part of the rebellion against Magicom. Willing the conversation to continue, he said, "Chadwick thinks you built Ashes for revenge."

August shrugged his shoulders. "Of course that's part of it, not just for me, but for every person who's joined the cause, including your brother. I hope you don't mind me saying, Roeden, but from what I understand, you're too young to remember your father. Phantex, however, is fifteen years older than you, and he remembers all too well the working conditions of Magicom's mines. He remembers how they led to your father's death." He paused. "But that's not all there is to it. Phantex also fights out of loyalty to me. Your brother is an incredible man,

Roeden, and I will free him at any cost."

"So … did Phantex know … Ashe … as well?" Roeden asked.

"Yes, a few of us used to train and undertake contracts together at Wing. Ashe, Phantex, myself, a couple of others." August shook his head. "There was one boy we called Felix."

"Felix? Like the character Felix from *Jarian the Dragon Hunter?*"

August laughed, and a genuine smile appeared on his face, the first Roeden had seen. It seemed to make him look younger somehow. "It wasn't his real name – Ashe christened him with it. Do you remember what the character was like in the stories?"

"Yes," replied Roeden fervently. Finally, this was a conversation in which he was an expert. "He was always late to everything. Like when Jarian had to battle the Chaos Dragon, and he needed the Shield of Ardinence as it could repel the dragon's flames. Felix had it and was tinkering with it while Jarian was nearly burnt to a crisp."

August leaned forward towards the fire, looking happy but as if he were somewhere else. "Our Felix was late for everything as well. Ashe used to say he was late for his own birth."

"What about Taurus? Was he at Wing with you?"

August snorted; another new behavioural trait. "Don't let him hear you say that," he said, sounding as amused as Roeden had ever heard him. "I'm not even sure Wing was around when he was the right age. Taurus I met afterwards – and he's been one of my most loyal and reliable soldiers since."

Roeden said nothing. Mentioning Taurus reminded him of how worried he was for his mother. What if Magicom had done something to harm her?

"Taurus will keep her safe," said August, watching Roeden closely. Roeden said nothing but nodded and turned away, looking at the flames of the fire so the Ashes leader would not see the tears that had appeared. He felt August's hand on his shoulder before August moved away, seeming to signal the conversation was at an end. Roeden sighed, took a deep breath, and moved back to where his blankets were.

As he did so, a sudden feeling of being watched came over him. He glanced in Chadwick's direction, but Chadwick's eyes were closed and his breathing even.

Putting it out of his mind, Roeden rolled himself in his blankets and went back to sleep.

CHAPTER TEN

August returned to his aloofness the following morning. After repeating his warning about keeping their distance from the water, he took the lead in silence, seemingly intent on making sure he was always in sight but never close enough for conversation.

"We'll be back on the plains by the end of today," Chadwick told Roeden after taking out his flask and having his customary morning swig. "After that, it'll only be a day's march south until we reach Doscadia's western gate."

The path continued to wind between spindly trees and green shrubbery. The river remained calm and gentle through most of the day but, by late afternoon, had picked up considerable speed.

Not long after, they stepped out into the open. But they were not on the plains yet. Stumps of trees littered the grassy floor, but ahead, the woodland continued.

"This must be where the Doscadians collect their timber from," mused Chadwick.

"The trunks are thicker here," agreed August. He looked up. "We're barely concealed from the Doscadian Road."

Following his gaze above the rise, Roeden saw what he meant. There was some shrubbery at the top, but beyond that, it was easy to see where the ground was flat and well-trodden. *Anyone passing would see us if they looked down*. It confused him then when August said, "We shall stop here."

Chadwick appeared to be having the same thought. "We're in plain sight," he said, his brow furrowed.

"I meant to say, we'll stop here, but back under cover of the trees."

When the three were back under the canopy again, August spoke. "We'll camp somewhere close tonight and take the road south in the morning." He looked at them both in turn, and Roeden felt a surge of pride at being included in this most important conversation. "There's a way into the city from the dam that controls the river – it involves a fair bit of climbing, but I've been that way before. I'll leave the road as soon as I can and cut across the fields while you two continue on and make your way inside through the city gates. We meet at an inn called the Hairy Dog – that's where some of the others are. It's in the Scholastic District."

"Why can't we come with you?" asked Roeden, the pride he felt turning to disappointment. Going via the dam sounded much more interesting … and adventurous.

"It would be silly for you to risk the climb when you could enter through the gates. I have to climb, as it's riskier for me to try to walk into Doscadia through the conventional route." August fixed Roeden with a look. "I might be recognised." August waited for him to nod before he continued. "I'm going to do some scouting. There's a precaution we need to take before we take to the plains."

"What does he mean, precaution?" asked Roeden, turning to Chadwick once August had disappeared back into the opening and out of sight.

"I'm not sure." But Roeden did not miss the hesitation

in Chadwick's reply. *He does know, or at least suspects.* "August is the strategist, not me." He stepped away from Roeden and looked into the river, as deep as it had been their entire journey, his hands making their way into the folds of his cloak. Roeden joined him. "That's how history will remember him, I think, as long as Ashes survive long enough to make a difference. It makes you wonder how things would be if August was the head of Magicom's forces instead of Rox Salvamal. August with all their resources – now, that would be frightening."

The way Chadwick spoke did not sound to Roeden like he found it frightening at all; in fact, he sounded positively enamoured by the idea. *And what does he mean if Ashes survive long enough to make a difference?*

"You're really not like the rest of Ashes, are you?" said Roeden.

Chadwick snorted. "Maybe wait until you've met the rest of Ashes before saying things like that, Roeden."

The rest of the afternoon drifted by slowly as they waited for August to return. Roeden spent most of it sitting on a log, staring at the deep, blue water while imagining what it would be like to create magic. A couple of times, he placed his hand out, remembering how August had conjured the spinning ball of water.

Chadwick, it seemed, had his own way of passing the time. An hour or so after August's departure, he took a wooden pencil and miniature leather-bound book from his pack and sat with his back to a nearby trunk, scribbling something down.

"What are you writing about?" asked Roeden after watching him curiously for a few moments.

Chadwick didn't look up. "Our journey."

"Why?"

Chadwick shrugged. "This is all history in the making.

Someone should be recording these events, and if not me, who will?"

By the time August returned, the sun was setting and the woodland was alive with the sound of crickets. Roeden and Chadwick had not set a fire but were wrapped in their blankets when he crashed through the trees.

"Make sure you're as far away from the river as possible," he said hurriedly, not looking at them but making his way over to the water. He took a vial of black liquid out of his pack, threw it in the air, and shot a blast of wind at it. It exploded, the liquid and glass soon lost in the water. Roeden stood up in shock. *That's arcannen!*

"What are you doing?" Chadwick exclaimed, echoing his thoughts. "That might attract whatever lives in there!"

August's response was to march over to Chadwick, which made the other man take a step back. But when August reached him, he gripped Chadwick's shoulder and spoke to him calmly.

"You're not a fighter, Chadwick, so whatever comes next, your job is to keep Roeden safe." August took the pack off his shoulder and handed it to Chadwick, who accepted it without a word. "Now, do as I say and step away. Both of you. There are people coming for us."

People? Roeden was confused, but Chadwick seemed to understand and, with a look of grim acceptance, placed an arm around Roeden, leading them back as far as they could go without having to step into the shrubbery so they were almost at the slope, where they dropped their blankets. August stepped into the widest part of the pathway and waited.

At first, nothing happened. All Roeden could hear was the rustle of the leaves and the crickets chirping. It was so quiet he felt as if he could hear his own heart beating within his chest. *Have Magicom finally caught up with us?* But no, August would have said if that was the case, and he had said 'people', not 'Magicom'. It was something else, something to do with the plan he seemed to have. Roeden was just beginning to wonder if August had made a mistake when the sound of several sets of footsteps could be heard, along with the crunching of branches. From the woodland ahead, four men appeared. As they spotted August and stopped short, Roeden could see that two of them were Raff and Baton. Aside from Raff, they were all carrying pistols in their hands.

The men seemed surprised that August was standing in the path, waiting for them. Raff recovered quickest and looked around until he spotted Roeden and Chadwick. The smile he gave them made Roeden feel sick.

"I wondered if we would run into each other again, friend," Raff said, turning back to August.

August said nothing but waited. Or at least seemed to. It was only because Roeden was watching him closely, and from the angle he was standing at, that he could see August was rotating his hand behind his back. *What is he doing?*

"It's strange, I thought I recognised you," Raff continued, unperturbed, "and then when we went back to the hub, and I saw those posters, I realised where I'd seen you before. Or your likeness, at least. You're August Silvershield."

Baton began to snigger, his eyes wide with excitement, and the other two men, who looked as dirty and unkempt as Raff and his partner, slowly moved around August so that one was beside the river and the other behind the Ashes leader. August's hand was still rotating, and he seemed completely unconcerned.

"The best thing you can do right now is leave," he told Raff.

The other man laughed. "Leave? Even if we split that reward four ways, we'll have enough coin to last us for months. The best thing *you* can do is come quietly. If you do that, you have my word we'll leave your friends be." He gave Chadwick and Roeden a contemptuous glance. "Is this Ashes? Cowards and little boys? I'd heard you were a force to be reckoned with – I was even considering joining myself – but now I'm just disappointed."

August looked around at them coldly. "I would never take in scum like you."

"Scum like us? We're just trying to make a bit of coin. You're the wanted criminal."

"Making a bit of coin, no matter who it's at the expense of. That's why you followed my friends into the woods."

Raff shrugged. "We're a bit low at the moment, and it seemed too good an opportunity to miss. Arcannen's expensive, you know, and we need to eat. We wouldn't have hurt them as long as they didn't resist. Besides, the whole of Ashes are a band of thieves; everyone knows that. How is what we do any different?"

"We steal from Magicom clinics and only take arcannen; you target people you think might be vulnerable. Do not compare us." Roeden had never heard such contempt in August's voice. "I'm going to give you one last chance to leave; if you don't, you may not make it out of this woodland alive."

If he or Chadwick had said that, Roeden thought the men would have laughed. As it was, Raff didn't do more than sneer, but the others looked uneasy. *Can August really hold his own against all of them? He fought half a dozen soldiers at the farmyard, but they were taken by surprise – these men are ready for him.* Whatever inner battle Raff was having himself, greed seemed to win. "There's four of us and two and a half of you," he said, holding out his hands in placation, "and I doubt the boy can use magic. You're not the one who should be making threats."

Roeden didn't like the way Raff's hands were spread, as if he were about to thrust them forward. He opened his mouth to shout a warning, but before he could, there came an almighty crash from the river. They all spun in its direction, and although Chadwick's grip hardened on his shoulders, it wasn't that which caused Roeden to cry out in alarm.

The head and body of a gigantic creature were ascending from the water. It rose above the trees, wing-like ears from either side of its greyish-blue head blocking out the sun. Its body was the same colour, long, thin and coiling like a snake's, with scales that covered every inch. Roeden's first instinct was to run, but all he could do was stare in horror. *A leviathan!* his mind screamed, reminded of illustrations he'd seen in *Jarian's Adventures with Balon the Shipwright.* As it opened its powerful-looking jaws, six larger fangs stood amongst at least two dozen smaller teeth. It screeched, a sound so shrill Roeden had to cover his ears.

The man closest to the river never stood a chance. One moment he was staring up in terror; the next, the leviathan descended. The man's scream was cut off as it took him in its jaws and crashed back into the water. The other men shouted and backed away, Raff drawing fire into his hand. August, however, sprinted to Roeden and Chadwick, pushing them behind a giant trunk as the creature ascended again and gunshots rang out.

Barely seconds had passed before Chadwick let out a sound of dismay. Roeden felt the pressure on his shoulders loosen, and before he knew it, Chadwick was sprinting away from them, back in the direction of the river. Roeden looked around the trunk in disbelief. *What is he doing?*

"Chadwick!" called August, sounding as alarmed as Roeden felt.

But Chadwick ignored him, running to the spot where he'd deposited his pack, near to the bank. He was unnoticed by the men, who were still firing, or in Raff's case, shooting fireballs. The bullets and magic were having little to no effect on the manabeast other than causing it to turn its head as if bothered by gnats. But Chadwick's movement seemed to draw its gaze. As Chadwick knelt down to pick up his pack, the leviathan opened its jaws wide and shot towards him.

Too late, Chadwick realised the danger he was in. His mouth dropped, and his eyes bulged, but he could seem to do no more than stare upwards.

Then August was there. The Ashes leader had charged after him, bundling him out of the way just before the leviathan found its target, its fangs snapping on nothing. Letting out another shrill scream, it rose again and opened its jaws, gaping wide, a ball of pure blue energy spiralling from within. August and Chadwick, the latter clutching his pack, scrambled back to their feet and ran towards Roeden while the other men fled back in the direction they'd arrived from. To Roeden's immense relief, the manabeast seemed to decide the bandits were its target this time, and the energy beam it shot streamed along the pathway they were on, enveloping everything in its path. Roeden caught a glimpse of Raff's panic-stricken face before the man was engulfed, along with the others. Roeden shut his eyes and looked away as the other two reached him and brought him back around the trunk, knowing he'd never forget what he'd just seen. Then there was silence, with no sign as to what had happened aside from the smell of burning in the air. A few moments later, there was a crunching, dragging sound, followed by another splash, then nothing again.

When Roeden felt the other two stirring, he took it as a sign to open his eyes and look back around the trunk. By the river, he saw nothing left of the pathway or nearby trees but a black mould and charred stumps; and the only sign of the four men was the scarlet stains of their blood on the ground.

CHAPTER ELEVEN

Pink narrowly sidestepped another burst of Sol's wind magic, forming an air shield as he continued to shoot wave after wave at her.

When Sol had asked to train together that morning, Pink's first instinct had been to find a reason not to. He'd hardly been easy to work with during their trip to Poulsen, and his anti-Ashes rhetoric made her uncomfortable. But an opportunity to train with someone, even Sol, felt too good to miss – especially since she'd received no offer to practise with her new mentor.

She concentrated, keeping her barrier in place, the strength of Sol's magic forcing her to step backwards, the sound muffled from her own displaced air. Before long, she found herself in the corner of the training ground where the two fences met, beads of sweat trickling down her forehead and neck. The battle had, much to her displeasure, created a bit of a crowd. She could hear Jase shouting encouragement from the outside pathway, along with Sol's group of friends and others who'd stopped to watch. Dropping her shield, she ducked and, attempting to catch Sol off guard, pushed out her hands, shooting her own wind magic, hoping to knock him off his feet.

He rolled out of the way just in time. But it had given Pink a chance to take the offensive. She straightened, and now it was her turn to shoot constant blasts of wind, causing him to adopt his own air shield as he stepped back. Almost too late, she realised he'd dropped his left hand. *What is he doing?* The question was soon answered as he formed a spiralling ball of water and shot it towards her. The liquid momentarily obscured her vision as it met the resistance of her shield, but she kept her composure. Releasing her shield, which in turn caused the water to splash on the ground, she shot another blast of wind at him just as he did the same, resulting in them both being knocked off their feet.

They sat up at the same time, and as their eyes locked, he raised his hands. Understanding the gesture, she nodded. They made their way to their feet and walked towards one another in the middle. Many of the bystanders, seeming to lose interest, started to wander away, although Jase stayed, his face screwed up in disgust.

"You fought well," Pink admitted as they came together, a little breathless. "I needed that."

Sol seemed pleased at the compliment. "You as well. I heard you were something of a talent among the trainees; I can see those rumours were not unfounded."

Pink shrugged, then gave him a wry smile. "Water magic? Thought I'd need cooling down, did you?"

Sol let out a snort but didn't say anything in reply. It was a good tactic; they both knew it. "Has anything been done about what we discovered at the dukesbane site?" he asked as they started to walk off the training ground together.

Pink shook her head. "I've not heard from Instructor Texeria or Gabriel since we've been back."

"You sound frustrated. Why don't you follow up?"

She didn't answer. It was now the fourth day since their return from Poulsen, and even if there was nothing new to report, she would've at least expected Instructor Texeria to undertake some combat training with her, which was common practice for new mages and their mentors. His affiliation with the Magicom soldiers bothered her as well – clearly, he'd been trading something with them, but what? She was still mulling over the question when they reached the pathway where Jase was waiting for them.

"Well done, Pink," he said, talking to her as if Sol wasn't there. "You had that one won."

"That was practice. It wasn't about winning or losing," retorted Sol before Pink could reply.

"I suppose you would say that after yielding first." Jase didn't meet Sol's eyes, but he gave Pink a look that suggested they were sharing some private joke. She shook her head slightly, trying to signal that his comments weren't necessary, but he seemed not to notice. "I guess you thought a newly qualified mage would be an easy target."

Sol's laughter was derisive. "Quite the opposite. If I wanted an easy target, I would have invited you to the training courts."

Jase did turn to Sol now, face contorted. Pink spoke before he could say anything. "I'm going to find Instructor Texeria. I'll see you both later."

She took off, having had enough of their exchange. She knew she should support Jase, but *he* had been the one to start that argument. Besides, Sol was right – if she wanted to know what was going on, Keat Texeria was the person to speak to. *Four days without word is too long, especially this early in the mentorship. Even Jase has had some time in the courts with Gabriel.*

She made her way along the eastern slopes of Highstone Hill, frustration growing in her mind. *How can*

I be the best mage at Wing if I don't have a mentor who supports me?

Reaching the door of East House, she knocked once and waited for an answer. When none came, she let herself in, her frustration overriding etiquette. The main room of the building was empty, but she'd barely shut the door when she heard footsteps coming from the hallway leading to the storage area.

"Sara!" Gabriel exclaimed as he entered the room, looking startled to see her there.

"Assistant Master." Suddenly coming in without an invitation didn't seem a great idea. "I … er … knocked, but nobody answered." He didn't reply but continued to stare at her, making her feel even more awkward. "I needed to see Instructor Texeria," she added somewhat lamely.

Something was bothering Gabriel. She could see it right away. *Is he that upset I came in without permission?* "I received a letter from a Miriam Shawgrave this morning," he said at last, throwing Pink off balance, "complaining that four Wing mages had been harassing her staff at a cultivation site near Poulsen."

"Madam Shawgrave complained about *us*?" Pink screwed up her face. *That doesn't make sense. She was the one who convinced the Magicom soldiers to let us in!* Pink thought back. *She was happy to talk about Corey Leathers, the man who went missing. But when we wanted to talk to Cylan Wight she seemed uncomfortable. Could this be something to do with that?*

Gabriel nodded. "I've already spoken to Instructor Texeria, who informs me he sent you there as part of a contract. However, I suggest you leave that site alone in future. It's owned by Magicom, and this facility would not benefit from more of their interference at the moment. Instructor Texeria understands this – I believe he won't try to send you again."

There was a slight uncertainty in Gabriel's voice at that last statement, and Pink thought she knew why. *He's found that trying to have a conversation with Instructor Texeria isn't the easiest task in the world.*

"I understand, Assistant Master," replied Pink, disappointed. "Did Instructor Texeria inform you of what we discovered there? About this unknown type of manabeast we think might be responsible for the missing townsfolk?"

Gabriel looked at her in puzzlement. "He informed me there might be a manabeast lair on the day you returned, and I took a group of instructors to investigate that evening. We found no evidence of any type of manabeast in the vicinity. I'm surprised he didn't tell you." With a curt nod, Gabriel left the building, leaving Pink to stand there in disbelief. Why *hadn't* Instructor Texeria felt the need to tell her of this development? They were the ones who had put in all the work, after all, while he … he'd been busy mixing with Magicom soldiers!

She stormed through the corridor and into Texeria's storage room, finding the instructor engaged in something on his table by the glass cage. There was a new rusted metal container, about the size of a cart, standing against one side of the wall, but everything else looked just as disorganised as last time. As she approached him – sparing a glance for the squeaking armadillo-types scurrying on the cage floor – she saw he was attempting to attach a fan with blades made from thin sheets of metal to some sort of bronze cylinder.

She hesitated, her frustration tempered by curiosity. "What are you working on?" she asked, curiosity winning out.

"Something I picked up in Poulsen," replied Texeria,

showing no signs of surprise at her arrival but letting out a satisfied breath as the fan locked onto a copper pipe jutting from the cylinder. He held it in one hand and, with a click of his fingers, conjured a flame to appear above his free index finger, which he held under the cylinder. Pink cocked an eyebrow. *If that's arcannen from Wing's stores, he'd better hope Gabriel doesn't find out how he's been using it.* They stood there and watched.

"Nothing's happening," Pink said after a couple of minutes.

"Just wait," muttered Texeria, his eyes never leaving the contraption.

He'd barely finished speaking when the cylinder began to hiss. He knocked the glass of the cage with the side of his boot, which caused the armadillo-types to squeak and scurry away from the area he'd struck. Pink stared as black dust appeared and spread across their bodies, making patterns on their shells. As each intricate line joined with another, she was reminded of a spider weaving its web. But it was what happened next that truly amazed her. Most of the black dust disappeared, along with the manabeasts! First, their shell at the back, then their snouts, tails and legs. She'd almost forgotten about the contraption when she heard a whirring noise and saw the fan rotating in his hand. He held it over the side of the cage, swirling the excess dust floating inside.

Texeria then dropped his other hand into the cage. At first, Pink thought he was going to pick up one of the manabeasts, which she could still hear scurrying and see displacing the sticks and straw below, but he left it suspended about halfway down until the same pattern appeared on his skin. She let out a sharp breath as his hand faded until there was nothing left of its shape aside from a faint shimmer in the air.

"Imagine," he said, holding it up in front of him, "the advantage you would have in battle if your enemy couldn't see you."

"Incredible," breathed Pink, but then she looked at Texeria, frowning. "It's all very well making your hand disappear, but what about the rest of you? If you were trying to make your whole body invisible, wouldn't your clothes … get in the way?" A bizarre image appeared in Pink's mind of a Wing uniform running around with nothing inside it.

Texeria shrugged. "The armadillo-types aren't becoming invisible themselves. Rather, the dust particles are connecting and creating a field of displaced air *around* them. Which makes it *seem* as if nothing's there, but in reality, it's like being enclosed in a light-reflecting bubble. The dust creates this bubble by connecting around the shape of the physical specimen, clothes and all. The biggest issue with using the dust on humans is you need a whole lot more of it."

"So you're visible, but nobody can see you're visible."

"Exactly."

"Isn't that the same as being invisible?"

Texeria smiled and then inclined his head. "How about invisible but not transparent?"

He's far too impressed with himself, thought Pink, although she did admire his creativity. She looked at the contraption, then at Texeria. "This is what you bought from those soldiers the other day."

It was more of a statement than a question, and Texeria took it as such. "They have all sorts of spare parts in those steam vans of theirs. The fan I was able to construct myself, but the cylinder – which I'm actually using as a boiler – I had to purchase from them, and quickly. Who knows how long they'd be around for? This was something I had begun to experiment with for my performances in Holding, but being back at Wing reminded me it could have other uses."

"I came to ask you about the Poulsen contract," she said, deciding it was time to get to the matter at hand. She was relieved his involvement with the Magicom soldiers had been explained, but despite the distraction of the manabeast magic, she was still frustrated at his lack of engagement since their return to Highstone Hill.

"Ah, yes," he said, detaching his equipment and returning it to the table with a clank, "I have an update on that front, actually. There have been further disappearances since your visit to the dukesbane site."

"What? When?"

"Just this morning. I had planned to send for you, but my progress with the armadillo-types put it out of my mind." He faced her, crossing his arms as Pink, with great difficulty, managed to restrain herself from responding to that last comment – at least, until he had told her everything. "It seems the mayor's own son has gone missing this time, along with the man you interviewed, Cylan Wight. They journeyed to Katton a couple of days ago and never returned. The mayor sounded most concerned in his letter."

Pink's eyes bulged. "But … Instructor, there must be some sort of connection! Out of all the people in Poulsen who might have gone missing, the one who saw an unusual manabeast in the area is the one who has!"

"My thoughts exactly. Although some might argue that they just happened to be the only ones foolish enough to travel the wilderness, despite this apparent danger."

Pink thought about Scottie Sharp's behaviour at the Salted Pig and Cylan Wight travelling at night to retrieve his coins and couldn't disagree.

"Katton is near Poulsen," she said instead, trying to reason out loud, "but the disappearances have all been residents from Poulsen, and this case is no different. Our biggest lead so far is the manabeast Wight saw near the dukesbane site – but we can't go back there, according to Gabriel."

"I may have ... forgotten to mention this development to the assistant master," said Texeria, "but I don't think he would have any problem with a recon to Katton. As luck would have it, I know the administrator who runs the place, so complaints are less likely. Lovely lady by the name of Alma Ratchette. Very flexible."

Pink decided not to respond to that last comment, either. Instead, she said, "Administrator … is that like a mayor?"

"Katton is a small place. Some do live there, but it's more of a business district than a town. Ratchette oversees its projects. Why don't you take Jase, Bale and Sol and head down that way today? She might give you some idea of Sharp and Wight's movements, which might lead us to some answers."

"I don't think there's any need to take Sol," muttered Pink.

Texeria chuckled. "There's every need. He's part of this now. Besides, the more of you there are, the better – strength in numbers."

Pink grimaced. *Sol goes then. Wonderful, that means I'll have to listen to him and Jase bicker the entire time.* "Are you not coming too, Instructor?" she asked, trying to keep her voice polite.

He smiled. "I still have a lot of work to do here. I'm on a bit of a deadline." He gave her a shrewd look. "When I'm finished, I'll make sure you have some proper combat practice, I promise." She nodded, looking down at his hand as she did so. Parts of it were visible again. It almost looked like dismembered fingers floating in the air.

She wondered what he meant by being on a deadline. A deadline for whom? She opened her mouth to ask, but a low growl caught her attention, muffled but familiar. She looked around the storeroom and realised it was coming from the metal container in the corner. *No, not a container,* she realised in horror, *another cage!*

"Instructor, you've got a wolf-type in there!"

"Oh, that? Gabriel let me have it for my work. I'm analysing its magic."

Pink stared at him, then back at the cage. She couldn't see inside, the bars must have been facing the opposite way, but yellow, feral eyes appeared in her mind, and she felt it could *see* her.

She realised her mentor was watching her closely, so she hastily made her excuses and left, deciding against asking him about his deadline after all. She didn't want to spend a moment longer in that room than necessary.

CHAPTER TWELVE

There didn't seem much point in waiting, so as soon as she left East House, Pink rounded up the others, intent on leaving right away and getting back before nightfall. Jase and Bale agreed to join her as soon as she told them her intentions, as did Sol, whom she found with his small group of friends still on the training ground.

"I'm glad you followed my advice," he said. "If others are missing, we need to follow up right away."

Pink fought to keep her expression neutral. He assumed she'd gone to Instructor Texeria just because of his say-so, did he? Checking the grudging respect she'd afforded him from their combat training, she told him to meet them at the stables and stomped away, the stares and whispers of his friends following her as she left.

They were riding across the plains within the hour, delayed only by Bale and Jase acquiring arcannen potions from the infirmary, where request forms were filled and potions stored. The afternoon sun was high in the sky by the time they spotted the first sign of Katton – a blimp floating in the distance, held in place by a long thick rope, with the name of the settlement painted across its envelope. As they rode to the top of a hill, they caught sight of dozens of brick buildings below, tall chimneys with smoke puffing out from many, as well as flatter but wider buildings that had the look of warehouses, with their roofs and walls made from sheets of metal. There was little else aside from a single track that ran east across the plains. Nearer the settlement, the track bypassed a concrete platform and separated into many others, disappearing into a large shed like fingers on a metal hand.

"There's no wall," said Jase as they reined in.

"There's probably too few people living here," said Pink, "not worth the cost."

"I'm sure they protect themselves in other ways," said Sol as he joined them, looking upwards. "They wouldn't have an airborne blimp just as a glorified signpost. No doubt there's a person watching the wilderness from the gondola. The metal cabin," he added in response to a perplexed-looking Jase. "They'll have some way of signalling those below if they see manabeasts."

"I read something in *Severity News* about Sermouth designing engines for their blimps so they can travel," said Bale, speaking up unexpectedly.

"Magicom have been working on that as well," said Sol. "Soon, we might have to call them airships."

"Ships in the air?" Jase laughed nervously. "No, thank you."

But Pink gazed up at the blimp in wonder. *Imagine that … to be as high as the clouds, watching the wilderness as it passes below …* She turned to face the others, expecting their reactions to mirror her own. Jase and Bale were still looking upwards, neither looking particularly impressed, but Sol turned to her, and his eyes shone.

I think that's the first time I've seen him smile. He should really do it more often.

Tapping her heels to her mount, Pink led the others to the buildings, where a distinct smell of oil and smoke filled the air. As they neared, the people who lived and worked in the settlement came into sight. Most wore baggy shirts and trousers of wool and cotton, looking busy as they hurried from one place to another, while some were pushing wheelbarrows, holding bricks or metal or some other commodity, wheels scraping stone pathways as they went. Pink and the others received a few curious glances, but nobody stopped to speak.

They found nearby stables for their horses and, after receiving directions for Alma Ratchette's office from the stable master, proceeded to take a wide, flat road made from grey brick that led to the settlement's centre, the buildings and warehouses running adjacent on either side. They walked in silence, the nearby clanging of metal the only sound accompanying their footsteps. When they reached their destination, they discovered it to be nothing more than a brick house, sitting on a road with many others, identified by a metal sign set within its stone wall that read 'Administrator's Office'. They followed the pathway through the front gate, passing a neatly trimmed garden, before stepping through the open doorway into what was clearly a reception area. Sofas lined the walls, a staircase was cordoned off with rope, and an elderly lady sat behind a desk, scrawling something on a sheet of paper.

"We're here to see Administrator Ratchette," said Pink, meeting the receptionist's enquiring look.

Pink thought they might have to wait a while – the sofas certainly suggested that might be the case – but the administrator stepped out moments after her receptionist had announced their presence. She wasn't what Pink had expected. Pink supposed she'd thought Ratchette might be someone a bit like Miriam Shawgrave, but aside from their ages, they couldn't have been more different. Ratchette had her dark hair tied up, with a wooden pencil placed conspicuously in the bun, and wore a dress of flowing black silks.

"Wing mages!" she said, a little breathless, blotches of red appearing on her tanned cheeks. "I am curious to know why you've arrived at *my* doorstep. I do have another appointment, but … no, come in, come in!"

As they followed Ratchette into the room, Pink caught Jase's eye. "I can tell she's Instructor Texeria's friend," he muttered.

"Did you say Texeria?" said Ratchette, looking over her shoulder. Apparently, she also had very good hearing. Pink snorted as Jase's cheeks burned. "Don't tell me he sent you – what does he want? Haven't we built enough cages for him?"

A long oaken desk faced them as they moved through the doorway, piles of papers dominating its surface, while a ticking longcase clock stood to one side. Something else grabbed Pink's attention, though. On the wall opposite the longcase clock, set within the patterned wallpaper, an oil painting hung, with Ratchette's likeness standing behind a chair and a small girl of about five or six with a similar look sitting on it. Pink couldn't help but smile – the girl's happy expression seemed to bring the painting alive. A noise drew her gaze to a small, slightly ajar nearby window, but it was just a ginger cat stretching on the sill, who meowed at her before disappearing outside. Pink walked to the window and peered through the glass pane but saw nothing aside from an alleyway separating Ratchette's office from the next building.

"Why does Instructor Texeria have cages?" asked Sol, bringing her attention back.

"He keeps manabeasts in his storage room," responded Jase, who was near Sol. He shot Sol a look as if suddenly remembering they were not supposed to be on friendly terms before moving as far away as possible.

"Why am I not surprised?" muttered Sol, not noticing. "How do you know him?" he asked, turning his attention to Ratchette.

"I served as his assistant on several of his illusionist shows." They stared at her as she sat down behind her desk. *I guess that explains the 'flexible' comment.* Ratchette frowned up at them. "What? My daughter was only a toddler at the time, and I had to bring her up by myself. I had to find some way to make coin."

"Apologies, it's just … this is quite a change of occupation," said Sol sheepishly.

"Well, I had many jobs in Holding, *most* engineering-based. I was good at them, which is why I was given the position of overseeing things here in Katton. Did you say Keat Texeria's an instructor now? He's had as many jobs as I, but I would never have guessed he'd go down that route. It seems out of character for him to … give back."

"Instructor Texeria's actually the reason we're here," said Pink, deciding now was the time to get to the matter at hand. "He's running a contract requested by Spencer Sharp, the Mayor of Poulsen. We need to locate Mayor Sharp's son, Scottie, and another man named Cylan Wight. Apparently, they came here to fish but never made the return journey."

Ratchette scratched her nose. "They were here. I know this because of the complaints I received. They arrived one evening, got drunk in the inn, stayed the night, got drunk again in the morning, and then took themselves to the river that runs near the station. You say they went missing? I wouldn't be surprised if they fell in."

Before Pink could open her mouth to reply, the door to Ratchette's office burst open. She spun with the others to find a scowling Magicom soldier striding in, changing the atmosphere in an instant. He was tall and fair-skinned, with neatly brushed grey hair and three red stripes on the sleeve of his uniform. Pink's eyes widened. *Wait, doesn't that mean …?*

The receptionist followed from behind. "Sorry, ma'am, he insisted on coming straight in …"

"It's fine," said Ratchette. She looked apprehensive. "Welcome, General Salvamal. I think our business is concluded, mages. If I could ask you to …"

"Just a moment," said Salvamal, holding up his hand as he looked them over. "What are four Wing mages doing here?"

Pink felt her heartbeat quicken. *Get a hold of yourself. There's no way for him to know who you are.*

A look of annoyance flashed across his features when no one answered. "Speak!"

"We're here on a contract," said Sol. "Looking for two individuals. Administrator Ratchette here has been giving us some information on the matter." He took a deep breath. "Can I just say it's an honour to meet you, General? You are highly revered by many at Wing."

If Pink hadn't been so frozen in place, she might have rolled her eyes. Salvamal, however, looked at Sol as if he wasn't sure how truthful he was being. "I was under the impression that many at Wing are sympathetic to Ashes, given the facility's affiliation with August Silvershield."

"Wing is a diverse place," said Sol. Pink shot a quick glance at Jase, fearful he might try to contradict him. But her friend, thankfully, was staring at the ground. "Many of us are hopeful of joining Magicom when we've finished our service," Sol added.

Salvamal seemed to mull over that for a moment. When he spoke again, his voice had taken on a curt quality reminiscent of Gabriel's. "Well, if that's really the case, then know this: if anyone at Highstone Hill happens to hear anything, anything at all, about August Silvershield or any members of Ashes that leads to their capture, Magicom would reward them handsomely. Paying off their service for a start, and welcoming them into the army, if that's what they choose. It's a generous offer – Magicom are the future of Blake. Tell any who might be interested. Speaking of Ashes," – he looked past them to Ratchette – "that's partly why I'm here."

He stood to one side as if dismissing them. Happy to comply, Pink led the way out, head down. The others followed closely behind. In the reception area, two more soldiers waited with the now concerned-looking receptionist while more stood guard outside. None spoke, but Pink felt their glares.

As they headed back towards the outskirts, the other three began to discuss the best way to get to the bridge. Pink's mind, however, was far removed from their conversation.

Speaking of Ashes, that's partly why I'm here.

Right now, in Ratchette's office, Salvamal was likely talking about his plans for her brother. She felt a heaviness in her legs as if her very body was trying to slow her. Should she be walking away from this? She had long made peace with August's decision to fight Magicom and, for the last year, had been resolved to find her own path at Wing. August had always made it clear he didn't want her involved in anything Ashes-related anyway. But, if luck and fate had conspired to give her an insight into Salvamal's plans, should she not take it?

Especially since she had a way to listen in.

"I'll meet you guys at the bridge," she said, coming to a halt.

"What? Why?" asked Sol as he and the others stopped

in their tracks. Jase tried to discreetly shake his head at her.

"Call of nature. I saw a public bathroom nearby," she said with a fake laugh. "I'll catch up with you guys – go!" She turned on her heel and left before they could ask further questions.

She hurried back to the centre, moving towards Ratchette's office, trying to act nonchalant as she passed the soldiers congregating around the building. After glancing back to make sure they weren't watching, she found the alleyway next to the building and stepped into it. The cat she'd seen earlier had vanished, but she quickly found the small window it had exited Ratchette's office from. Kneeling down, her heart beating rapidly again, she listened in.

"… can't take all of them," Ratchette was saying.

"It's essential, I'm afraid." Salvamal's voice was firm. "I need those blimps airborne. Holding needs to see that Ashes' attack last month was nothing more than an inconvenience. I've waited too long for parts, and your workers know what they're doing more than my Technological Department. It saddens me that I have to come here myself to have this conversation."

"*I'm* afraid the answer's no, General," said Ratchette. "I can maybe send someone to oversee your project, but that's it."

Salvamal said nothing. As the silence extended, Pink risked a look through the window and saw Salvamal studying Ratchette's portrait, his hands behind his back.

"You have a beautiful daughter, Administrator," said Salvamal.

Pink could only see the back of Ratchette's head but could imagine her horrified look as she gasped. "I am a government-appointed administrator! And she is a child! You can't come in here threatening my daughter,

Salvamal. I won't allow …"

"Threats? I don't know what you're talking about." Salvamal's voice was soft. "I was merely commenting on something that's obviously precious to you. Family is so important, isn't it? It pains me to see parents and children separated, but Alsing is full of people who haven't put their families first. I hope you never find yourself in a cell there, Administrator, but who knows what we might find if we search your office? It's … cruel to leave a child all alone in the world."

"General Salvamal … I …" Ratchette sounded like she was almost in tears. Pink felt sick. "The Governmental Council placed me here to do a job …"

Pink ducked as Salvamal turned to look at Ratchette. "And I have my own job to do. I assure you, my requests are more important than theirs."

There was silence. Then – "Very well," came Ratchette's strained voice.

"And another thing – I will have to station a unit of soldiers here in case Silvershield turns up."

"General, do you know how many workers we'll lose if Magicom soldiers are around? Is it worth it for one man? We don't even have a clinic here."

"Anything is worth disposing of that rat," snarled Salvamal. "Ashes have scurried back into their holes since Holding Castle, but this place is the perfect next target for them. Not only because of the blimps. Many of the trains are built here, and they are essential in the delivery of arcannen potions across Blake."

Pink froze as she felt something touch her arm. Her head shot up, but it was just Sol. He put a finger to his lips and inclined his head. She nodded and followed, saddened at how little she could do for Ratchette. At least Salvamal was wrong about August. She knew her brother – he would only attack Magicom directly; he wouldn't attack those who helped the company by proxy. His revenge drove him, but it didn't blind him. Salvamal was wasting his time stationing soldiers in Katton.

At least, she thought so.

Sol took her all the way back to the signpost before rounding on her. "What are you doing?" he demanded, glancing around to make sure no one was close enough to hear. "What madness drove you to spy on the general of Magicom's forces?"

"I was passing and heard …"

"I know what you were doing – Jase told us."

Pink froze.

"Well, more accurately, we all guessed. You *were* rather obvious about it. But Jase explained the reason: you're worried General Salvamal's stopping here on his way to Wing."

If Sol hadn't been looking straight at her, Pink would have breathed a huge sigh of relief. Instead, she puffed out her cheeks and nodded. His voice softened.

"Quite frankly, I'm surprised. You don't seem like the sort to go off-mission like this, and it seems unlikely that Magicom would return so soon or that General Salvamal would talk to Administrator Ratchette about it." He looked more closely at her then. "But you'll know better than I. He mentioned Ashes. Did you find out why?"

"I think he just wanted her to keep a lookout for them," said Pink. "He … he was more concerned about their blimps. I didn't hear anything about Wing."

"Well, there you go." Sol gave her a small smile. "Remember, we're a team." He rubbed his arm, glancing towards the direction of the station. "Even if some of us don't like one another very much. We need to stick together, not go charging off looking for some imagined

Magicom plot."

If only you could have heard the leader of Magicom's forces blackmailing Ratchette, thought Pink. But she was sure he'd have a response for that, and she didn't want to talk Ashes with him. Maybe one day he'd understand August's band had formed because of what the company had done to people like her brother. *And yet Sol hates Ashes in part because of what happened to his mother. You need to be a bit less reckless, August. You don't want as many enemies as them.* She supposed if their roles were reversed, she might feel a similar way. But Pink had never known her mother or father. Like many in her generation, her parents had been killed in the Spirit Mage Wars.

"Let's return to the others," she said, not wishing to dwell on something she had long put to one side. "Like you said, we have to stay on mission."

He placed a hand on her arm as if to comfort her. She looked back at him, raising an eyebrow. He patted her arm, looking awkward, and hurried away. As she followed, her thoughts drifted back to Ratchette, and her mood darkened. Whatever Sol thought about Magicom, the general of their army was a monster.

***

The bridge was joined to a road of gravel on either side. Pink walked to its centre, running her fingers along its bumpy brick wall, looking first over its edge at the clear blue water flowing underneath and then at the surrounding land. Katton's station, along with the rest of the settlement, stood to the west, and the plains of the wilderness to the north, south and east, with the road travelling across the latter. She could see no sign of Scottie Sharp and Cylan Wight anywhere. The others, who'd started their search on the banks, didn't seem to be faring any better. Letting out a sigh, she was beginning to wonder if they were wasting their time when Jase called out.

She hurried over to where he was waving his arms, about twenty feet away from the bridge down by the riverside. Bale and Sol reached him at the same time. When they arrived, Jase, who looked like he could barely contain himself, pointed at the ground, where two parallel lines had indented the soil and flattened the grass.

"Tracks," muttered Sol.

"Made by tyres," added Bale. He looked sideways at Sol. "Large tyres. There's only one vehicle I can think of that could have made these tracks."

"A Magicom steam van," agreed Sol. He crossed his arms. "But I don't understand. If the soldiers in Katton arrived by steam van, they must have parked somewhere else. Why would there be tracks here by the bank?"

His unanswered question hung in the air. Jase's arm dropped, and his eyes narrowed while Pink and Bale exchanged a glance.

"Oh, come off it," huffed Sol, raising his arms in exasperation. "Surely you don't think Magicom took the mayor's son and his friend?"

"It does look suspicious, Sol," said Pink. "This is exactly the spot where they went missing."

"Could these tracks not be here for some other reason?"

"They could … I suppose." But Pink didn't like the coincidence.

"I thought we were under the assumption that this manabeast was responsible for the missing people," pressed Sol. "What's that got to do with Magicom? Why would they have anything to do with Scottie Sharp and

Cylan Wight?"

"So you've just conveniently forgotten what happened at the Salted Pig?" said Jase.

Not this again, thought Pink, as Sol turned sharply to Jase. When he spoke, however, his voice was deliberately soft. "I just think we ought to know all the facts before we come to a conclusion."

"We do," agreed Pink, which seemed to appease him. Jase looked incredulous; Bale merely watched her as if she was mildly amusing. "But to do so, we need to find out what Magicom were doing here and what the connection is to these manabeasts. Jase is right about the mayor's son, but why take Cylan Wight? Was it by association? Or is it somehow related to the manabeast he saw?"

"Investigating missing townsfolk is one thing," said Bale, "but investigating Magicom is another. If they find out we're looking for this connection, we could put ourselves in danger."

Pink's mind flashed back to what she'd witnessed in Ratchette's office. "We could," Pink said, "but we're going to have to take that risk or give up now." She looked round to them. "Does anyone want to give up?"

Jase and Sol looked uncomfortable, but neither voiced any objections. Bale merely crossed his arms and shook his head.

"Let's return to Wing then," said Pink grimly, "and plan our next steps."

CHAPTER THIRTEEN

The walls of Doscadia were a great expanse of concrete rising at least a hundred feet in the air, a mass of architecture dominating the plains they were sitting on. When Roeden had stepped out of the woodland with August and Chadwick and seen them for the first time, his awe had been all-consuming. Now, hours later, as he and Chadwick trod the road running southeast to the city, he still couldn't stop himself from taking frequent glances.

August had left as soon as the walls had come into sight, diverting off the road and onto the plains, not wishing to be seen by other travellers, who would only increase in number nearer to the city's western gate. After promising once again to meet them at the tavern known as the Hairy Dog, he'd headed in the direction of the dam.

As August had predicted, it took Roeden and Chadwick nearly the whole day to reach Doscadia's western gate, making Roeden appreciate just how large the city actually was. As they neared, Roeden could see the sense in August's decision to go his own way. When the River Road first joined the Doscadian Road, there had been a few other travellers here and there, ahead and behind; but now dozens of other small roads had joined theirs, and they'd become part of a procession of hundreds. Some were on horseback or driving wagons, but many were on foot like them.

"The number of people here must equal all of Bodham," said Roeden, gaping as they joined the back of the line, the volume of noise reminding him of his town's marketplace.

Chadwick grunted, but Roeden could tell he was pleased with his amazement. He always seemed to appreciate Roeden's wonder at the world outside Bodham. "No doubt they all need to enter the city before dusk, which is nearing," he said. "You can't underestimate the safety of being inside those walls." Chadwick emptied the last drops from his flask into his mouth and looked towards the city with longing. "I hope it doesn't take too long to get in."

As it happened, it took them only half an hour or so to reach the gateway, which waited at the end of two parallel stone walls. Men and women in shiny, golden syntaxicite, partially covered by red cloaks, flanked them from within – the city guard, Chadwick told him before he could ask.

"They have swords," said Roeden, spotting the weapons sheathed beneath their cloaks, "like Magicom soldiers. Can they use magic as well?"

"I would wager they're all trained to use magic and carry potions on them at all times," replied Chadwick, sparing them a quick glance, "but, like Magicom soldiers, they won't use them unless needed. Arcannen costs, remember?"

Once inside the city, they were greeted by a mass of tall buildings, brick houses, wide streets, cafes and shops. The circular area they found themselves in was so crowded and loud that Roeden could barely hear himself speak. Boys and girls around his age stood by stands with posters that read '*Severity News*', waving copies of the publication and calling out the day's headline: "Blimp reconstruction starts at Holding Castle!" The smells of cooked meat and spices wafted from stalls at every corner. Small rivers flowed right through the heart of the city, walkways and bridges separating different areas, while canoes took people from place to place, docking at small wooden piers.

However, as Roeden finished drinking in the architecture, he also saw hundreds of people dressed in what could only be described as rags, seemingly pushed to one side of the gate, some huddled around metal burn barrels, others trying to sell flowers or some other ware to the new arrivals. Largely, they were ignored. Roeden wondered if these were the people Chadwick had meant on the River Road, the ones living on the outskirts of the city proper. Many had set up their tin shelters or tents against the wall itself, while others seemed to have no more than a tatty blanket and were wrapped in these asleep – or worse. Suddenly, the city wasn't quite as magnificent as Roeden had thought.

"Better inside the walls than out," muttered Chadwick as he motioned away an elderly lady offering wilted roses with a wave of his hand.

Once they were through the crowds, Chadwick paid a rower from one of the stations to take them to the Scholastic District. They sat on a bench built into the bow and were soon drifting through the city, passing by streets holding shops looking as if they were shutting for the day or the odd tavern starting to fill up, the faint sound of a flute or violin coming from within.

Roeden noticed that much of Doscadia seemed to rise and fall. He saw brick stairs ascend and descend to different platforms, and in places, the river travelled down waterways. At one point, Chadwick pointed out a house of worship. The sheer size of the building was incredible to Roeden, much larger and grander than the one situated in his home town. It had stained-glass windows full of shapes and colours, images of boats, trees and stars set within, as well as other symbols he didn't recognise. As they passed, Roeden watched black- and brown-robed priests of the Trinity tending plants that grew from pots at the front of the building.

By the time they got to the Scholastic District, the area seemed flatter, as if the district was at the bottom of the city, and quieter, with wider streets and pathways made from brick rather than cobblestone. They passed under a bridge and stopped at a wooden platform, not far from which Roeden could see another tavern on the corner, this one with a sign that read 'The Hairy Dog'.

Chadwick paid their rower a few bronze wyrms, and they stepped off the canoe. Roeden could still feel the movement when they were on the pavement and laughed aloud at the feeling while Chadwick looked at him like he was mad. As the canoe pulled away, Roeden spotted a Magicom clinic across the bridge, the white marble walls reflecting the now-lit streetlamps. It stood on either side of brick buildings, many of which rose several storeys higher (offices, Chadwick had told him on the canoe). These ran adjacent to the river on both sides, with their windows neatly arranged into rows and columns and their slanted roofs identical. The road on their side of the river was very wide and quiet, with no sign of traffic. Seeing Chadwick moving towards the tavern, Roeden pulled his eyes from their surroundings and followed.

Inside, the Hairy Dog was comprised of several rooms separated by beams and half-walls, holding dozens of wooden tables and candles. Some of these were occupied by dining men and women, most dressed in expensive-looking suits or dresses, the appetising smell of their cooked food thick in the air. The looks Roeden and Chadwick received suggested that their cloaks were starting to look considerably travel-worn.

Chadwick stepped to the bar, where they were greeted by a young girl in a waistcoat, dark trousers and, to Roeden's astonishment, pastel-blue, straight hair that framed her tawny-beige features and fell past her shoulders. Her green eyes widened when she saw Chadwick, yet they exchanged no more than a few pleasantries as he ordered a mug of ale and a small one for Roeden. When Chadwick handed over the coin for his drink, however, she leaned over the bar and whispered in a nervous-sounding voice,

"I'll send someone for Rush."

Chadwick nodded before taking their drinks to the room furthest from the entrance, where they sat at one of several empty tables.

"Who was that?" asked Roeden as soon as they were seated. "Someone from Ashes? Who's Rush?"

"Better wait for August before I answer those questions."

Roeden was impatient to find out more but let the matter drop. "I've never seen anyone with blue hair before," he commented instead, sipping his drink before almost instantly spitting it back into the mug. "That's disgusting!"

Chadwick chuckled. "A little more bitter than you were expecting?"

Roeden shot him an angry glance. "It's not funny!"

Chadwick continued to laugh. Roeden glared at him until the man put his hands up in a placating gesture. "Fine, Roeden, I'll stop. Look, I'll even tell you about the magic-born to make up for it."

"The who?" spat Roeden, still irritated by the other's laughter.

"Those born with unusual hair colour. They're sometimes called the magic-born – it's believed their appearances were altered by access to arcannen while still in the womb. By way of mothers who took arcannen potions whilst pregnant," he added in response to Roeden's raised eyebrows. "The belief comes from the fact that this phenomenon didn't appear until *after* Tette Tesyn discovered how to create arcannen potions. Naturally, these individuals are all of the younger generation."

He says it's for my benefit, yet he loves sounding like a know-it-all. But that did not stop Roeden from enquiring after every person Chadwick had ever seen or met who had unusual hair colour until they were joined by a dark, hooded figure.

"You two seem to be enjoying yourselves," said August, lowering his hood and placing his hands on the back of an empty chair. Water dripped from his long hair, and his cloak looked as if it'd recently been wet. "What is it you're discussing?"

"The magic-born," said Roeden, liking the sound of this newly learned phrase on his tongue. "Do you know any, August?"

Something dangerous flashed in August's eyes, a look so sudden Roeden flinched despite himself. Chadwick frowned and turned to August to see what the matter was, but by then, the Ashes leader's features had smoothed.

"I've come across a few." August shrugged indifferently. "What made you discuss such things?"

"The girl at the bar – she has blue hair."

"Ah, Sapphire. Of course." August seemed to relax. "She has, in fact, arranged rooms for us. We should go to them."

Chadwick scowled but made his way to his feet, picking up his mug of ale. Roeden, still wondering what had caused such a reaction from August, left his behind. The blue-haired girl, Sapphire, was waiting for them at the side of the bar. She gestured for them to follow and led them up a nearby wooden staircase to a landing on the first floor lined with doors on either side. They were taken to one at the end, finding a room with three beds and blankets, a crackling fireplace and an old rounded wooden table near the small window, complete with a few lit candles.

"Thank you, Sapphire," said August as she turned to leave. He placed a hand on her arm. "It's good to see you," he added quietly.

The girl looked grateful and nodded before shutting the door behind her. August took himself to the table, slung his pack into the corner and removed his cloak, flinging it onto one of the beds. *He looked strange in just his syntaxicite,* Roeden thought, *almost like a distorted version of the city guard.* Roeden watched as August grabbed a chair and took it to the fireplace, sitting himself in front of it, wet hair falling over his face.

"I'm afraid I must steal the fire for a while," he said, placing his hands towards the flames, grunting in satisfaction before turning his head to look at the other two. "It's not much, this place. But it's a quiet tavern and one not often frequented by the city guard – which is useful, as the majority have probably seen my likeness on those charming posters."

Roeden looked around. A bed, a fireplace, blankets. "I've never been so glad to be inside," he said.

Chadwick laughed, and even August let out a dry chuckle. "Your first journey in the wilderness," said

Chadwick merrily. "Makes you appreciate the comforts of shelter." He took a swig of his ale as if to emphasise the point.

"We'll make a traveller out of you yet, Roeden," said August. He turned back to the fireplace, where he fell silent, staring into its depths. Chadwick seemed content to sit at the table and drink, so Roeden looked out of the window. There wasn't much to look at, but he could see the street lamps reflecting off the water and just make out the Magicom clinic in the distance.

It wasn't long before there was a knock at the door. August leapt up and opened it, allowing a lady with pale features and long, dark hair, wearing an outfit similar to Sapphire's, to stride into the room. She took in Chadwick and Roeden before turning to August.

"I heard that an ill-begotten rogue who smells like he's been travelling for days is staying at the Hairy Dog. Looks like my information was correct."

Roeden's heart skipped a beat. *I thought this person was the friend August had been waiting for!* However, August chuckled.

"Don't be an idiot, Rush," he said as they clasped hands.

Rush grinned. "Chadwick, good to see you," she said, moving over and doing the same. Chadwick seemed more awkward than August had been. Her sharp blue eyes travelled to Roeden, and she looked at him questioningly. "And … who's this?"

"Roeden, meet Rush Chambers. Rush, this is Roeden Mason."

"Phantex's brother?" Rush looked to August in surprise. "Seems like there's a story to tell here."

"Let's wait for Sapphire. Then we can all talk together."

"Are you in Ashes?" Roeden asked.

Rush looked at him for a moment before shaking her head. "Should a boy of this age be around us at this time?" she asked, turning to August. "Seems a bit reckless, even for you, August."

"I trust him," said August quietly, at which Roeden felt a surge of pride. Rush shrugged her agreement before – to Roeden's amazement – removing the hair from her head. Roeden's gasp caused both August and Chadwick to laugh this time. Chadwick even had the nerve to slap his knee.

"Rush is a master of disguise," said August, as Rush ran a hand over her shaved pate, winking, and the door to the room opened once more, admitting Sapphire. "That's one of the reasons we need her. She also comes from a long line of smugglers, which has proved useful before."

Rush dipped her head in acknowledgement before crossing her arms. "Enough pleasantries. I want to know what the plan is."

August's response was to move his chair back to the table, inclining his hand for Rush and Sapphire to sit. They squeezed onto the chair together, looking towards him expectantly as he stood before them. August's whole manner seemed to change in an instant – he held himself upright and still, with his hands clasped before him and his expression serious. *Like a general,* thought Roeden, remembering Chadwick's words from the River Road.

"Our next step was always to restock our arcannen supply," August said, his eyes moving to each of them in turn, "and increase our numbers. It's something Taurus and I have been working on: creating allies, and finding people who could make a difference. Our end goal remains the same – to remove Magicom and their corruption from the face of Blake, to make arcannen available to all. Yet our priorities have changed. Phantex was targeted by Magicom in an effort to get to me, and so the first thing we must do is secure his liberty. For that, we're going to need more arcannen.

"Since Holding Castle, I've been sheltered by Verity Ravenscar. She, in fact, helped me orchestrate the Holding Castle mission. Verity is sympathetic to our cause but cannot be openly so. However, we can use her position to our advantage. The reason why I've come back into the open now and journeyed all the way to Doscadia is due to a meeting she's having with a Magicom representative tomorrow. That meeting is to take place at the Magicom clinic opposite this very building at noon."

"The one just over the bridge?" asked Roeden, his mind working quickly. "You can see it from the window!"

"That is no accident," replied August, smiling. "I wrote to Rush and Sapphire when Verity and I first came up with the plan, trying to get everything in readiness. That's how Sapphire was able to secure a job at the nearest tavern before I arrived."

"It's as we thought then," said Rush, indicating herself and Sapphire. "We're hitting the clinic for arcannen. And that means," – she waved the wig in the air – "you want me to be our good Minister for Agriculture."

August grinned. "Verity wouldn't help with the robbery herself, but she's going to ensure she suffers a delay on the way. One that will give us enough time for you to get in and do what we need."

"What if someone recognises Rush is not Verity Ravenscar?" asked Chadwick.

"Verity assures me she has never met the representative in question nor been to Doscadia for a number of years. Although Rush is a little younger, she has the same look and build, so I don't think recognition should be a problem. Especially as Verity has given me papers that authenticate her as a government official, which I'll pass on." His gaze passed to Rush. "What I'm more concerned about is leaving you alone in there to discuss a subject matter with which you're not entirely familiar."

"This isn't my first deception," said Rush, at which August inclined his head.

"Hold on, I'm not following this," said Chadwick. "Why does Rush need to be Verity Ravenscar for us to steal arcannen? She's never had to do so before."

"Things aren't like before," answered August, his features grave. "Magicom know we can hit any clinic at any time, so the amount of arcannen they keep on their shop floors has greatly decreased. You can understand Salvamal's way of thinking – if we're successful in stealing arcannen, he wants us to get as little as possible."

"*You* can understand Salvamal's way of thinking," Chadwick muttered.

August shrugged. "The point is, they've adapted; therefore, so must we. Besides," August rubbed his arm, looking uncharacteristically uncomfortable, "I regret what happened at Rynn. That mustn't happen again. They may work for Magicom, but those clinic clerks are no soldiers. If we want the people of Blake behind us, we have to ensure our arcannen retrieval is done in the right way."

The others nodded, seeming to understand, but Roeden did not. *What happened at Rynn?* He opened his mouth to ask, but August continued before he could get the words out.

"Verity showed me a floor plan of this district's clinic. There's a storeroom located near the back of the building, accessible through a secure door on the shop floor or through the back door itself. They have been designed so neither can be blasted open with magic. One of the soldiers will have the key, but attacking a fully trained Magicom soldier in broad daylight is not a sensible option. That's where Rush comes in. As the Minister for Agriculture, she'll be taken to the meeting room at the back of the building." He turned to Rush. "After that, you'll need to find some excuse to step out so you can find the back door and unbolt it. Say you have to use the bathroom or something. If we time everything correctly, the rest of us will be waiting, and you and I can fill up our satchels with arcannen potions from the storeroom while Sapphire and Chadwick – taking Taurus' place – wait with horses for our escape. We can be in and out within minutes. By the time the representative realises you're not coming back, we'll be long gone." The corner of his mouth twisted into a smile. "This will only work once, so let's make it count."

"I can go with Sapphire and Chadwick to get the horses. They may need help," suggested Roeden, hopeful he might play some part in this exciting plan.

"I'm afraid not, Roeden. I don't want anyone to give your description to Magicom, even if it's just a stable master. As it stands, they have no idea where you went after Taurus' farm. When it's time, you'll come with me to meet Sapphire and Chadwick, then you'll need to stick with Chadwick while Rush and I collect the arcannen from the clinic. He's proven competent at looking after you."

Roeden felt mutinous. Had he come all this way to do nothing? Chadwick gave him a sympathetic smile, but August seemed not to notice as he addressed the others. "Any number of things could go wrong," he told them. "If things go awry, we leave at once – with or without the potions. Does everyone understand that?" He waited until he had all their nods of agreement before adding, "With any luck, we'll be on our way out of Doscadia tomorrow on horseback with enough arcannen to help Phantex."

"And Verity Ravenscar?" asked Chadwick. "What if someone works out she helped us?"

"She's taken steps to ensure nothing gets back to her. The papers Rush will carry are fraudulent, so she can't be blamed in any way for them, and we could have found out about the meeting in any number of ways. Besides, anyone who claims she's helping Ashes will be making a powerful enemy." August met Chadwick's eyes. "She's very dangerous in her own way."

Rush frowned. "You're not selling her to us, August. Can we really trust her?"

August shrugged. "This will never succeed if we don't."

CHAPTER FOURTEEN

Roeden was surprised to find he slept well that night. His frustrations at not being involved in the mission – and a renewed sense of worry for Phantex if it went wrong – were outweighed by his exhaustion, it seemed. Spending those nights in the wilderness had not afforded him much rest nor comfort, but sleeping in a real bed gave his aching limbs both.

He was woken the next morning by the sound of Sapphire bringing in a tray of baked bread, butter and boiled eggs. Rush – wearing the dark wig and dressed in a smart grey woollen suit – followed closely behind. August was sat at the table, making Roeden wonder if he'd gone to bed at all.

"Is everything in readiness?" August asked Rush, thanking Sapphire as she deposited the tray in front of him but ignoring its contents. Roeden was starving after his full night's sleep, and the smell of the food was enough to make his mouth salivate. He scrambled over almost as quickly as Chadwick.

"We're all set," replied Rush, watching them with a crooked smile.

The morning passed slowly. After they'd eaten, Rush and Chadwick took to the table to play Elementals, retrieved from the common room by Sapphire. Roeden watched them, trying to pick up on how the wooden pieces moved. By the end of the first game, he thought he had it. *The fire mages can only move forward, but the wind mages can move forwards and backwards; the water mages can move diagonally, and the earth mages horizontally. If they meet, the wooden discs battle, and a roll of the dice decides who wins.* His eyes moved to where Chadwick had stacked half a dozen of Rush's painted stones. *The idea is to use the mages to pick up all the stones, but the trick is to stop the other player from doing so.* August seemed content to gaze out of the window, although Roeden didn't think he was really watching anything.

An hour before noon, once the game was packed away, Sapphire returned to their room and was handed a pouch of coins by August. "That's more or less the last of what I have," he told her. She nodded, took a deep breath, and together she and Chadwick headed for the door, the latter giving Roeden what he obviously felt was a reassuring smile, yet Roeden thought was more of a grimace.

As noon approached, August announced it was time. From her waistcoat pocket, Rush produced two silver pocket watches and handed one to August. Roeden watched curiously as they compared the two faces before nodding in some sort of agreement.

August noticed him watching. "We have to ensure Rush opens the back door around the same time we arrive," he told Roeden, "in order to limit how long we're outside for. If anyone sees us and thinks it suspicious, we want to be away before they can report it to the city guard."

"See you in ten minutes," said Rush, winking as she took her leave, but Roeden didn't miss the slight tremble in her hands.

That left just August and Roeden. August took to the

window, looking down at the street. Roeden moved alongside him, noticing how much busier it was than the previous evening, many going about their business on foot, carriage or horseback, the clip-clop of hooves reaching them where they stood. After a few moments, he saw Rush crossing the bridge and heading towards the clinic, where two Magicom soldiers stood guard. She approached them, held up something and followed one inside.

At that moment, August let out a hiss.

Roeden looked at August in confusion. Everything had gone to plan, hadn't it? But then he saw August wasn't looking at Rush but at a handful of men and women stepping out of a black carriage parked on their side of the river, fresh-looking paint glinting in the sunlight. The two who were helping the others out were in black syntaxicite, much like August's, but the rest were dressed in suits similar to Rush's attire.

"Who are they?" Roeden asked.

But August was already moving. He grabbed his pack from where it had been waiting by the door and started rummaging through it.

"August?"

"That's Verity Ravenscar down there," August spat. "The *real* Verity Ravenscar. She was meant to be delayed, remember? She's arrived on time after all – with an escort, it seems."

Roeden looked back, making out a dark-haired woman from the window. She seemed to be glancing around a lot. "I don't understand," he said. "Why isn't she sticking to the plan? Has she betrayed you?"

"If that was the case, why would she even show? Perhaps something has happened outside her control. Either way, Rush is in danger. As soon as they reach the clinic's soldiers, they'll realise there's an imposter inside."

Roeden could hear a lot of rustling, like the changing of clothes. He glanced behind to see August pulling on a grey syntaxicite top. On the chest was a red M symbol. "You're wearing a Magicom uniform!" Roeden exclaimed.

"I've had it since our mission at Holding Castle, just in case," August said as he took a vial of arcannen from his pack, uncorked the stopper and downed the liquid. He glanced back at Roeden, a troubled look on his features as if he was making some difficult decision.

"There's no help for it," he said at last. "I can't leave you here alone, and the others need to know what's happened. You'll have to tell them while I keep the officials away from the clinic. Take yourself over the bridge and through the alley to the left of the building. At its end, you'll find a yard where Sapphire and Chadwick should be waiting with the horses. Tell them the plan's off and to get out of the city with Rush at once. They'll need to head for the town of Rothmount. I'll either catch you all up on the road or meet you there." He walked to Roeden and placed a hand on his shoulder, his dark eyes boring into Roeden's own. "Roeden, you need to do everything exactly as I say. Can you do that?"

"Yes," said Roeden at once.

August nodded. He thrust the pack at Roeden. "Keep this safe for me. Tell me the name of the town again."

"Rothmount."

"Good. Wait one minute, then follow."

A moment later, he was gone.

***

August was not, in fact, entirely convinced of Verity Ravenscar's loyalty. As he moved through the hallway and down the steps that led to the tavern's ground floor, his mind worked quickly, trying to assess the situation. During the time he'd spent with her, Verity could've given him up any number of times, yet she hadn't. On top of that, she *had* seemed to truly believe in the cause. Yet he would never fully trust a government official. The only people he did trust, aside from his sister and uncle, were his brothers and sisters in Ashes. *Well, most of them, anyway.*

He spared a quick thought for Roeden. He'd intended to keep the boy from being involved, but circumstances had conspired against him. Hopefully, Roeden would follow his instructions, but that was hardly a certainty given Roeden's stubborn streak. *The decision's made. I can't go back on it now. I have to keep my mind on what I can control.*

He crossed the empty common room and stepped out into the daylight, spotting Verity at once. She was speaking with a white-haired, amber-skinned man with a bronze arm, one whom August knew by reputation. Linus Atkins – one of the figures on the Governmental Council, those who passed the laws in Blake and technically ran the country. The other suits were probably part of the same council, and the two men in syntaxicite were likely hired mages there to offer security and protection.

They may yet get a chance to prove their worth.

"Ladies, gentlemen," August said, calling to them as he approached, an inkling of an idea coming to him even as he spoke. Half a dozen faces turned to look at him; surprise mirrored in their features. He could see them take in the uniform at once, and that surprise turn to a mixture of confusion, fear and loathing, the exception being Verity, who merely paled. Another complication was the two soldiers who stood guard outside the clinic. If he could see them, they could see him and might wonder why one of their fellows was having a discussion with the officials. The question was, would it cause them to leave their posts?

He cleared his throat. *One thing at a time.* "Correct me if I'm wrong, but I'm assuming you have a meeting scheduled at our clinic today?"

"You are not wrong," replied Linus Atkins, eyeing him warily.

"There is a situation. The rest of my unit are inside at the moment dealing with it. For your safety, ladies and gentlemen, I must insist you wait here until its conclusion." August spread his left arm out in the direction of some nearby wooden benches facing the river to emphasise this was not a request. "There is seating, so you should be comfortable."

And now to see if this'll work. The two officials August did not know seemed to be looking at Atkins for his decision. Verity continued to stare at August, clear eyes imploring as if she was trying to speak without words. *I suppose she'd have raised the alarm by now if she'd sold me out. That's some consolation, at least.* He resisted the temptation to check if Roeden had followed him from the tavern yet.

A small smirk appeared on Linus Atkins' lips. He dipped his head curtly, seated himself on one of the benches, and looked out to the river. The others followed his lead. August took up a position behind some nearby potted plants, the rising stems and leaves partly concealing him from those outside the clinic. *Now Roeden just needs to get the others out of there.*

Linus Atkins looked up at August as if wondering what he was still doing there. "If there is a matter at the clinic, wouldn't it be wise to call the city guard to assist?" His voice, while smooth, betrayed a hint of annoyance.

The other two officials were muttering to each other, clearly unhappy. Verity, who was nearest to Atkins, continued to stare straight ahead at the river, but August could tell she was listening to every word. *What would a Magicom soldier say?* "This is a Magicom matter," he decided.

Atkins scoffed. "And I'm sure it's a matter your superiors want dealt with discreetly, but what could be happening at a clinic that can't be dealt with swiftly? You say your whole unit's in there, which must mean there is some operation going on, especially since two of your guards are still standing outside, making it seem as if everything's normal. Tell me, soldier, is this something to do with Ashes?"

He's missed the point, but you can't fault his reasoning, given the information I supplied him with. This man was dangerous. August would have to be careful.

Atkins, who clearly took his silence for something else, smiled smugly. "I thought so. Well, they're after more arcannen, no doubt. By the Trinity, you have to admire their audacity."

"Be careful what you say, Linus," said Verity, keeping her eyes on the river, her usually refined voice flat.

Atkins let out a snort before taking in August once more. "What's your name, soldier?"

Damn. "Jarian Green," August replied, the first name that came into his head.

"Do not misunderstand Linus," said Verity suddenly, as if she was trying to draw his attention away from who August was. "He doesn't mean he supports Ashes."

"No, of course not," said Atkins in a bored voice. "I merely appreciate bravery and the tactics of warfare. Ashes have always shown great cunning. I was at Holding Castle when they pulled that little stunt; Rox Salvamal will never forgive them for making such a fool of him." Atkins sounded as if he found the thought amusing. "Of course, none of that changes the illegality of Ashes' actions. Now, how long do you expect us to stay out here for, Mr Green?"

"As long as it takes for my unit to secure the area," replied August, trying to sound put out by the question.

"Just think, Linus," said one of the other officials. "We only joined with Verity at the last moment to help support her in these talks. We all thought this would be an uneventful trip. But now we might get to see August Silvershield arrested – what a coincidence that would be!"

"Yes, quite …" murmured Atkins. He looked back up to August, a small crease appearing on his brow. At that same moment, August caught sight of Roeden crossing the bridge. *Good lad.* Then he saw something else. Half a dozen city guard had appeared from around the corner of a nearby building and were approaching their position.

***

"That's the Minister for Agriculture? The lady from the Ravenscar family? She's younger than I expected."

"Still too old for you. Did you think she looked nervous?"

"Nervous? Nah, what does she have to be nervous about? They're just having one of those never-ending meetings in there, right?"

Roeden tried to act nonchalant as he passed the Magicom soldiers. Aside from a perfunctory glance from one, they paid him no heed, continuing their conversation about whom they believed to be Verity Ravenscar. Thankfully, they had yet to notice the gathering on the other side of the river.

When he reached the end of the marble walls and turned the corner into the alley August had mentioned, he broke into a run. At the end, he found Chadwick and Sapphire already in the concrete yard, each atop a mount, both holding the reins of another. Aside from them, the yard was deserted, but the streets were visible from areas not covered by the back of buildings.

"Roeden!" said Chadwick, noticing at once something was wrong. "Where's August?"

"There's a problem," Roeden replied just as a metal door from the back of the clinic opened, and Rush poked her head out. At any other time, Roeden might have asked why the back of the clinic was made from brick instead of marble, but there were more important matters at hand. Rush looked from him to Chadwick as Roeden continued. "The real Verity Ravenscar's turned up with other officials and two men in syntaxicite. And that's not all! I saw some of the city guard just now. August says to … he says to …"

"To abort?" Rush asked quietly.

"Yes, but …" Despite what August had told him, Roeden refused to give up on the mission. It was clearly vital in saving Phantex. "We need that arcannen," he told them, "so … so I'll take August's place! I even have his pack! He seems to have those officials distracted, quick – we should still have time!"

"I don't think August will like …"

But Roeden was already moving, ignoring Chadwick's words and startled cry, mirroring August's quick decision-making from minutes before. He knew the others would try to stop him, so he ducked under Rush's arm before she could do anything other than frown.

He found himself in a corridor. Oil lamps lined the brick walls, which had been painted white. Ahead, it ran in two directions, one intersecting left and the other carrying on to a metal door similar to the one he'd just bypassed. There was an opening a little ahead to his right, and as he hurried forward, Roeden realised it led into a small square room.

Peering around the corner, Roeden saw a number of open wooden crates on the concrete ground, each filled with arcannen potions, the black liquid glistening within their vials. *So many!* There was nothing else in the space aside from more oil lamps and a table holding neatly arranged leather bags, which, from the way they bulged, Roeden assumed were filled with coins. Ignoring these, he unclasped August's pack and started loading the arcannen potions from the nearest crate into it.

"August is not going to be happy about this," came Rush's voice from the opening. Roeden glanced back to find her watching from behind the curtains of her fake hair. She wore an amused look on her face. "But then again," she said as she joined him, kneeling down and loading arcannen into her own pack, "this is exactly the sort of thing Phantex would've done."

Roeden didn't respond, but a grin spread across his features.

Once their packs were filled, they exchanged a glance to confirm the other was finished before moving back towards the opening, the stolen vials clinking together as they went. As he passed the table, Roeden paused, looking at the bags of coins. He grabbed one, pocketed it and followed Rush outside.

"Now what?" asked Chadwick, clearly anxious, as Rush attached her pack to one of the spare horse's saddles. Roeden watched her fingers work with the strap and ties and attempted to do the same with Chadwick's horse.

"Roeden's message from August was to leave," said Sapphire quietly. She looked to Rush as if for a decision, but Rush merely looked uncomfortable.

Another idea came to Roeden then. "We'll leave with August," he said, tightening the last strap before running back to the alley and looking over his shoulder. "Wait here!"

Once again, he ignored their protests.

***

"Is everything all right?" one of the city guard asked, taking in August and the officials.

"Everything's fine," Verity told them.

"Not everything," said Atkins. "We have a meeting at the clinic, and apparently Magicom are apprehending Ashes members inside, although all seems quiet, and look there's a guard heading in our direction …"

August readied his magic. The soldiers had finally noticed their crowd, and one of them was crossing the bridge. Even from where he was standing, August could see the questioning look on the soldier's face. Linus Atkins turned to August, opening his mouth to speak, but at that point, Roeden appeared from behind the soldier on the bridge, overtook him, and yelled,

"Guards! Quick! August Silvershield is in the Hairy Dog!"

The city guard looked at one another before charging towards the tavern, red cloaks billowing in their wake, many removing vials of arcannen from somewhere within their clothing and downing them as they entered.

"Follow!" Verity commanded the officials' security.

The two mages went in behind the city guard. The soldier on the bridge hesitated and exchanged a look with the one at the doorway. It was likely they had orders not to leave sight of the clinic. August, knowing this confusion was the only chance he had, made eye contact with Roeden and nodded back to the direction of the alley before moving to follow. Before he could, however, Linus Atkins grabbed his arm.

"It seems strange," said the government official quietly, "that a boy who left the tavern moments ago would only say Silvershield was in there *after* he'd gone over the bridge." He looked into August's eyes. *Does he know?* But Atkins let go of his arm and smiled. August took off at once, following Roeden.

"What's going on?" the soldier on the bridge asked, stepping in front of August as he was halfway across, preventing him from getting any further. "I don't recognise you, soldier. Whose unit are you in?"

"I was ordered here to protect Verity Ravenscar," said August, ignoring the question he couldn't answer. "This is a secret operation, and I need to find her at once, so you need to step aside. I'm sure everything will be explained in due course."

"Hold on, none of this makes sense. Who are those people you were talking to? And since you don't have guard duty, isn't it more important you assist the city guard in apprehending Silvershield? Look, they're coming out now. By the Trinity, they don't look happy."

"Soldier, we don't have time to discuss this."

"I'm afraid you're going to have to make the time." It was clear by his tone that the soldier suspected August was not who he claimed to be, so when he made a movement with his hand, August did not mistake his intention. Before the soldier could act, August blasted him with wind, sending him over the side of the bridge and into the river with a splash. He shot another blast at the soldier still by the clinic, slamming him against the marble with a thud. The soldier landed in a heap and did not get back up. August ran for the alley, ignoring both the cries of the officials and the calls from the city guard to halt. Wind magic struck the archway of the opening moments after he'd gone through, the sound of crumbling brick following in his wake.

The others were waiting in the yard, all mounted, with Roeden behind Chadwick. August charged to the last free mount, held by Chadwick, who was almost pulled from his own horse as August hoisted himself onto the saddle. August's horse snorted, clearly spooked by the sudden movement and weight.

"What are you waiting for?" August yelled, putting his heels to his mount as Chadwick released the attached rope. "The city guard are coming. Go!"

Within seconds they were galloping across the yard and onto the streets, Rush taking the lead as they manoeuvred their way through the city, crossing bridges at places where the river intersected, the brickwork of the various buildings blurring as they passed. Rush was obviously trying to lead them through the quieter routes, but occasionally they came across someone who would have to dart out of the way. Many shouts and curses were lost in the hammering of hooves.

The streets became more crowded as the western gate came into sight, and they were forced to slow to a trot as they drew near, manoeuvring around the stalls and people. Another group of city guard standing by the alcove in the wall watched them approach, perhaps wondering why a Magicom soldier was keeping such odd company. *I need a good excuse, but one that doesn't take too long. Who knows how close pursuit is behind?*

As if on cue, sudden shouts made August swivel in his saddle. *Damn!* But the commotion wasn't coming from the direction they'd fled from. It was coming from the area to the side of the gate where the poorer populace resided. There was a frantic crowd forming around something golden glinting on the ground, pushing and shoving one another as their excited cries filled the air.

Are those ... phoenix coins? But ... where did they come from?

He turned to the others and saw, beyond an exasperated-looking Chadwick, Roeden grinning. August, working out what had happened, let out a snort of amused disbelief. *Bringing the boy paid off after all.*

The city guard at the gates vacated their post to investigate, and August's group were able to leave the city unchallenged.

CHAPTER FIFTEEN

The first task Pink undertook on their return to Wing was to brief Instructor Texeria about the steam van tracks, as well as the conversation she'd overheard between Ratchette and General Salvamal. He'd responded in his normal nonchalant way, suggesting she take the information to Gabriel to sec what the assistant master advised.

Before, she might have seen this as a lack of interest in their investigation, but she had since got used to Keat Texeria's quirks and decided he likely needed time to mull things over. As for Ratchette, Pink had kept the blackmailing from the others, even Jase, in order to keep the conversations regarding Ashes to a minimum. Instructor Texeria was, however, Ratchette's friend, and Pink thought he deserved to know she was in difficulty. Whether he would do anything to support her was another matter entirely.

Gabriel's cottage was one of many built on the eastern side of the hill, all thatched roofs and tidy brickwork. Pink made her way there early the following morning, walking the well-trodden paths, the sunlight warming her skin despite the morning's crisp air. At the entrance, she knocked and waited.

After a few moments, the door opened, and Gabriel

appeared at the threshold. He was dressed in his Wing uniform, clutching a piece of paper in his left hand.

"Sara!" he said, clearly surprised. He took a glance behind her before adding, "You had better come in."

She followed him into his cottage's sitting room. This one was plainer than East House's, furnished only with a couple of brass candlesticks that stood on a mantelpiece, a rug on the floor and a few armchairs. Gabriel sat in one of these and directed her to another with a wave of his hand.

"Just now, I received a letter from Mayor Sharp of Poulsen," he said without preamble, his dark eyes fixed on hers.

That was quick! I hope it's not like the letter he received from Madam Shawgrave. "Yes, that's what I've come to talk to you about. Instructor Texeria also received a letter from Mayor Sharp yesterday …"

He nodded along as she briefly recounted their outing – a little too quickly, she thought, as if he was doing nothing more than humouring her, although a small crease did appear on his brow when she mentioned the steam van tracks.

"I'm afraid there's more to it than you know," he said when she'd finished, waving the letter in his hand. "A rider delivered this with some haste earlier. Apparently, workers found Poulsen's coal mines overrun with manabeasts this morning. Mayor Sharp has asked for an additional contract to purge the beasts."

And discover any clues about his son's whereabouts, no doubt. "This is very strange, Assistant Master," Pink said, her mind working quickly. "No manabeasts for weeks, and suddenly now they're all in one mine? How has that happened?"

"A question I very much hope to find the answer to.

This can no longer be a project of Keat Texeria's, of which he will tell me very little." Gabriel shook his head, and Pink could sense his frustration with her mentor. "This contract will be overseen by me. I will send a team of mages right away, with a few experienced instructors to lead them."

"Can I have permission to be part of this team?" she asked hopefully.

Gabriel sat back in his armchair, tapping a fist to his mouth. "I feel your time would be better spent working on the original contract. If we discover anything that supports your investigation, it will be passed on, of course."

"Very well," said Pink, knowing when not to push a point. "But whoever you do send will need to be careful, Assistant Master. We still don't know what's going on. Based on those steam van tracks, it may be that Magicom are involved in this."

Gabriel raised his eyebrows. "You need to be careful saying things like that, Sara."

"I'm aware of that. But it doesn't change the facts. What if this is some kind of Magicom trick?"

Gabriel sighed. "Before, I was told that a strange type of manabeast had been spotted by the old arcannen mines. I listened and took a team to investigate. There, we found nothing. Now you're saying it's not a manabeast responsible for these missing people, but Magicom? To what purpose?"

"I don't know, but I think the two are linked."

"Perhaps. But that doesn't change the fact that manabeasts have been seen this morning in those mines. Manabeasts, not Magicom."

"Magicom must have an endgame," said Pink. "You'll need to send a proper force, and they'll need to take precautions …"

"I am the assistant master here," said Gabriel, cutting her off. His tone was cold. "Not you, Sara. Or Instructor Texeria. I don't know what encouraged Master Wing to give him his position out of nowhere, but I have a facility to run, and I intend to run it the right way."

"Apologies," said Pink quickly. "I only meant … based on what I'd seen … to make sure you had all the facts …"

"Duly noted," said Gabriel, "and you can let Instructor Texeria know you've passed those facts on to me – I assume he sent you, so he didn't have to come himself. Perhaps, in turn, you might remind him that although his role as an instructor is to mentor new mages, it is also to teach trainees, something he seems to have avoided thus far." He nodded towards the door. "Now, I have much to prepare for."

She departed, accepting the dismissal wordlessly but uncomfortable with the way the conversation had ended, although part of her recognised it wasn't really her Gabriel was frustrated with. Whatever was going on between the two instructors was … well, between them. She was less uneasy with that than she was about his scepticism of Magicom's involvement. Sol had been the same on their return from the wilderness the previous evening. What, he had argued, about this manabeast that had been seen by the dukesbane site? What had happened to all the wolf-types in the area? Had Magicom taken them as well? What possible reason could they have for doing so? Pink thought they were entirely reasonable questions, but despite the fact it seemed some form of manabeasts had reappeared, she still believed Magicom were involved. Steam van tracks, missing people, retaliation for Scottie Sharp's outburst in the Salted Pig – it had the company's mark all over it. Sol would be biased, of course. She'd expected that from him. Gabriel, on the other hand …

She found Jase in the Box and told him everything. He believed as she did, but neither of them was able to say exactly *how* Magicom were involved, only that there were too many coincidences for them not to be. She would have liked to mull things over with Sol and Bale as well but could see neither inside, despite Sol's group of friends sitting in one corner.

Keen to practise her magic, she convinced Jase to join her on the training courts. They had been training for almost an hour when they saw Instructors Strong, Krank and Birch descending the hill with a dozen or so mages, Bale among them. This caused quite a stir within the courts, with many of the other mages stopping their own training to watch. Bale caught Pink's eye and gave a shrug of his shoulders before continuing on his way.

A twinge of apprehension ran through Pink, but she quickly pushed it down. Whatever was happening at those mines, this was a group of well-trained instructors and mages. Bale and the others would be able to protect themselves.

"How long do you think it'll be before everyone knows where they've gone and why?" Jase muttered to Pink.

"Within the hour," she replied with a smile, thinking it would be Jase who told them.

***

He did not disappoint. After they had spent a little more time training, they took themselves back to the Box to eat, collecting vegetable-filled pastries set out on the main table and taking them to one of the crowded benches. There, Jase pretty much confirmed to anyone who would listen that the three instructors and mages were going to the coal mines to take out a manabeast infestation.

"But I've been wondering," he said, turning back to Pink after his latest retelling. "When they say the coal mines have been overrun by manabeasts, do they mean wolf-types or the other type Cylan Wight saw by the dukesbane site?"

Pink, who was still eating, chewed her food thoughtfully.

Jase watched her closely. "You think this is all Magicom's doing? That there aren't any manabeasts?"

"It seems more than possible that Scottie Sharp and Cylan Wight were taken by Magicom soldiers, not attacked by manabeasts. Although we can't discount manabeasts, especially as the coal mines are suddenly overrun with them. But if they *are* the wolf-types, where have they been all this time? I'm sure there's some connection. I just can't see what it is."

"They should be back soon anyway," said Jase. "Poulsen's coal mines are actually nearer to Wing than Poulsen. It'll take them, what, a couple of hours to get there? I shouldn't think it would take long to exterminate the manabeasts, then journey back. They'll return by noon. Then we'll find out one way or the other. Bale will tell us."

"We keep talking about this unknown type of manabeast Cylan Wight saw, but I've never heard of any type of manabeast in this area other than the wolf-type," said Pink, her fingers rattling on the table. "That doesn't mean other manabeasts haven't wandered into a different territory, of course, and that would certainly explain why the wolf-types went missing." Her fingers stopped their rattling. "We could check the library for information about manabeasts known for this pattern of behaviour. It'll give us something to do while we wait."

"Jase! Pink!" A flushed Rodric fell on the bench beside Jase before he could reply. Jase turned his head with an expression of polite bewilderment. "Is it true Gabriel's sent *three* instructors and a bunch of mages to the coal mines south? Do you know why?"

"You know what, Jase," said Pink with a half-smile, "you fill Rodric in. I'll let you know if I find anything."

Jase launched into speech the moment she stood.

***

Wing's library was a room tucked away in the attic of the Tesyn Building. It was an essential part of the complex, in Pink's opinion, as mages and trainees needed some way to spend their downtime when they weren't out on contracts or training. There were only so many times you could play Elementals. As she entered the spacious room, with its high beams and triangular ceiling, she found just one occupant among the bookcases, sitting at an oaken table by one of the windows.

"So this is where you've been hiding yourself away," said Pink to Sol, finding, to her surprise, how pleased she was to see him.

He looked up with a start. "Not hiding," he said, waving a hand airily, although she couldn't help but notice his lack of eye contact. "I like to read."

"Uh-huh." Pink sat down next to him and watched in amusement as he tried to continue.

Sol sighed and lifted his eyes to meet hers. "Was there anything else?"

She snorted and jumped up, moving to the nearest bookshelf. "I'm doing some research for the contract, trying to identify Cylan Wight's manabeast."

"I thought you were working under the impression

that Wight was taken by Magicom?" he asked slyly.

That's the Sol I know. "They're not off the hook yet," said Pink, "but I spoke to Gabriel today." She told him about the mayor's letter and the group that had been sent to deal with the manabeasts. "It's clear the coal mines are infested with manabeasts," she finished. "So, whatever's happening, maybe we can find something that fits Cylan Wight's description or a type of manabeast that's known for invading the territory of others. Are you going to help? Or are you going to sit there and read your stories, Mr I Like to Read?"

Sol grinned as he got to his feet. "So how did Wight describe it?" he asked, joining her and picking up a leather-bound book from one of the shelves. He flicked through its pages. "Yellow eyes, moving on four legs, quick?"

"Something like that," replied Pink, distracted as she tried to read her own.

"You know I'm not the only one who likes to read," said Sol. Out of the corner of her eye, she saw him glance at her. "I've seen you up here plenty of times. Usually on your own."

"That's an odd comment to make about someone you'd never met before this contract."

"Well, you're hard to miss. With your hair …"

"Are you sure you come up here to read, Sol? Or is it just an excuse to stare at girls?"

Sol spun in her direction, looking horrified, but Pink gave him a smirk before replacing the book and picking up another. *He is just too fun to tease.*

"Ah, you're messing with me."

"Don't worry," she said happily, "I know my hair makes me stand out."

They continued looking for titles relating to the

properties and behaviour of manabeasts, of which there were many. They shared what they found but, as the hours slipped by, seemed to get no further to identifying the manabeast they were looking for.

"It's the same types we keep coming back to," Pink said at one point, running a hand over a scratchy page that had a drawing of a cougar-type, with a description below. "But … nothing stands out."

"He seemed quite sure it wasn't a wolf-type," said Sol, looking thoughtful as he flicked through a particularly weathered-looking tome called *Manabeast Lore*. "But manabeasts are just animals, or they were at one time. Lots of animals move on four legs."

"Well, it could have been. But he seemed so sure it was something else. Something that sort of … crawled … maybe like a spider?"

Sol laughed. "I certainly hope not."

"But it fired energy, remember? Many mammal spawns have that as an offensive type of magic. I've read that point in a dozen of these books. Besides, spiders have eight legs, not four."

"Well, at least we know what type of magic it uses if we come across one," said Sol, slamming the book shut, dust shooting in the air. His enthusiasm for their research had not diminished with time. Pink thought that, deep down, he knew Magicom must be involved in some way. He just didn't want to admit it to anybody – that was probably why he'd been cooped up in the library. "We'll be able to defend ourselves accordingly. Why don't we see if Bale's group has returned? I want to find out what happened."

Yet, despite the fact that it was now a couple of hours after noon, a quick recon of the Box and the training grounds told them that no one had seen the three instructors nor their mages. Pink thought to discuss the matter with Instructor Texeria, but East House was locked, and no one answered when they knocked on the front door or the shutter that led into the storage area.

Now starting to feel a bit uneasy, Pink suggested to Sol they train for a bit. Another hour passed with no sign of the returning group. Nor any the hour after. Eventually, they had had enough and decided to return to the Box for supper. Pink joined Jase, noting he hadn't moved since she'd last been there, while Sol joined his group of friends. She didn't stay for long. After passing on what she'd learned in the library (which was very little) and shutting down Jase's questions about why she'd been spending so much time with Sol, she told her friend she was going for a walk, wanting to sort through the thoughts in her head. Once outside, she took the path leading away from the buildings of Wing.

Had Bale's group run into some kind of trouble? And, if so, what form had it taken? Was it Magicom-related? She looked across the plains, much of it now shadowed by Highstone Hill, the sun starting to dip in the sky behind her in the west. She could feel the warmth on the back of her neck. *What will happen if they don't return before dark? When we found the tracks, Bale warned us that looking into Magicom's activities might prove dangerous. Was he right?*

"You're here for the same reason I am, I see," said a voice behind her.

She turned to see Gabriel walking up the path. He wore a small smile.

"The instructors and mages I sent were due back hours ago." He came to stand next to her, the cloak he now wore wrapped tightly around him, looking out across the plains. The wind was starting to pick up and whistled in the air as if in warning. "Why haven't they sent a runner back?" he murmured, more to himself than her, she thought.

"So send someone after them," she said. He looked at her with his eyebrows raised. "Sorry, I'm not trying to tell you what to do."

"No, it is I who should be sorry. I was rather short with you earlier – I apologise. You were only trying to tell me what you thought I needed to know. I've been under a lot of stress lately. Running Wing is not easy – I'm starting to see why Master Wing wanted to get away for a while." He sighed. "If I send others, by the time they arrive it'll be dusk. I couldn't possibly sanction that with the number of manabeasts roaming the wilderness at night. It seems unless they return or word is sent back, that I'm going to have to wait until morning." He shook his head, and Pink began to feel a little uncomfortable. She'd never seen him look so despondent. "I don't think I'll be getting much sleep tonight. Anyway, I'll leave you to your vigil. Let me know if you see anything."

Pink watched him leave, feeling a great deal of sympathy for the assistant master. She supposed she understood his reasoning for not sending anyone else to the mines just before dusk. *But what if someone else took it upon themselves to investigate?* she thought suddenly. *Someone who wasn't following his orders, thus rendering him blameless?* Nervous excitement rose in her. *I don't have the same reservations about travelling so close to dusk. He probably doesn't put too much store in our findings at the dukesbane site, especially since Cylan Wight's manabeast wasn't where he was told it might be. But it seems that whatever danger there is tonight will be in the coal mines, not in the wilderness. And if I was just to look from afar* … But even as she had that thought, she knew it would be too dangerous to go alone.

She needed Jase and Sol.

Energised by her conviction, she ran back up the path

and into the Box. Sidestepping other mages with rushed apologies, she hurried to where Jase sat. Sol saw her rush in, and she waved him over as she placed herself next to her friend, the bench shuddering with the force of her landing.

"We should go to the coal mines," she said once Sol had joined them.

They both stared at her. Sol was the first to speak. "And why would we do that?"

"Because Gabriel can't send anyone else this close to dusk," she replied, her answers ready, "because he can't leave himself as assistant master and because nobody knows more about this business than we do. Think about it. We know there aren't likely to be any manabeasts out in the wilderness around here because that's the very thing we've been investigating. We'll have to be careful when we get to the coal mines, but the journey itself shouldn't be dangerous at all."

"But Pink," started Jase, wide-eyed still, "what if we *do* run into manabeasts out there? We've only just passed our assessments!"

"Speak for yourself," muttered Sol.

Pink was undeterred. "There's three of us, and we're all *trained* to fight manabeasts. Come on, what do you say? We won't be able to go on horseback because otherwise, we'd have to tell Ored what we're about. But the sooner we leave, the more sunlight we'll get. Besides, what about Bale? I know we don't know him well, but he would have our backs if needed." She paused. "He did at the Salted Pig."

"I'm in," said Sol, who had been watching her with rapt attention.

She swivelled her head to look directly at Jase. She could tell that the thought of travelling at night frightened him, yet he was clearly battling with something else – it was written all over his face. "We won't think any less of you if you decide to stay," she said to him kindly.

"Yes, you would," replied Jase at once. "At least, one of you would." His eyes shifted to Sol and he let out a long breath. "Fine – let's go find Bale."

CHAPTER SIXTEEN

The sun was a glowing red orb in the sky as they departed, large and bright and dipping behind Highstone Hill. They headed east, wrapped in black cloaks, knowing their syntaxicite wouldn't be enough to keep them warm when dusk finally fell. They carried small waterskins, which they'd attached to their belts, and Pink had grabbed a few warmed bread rolls from the Box since she hadn't eaten supper, but nothing else.

She'd briefly considered trying to reach out to Instructor Texeria again. After all, this had all stemmed from the contract he'd given them – shouldn't he be involved? But, after some deliberation, she'd decided not to take the risk that he might try to stop them. Even if he didn't, what they were doing was their choice, their responsibility. She shouldn't drag her mentor into it by having him know what they were about. *Not our responsibility,* my *responsibility,* she corrected herself. *I was the one who convinced the others.* She wondered whether there was some other reason she hadn't told Instructor Texeria – there was something Gabriel had said about her mentor back in his cottage that had bothered her. She was still trying to remember what it was when Jase moved close and spoke quietly in her ear.

"If Magicom are involved," he said, "then *he's* the only

one who can do anything about it. Anyone else would be in danger if they tried to act … but August …"

"Is already in enough danger," finished Pink. Jase, to his credit, nodded and moved away. His words lingered, though, and Pink found she could not help but weigh the point in her mind. *What'll happen if Magicom are involved? Who will hold them to account? Most people would be too afraid to do anything. Will it make a difference if we can provide evidence of their guilt? We could pass that evidence on to Gabriel, who could take it to the government … and then what? I'm not sure even they could do anything about it.*

Was she going to have to drag August into this after all?

With these thoughts still in the forefront of her mind, she picked up the pace, keen to reach the coal mines quickly, and they took another pathway heading south. As expected, they met no other travellers so late in the afternoon, a few rabbits and birds the only other signs of life. Dusk had fallen, and they had all long since conjured a flame to see by when they stumbled across the horses. Up a small rise, they found the grazing animals tied to pickets that must have been set up by their riders. Of those, there was no sign.

Pink shone her flame over the surrounding grassland, an area predominantly covered by a few smaller trees, thistle bushes and sporadic rock, until the fire illuminated a hole built into another rise a little further on, surrounded by wooden boards like a door frame.

"You think they went through there?" asked Jase, coming to her side.

"Probably," replied Pink. "This is where their horses are … I don't see where else they could be. But they must've gone in hours ago. Why haven't they come back out?"

She turned towards the others. Jase was running a hand down his face, but Sol was watching her keenly.

"You mean to go in, don't you?" he asked quietly.

"W … wait, Pink," stammered Jase, his hand frozen over his mouth. "We can't go inside! There are only three of us!"

"He has a point," said Sol. "From what we've heard, this is now a manabeast lair."

"And what about Bale and all the other mages and instructors?" returned Pink. "What if they're trapped inside somewhere or hurt?"

They both looked uncomfortable.

"Well, we won't find out by standing here," said Pink, impatient with the pair of them. Didn't they understand the importance of moving quickly? She heard Sol swear from behind as she took off, stomping down the little rise and towards the entrance. Both Sol and Jase followed, trying to convince her to stop, to consider, to think things through, but she ignored them, determined in her decision. She entered the rocky face with an assuredness that surprised even her.

Immediately that belief faltered. Perhaps it was because ahead, all was pitch black, like a tunnel into oblivion, or perhaps it was the instant cold and dampness she felt in the air, making her feel like they'd stepped into a tomb. She stopped short, took a deep breath to steady herself and then took another tentative step forward, using the flame in her hand to take in the rocky, arched walls. From the entrance, Sol and Jase appeared, the light of their flames creating deep shadows under their eyes. They seemed to have stopped trying to talk her out of going any further. With her free hand, she pointed forwards, at which she received reluctant nods.

A wooden cart blocked their way a few steps in. They

moved forwards by shuffling to one side of it, their hands and backs against the jagged rock. On the other side, they could see the cart was on top of a metal track running downwards. They followed it, the air getting even cooler as they descended, their steady breathing audible as they inched deeper into the earth.

Eventually, the tunnel opened up, and they found themselves in a cavern littered with crates, pickaxes and upturned carts. A wooden barrier stood at the end of the track. Pink moved closer to one of the crates, noticing chunks of black rock within.

A sudden crumbling from behind made her jump. She spun with the others, but their flames revealed nothing untoward. Jase gave a nervous laugh. *Relax,* Pink told herself as they continued on. R*ock probably crumbles all the time under the surface.* Still, she found the need to glance backwards a few more times as they followed a track leading to a second descending tunnel.

There was a faint smell in the next area, like the aftermath of burning and smoke. They walked from the tunnel into the open space, bypassing another wooden barrier, flames held before them, examining the connected tunnels, of which there were now many. It was at this point Pink caught a glimpse of an unusual shape against the circumference of the area, one that had been hidden by the lack of light. She went for a closer look, lowering her hand to bring whatever it was into focus.

It was a body.

She gasped, took an instinctual step back, and her flame revealed many others. They were piled on top of one another, blackened and covered with blood, the green syntaxicite they were wearing barely noticeable. They had found the missing team of instructors and mages.

Cries from the other two told her they had seen what

she had. She heard retching from behind. She was frozen, unable to move, unable to look away.

"Pink, we should go." Sol had come to her side, a rare shakiness to his voice. He placed a hand on her arm when she didn't respond. "*Now.*"

She turned to see Jase wiping his mouth, his hand shaking, staring at another part of the wall, where Pink realised more bodies had been piled up. The colour seemed to have completely drained from Sol's face. "We need to find Bale," was all she was able to say hoarsely. Jase turned to look at her and nodded vehemently. He understood. Sol looked like he might try to argue, but the look she gave him seemed to make him reconsider.

Sol kept his flame alight while Pink and Jase moved the bodies away from the wall, which they did as respectfully as they could. Pink, with trembling fingers, checked their pulses as they went but, to her dismay, found no signs of life from any of them. She tried to avoid looking directly at their faces – despite her lack of attachments, these were people she'd seen around Highstone Hill over the last year, people who'd had their whole futures ahead of them. The bodies were heavy, and Pink hated the sound they made as they were dragged across the ground, but she kept her mind on Bale. Deep down, she knew what they would find, but she needed to see it anyway. Eventually, the last body was moved, and they found him.

Bale's uniform was torn and the skin underneath blackened, his face a mass of soot and blood. She swallowed a sob and tenderly moved two fingers to his neck.

Where she found a faint pulse.

She gasped despite herself. Amazingly, Bale seemed to hear, and his eyes flickered open. Jase let out a breath of relief and Sol a disbelieving laugh. Bale moved his lips as if trying to mouth something, but then his eyes closed again.

"He's hurt and badly," said Pink, forcing her voice to remain calm. "We have to get him back to Highstone Hill. Now."

"What about the others?" said Jase. "What if anyone else is alive down here?"

"We have to leave them," said Pink, hating herself for saying it but knowing a decision had to be reached quickly. "It doesn't look like anyone else is, but … even if they are … it will take two of us to carry Bale and one to hold a flame. It wouldn't be possible to take anyone else. We'll raise the alarm as soon as we get to Wing and come back in force. That's … the right decision."

If possible, Jase looked even sicker than before, but he nodded, and together they eased Bale off the ground until his arms were over their shoulders.

"We'll use their horses," Pink said. "They … they won't be needing them anymore."

Moving whilst supporting Bale was awkward, but they managed to move across the cavern fairly quickly – that was until Sol, who had been in the lead, stopped short. Pink was about to ask what the matter was when she heard a shuffling sound. Sol moved his flame towards the exit. There was nothing, but the sound became clearer and clearer until, finally, a man appeared from the tunnel. He moved with a limp as if one of his legs were broken. With a shock, Pink recognised him. It was Scottie Sharp – they'd found the mayor's son! Yet something was wrong, and as he shuffled closer, she realised what it was.

His eyes were glowing yellow.

They all took a step back, but at the same time, Scottie stopped and pushed both his arms out, moaning softly. A ball of pure, blue light began to form in front of his outstretched hands. They all yelled, and Pink held Bale tight as she dove to one side, pulling her injured comrade from Jase's grip and with her to the ground just as the magic flew in their direction.

There was a crash of falling rock, a smell of burning and darkness as Sol's fire extinguished, followed by another whooshing and crashing sound. Then there was light again. Sol was holding a ball of fire in cupped hands, and Scottie Sharp was no longer standing where he'd been.

"Move!" he screamed. "Now!"

She didn't need telling twice. Jase rejoined her, and together they placed Bale's arms back over their shoulders and scrambled for the tunnel behind Sol. Pink didn't know what had happened to their attacker but guessed they had Sol to thank for that.

They hastened back the way they'd come, the sound of their heavy breathing echoing around them. When they were back in the first tunnel, Sol looked behind him, an alarmed look on his features as he cried,

"That wasn't one of the elements! That was pure energy! Manabeast magic!"

Another explosion sounded from behind, showering Pink's head and back with little fragments of rock. She was starting to feel the burden of Bale's weight but knew she couldn't pause. The unmistakable scuffling of feet followed. Sol glanced behind him and yelled,

"Duck!"

At first, Pink thought they were the target of more manabeast magic. But, as she and Jase followed Sol's command, he projected the ball of fire in his hands over their heads, where it exploded behind them with a deafening bang. He conjured another over the sound of falling rock, and they continued through the tunnel. Eventually, they arrived at the first cart they'd encountered. Pink held Bale under the arms, and Jase took hold of his legs, and together they carefully lifted him over and past it while Sol waited ready with his flame, keeping his eyes fixed for any signs of pursuit.

Finally, at last, they reached the entrance and were back out in the open, with the moon and stars shining above. They had barely stumbled out when Victorian came into view, cloakless but fully dressed in her green syntaxicite, an astonished look on her face as she recognised them.

"What happened?" she demanded, coming forward to place a hand on Bale's face. "Manabeasts?"

"No," replied Pink, glancing behind her before looking back. She didn't know what the instructor was doing here, but that wasn't important right now. "The mayor's son from Poulsen. But he's not himself, Instructor Dex. He's able to use … manabeast magic."

There was a brief pause. "That's not possible," said Victorian at last.

"We saw it. We all saw it," said Sol. Jase and Pink murmured noises of agreement.

"I … look, Pink, you and the others had better secure Bale to one of those horses so we can take him back to Wing. I'll wait here until you do, just in case anything … follows."

Pink didn't want to leave Victorian, but now wasn't the time to disobey a direct order. Reluctantly, she and Jase helped Bale towards the horses. They were halfway to the rise when she heard Victorian's shout. Looking over her shoulder, she saw the instructor backing away from the entrance, yelling at someone to stop. A blue blast filled the hole in the earth but seemed to strike the inside of the wall, exploding rock and wood. Pink's shout was lost in the noise. The dust and earth filling the air meant they could see nothing at first, but when it cleared, Victorian emerged, moving gingerly, with blood dripping from her forehead. The entrance had now completely disappeared, replaced by a pile of rock, stone and earth, but Scottie Sharp stood before it, as still as the night. And then they heard the moaning and guttural sounds.

Men and women wearing little more than rags staggered into view from the rising land around the entrance, yellow eyes glowing in the dark, a dozen strong. Some of them were shuffling on two legs like Scottie Sharp had; others moved on all fours. In moments, Victorian was trapped in a ring. Pink almost choked as she recognised one as Cylan Wight, his clothes in rags, his face contorted in a snarl.

"The missing townsfolk," breathed Sol, speaking aloud her thoughts. Jase cursed over and over again. "They're … they're the missing townsfolk," Sol repeated dumbly.

The townsfolk drew nearer to Victorian, their intention clear. Then one broke out into a run, and the others followed, moving in a jerky manner as if they didn't have full control of their limbs. The instructor acted at once, moving quicker than Pink would have thought possible, shooting wind magic to send them flying backwards as they descended upon her. But her attackers were soon back on their feet, arms forward, blue balls of energy appearing from all directions. Victorian rolled as several of them struck where she'd just been, exploding the earth upwards.

"We need to get to those horses quickly," said Sol, an unmistakable note of panic in his voice.

Pink moved a few steps with the others but had to look

back, and when she did, she saw Victorian in trouble. The instructor was moving towards them but limping badly, and her syntaxicite had been completely ripped on one side, her skin as blackened as those bodies inside the mines. Victorian attempted to deflect more shots of energy with quick air shields, but one struck her legs, and she fell to the ground with a cry. Again, she rose to her feet, but her movements were laborious, and the pain evident on her face. The instructor shot a fireball as one came too close, but then a beam of blue hit her squarely in the back. She went down in a blur of orange hair, and her attackers were on her at once.

"No!" screamed Pink.

All thoughts of staying back forgotten, she gave Bale's weight over to Jase, who grunted. She ran towards the fallen instructor, conjuring a fireball, then shooting it in the direction of Victorian's attackers. It exploded in their midst, causing them to spin around, snarling and backing away from the flames now licking the grassy ground.

Pink was running down the rise, shooting more blasts of magic as she went: wind and fire. When she reached Victorian's limp form, she stood a few feet in front of it protectively. The townsfolk regrouped and, following a collective raising of their arms, fired more beams of energy. She soon found herself in the same situation as the instructor, trying to dodge and using wind to deflect the blasts whilst having no opportunity to counterattack.

But then Jase was there, and Sol. Side by side, they exchanged blasts of magic with the attackers, deflecting and dodging every time a blue beam of energy came their way. For a moment, she thought they might have the upper hand, but they were outnumbered and losing ground fast until finally, Pink had stepped so far back she was almost standing on top of Victorian. Her ability to draw magic quickly was waning with her exhaustion, and the rapid breathing of the other two suggested they felt the same. *Even if we flee, we'll never make it back to the horses with our backs turned, and that would mean deserting Victorian and probably Bale.*

"Create a fire on the ground!" she called over the noise, her training kicking in, helping her to put aside her panic. "There's too many to fight!"

Jase and Sol seemed to understand at once what she meant. Together, they targeted their magic not at their attackers but at the grassy mounds, shrubs and other vegetation in front of them. Between the three of them, they were able to create a wall of flames, which separated them from the townsfolk.

"Now!" shouted Pink. Sol helped her to lift Victorian, putting her arms around their shoulders. They moved towards the rise as quickly as they could, Sol swearing with every stumble. Pink took frequent glances back at the flames, ready to halt and make another stand if needed, but saw no immediate signs of pursuit. By the time they'd reached the horses, the animals were whinnying and panic-stricken. It wasn't an easy job calming them, but Pink and Sol somehow managed to get Victorian onto the saddle of one. Pink hoisted herself behind the instructor, gripping onto the reins firmly. *We'll have to send back for the other horses if they live that long.* Sol went back to help Jase, who had gone back to where he'd left Bale on the grass. Together they supported Bale onto another horse, Sol speaking words of encouragement to the animal all the while. Pink kept her eyes on where the crackling flames were, but either the fire had frightened the townsfolk, or they hadn't the intelligence to move around it.

Finally, Bale was secured to the saddle, allowing Jase to climb on behind. Sol grabbed the reins of another and passed it to Jase before sprinting to the pickets and hurriedly detaching the horses. He ran back and clambered on his own. They set their heels to their mounts, shouting encouragement as they galloped away from the flames.

She risked another glance back, but all she could see was the fine dust of their parting.

CHAPTER SEVENTEEN

Against the horizon, over the flatlands of the wilderness, the stone wall, roofs and chimneys of a town August had once known well came into view. He longed to go there: to tread the streets he had as a child, to see the people he'd grown up around. But the setting sun served as a reminder of their need for shelter before nightfall. He didn't want to use up his arcannen protecting them from manabeasts; he would have need for their newly acquired potions in Holding.

"Rothmount," August said to his travelling companions as they reined in their horses alongside him, Rush and Sapphire on his left and Chadwick, with Roeden sitting behind, on his right. August pointed in the direction of the town. "This is where I was born and raised until my training at Wing." He sighed. "It's best we pass by, for the fewer people who see me, the better. Especially after what happened in Doscadia." He paused. The time had now come to deal with a matter that could not be put off any longer, and as close as they were to the town, this was the place to do it.

"Chadwick, get Roeden down from that horse for a moment," he said, lowering himself off his own saddle but keeping hold of the reins. Chadwick looked confused but did as he was told, helping Roeden off the saddle. August beckoned Roeden over and lifted the boy up onto his mount before turning to a now-frowning Chadwick.

"Please keep the horse, and find yourself somewhere safe. There will be plenty of places to stay in the town. Your time travelling with us has come to an end."

Silence followed these words. Rush and Sapphire were looking from August to Chadwick, trying to work out what was going on. Chadwick merely nodded to himself as if he was confirming something. A small smile played on his lips.

Roeden, however, looked thunderstruck. "Why does Chadwick have to leave?"

"It's fine, Roeden," said Chadwick. He looked back at August shrewdly. "How long have you known?"

"More or less the entire time."

"Hold on, August, what's going on?" asked Rush. She shot Chadwick a suspicious glance as he climbed back on his saddle. "What do you know?"

"It was Taurus who first found out," said August, looking over his shoulder in reply. "He and I have always been careful about who we allow in Ashes. Usually we recruit members ourselves, like you and Sapphire. Others I've known and trusted from my time in Wing, like Phantex. If we didn't, anyone could join and pass on our plans to Magicom." August turned back to look at the man on the horse. "So when we first met you, Chadwick – on an arcannen-filled train to Holding, cuffed and guarded by two private security mages for the very same crime we were about to commit – not only did you seem like an ideal Ashes candidate, you also seemed like a potential Magicom trap."

"Chadwick works for Magicom?" Roeden's voice was distraught.

"Not quite," replied August. "We found no Magicom

connections. Taurus did, however, discover that a reporter named Chadwick Chase was working for Severity News. We both read it as often as we can to see what's being fed to the public about Ashes, despite its pro-Magicom nature." He nodded his head at Chadwick. "You changed your second name but not your first. Why was that? We would've remained suspicious, but we might not have found out who you were so quickly."

"I thought I might get confused and give myself away if called by a different name," replied Chadwick. August was glad he was making no attempt to deny it. He had looked a little wary through most of the exchange, but now there was something in his expression that August couldn't read. Relief, perhaps? "I can now see that was a mistake. But, forgive me, *you* are wrong about one thing, August Silvershield. *Severity News* isn't all pro-Magicom. It's true our editor ensures anything too critical of Magicom is filtered out, but there are many who work there who are far from Magicom supporters, including myself. An article unveiling the leader of Ashes would've been the biggest story of my career, but I had no intention of furthering Magicom's agenda more than I had to. Your name became public knowledge almost as soon as I 'joined', but that didn't deter me. If anything, it would've made my article even more of a sensation."

"That's why I allowed you to stay," said August, "despite Taurus' protests. I wanted Blake to know about me. I wanted them to see that there are those who will stand up to Magicom, whatever light you painted me in. So I allowed your careful questioning whilst keeping a close eye on your actions. You can write your story, but you'll have to witness the grand finale from the outside, I'm afraid. I cannot allow you to remain with us any longer. We have different priorities, which makes it too much of a risk with Phantex's safety in the balance."

"Are you really going to let him go, August?" Rush asked, eyeing Chadwick with distaste. "What if he goes straight to Magicom and lets them know where we are? What if he tells them of our plan to rescue Phantex?"

"I doubt he'll go anywhere far tonight," August answered. "Travelling alone in the wilderness at night? No reward would be worth the risk. He'll take my advice and find somewhere to stay in Rothmount. But I don't think he'll go to Magicom – he won't want them to know how long he spent with us and kept my location secret, and he'll never be able to give it to them now. Nor does it matter if he tells Magicom we're on our way to rescue Phantex. They know we're going to try that anyway. On top of that, I saved his life on the River Road – he owes me for that. He'll write his article but will make sure his connection to Ashes remains unknown. I'm sure reporters have lots of sources of information. Do I hit wide of the mark, Chadwick?"

"You hit straight on the mark," replied Chadwick, "as can be expected of you, August. Well, I suppose there's nothing more to say other than farewell." He trotted his horse forward as if he was going to clasp arms with Rush and Sapphire, but he must have seen something in their expressions, for he quickly changed direction and headed towards August and Roeden instead. For his part, August felt no anger towards the man. He'd been doing exactly as expected of someone in his position, and August had manipulated him just as much as the other way around. Besides, August had not forgotten how Chadwick had travelled to Bodham to warn Phantex of the danger he was in. He might have arrived too late, but he had saved Roeden from capture.

"Goodbye then, Roeden," Chadwick said softly to the

boy, reining in close. "I've enjoyed journeying with you."

Roeden said nothing. He was looking at Chadwick as if he'd never seen him before. The reporter nodded once at August, who returned it with a wry smile, then turned his horse southwest and rode off in the direction of Rothmount.

"And now we must ride hard," said August, climbing back onto the saddle in front of Roeden. He reined his horse around to face Rush and Sapphire. "We're going to seek shelter at a lodge north of here. It belongs to my uncle – that's the reason why now was the right time to say goodbye to our hidden reporter. I will not take any risks with my family's safety. It should take us no more than an hour to get there."

Rush and Sapphire looked as if they wanted to discuss what had just happened, but August forced his horse into a gallop before either had a chance to say anything. There was no avoiding Roeden, though. After a few minutes of contemplative silence, he spoke up like August had known he would.

"Do you think Chadwick is a bad person?"

The question caught August by surprise. He mulled over the answer. "That's a hard question to answer," he said finally. "I don't think you can say that anyone is a fully good or bad person. The world is not like *Jarian the Dragon Hunter.* We all do what we must."

It's a shame, August thought to himself as Roeden lapsed into another thoughtful silence. *Chadwick was good for the boy.* His mind turned to Chadwick's article. No matter its tone, it would support August's recruitment. Ashes would need more allies if they were ever going to be more than a small band that stole arcannen potions, and for every reader who despised them, there might be another sympathetic to their cause. Numbers were key in liberating Blake from Magicom's influence. *And making them pay for Ashe's murder.*

He felt a familiar pang. After all these years, her absence was still like a wound in his very being, one he knew would never completely heal. She was never far from his thoughts, but their proximity to Rothmount had brought back a memory of a similar journey, one taken many years before.

Strands of her chestnut-brown hair tangled and whipped about as she raced him, the wind pulling her Wing uniform against her lithe frame. *She might have won the last race, but she won't beat me to Rothmount.* Unexpectedly, however, she slowed to a trot before the town came into sight. He did the same and looked at her questioningly.

"Have any of the others ever visited your uncle?" she asked him, her brown eyes uncharacteristically serious.

"Only Felix, and only once."

"Felix, huh?" The serious look faded almost at once. There was a smirk on her face now. "I thought I might have been the first from Wing introduced to your family. I'm almost disappointed …"

He laughed. "Are you jealous of Felix?"

"Oh, yes, who wouldn't be jealous of a man who eats his breakfast in the afternoon?"

"Well, Uncle and Sara are away at the moment, so you won't meet them anyway. We'll have the place to ourselves; you can have all the afternoon breakfasts you want."

Her eyes twinkled. "Now I see why you've brought me here, August Silvershield."

And with that, she pulled her reins, galloping away.

You have no idea why I brought you here, Ashe, thought August as he did the same, his mind on the ring stored safely in his pack. He wondered how her eyes would look when he asked the question. The memories faded and took him, as they always did, to the last time he'd seen her alive.

"I'm so cold," she whispered, on her back, crooked metal pipework jutting through her stomach. Bodies lay everywhere, remnants of the Spirit Mage faction, the Magicom soldiers long gone. They hadn't even bothered to try to save her; they'd just left her to die.

In agony.

He held her hand and placed his other around the metal, tears in his eyes as he tried in vain to stop the bleeding. She gripped his hand tight as if clinging on would help her cling on to life. She couldn't die, he told himself, over and over again, as he spoke reassuring words, telling her everything would be all right, that help would come soon. But by the time Phantex and Felix found him, those brown eyes were fixed and staring. The memory of what came next was blurry, but he did remember the screaming and Phantex gently pulling him from her body.

Back in the present, he gripped the reins more tightly, trying to manage the cold fury raging through his body.

One thing at a time, he thought as he looked back towards the rolling hills ahead. *I will avenge Ashe – but first, I have to ensure Phantex doesn't go the same way.*

***

True to his word, the company arrived at a wooden lodge within the hour as the last light of day faded. Lit by lanterns shining from within its open windows, and with many different-coloured flowers growing from pots along its ledges, it was as welcome a sight as any after a long journey through the wilderness. As the group neared, August could hear the sound of chopping wood coming from a nearby small woodland. They brought their horses around the side of the building where two others were already tethered. *Why are there two? I wonder …* They tied their horses to the nearest trees as his uncle, Ethan Luz, materialised from under their shadow, carrying several logs in his arms. August felt his body relax, realising how taut he'd been. He'd thought his uncle would be safe out here, away from Rothmount, but doubts had gnawed at him on the journey. Ethan Luz could protect himself from manabeasts if need be, but if Magicom ever found him …

Ethan Luz was a fairly small man with brown hair and tanned skin on his weathered face, a result of spending most of his days working under the sun. His arms were thin but corded with muscle, and his hands calloused. "August," he greeted in a quiet voice as if his nephew dropped around all the time. "I was wondering when you'd arrive."

"Everyone, this is my uncle, Ethan Luz." August introduced each friend in turn. August thought he might question Roeden being there, but his uncle's eyes moved from person to person without stopping. "You were expecting me, Uncle?" August said, at last, fixing his uncle with a quizzical smile.

"You're not the first visitor I've had today," answered Ethan Luz. "Come inside."

Keeping the logs in his arms, Ethan Luz led them into the lodge. The doorway opened up into a spacious room in which a fire burned merrily, and his uncle deposited the logs in a metal container beside it. The room was as August remembered from his last visit, with a large wooden table and stools in its centre. August was about to ask his uncle where this first visitor was when a large figure appeared from a second doorway, his bulk barely able to get through.

"Taurus!" August laughed in delight at seeing his friend, and they embraced warmly. Taurus gave the others a hug in turn, and Roeden, in particular, seemed pleased to see him, laughing along with the others.

"Your mother is safe," Taurus said to him as he held the boy at arm's length. "I sent her to Sermouth as she originally planned. She was desperate to come with me, but I didn't want her journeying north when Magicom would almost certainly be looking for her. I assured her you were being well cared for, and I would send you to her right away."

"What about Axe?"

Taurus laughed again. "That old mutt you have? She insisted he went with her." He looked to August now. "She was under house arrest. Thankfully, I was able to sneak her out. It wasn't easy, and it's probably best she never meets you, August." August nodded, the relief he was feeling tinged bittersweet by Taurus' words. *I can't blame her – her whole family have been put in danger because of me.* Taurus turned back to Roeden. "She was relieved beyond words you'd got away, and she's looking forward to seeing you again soon."

"After we rescue Phantex?"

Taurus hesitated, so August stepped in. It was time to be open with the boy. "Like Chadwick, you've gone far enough, Roeden. I can't take you into Holding – it's far too dangerous."

"But I can help! I helped us in Doscadia, didn't I?"

August came over to Roeden and knelt down, placing one hand on his shoulder. "Absolutely you did," he said, facing the boy's defiance, "and in the future, I'm sure you'll continue to, just like Phantex."

"I don't want to be sent away," said Roeden, eyes wet with tears. "I want to stay and fight."

August suddenly felt weary – the boy's courage was admirable, but with it came a stubborn streak. "The answer is no," he said firmly, taking his hand off Roeden's shoulder. "Do as I say, Roeden. Ethan Luz will take you to Sermouth to be with your mother if he's willing." He stood and looked at his uncle, who had been watching this exchange with a curious look on his features.

"I will take him. Roeden, is it? I'm assuming from your conversation he's Phantex Mason's younger brother?"

August nodded and saw his uncle share a look with Taurus. *I don't like the look of that.* They said nothing, and August didn't ask, deeming it something that should not be said in front of Roeden, who was now hanging his head.

"A rider brought this for you," Ethan Luz said, handing August a brown leather bag fastened with a drawstring. August looked at it curiously. It was very light. He opened it up and pulled out a white piece of paper that had been folded into a small square. There were many more inside. He didn't need to open the paper to know what it contained. He grinned. He now knew how they were going to rescue Phantex.

***

The large table was soon filled with salted beef and gammon, fresh bread and slabs of butter, baked vegetables, ripe red apples and yellow and orange cheeses. The others washed their meal down with a clear ale from a keg that Ethan Luz kept on a smaller table in the room, and Roeden had fresh milk. It seemed that August's uncle had a cow and a few chickens in a pen around the back of his lodge, and he was fairly self-sufficient, only needing to go to Rothmount every now and then to trade.

Despite his contentment with the food and drink, Roeden's mood improved little as the evening progressed. The words of August gnawed at him. Why should he run off to safety while all the others risked themselves for the sake of Phantex? Wasn't Phantex *his* brother? Shouldn't *he* get a say in the matter? Roeden understood he couldn't fight in the same way they could, with magic, but he had his own set of skills – and hadn't he already proven how useful they could be? And what was that package all about? August hadn't bothered to explain. He had put it inside his pack and carried on like nothing untoward had happened. How would anyone even know to deliver something to August at his uncle's? Roeden had thought that information was meant to be secret. It was with these thoughts running through his mind that Roeden had forgotten about Chadwick, and when he remembered, it was like feeling the pang of loss all over again. It was strange. The only one who'd treated Roeden like he was a member of Ashes was the one who'd been pretending to be in it.

"Why so quiet, Roeden?" asked Taurus at one point. The big man was sitting on the stool next to him. "Not happy about going to Sermouth?" Roeden didn't reply, but Taurus' smile was a little too understanding. He dropped his voice and leaned over. "Well, I'll tell you this, lad. I can't promise we'll save Phantex, but if anyone can find a way to do it, it's August. The man's got more tricks up his sleeve than anyone I've ever met."

"I just want to be there when Phantex is freed," said Roeden. "I know I can help. Can't you say something to him?"

Taurus looked at him thoughtfully. "I can't," he said, dashing Roeden's last hopes. "I agree with him on this one – things will get too dangerous in Holding. And you don't have magic to protect yourself."

Taurus' words stayed with Roeden even after the big man turned away to listen to something Ethan Luz was saying about Magicom's blimps. *Magic to protect yourself.* A thought sparked in his mind, evolving until it became an idea. An amazing, risky, possibly foolish idea. But one that, now it had its grip on him, he couldn't shake off.

A little while later, Taurus, August and Ethan Luz went outside together. Roeden, wondering if this was something to do with the curious look he'd seen Ethan Luz and Taurus exchange earlier, followed them unnoticed. They'd gone around the corner of the lodge and were talking in low voices. Roeden snuck to the nearby trees and crouched down by one of the trunks, listening in on what was being said. He was surprised when he heard his name.

"Roeden wants to go. He won't give up, you know. There's a lot of Phantex in him," Taurus was saying.

"He'll have to accept it," said August gravely. "Any news on Phantex?"

"I'm afraid it's not good, August," came his uncle's lower voice. Roeden could see little puffs of smoke coming from a pipe in his mouth. "I visited Rothmount yesterday. Word is a member of Ashes is being executed in Holding Square at week's end. They've put up posters alongside your own. No doubt this is Magicom's way of ensuring the information gets back to you."

The three were silent for a while. It took all Roeden had not to call out. Executed? His brother? His eyes burned, and his heart quickened, but with it, his resolve deepened. *I will not be left behind.*

Eventually, August spoke again. Despite not being able to see his face, Roeden could hear from his voice that his reaction had been similar to Roeden's own. "This doesn't change our immediate plans. We'll leave the day after tomorrow so we can rest and work out what we're going to do. I have something in mind – I need to think through the finer points, then I'll run it past everyone. Holding is a two-day ride from here; we should be able to get ourselves organised and there by week's end."

Roeden hoped one of the others would ask about August's plan, but Taurus' gruff voice merely said, "This may work in our favour, August."

"How do you mean?"

"Although this is almost certainly a trap, Salvamal's impatience to get his hands on you means we don't have to find a way to break into Alsing."

August nodded before turning to Ethan Luz. "Uncle, I need you to send a bird to Holding. We're going to need some extra help."

"You mean Dele and the others?" asked Taurus sharply.

"I know how you feel about them, but they see themselves as members of Ashes – and with what I have in mind, I think we're going to need them."

Taurus sighed. "That doesn't fill me with confidence. Anyway, this may be the last chance we have to rest for a while. We should take the opportunity."

Roeden moved quickly and made his way back inside before they returned. Sapphire was sitting in Rush's lap and talking quietly in her ear – it didn't seem they'd even noticed he was gone. Before long, Ethan Luz's guests cleared the table and said their goodnights. The room was large enough for them all to sleep in, so they rolled out their blankets on the wooden floorboards. The fire continued to crackle soothingly, but, despite his exhaustion, Roeden made sure he stayed awake until everyone else was breathing deeply, thinking about his brother and how Phantex needed him now more than ever.

When he felt the time was right, Roeden rose and crept to the corner of the room where they'd deposited their packs. Nimbly, he undid the clasp of the one he knew to be August's and opened the top.

A sudden grunt from behind caused him to freeze. He turned, his heart beating furiously in his chest, but it was only Taurus making noises in his sleep. Letting out the breath he hadn't realised he'd been holding, Roeden placed his hand into the pack, his fingertips feeling the smooth fabric of the Magicom syntaxicite on their way to the cold, glass vials of arcannen at the bottom. He took hold of one and was carefully lifting it out when he felt something else. *One of those square bits of paper!* He hesitated. Was taking one of those as well going too far? *I've done my part. I helped out in Doscadia. I deserve a share of the spoils as much as anyone else.* The decision made, he took hold of the paper (which felt like it had something grainy inside), along with the arcannen vial, and returned to his blanket. As he didn't have his own pack, he placed the vial in one of the folds of his shirt, which sat beside him.

Sitting cross-legged, he twirled the folded paper around his fingers before opening one of the edges. A sudden shuffling sound, like someone sitting up, encouraged him to lie back down. He didn't dare risk a look – what if it was August, and he became suspicious of Roeden being awake? August might decide to check his pack, and then, if he discovered something was missing, he would take it off Roeden right away. If that happened, Roeden's plan would have failed.

Besides, the thought of those intense eyes locked onto him, displeased, made Roeden shudder.

With that in mind, he decided he'd be better off checking the square paper when he had a chance tomorrow. *I won't be left behind,* was his last thought before he drifted off to his long-awaited sleep.

CHAPTER EIGHTEEN

"So, you think Magicom are responsible for what happened to those instructors and mages?"

As Pink nodded in reply, she noticed there was a heat to Victorian's voice, one she had never heard before. They were both in the infirmary, Pink sitting on a hard, wooden chair and Victorian lying in one of the beds, looking like she'd been hit by a steam train. The linen covers were pulled up to her stomach, but above that, her skin was covered in burns and bandages. Pink could barely look at her. *Another responsibility I have to take the blame for, along with almost getting my friends killed.*

"What exactly was done to them, Instructor?" Pink could tell Victorian knew who she meant – the instructor had seen Scottie Sharp and the other townsfolk. "They acted like manabeasts. They even had manabeast magic. That's impossible, isn't it? It goes against the very laws of nature."

Grimacing in pain, Victorian tried to sit up. Pink thought for a moment about telling the instructor to take it easy, but the warning glint in Victorian's eyes made her think better of it.

"First of all, it's Victorian, not Instructor. We've been through enough together now, Pink. You're too formal by far." Victorian's stare suggested she wasn't going to say anything further until she received a response, so Pink gave a reluctant nod. Victorian, seemingly satisfied, continued. "I don't know what happened to them. From what you've told me, it sounds like they were taken and something … done. The others … Strong, Krank, Birch, all those mages …" She shook her head. "They never stood a chance."

"How we managed to survive, I'll never know," muttered Pink.

Victorian gave her a sharp look. "We survived because of you – and the others." When Pink didn't reply, she sighed, and her look softened. "What happened to me is not your fault. Besides, I doubt Bale would've survived the night in those mines. By going in, you saved his life."

"What will happen next?" asked Pink, in part to change the subject. Victorian was being kind, but it was too early to say whether Bale might live or not. She briefly glanced along the row of beds to where Bale lay. He hadn't woken since their return the day before yesterday. His skin had lost much of its colouring, and Pink wouldn't have thought him breathing at all if not for Victorian's assurances. As for the others in the group Gabriel had sent, there hadn't been a single survivor.

"Gabriel has been very quiet about this, which suggests to me he's very angry," said Victorian, drawing her attention back. "He's not the sort who will act on impulse." For some reason, she gave Pink a wry look as she said this. "He's currently with some of the other instructors, scouring the wilderness for the townsfolk we saw, ready to … restrain them if needed. I expect he'll attempt to contact Master Wing as well. You say Magicom have done this – I agree. I can't think who else would have gone to such measures and with such disregard for human life. The problem is evidence. There's nothing to prove they were involved aside from the steam van tracks you say were present where Scottie Sharp and Cylan Wight were taken. And you can bet Magicom will deny everything." She paused. "I'm just glad I discovered what you were about. You have your mentor to thank for that. I'd just returned from an assignment when he mentioned he couldn't find you. Once he told me the situation with the coal mines, I guessed that's where you'd gone and followed."

Victorian looked towards Bale. "Speaking about Keat Texeria, he came to see Bale. It looked like he was examining him."

Pink gave her a puzzled look. Examining? What did he hope to learn? She shook her head. Trying to work out Keat Texeria was a near-impossible job – why even bother?

"You know, I remembered something about him," said Victorian. "Back before I was an instructor. It's quite a strange thing, actually. He was …"

"You look tired, Victorian. Time to get some more rest, I think."

Oxlade Perola, Wing's healer, had walked in from his office, which connected the infirmary to the grounds outside. He was a small, bald man with glasses and what Pink had always found to be a kindly disposition, though he currently looked stern. Pink decided that whatever Victorian had been about to say could wait and said goodbye. Victorian fixed her with a fond – albeit tired – smile as she left.

As Pink stepped outside, she spotted a familiar face walking the pathway to the infirmary. Sol's movements slowed as he spotted her, but he didn't stop – not until they stood face to face anyway.

"How's Bale?" he asked.

She shook her head. "There's no change. He hasn't

regained consciousness since we returned. Healer Perola's given him a potion to bring the fever down but says he needs to wake up on his own."

Sol nodded as if he'd expected as much. "I came to see him, but I suppose he wouldn't even know if I was there or not."

Pink gave him an understanding smile. There was silence for a moment, interrupted only by the wind rustling the leaves of nearby trees.

"Sol … about taking you inside the mines," she said at last. An image of blood and charred flesh flashed in her mind. She looked down. "You and Jase could have gone the same way as the others. I'm … sorry."

Unexpectedly, Sol put his arms around her. She froze for a moment, then relaxed into him, her head momentarily resting against his chest, surprised at how much comfort she found in the contact.

"Feel better, do you?" she asked as they broke apart. Sol chuckled. Over his shoulder, she spotted Jase approaching. He had his eyes on them and wore a frown.

"Hello, Jase," said Sol stiffly as he joined them.

Jase nodded a greeting before turning to Pink. "What did Victorian say?"

"What we thought. She said that Gabriel and some of the other instructors went into the wilderness to find and restrain the townsfolk."

A look passed between them in which Pink knew they were both thinking the same thing. Victorian might have said 'restrain', but if that wasn't possible, would the instructors treat them like manabeasts?

"What happened to them, Pink?" Jase whispered. Pink saw the fear in his eyes. It was that, in a way, that prevented her from reminding him about the number of times he'd already asked that question. "Did Victorian have any ideas?" he added as if he'd realised himself.

Pink shook her head.

"How is it possible that Magicom managed to change them so?" he continued, running his hand down his face. Another question he'd been asking time and time again as if that would help him understand it. "They acted like manabeasts; they used manabeast magic. That shouldn't be possible."

"We still don't know Magicom are behind this," said Sol calmly. "No, please hear me out," he said, for Jase was about to speak again. "I know you think I'm biased, but have a real think about what we know and what we don't. We know that someone or something must be responsible. From what the mayor told us, we know that it's been going on for some time. But the only reason you think Magicom are involved is because of some steam van tracks. For all we know, this could be some sort of illness."

"An illness wouldn't have caused these people to disappear in the first place," said Pink quietly.

"Okay – that's true. But the point I'm trying to make is that there could be reasons we've yet to think of."

"Whoever's responsible, the coal mines felt like a trap," said Pink. "Think about it. Wing were sent to deal with the sudden reappearance of manabeasts. The instructors and mages arrived, and those … townsfolk … were waiting for them." She paused, and they all looked a little uncomfortable. *Those things,* she'd almost said.

"Which means that us getting Bale out wasn't part of the plan. Perhaps he knows something," said Jase, filling the silence.

"Jase is right," said Sol, causing Jase to shoot him an astonished look. "Bale may have seen something, but he's not able to help us right now, and everything else we have is pure speculation. Gabriel hasn't given us any further information or directives aside from asking us not to speak to the other mages about this."

"And who knows when he'll be back?" added Jase. "I can't see him returning until he's found the townsfolk." For the first time in days, Pink felt a tinge of something other than sadness or guilt. *Are Sol and Jase actually having a civil conversation?*

"It's up to us to decide what to do then," said Sol. He turned to Pink. "We need to decide our next move."

Pink's surprise turned to wariness. "Next move?"

"Well, yes. Those manabeasts … townsfolk … whatever they are, they must have gone somewhere. And where were they before that? Perhaps another visit to Poulsen might afford us some answers."

Jase nodded. "We can find out if anyone knows anything."

Pink looked between them, incredulous. "We *found* the townsfolk. The contract's over."

"But we haven't found those responsible for their condition," said Sol.

"Nor have we been ordered to. Look at what happened last time we did things on our own. We were almost all killed!"

"Just … hear me out," said Sol, holding out his hands as if to placate her while Jase looked uncomfortable. She remembered how calm Sol had been at the coal mines, how he'd probably saved their lives. It was that, more than anything, that prevented her from telling him how foolish he was being. She gave him a curt nod, and he continued. "I understand your reluctance to go, but we don't have to do anything unnecessary. Why don't we visit Mayor Sharp? I assume Gabriel's informed him of what happened. We might not be involved in finding the townsfolk, but we owe the mayor our condolences if nothing else. We're the ones who found his son, after all."

Pink sighed. "That and nothing else?" she asked.

"Nothing else," affirmed Sol, looking relieved. *We shouldn't be doing this without orders. But I understand. After everything we've seen, they want to see this through to the end.* She thought for a moment. *And so do I.*

***

The mood of Wing was sombre, so in a way, Pink was glad to withdraw from its presence for a few hours. The training grounds were deserted as they left – which was unsurprising, really, given what had happened. They passed a couple of sobbing girls on a bench, one with her arm around the other. They weren't the first mages Pink had seen in tears for their friends and mentors.

There was one thing she was grateful for, despite her guilt for feeling it – none of the other mages knew they'd been the ones to find the missing party. They'd returned with Victorian late in the night, and only Gabriel, the instructors and Oxlade Perola knew of their involvement. As far as the rest of Wing knew, Victorian had managed to return with Bale alone, which meant they wouldn't have to answer any questions about what they'd seen. Or so Pink thought.

She wasn't in the mood for any sort of confrontation, so when she heard Lena call her name on their way to the stables, Pink felt nearly every part of her body tense. She turned and waited on the pathway as Lena approached from the direction of the buildings.

"I heard something from Rodric," Lena said at once, sounding a little breathless. Her dark eyes locked onto Pink's own, and to Pink's surprise, she saw none of the usual malice there, only … *uncertainty?* She remained silent, waiting for Lena to speak again. "He said he saw you three return with Victorian and Bale in the middle of the night, looking like you'd been in some kind of terrible battle."

"We were at the mines," said Pink, deciding there was no point in denying it. "We were the ones who found the others."

"In that case, I want to say … thank you," said Lena. The confusion Pink felt must have shown on her face because Lena added, "Instructor Birch was my mentor. I know he must have already been … gone by the time you got there. But you went after him and the others. I only wish I'd done the same."

Lena held out her hand. Pink stared at it for a moment. Was this really happening?

She reached out and shook it.

***

The day was overcast as if the heavens reflected the very mood of Highstone Hill itself, and the dark clouds still hadn't cleared up by the time Pink, Jase and Sol stabled their mounts in Poulsen. Moments later, they were in the Salted Pig and, after a quick conversation with the innkeeper, had procured Spencer Sharp's address.

The mayor's residence was located at the end of a street on the other side of the marketplace, one with well-maintained tarmac roads and large brick houses. It was hard to miss – a building even larger than the others, standing behind a black iron gate, all polished metal and spikes. Pink took hold of one of the smooth bars and, finding the gate unlocked, pushed it open to the sound of creaking hinges.

The winding path they found themselves on led

through a garden as well tended as anything on the street, roses and tulips among the many colourful plants growing amid the bushes, their fragrance thick in the air. A fountain stood in the centre of it all, birdsong accompanying the trickle of the water. Beyond all this, they found the mayor. He was perched on a small wooden bench near his front door, wrapped in a thick cloak clutched tightly around his body, staring at the ground.

"I thought you might come," he said without looking up. Pink was sure that the others, like her, could sense something was amiss.

The silence following these words was filled only by the fountain's gurgling. "Why did you think that, Mayor?" asked Pink, since neither Sol nor Jase seemed prepared to ask the question.

"For the same reason your assistant master was here earlier," he replied, still not looking up. "Oh, he could present it any way he liked, pretending he'd come to inform me of my son's fate. But all he really wanted to know was where Scottie was – so Wing could finish the job, I assume. Now you've come to ask me the same."

"Mayor Sharp, that's really not the case. We wish to offer our condolences. We aren't here to ask about your son's whereabouts."

"Whereabouts!" Bizarrely, Spencer Sharp's body seemed to shake with suppressed laughter. Then he looked up, and Pink saw the tears in his eyes. "His whereabouts are under the earth. We buried him. And the others. They're all dead." He began to sob, burying his head in his hands. Pink exchanged a look with the others and saw shock mingled with sympathy and awkwardness. Pink sat down next to the mayor on the bench, placing a hand where the rough fabric covered his arm.

"It wasn't clear what had killed them," he said after a

few moments. He looked directly at Pink now. "But I can deduce it was a result of their condition. They were discovered this morning in the wilderness, after that Gabriel had been here. He told me something had been done to them, something … unnatural. Well, I think we all know who is responsible."

"Magicom," said Jase.

"Magicom," spat the mayor. "And that damn dukesbane company."

"The dukesbane company?" asked Pink, surprised. "What makes you say that?"

Slowly, something in the mayor's face changed. It reminded Pink of the shrewdness she'd noticed when they'd first met, back in the Salted Pig when he'd convinced the Magicom soldiers to leave his son be. "Commander Riccard was the one who told me of the manabeasts at the coal mines. Almost as soon as he had done so, all the workers were let go from the dukesbane site. Since then, hosts of Magicom soldiers have been seen coming and going from there with those steam vans of theirs. That seems more than mere coincidence to me. They're trying to hide something."

"But they're just cultivating there," said Pink. "It's for an elixir they're creating. We saw it."

"There's always more going on than meets the eye," said the mayor. "That's the way of the world. A useful thing to learn quickly, my friends. There are too many soldiers coming and going for them to be there for mere security. I hadn't thought Magicom had anything to do with our missing people when I contacted Wing about this, but now I know better." He shook his head. "Forgive my accusations. I'm … not myself, but I hope you can do something with this information. I doubt it – Magicom have always been able to do what they like. My predecessor opposed the way the soldiers stationed at their clinic bullied those living in Poulsen. Soon after he'd made his complaints known, a government decree stripped him of his title and ordered him to depart the town. But Wing belongs to Articulas Wing. That gives you some form of protection. There's nothing I can do to get back at them, but if you uncover anything, I hope you spread it as far and wide as you can."

"Thank you," said Pink gently, "for telling us."

The mayor nodded but seemed unable to say anything more. As they said their goodbyes, Pink placed a hand on Spencer Sharp's shoulder. He nodded as if in response but did not look up again. They waited until they were out of the garden and were back on the street before Sol, looking round to see if anyone was nearby, spoke.

"We should go to the dukesbane site."

Pink was saved the trouble of replying by Jase. "You think Magicom *are* involved in this now?"

"I didn't say that," replied Sol, looking askance at Jase. "What the mayor said doesn't change anything – we still don't know what's going on. But we should have a look while we're nearby. Just a bit of recon. What do you think, Pink? You must agree?"

"I think we should pass on Mayor Sharp's words to Gabriel and Instructor Texeria," replied Pink before Jase could say anything about Sol's unwavering defence of the company. "Then I think we should step aside until ordered otherwise." Pink could read the disappointment on Sol's face. She felt ashamed, then irritated that what he thought mattered to her. "I'm not eager to put any of my friends in further danger," she said, meeting his eyes.

Sol gritted his teeth and looked at Jase. "I assume you're of the same mind?"

"I'm with Pink," said Jase, managing to look pleased

as Sol looked away in disgust.

There didn't seem to be anything left to say after that, so they walked back to the stables in silence, Sol's eyes boring ahead the entire time as if he was determined not to look at either of them. On their way to visit Mayor Sharp, Pink hadn't paid much heed to the town's clinic, her mind too focused on the missing townsfolk to notice much about their surroundings. But as they passed, she realised the usual soldiers standing guard were missing, while a 'closed' sign was visible on the glass windows of the door. *Are they at the dukesbane site, like the mayor mentioned?* She shook her head. *It doesn't matter – we shouldn't be going there, not without orders.* There was something else that drew her attention, however – a large poster that had been stuck above the sign on the glass window, one like August's wanted posters, but without a profile. She stepped away from the direction the others were taking and walked closer to read:

PUBLIC EXECUTION

PHANTEX MASON

FOR TAKING PART IN ILLEGAL ACTIVITIES AGAINST THE STATE WITH THE GROUP KNOWN AS ASHES, INCLUDING, BUT NOT LIMITED TO, THIEVERY AND ASSAULT OF MAGICOM SOLDIERS. HANGING WILL TAKE PLACE MIDDAY AT HOLDING SQUARE AT WEEK'S END.

"A hanging," Jase said as he joined her, a disgusted edge to his voice, "in front of the whole city?"

"It's not just anyone," replied Pink, trying to keep the emotion from her voice. "It's someone from Ashes. That demands a spectacle; it teaches everyone else how to behave, doesn't it? But … there's more to it than that, Jase. Don't you see?"

"They're trying to draw someone in," said Jase, suddenly comprehending.

"Nothing to do with us, anyway," said Pink hurriedly as Sol walked over to see what they were looking at.

"Ashes," spat Sol, evidently still in a bad mood. "I hope this Phantex Mason gets what's coming to him."

"Because you know him so well," muttered Jase.

Sol shot him a dirty look and stormed off. Pink didn't pay Sol any heed. She was too busy thinking of the poster's implications.

CHAPTER NINETEEN

Pink dreamt of yellow eyes. They appeared from the darkness with black slits and a predatory gaze, drawing ever closer as she remained frozen in place. The muzzle and razor-sharp fangs of a wolf-type came into focus. As it opened its jaws, she could smell its rancid breath and see a ball of pure, blue energy start to form from within.

But suddenly, it became a man's face – the face of Scottie Sharp, but horribly distorted. It retained most of what made it human, but the yellow eyes and sharp fangs of the manabeast remained. It lunged at her, and those fangs tore into the soft flesh of her neck. She could feel warm blood drip down her skin and opened her mouth to scream, yet when she tried, no sound came out …

"Pink! Pink!"

Pink sat upright in her bed. She turned her head and recognised Jase's face, but with manabeast features. Pink flinched and the image vanished. She realised his eyes were not yellow but clear blue and full of concern.

"Jase," she gasped, a little embarrassed. She took a moment to steady herself, breathing in the familiar smells of her dormitory room, from the cotton sheets to the fresh air coming through the small window she often left ajar. It helped to slow the rapid beating of her heart. Jase must've been trying to shake her awake – that was why he'd just taken his hands off her arms. She stared at him for a moment before shutting her eyes tightly and flopping back down on her bed as if that would shatter the uneasy spell the dream had left on her. She tried not to think of Scottie Sharp sinking his fangs into her neck.

Teeth, not fangs. Humans don't have fangs.

"Why are you here, Jase?" she moaned, opening her eyes.

"It's Bale!" he said. "He's missing!"

It was only now she heard (and saw) his panic. She sat up at once and shifted her weight until her feet were on the floor. Jase looked away – she wasn't in her uniform yet, only a loose old shirt she wore to bed. "How do you know this?" she asked.

"I went to visit him," he replied. "I was up early. I couldn't sleep." As he ran a hand down his face, Pink suspected she wasn't the only one having nightmares. "Healer Perola and Gabriel were talking about it outside the infirmary."

What exactly is going on? Despite her desire to no longer be involved without orders, if Bale had gone missing … well, that changed things. "Keep looking that way," she said to Jase, who obliged as she grabbed her uniform from under her bed and started to dress. "Is Victorian okay?" she said to his back.

"I don't know."

They were soon hurrying through the corridors of the dormitories and, once outside, moving along the pathway that led to the infirmary. Above, the sky's deep purple was giving way to dawn's first light. Crashing through the infirmary's door, they found the healer in discussion with a still-bedridden Victorian.

"Pink!" Victorian said, eyes widening. "What's wrong?"

Pink's eyes travelled to Bale's empty bed. "We heard that Bale was missing."

"There are three … no, four people who know that information," said Perola, aghast. "How is it that you do?"

"Don't underestimate these two, Oxlade," said Victorian wryly. "They probably know more than we do."

"You mentioned four people," said Pink. Something at the back of her mind stirred a thought that had been developing but only now came to the forefront. "You two, Assistant Master Gabriel – who's the other?"

"I see no reason to say," grunted Perola.

"Pink already knows," said Victorian. The instructor was watching her closely. "Don't you, Pink?"

"Instructor Texeria," she said, at which Jase glanced at her sharply.

Victorian nodded. "We suspect he's taken Bale."

"But … why would he take Bale? *How* could he take him?"

"Not just Bale, but those manabeast pets of his as well. He bumbled in late last night and said he was monitoring Bale's condition, seeing if there was anything he could do to help. When Gabriel came to check on Bale this morning, he was gone. I was trying to keep an eye on what Texeria was doing but must've fallen asleep … I can't stay awake with the potions this man keeps forcing down my throat." She shot the healer a nasty glance.

"You've suffered some very serious injuries!" said Perola defensively.

Victorian snorted but turned back to Pink. "Gabriel went to check his quarters, but he and those beasts were long gone. He must have taken them and Bale in a wagon or something. Where he is now is anyone's guess – if this happened during the night, he could be leagues away by now, in who knows what direction. No one saw him leave."

"I don't understand, though," said Jase, turning to Pink. "I've never trusted the man, but why take Bale?"

Pink bit her lip thoughtfully. "He's obviously interested in manabeasts and their abilities. But … does this mean he's involved in some way?"

"With the townsfolk?" asked Jase.

Pink nodded. "He was experimenting on manabeasts; what's to say he wasn't experimenting with humans? And the townsfolk … they were using the same magic as wolf-types like the one Instructor Texeria had in his storage room. Was he the one who found a way to … fuse them?"

Pink felt like she had been dealt a physical blow. Despite her misgivings about Instructor Texeria, she had trusted him. But she didn't understand. How was it possible that Master Wing had sent the very person who was responsible for all this to Highstone Hill?

Something wasn't adding up.

"Where's Gabriel?" she asked Victorian.

"He took off not long ago – he said something about following Keat Texeria's trail." The instructor looked apprehensive. "I think he feels somewhat responsible."

Pink nodded, distracted. *If Instructor Texeria is involved in this, where would he go?*

"Healer Perola, we're going to need two arcannen potions," said Pink, the answer coming to her. *What about Sol? No, there's no time!* "We have to go after Gabriel. I think … I think I might know where Instructor Texeria is."

Perola shook his head. "Gabriel himself ordered me to deny all requests for arcannen today. He didn't want anyone leaving Highstone Hill."

"It's almost like he thought you might do this," mumbled Victorian.

Pink opened her mouth to argue, but Jase's hand on

her arm cut her short. "Perhaps we can catch Gabriel before he leaves."

"Right," said Pink. She nodded curtly at the healer and instructor before heading out of the door, Jase following. She thought she might have heard Victorian call after them, but Jase was right. If Gabriel was still at Highstone Hill, they needed to speak with him right away. She didn't think he'd let them back him up, but he couldn't turn down the information they had.

When they got to the stables, however, the assistant master was nowhere in sight.

"You two," came a rough voice from within. Ored shuffled towards them, holding up a brown package. "I may look after the birds as well as the horses, but do I *look* like a carrier pigeon to you?"

Pink's eyes rose to his white hair. "Do you really want me to answer that question, Ored?"

His reply was to shove the package at her. "This was left here for you – see, someone's written your name on the top. Must've been last night. Obviously thought I would deliver it to you – hah! Like that was going to happen." He squinted at them in the sunlight, chewing the flesh inside his mouth as if he wanted to say more. Pink waited politely until he did. "I heard some of what happened, you know. You two – and the other boy – freed my horses when you took it upon yourselves to go to those mines. I was able to retrieve them with the aid of some of the instructors. I am … grateful to you for your help in getting the animals back safely, so if you want to follow that foolish assistant master, you won't get any trouble from me." Evidently, having said what he'd needed to say, he shuffled back inside, leaving them staring after him in shock.

"Did … did Ored just thank us?" asked Jase weakly.

"I think he did," replied Pink, looking down at the brown package, curiosity overcoming her surprise at the stable master's unexpected candour. Descending to her knees, she laid the package down on the grass, carefully unwrapping the string holding it together. She pulled away the wrapping and found three glass vials of black liquid.

"Arcannen," whispered Jase from over her shoulder. He knelt down next to her. "There's a note," he said.

Picking up the piece of square paper that Jase had noticed, she read the note, which had been written in block capitals.

JUST IN CASE.

"Who left it?" asked Jase.

"I don't know," replied Pink, chewing her lip. "Can't have been Victorian or Healer Perola. They were both against us leaving Highstone Hill."

"The mayor?" suggested Jase.

"Perhaps. But how would he know we needed them?"

"If you ask me, this is Gabriel's doing," said a familiar voice from behind. Pink shifted her position to find Sol standing over them. Despite the early hour, his hair was as meticulously styled as ever, and he was fully dressed in his Wing uniform. He shuffled his feet under her upwards stare. "Think about it. We haven't had much of a chance to speak to him lately, but he knows how involved we are in all this. He wants us to be protected."

"But Victorian said he didn't want any mages to have arcannen," said Pink, frowning. "Those were the orders he left."

Sol looked thoughtful. "Perhaps that was his wish. But if he thought we'd leave Highstone Hill regardless, he'd rather we were out in the wilderness with arcannen than without. That's why he left it at the stables, as opposed to handing it to us. He knew we would only receive it if we were intent on leaving. We *are* leaving, right? I heard enough of that to guess we're following Gabriel somewhere?"

"Whatever Gabriel intended," said Jase quietly from next to her, "we couldn't follow him without horses or arcannen, but now we have both."

Pink knew what was going on. Sol was convincing himself that Gabriel had reluctantly given them permission to come after him. It was possible, she had to admit, and if that was the case, they wouldn't be going against orders. She was worried about leading her friends into further danger – the bodies of Wing instructors and mages would forever be etched into her mind. But something had changed. With Bale taken and Gabriel acting recklessly, both of them were in grave danger if they *didn't* go. There was, of course, also the matter of Keat Texeria – he was her mentor, and she wanted to know his involvement in all this.

She realised then that they were watching her, waiting for her decision. Without speaking, she picked up one of the vials, uncorked the stopper and drank its contents. Almost immediately, she felt a tingle in her fingers as her body ached to draw the elements.

Almost as one, Jase and Sol did the same.

***

A little while later, clustered within a clump of trees and with their horses tied to the trunks, Pink stood with Jase and Sol monitoring the dukesbane site.

"I see no Magicom presence here," whispered Sol, brushing against Pink's arm as he leaned in to speak with her.

Pink gave him a sideways glance. On the way, they'd

filled him in on Bale's disappearance. He had been suspicious of Instructor Texeria at once but refused to be swayed by the idea Magicom were involved in his kidnapping of Bale. Pink wished she could see things from his point of view, but even if Instructor Texeria was behind everything, she could not see how he had done it all on his own. *And there's still the matter of the townsfolk going missing before he arrived at Wing.* She shook her head. *Perhaps I'm like Sol in a way. He refuses to accept Magicom are responsible; I make excuses for Instructor Texeria.*

"Shall we take a closer look at the warehouse?" suggested Sol.

Pink murmured her agreement, and together they left the shelter of the trees to move across the plains, Jase following closely behind. She felt exposed out in the open, yet she saw no sign of Magicom soldiers, nor anyone else for that matter, and they reached the entrance without incident.

"If Bale is here," muttered Jase, "why take the guards away?"

"It seems deserted," said Sol as he looked around the side of the building.

Pink tried opening the door but found it locked. They all exchanged a look, and moments later, the door had been blasted off its hinges by three lots of wind magic. Stepping over the splintered wood, they found themselves back in the familiar space of the warehouse. There was no sign of life – even the dukesbane flowers were gone.

"What now?" asked Jase, running a finger along one of the workstations and inspecting it for dust. "Back to Wing? Wasn't Instructor Texeria supposed to be here? Pink?"

But Pink wasn't listening. Her eyes had been drawn to the back of the building, towards a set of concrete steps.

I didn't notice those last time we were here; the crates must have hidden them. Jogging closer, she found they descended towards a wooden door.

"Let's take a look down there," she said, pointing as they joined her. Jase licked his lips, and Sol shuffled on his feet. Pink wondered if they, like her, were reminded of the entrance to the coal mines. However, when she stepped down, the sound of their footsteps accompanied her own. She reached the door and pushed it open to the sound of creaking hinges, a blast of cold air hitting her from within. There was no light, so Pink conjured a flame, which revealed the most unexpected sight. In front of them stood a series of upright beds with metal stands and wheels, each with a pair of leather belts attached. She moved closer and examined one, feeling the smooth fabric. *Is this to hold someone in place?*

Her flame was not enough to light the entire area, so Pink walked alongside the stone wall while the others followed closely behind. Eventually, she found a bracket and transferred her flame to the torch within. She had just stepped back when she heard a familiar voice.

"Pink ..."

Pink's heart skipped a beat as she realised the voice didn't belong to Jase or Sol. She turned slowly in its direction, finding she could now see another of the upright beds, one that wasn't empty.

"Bale!"

Their fellow mage was still dressed in the loose-fitting cotton blue shirt and trousers worn by infirmary patients. Pink ran over at once before the others had a chance to do anything more than gasp and curse. *He looks so vulnerable without syntaxicite.*

"Bale." She put the palm of her hand against his cheek. She didn't know if the lack of any warmth was a good or bad thing, considering his earlier fever, but the pallid tinge of his skin and his wet, bloodshot eyes didn't give him the look of a healthy person. "You're awake! Stay strong. We're going to get you out of here."

"I … don't know what's happened to me … my memory's … wrong … they gave me … something …"

"They? Do you mean Magicom?"

"Magicom … and … and … Wing."

"Wing?" Pink looked to the others. The torchlight dancing across their features mirrored her own confusion. "Bale, you've obviously been through a terrible ordeal," she said, turning back to meet his eyes. "If you mean Instructor Texeria, he's not truly …"

"Not … Texeria." Bale's eyes were wide – he seemed to be looking into the distance. "I mean … I mean … him."

It was then that Pink realised Bale was looking towards the doorway. She turned slowly, and there, standing by the entrance, stood Gabriel, flanked by two Magicom soldiers, his arm outstretched in their direction.

"What is …?" she started to say before wind magic threw her backwards, and everything went black.

CHAPTER TWENTY

Rox Salvamal sat at his desk in one of the high towers of Holding Castle, the steel nib in his hand stationary, his thoughts far removed from the tedious report before him.

Tomorrow, he and August Silvershield would be in the same place at the same time – how could he possibly think of anything else? Months of playing their cat-and-mouse game would come to an end. Once Silvershield was out of the picture, Salvamal could focus on projects more deserving of his attention.

Like the one going on underneath Holding Castle at that very moment.

The hammering of metal reached his ears through the window slit, the gondolas of his blimps being rebuilt in the courtyard below. Once airborne, they would show the futility of Ashes' little stunt. He scanned his circular office, bare aside from a desk (with his sword and belt propped against it), a rug on the stone floor and a few mementoes from his life as a soldier, his eyes falling at last to the shelf holding a decanter of brandy. Perhaps a drink was in order – it was early in the day, but it might help to put his active mind at rest. He was in the process of moving from his chair when he heard footsteps from the stone stairwell. Letting out a sigh, he lowered himself back down.

Rael Rookevelt's head appeared at the room's opening,

followed by the rest of him. Now that he was here, Salvamal found he was actually quite pleased to see his lieutenant – here was someone to share in his upcoming victory.

Maybe I'll even offer him a glass.

"General," greeted Rookevelt curtly, placing his hands behind his back.

"Lieutenant, how are the numbers looking?"

"Reports indicate that over two thousand people have entered the city since dawn. We expect more tomorrow."

Rookevelt looked as if he wanted to say more. Salvamal leaned back in his chair and intertwined his fingers, amused at the other man's indecision. "Is there a problem?"

"Not a problem, sir. More a small concern." Rookevelt rubbed his temple with his thumb and forefinger, frowning. "I understand the logic behind this execution, but surely having a crowd at Holding Square is more of an advantage for Ashes than for us. Doesn't it make more sense to keep Mason in Alsing? If the arcannen he stole from Doscadia is anything to go by, Silvershield's planning a rescue attempt, and the prison is much better defended than the square. On top of which, should Silvershield actually manage to free his man … in front of all those witnesses …"

Being reminded of the Doscadia incident soured Salvamal's mood instantly. Silvershield had now twice impersonated a Magicom soldier and got away with it. To say Salvamal had been furious when told of this latest theft was an understatement. *And those officials … so easily fooled. What use are these people?*

"Keeping Mason at Alsing also gives us the problem of not knowing *when* Silvershield will strike," Salvamal responded in a bored voice. "That has always been his advantage with the clinics. We never know which one he's going to target, so we have to spread our forces accordingly. But with Holding Square, we know when Silvershield will strike and where. As for the people, they will witness Magicom crushing Ashes. That makes all this worth it."

"Does how we look capturing Silvershield take priority over actually capturing him?"

Salvamal let a moment's silence follow those words. "Careful, Rookevelt."

Rookevelt bowed his head. "I'm merely trying to better prepare myself for tomorrow. I was hoping you might let me in on your plan of action. You've clearly been busy with something over the last couple of days. I can't help but wonder if your confidence stems from there."

Ahh, so we finally get to the crux of the matter. This is what you really want to know, Rookevelt. Salvamal tried to judge if Rookevelt was sincere, but the lieutenant was keeping his expression unreadable, a trait Salvamal had never liked about him.

He considered the other man for a moment longer. *Perhaps the time for secrecy is over. It was necessary at the time, while the project was still incomplete. But things have changed.* "It would be easier to show you," he said, coming to a decision. "Follow."

Despite Rookevelt's inscrutable expression, Salvamal was sure he detected a flash of relief. Together, they departed the tower and walked the parapets to the keep. Once inside, passageways and descending stairs led them into the castle's undercroft, an ancient storage area a level above the old dungeons, where flames burnt from torches along the walls and hundreds of bare wooden workstations stood in rows.

"This is where the Technological Department is

based," said Rookevelt, rubbing his hands against the cold. His eyes fell on the glass cabinets at the back of the room, where vials of arcannen were stored. "They do important work down here, synthesizing arcannen for Blake. Other potions as well, I've heard. But … where is everyone?"

"Most have been given the day off," replied Salvamal, walking towards the back of the room and motioning Rookevelt to follow. "A project has been going on down here recently, and it's on a need-to-know basis. We have stockpiles of arcannen potions – it doesn't matter if we temporarily ease off their manufacture."

Salvamal motioned Rookevelt to follow him through an opening at the back of the room into a dimly lit corridor. They passed by several smaller rooms until they reached the corridor's end, where a wooden door stood. Salvamal opened it and stepped aside so Rookevelt could enter first.

Rookevelt froze when he saw what was inside. "What is this?" he whispered.

Candlelight lit up a row of beds occupied by a dozen soldiers wearing black leather masks. Each bed had a pristine-looking metal table alongside it. A cabinet with a glass front, syringes neatly placed within, stood in one corner. Aside from the soldiers, there were two others in the room – a man and a woman, dressed in grey robes and standing over a bed at the end with clipboards. They nodded in greeting before going back to whatever discussion they were having in hushed tones.

"Why are they wearing those masks?" Rookevelt asked as he looked over the soldiers. Salvamal was glad to hear the unease that had crept into his voice. "Why … why are their eyes that colour?"

"We wish them to remain anonymous for now. As for

the eyes, they are a … side effect of a procedure they've had."

Rookevelt walked to the nearest bed, looking closely at its occupant, a man with a shock of blond hair whose sleeve had been pulled up, a bandage covering the skin between his forearm and bicep. The mask hid most of the man's other features, aside from a rectangular gap for his mouth and chin. The soldier, who was sitting upright, remained still, unnaturally so, but Salvamal could hear his shallow breathing as he met Rookevelt's gaze.

"Who are they?" Rookevelt asked, looking back at Salvamal.

"This is Commander Maynard, and the others are from his unit. Maynard's team were the ones who captured Phantex Mason and sent him to Holding but somehow allowed his ten-year-old brother to escape. They were also responsible for the mother's recent escape. Their lack of competence required consequences, so they were given a choice: face discharge from the army or remain and take part in an experiment allowing them to become the future of it. They unanimously chose the latter and are being looked after by researchers from the Technological Department."

"I'm not sure I understand," said Rookevelt. "What's the point in all this? You talk about experiments. What were you trying to achieve?"

Salvamal smiled. "Commander Maynard, please join us outside so we can demonstrate for the lieutenant."

With stiff movements, Maynard pushed himself off the bed, got to his feet and moved to the open doorway. As he passed the lieutenant, Rookevelt's hand moved ever so slightly towards the hilt of his sword. Forcing back a smile, Salvamal followed Maynard into the corridor with Rookevelt just behind.

Once outside, Maynard glanced back, and Salvamal nodded his confirmation. Facing forward, Maynard held out one arm, and a small ball of blue energy appeared above his fingertips. Rookevelt made a sound of disbelief and moved to say something, but Salvamal cut him off with a wave of his hand. The ball of blue energy grew larger, spiralled noisily, and then – as Rookevelt jumped back with a shout – shot through the space until it struck one of the walls, exploding in a shower of stone and dust. After it had cleared, the stone revealed dark, angry scorch marks.

"Manabeast magic!" gasped Rookevelt.

"The very same, Lieutenant. A simple transfusion of wolf-type blood gives them this ability *without* the need for arcannen. You can see why I am so confident about Holding Square tomorrow." Salvamal placed a hand on the other man's shoulder. "They have orders to target Silvershield and Silvershield only. The rest of Ashes can be dealt with afterwards."

Salvamal waited for a response but, as Rookevelt continued to stare at where the magic had struck, felt himself growing impatient. "This is the next step in the progress of magic, Lieutenant. Think about it! Soon, anyone willing to go through one simple procedure will be able to use energy-based magic forever."

"Soon?" asked Rookevelt. Finally, he looked at Salvamal. "You mean these experiments are incomplete?"

"We just need to wean them off the potion that keeps them … stable. But we will. A little more time and everything will be complete for other members of the army. Then we can use the manabeasts' own magic against them and make Blake a better place for everyone! You're a good man, Rookevelt. You don't just follow orders; you believe in what we're doing here at Magicom. I think it goes without saying you're with me on this?"

Rael Rookevelt was looking at Salvamal as if he'd never seen him before but, crucially, nodded.

The lieutenant was silent on their way back into the keep, but Salvamal paid him little attention. His anticipation for the following day, and all those after, had been increased by the demonstration.

I think I'll have that drink now.

CHAPTER TWENTY-ONE

Pink opened her eyes to a world of blurred shapes. She blinked to refocus, realising – as her senses returned – that she'd been strapped, with her arms and legs bound, to one of the upright beds. Bale, who was once again unconscious, was alongside her. Ringing filled her ears, and the back of her head felt sore and damp. One of the blurs ahead solidified into Gabriel, his attention diverted towards the Magicom soldiers – one of whom Pink recognised as Commander Riccard, the soldier who'd struck her in the Salted Pig – and a familiar woman in a suit. The commander and Gabriel were speaking as if from a great distance.

"… other equipment has been taken. This is the last of it, Gabriel."

"Which is why you need to take the mages. Now that the transfusions are working, they would make perfect test subjects."

"General Salvamal won't like it. He already has what he needs. You're just trying to avoid doing what needs to be done."

Disorientation gave way to disbelief. Gabriel had attacked them. Gabriel, the Assistant Master of Wing. A man who had trained hundreds of mages, including Jase; the man whom Articulas Wing had trusted to run his facility. *And now he's telling Magicom to use us as test subjects?*

"Pink … hsss … Pink." Jase was trying to get her attention from where he was strapped to another of the benches. He looked relieved when she looked over. She attempted to look beyond Jase to where she could see the legs and boots of Sol but could not tell what sort of state he was in. The movement caught Gabriel's attention.

"It seems I underestimated you children," he said softly, turning away from the commander. There was a predatory look in the assistant master's eyes Pink had never seen before. Instinctively she thought of her magic, but how could she direct it with her arms strapped? "I would have thought ordering Perola to refuse all arcannen requests would have kept you from leaving Highstone Hill."

Despite everything, a glimmer of hope rose in Pink. *He doesn't know we have magic!*

"You're planning to kill us?" Sol said from the side.

Gabriel turned to him. "It does seem a waste, but apparently, I'm being given no choice."

Jase moaned. *I have to find some way to keep us alive!* Pink tried to discreetly free her wrists from the bonds that held her to the bed. But it was no use. She would have to use considerable force to even change the angle of her palms, and if she did that, Gabriel would notice. *What if I mention August? Will that save us? No, if he's working with Magicom, he'll only use me as bait to draw August out. Then he'll kill the others anyway.* Pink fought hard against the creeping panic. *What should I do?*

"You should be dead already," said Gabriel, tilting his head to one side, seemingly oblivious to her attempts. "You were finding out too much, too quickly, so I had to talk Sara here into leading you all to the coal mines. She even thought it was her own idea." The satisfaction lacing his words morphed her fear into anger. *He played me.* She met his eyes, hating him.

"I knew you wouldn't be able to resist meddling," he told her, looking amused. "I sent those mages and instructors to test my hybrids in a battle situation. It was an added bonus that I might use them to take out Keat Texeria's little band of followers. But then Victorian had to get involved as well, didn't she? Well, she won't be here to save you this time." He sighed as if disappointed by their performance on the training ground. "You would've survived had you not followed me here."

"*Your* hybrids?" came Sol's voice again. "So you're the one behind what happened to the townsfolk." There was a pause. "And once they served their purpose, you exterminated them."

"Gabriel, we could have used them to do further tests," rebuked the woman Pink now realised was Miriam Shawgrave. She acted like they were all having a polite conversation, and Gabriel wasn't talking about murdering them. *Mad. They're both mad.* "You didn't need to eliminate them."

"We couldn't risk them coming back to themselves and implicating us," replied Gabriel with a shrug.

Just then, the wooden door flew open. Gabriel, Miriam Shawgrave and the two soldiers spun around, but there was nothing there. With their attention diverted, and while Riccard muttered something about the wind, Pink managed to change the angle of her right wrist so her fingertips pointed towards Gabriel. *There won't be a better chance than this. Maybe if I take him out, the others will be able to do the same to the other three.* It seemed unlikely, but she was desperate, and it was the only thing she could think of. She sparked the arcannen in her blood and summoned a burst of wind magic.

A whoosh of air, but her attempt was off-target and did no more than ruffle Gabriel's hair.

He turned back around; the surprise etched on his features giving way to renewed interest. "So you *do* have magic. Is that left over from a previous potion, or were you able to acquire more somehow?" He waited a moment, and when she didn't reply, he said, "Who are you, Sara Arrancove? Master Wing was very secretive about where you came from, even to us instructors. What is it about you he was trying to hide?"

"If you kill me, you'll never find out," responded Pink through gritted teeth, the back of her head throbbing.

Gabriel laughed. "My dear girl, that won't work any better than your ill attempt at magic just now. I am curious about you, though. Why is it you were the only mage assigned to Keat Texeria?"

"She doesn't know!" cried Jase.

Gabriel never took his eyes off her, so she forced herself to lift her chin and glare right back. "I believe that," he said at last. "I remember how you were pining for Victorian to be your mentor. She was furious, by the way. I'd already agreed to the request when a letter arrived from Master Wing with very specific instructions to put you under the guidance of another, one who'd be arriving shortly. I cared little – until I realised this new instructor was experimenting with manabeast magic himself. I soon worked out he was Master Wing's spy, of course, to keep an eye on what I was doing in his absence, especially when he snapped up that contract from Poulsen before I even became aware of it."

"So … Master Wing knows what's been going on?" asked Pink. *The longer we keep him talking, the more chance one of us has of getting free.*

"If he knows about your experiments, and you kill us,

he'll work out what happened and come for you," said Sol before Gabriel got a chance to reply. Pink nodded along, but she was sure that Gabriel, like her, could hear the desperation in Sol's voice.

Gabriel let out a long breath. "Perhaps, but General Salvamal will protect me. It may not even come to that. Master Wing is as much part of this as anyone."

This did give Pink pause. Gabriel seemed to notice her reaction.

"Why do you think he hired me in the first place?" he said, a small smile playing on his lips. "It was because we were both interested in finding a way for humans to access manabeast magic."

"I don't believe it," said Pink.

Gabriel sneered. "Why? Because everyone talks about how much of a *good* man Master Wing is? All that Spirit Mage Wars rubbish? By the Trinity, people of your age can be naive sometimes."

Commander Riccard placed a hand on Gabriel's arm. "Can we get on with this?"

But Gabriel shrugged him off. Talking about Master Wing seemed to have agitated him. "Years ago, the two of us set up a program with the purpose of administering blood transfusions to volunteers from wolf-types due to the latter's highly destructive magic. Blood has always been the key to elemental magic, so we thought it might be the same with manabeasts. The results, however, were disastrous.

"I knew we just had to tweak the procedure a bit, but Master Wing lost his nerve and no longer wanted to test on human subjects. Years passed, and when it appeared the master wouldn't be returning from his travels any time soon, I contacted Rox Salvamal, who had no such qualms. *He* understood that sacrifices had to be made for the sake of progress. He provided me with the equipment needed, and then it was just a case of … acquiring the right subjects." Gabriel's lips curved into a smile. "That's where the townsfolk came in. A jeweller who had acquired debts, a group of coal miners travelling the wilderness near dusk – people whose disappearances could be explained away. I set to work, changing the quantities of manabeast blood used, and, amazingly, found my theory to be correct. The subjects could use the wolf-types' magic! The problems with their mental state remained, though. Can you guess how we solved that?"

"The dukesbane compound," said Pink through gritted teeth.

Bizarrely, Gabriel clapped his hands and laughed. "Very good, Sara! General Salvamal suggested we try using a compound Magicom's Technological Department had been working on to counteract the side effects of my experiments. He sent Madam Shawgrave here, one of their researchers and a potions expert, to assist, working under the guise of her own independent company, so she could hire men and women from Poulsen to collect the plants, some of which remained here to be synthesised. Eventually, we were able to create hybrids docile enough to follow orders. We had no plans to use our own workers as subjects, but when Corey Leathers stumbled onto what we were doing, we had to take care of him, along with Cylan Wight, when he started supplying you with information."

"And Scottie Sharp," said Pink, not willing nor able to keep the disgust from her voice.

"He suffered the consequence of his disrespect." It was the commander who spoke now, a sneer on his face. "When we found him with Wight, the opportunity was too good to miss."

"No one's going to accept this," Sol called out. As soon as Gabriel looked in his direction, Pink attempted to free her wrists again. "You're just switching an arcannen potion for a dukesbane one. The magic might be different, but how many would allow themselves to go through those side effects just for that?"

"Fool!" spat Gabriel. "Do you really think I hadn't thought of that, Draeon? We're working out the kinks, but eventually, the subjects won't *need* the dukesbane. Their bodies will get used to the wolf-types' magic and fight off the manabeast corruption. It's amazing what the human body can do. Already, the new hybrids we've created require a lower dose of dukesbane than before." He paused, and when he spoke again, his voice had taken on a calmer quality. "As for the ones who were too far gone, General Salvamal suggested we use them to see how they fared against mages in the field. I deposited them in the coal mines, sent a team down, and well, you know better than any the results of that. Problems began to arise, though." He jerked his head at Bale. "One of the mages survived. He was injured, but I knew it would only be a matter of time before he talked about what he'd seen, especially since he'd been working under Keat Texeria. I was sure if that happened, Master Wing would suspect my involvement – and your friend here could be used as evidence against me. Then my plan to rid myself of the rest of you backfired, which in turn led to the instructors finding out about the experiments. I had to change tack. An idea came to me then – what if I framed someone else? Someone who was known for his own experiments? Someone who had arrived at Wing at a time suspiciously close to this incident? It would solve my problem and rid me of Articulas Wing's spy in one fell swoop. I guessed Keat Texeria would try to speak to Bale – and had Bale disappear just after he'd done so. I sowed the seeds of doubt in my most respected instructor to be sure he was suspected. I assume Victorian told you that Texeria was the last to see him? That damned illusionist disappeared before he could be detained, but it only served to make him look more guilty."

Pink was beside herself. "So, this is your plan now? To turn Wing into a place for your twisted experiments?"

Gabriel scoffed. "Wing is finished. Salvamal's been looking for an excuse to close it down ever since he learned August Silvershield trained there, or, to be more specific, Salvamal wants an excuse to turn it into a facility that trains mages exclusively for Magicom. And now he has one. He could do nothing before because of Articulas Wing. The master is a powerful man and has many allies in Holding, but when word gets out that one of his instructors was responsible for the death of their own mages, that will all change. It matters little to me – when I am master of Salvamal's new facility, I can continue my research."

Gabriel paused and regarded them a moment longer before looking at Commander Riccard and exchanging a nod. The commander and the other soldier moved closer. "I'm afraid Commander Riccard's right; you're too dangerous to keep alive." Gabriel let out a sigh. "Use air traps," he said to the soldiers, "we can at least keep it painless."

Pink started to struggle frantically as Gabriel neared. She could hear Jase pleading and Sol threatening from the side. Magic shot in the air from someone and struck the ceiling. It soon became clear that no matter how hard she struggled, she was never going to free herself in time. She became still and met Gabriel's eyes, the look of regret he wore not quite reaching them. *I'm sorry, August. I've given you one more reason to hate Magicom. I'm sorry, Jase, Bale, Sol.* She closed her eyes, a single tear running down her cheek.

And then she heard a growl.

Pink snapped open her eyes and saw Gabriel now facing the other way, looking towards something at the entrance. As he moved, she got a clear line of sight. A wolf-type stood in the opening at the bottom of the stairs, its hackles bristling and its sharp teeth displayed in a snarl.

Pink's eyes widened as Commander Riccard shot a fireball at it. The sound of the explosion reverberated around the room as Gabriel and Shawgrave yelled. At the opening, nothing could be seen but smoke. Their captors all had flames in their hands, and for a moment, everything was still. Then out of the smoke, the manabeast pounced, a ball of energy forming at its open mouth. The second soldier, who was nearest to the entrance, was struck before he'd even had a chance to defend himself. He gave a brief cry of what sounded like shock before he dropped to near Sol's feet, the smell of burning flesh filling the room.

Gabriel, Shawgrave and Riccard threw themselves into action then, firing blasts of wind and fire at the still-moving manabeast. Pink tried to follow their movements, but something shimmered in the air in front of her, distracting her from the battle.

"Sorry to keep you waiting," whispered a familiar drawl.

The voice was coming from the shimmer! As it unbuckled the leather straps around her wrists, Pink recognised the shape of a man.

"Free the others," it commanded once it had finished the ones on her ankles. "Quickly now, before they notice."

Between her and the shimmering figure, they managed

to unbuckle the leather cords that held Bale, Sol and Jase in less than a minute. Gabriel looked over and yelled, moving his arm back in their direction, but he had to swing it back to form an air shield as the manabeast's magic exploded within the room. The shimmering figure swung Bale over its shoulder and moved towards the entrance, creating a bizarre scene where Bale looked as if he was floating in the air. Gabriel turned back and tried to stop them from escaping again, but Riccard was down, smoke rising from his body, and Shawgrave had already fled. Diverting his attention between them and the wolf-type proved to be a mistake. As soon as he looked away, the manabeast was on him, bearing him to the ground.

For a moment, Pink felt like everything was happening in slow motion. Should she help Gabriel, or should they take advantage of the distraction and escape? Even as she hesitated, a fountain of blood sprayed into the air as the wolf-type sank its sharp fangs into Gabriel's neck, and the assistant master screamed in pain. She looked away, unable to watch, focusing instead on following the floating Bale up the steps.

The shimmering man, who was becoming more opaque by the second – revealing garb of green and brown and a mass of dark curly hair – shut the wooden door behind them, cutting off Gabriel's screaming.

They stared at the closed door, horrified.

CHAPTER TWENTY-TWO

"I can see why you're called an illusionist," said Sol to Texeria, tearing his eyes away first. Pink squeezed her eyes shut, trying not to imagine what was happening to Gabriel inside.

"Not right now," came Texeria's reply, his voice taking on a rare edge. "Let's get back to where your horses are. For all we know, more Magicom soldiers are on the way – at least we'll have cover there."

He retrieved Bale from where he had placed him, lifted him over his shoulder, and headed towards the exit. Pink and Jase exchanged a glance, and Sol raised his eyebrows; they had no choice but to follow him out of the building. As they crossed the grasslands towards the woods, she caught sight of Jase out of the corner of her eye. He looked dazed. She moved closer and put an arm around his waist.

"It's over now," she said kindly. "We're safe."

Her best friend gave a sort of whimper in response but was unable to offer anything else. It wasn't until they were back under the shelter of the trees with their horses that he found his voice.

"What about Gabriel?" he asked Texeria, who was laying Bale down gently on the forest floor. "Are we just going to leave him there?"

Texeria turned, looking at Jase in puzzlement. Sol's expression wasn't much different. But Pink understood. Jase was in shock – Gabriel was his mentor, after all.

She placed a hand on his arm. "Jase, he was going to kill us. He's been experimenting on humans. He pitted them against mages and instructors from Wing. He's a murderer."

Jase looked at her with glazed eyes. He nodded, but there was something very distant in the way he did it.

"Is he going to be okay?" Pink asked Texeria, inclining her head to Bale.

"Try to get some water in him," said Texeria, chucking a skin to Sol, who quickly obliged. "He'll be fine, I think," he said to Pink. "He's been drugged, and he's dehydrated. Once he's back resting at Wing, he should recover."

"That manabeast," said Pink. "It was the one from your storage room, wasn't it?"

Texeria nodded with a small smile. "I wasn't about to take on Gabriel, two Magicom soldiers and that dukesbane woman, not an inept instructor like myself."

Sol let out a snort of laughter and stood away from Bale. "You are many things, Keat Texeria, but inept is not one of them. Talking about Miriam Shawgrave, I saw her running from the room before you appeared. Should we be concerned?"

Texeria shrugged. "She'll either return to Holding or flee as far as she can in the opposite direction. There's not much we can do about her now."

Pink regarded the curly-haired instructor. The gratefulness she felt for him saving their lives was tempered by the fact that manabeast could easily have attacked them. *Why do I feel it's pointless to bring that up?* He watched her back, and she didn't miss the perspicacious look in his eyes before he slackened his face. "It's time you told us everything," she said.

Texeria chuckled. "Fine. Well … where to begin?" He ran a hand down his stubbly chin. "I knew something was wrong when Bale went missing. I was curious about the attack at the coal mines and visited the infirmary to speak with him, but he was unresponsive. When I tried again later that night, he was gone." The instructor gave them a wry smile. "As I had been the last to see him, I deemed it likely I would be blamed for his disappearance. Luckily, I still had the wagon I used to bring some of my equipment to Highstone Hill, so I took what I could and departed for Holding, hoping to find aid there. However, as I journeyed through the wilderness, I had time to think. I was already suspicious of Gabriel, but following the information you received from the mayor yesterday, I wondered anew about the involvement of the dukesbane site. If something was happening at that site, was that where Bale would be taken? I realised then that you would probably draw the same conclusions and the danger you'd be in if you did. I turned around at once. Unfortunately, I arrived after you, something I worked out after I found your horses. As I made for the building, I saw Gabriel, Shawgrave and the soldiers go inside. I used the armadillo-type's black powder and followed them."

"When the door opened?" Pink asked, suddenly remembering. "That was you?"

"That was how I knew of Gabriel's intentions. Thankfully, the lack of light prevented my outline from being seen. I returned at once to my wagon, which isn't too far from here, and got backup." He grinned. "The hardest part was using magic to get the wolf-type inside the building. After that, well, you know the rest. I'm disappointed to have run out of the black powder – I will have to start collecting again – but I suppose it was worth it."

Jase handed her a waterskin, and she accepted, taking a deep draught. It was cool and refreshing and gave her a moment to think. *He supposes it was worth it?* She shook her head.

"What are we going to do now?" she asked, deciding to be proactive. She was still a Wing mage, after all.

Texeria looked as if he'd been waiting for her to ask that question. "Leave it to me to settle things at Highstone Hill," he said, much to her relief. She could not imagine bringing back the news of what Gabriel had done – especially to Victorian. "Bale can confirm my story. As you can get there quicker than I, I want you to go to Holding in my place. Magicom's experiments won't stop with Gabriel's death, but there might be another way to stop them."

"How is that possible, though? Magicom can't be stopped by anyone. Even if what they're doing is illegal, they'll still get away with it."

"And can we really attribute the blame to Magicom?" asked Sol, coming forward.

"What do you mean?" asked Pink, shooting him a wary look. Out of the corner of her eye, she saw Jase's vacant expression start to sharpen.

"I mean, these experiments have been done under the authority of Gabriel and Rox Salvamal, correct? You're discussing this matter as if no blame can be attributed to Wing – and rightly so, before you say anything," he added, with a quick glance at Jase, who'd opened his mouth to speak. "The other instructors will be devastated when they hear of Gabriel's actions. But, by the same token, Magicom shouldn't be blamed for the actions of one man, nor should their soldiers be blamed for following orders."

"Rox Salvamal is the general of Magicom's army," said

Jase.

"And Gabriel is the Assistant Master of Wing. The general doesn't own Magicom. It may be those above him knew nothing of what Salvamal was up to like Master Wing knew nothing of what Gabriel was up to."

"I'm glad you brought him up," said Texeria, holding up his hands. Both Sol and Jase looked from one another to the instructor, each looking as if he was hopeful for support. "Master Wing might be the one person who could help us with all of this."

"Master Wing has been away from Highstone Hill for as long as we've all been there," said Sol. "None of us have even met him, as far as I'm aware."

"He returned to Holding last night. I imagine news reached him that Magicom were planning to publicly hang one of his former mages."

"We saw him on the posters!" said Jase excitedly. "Phantex Mason. Pink, do you remember?"

"I do," replied Pink, continuing to watch Keat Texeria.

"Master Wing has political sway in the city," said Texeria, scratching his cheek. "Perhaps enough to put a stop to these experiments. The problem for Magicom is that if the truth became public knowledge, they could have Ashes, Master Wing, the government and the general populace all opposing them. Even that would probably not be enough to stop them in their entirety, but it would cause considerable problems for those who run the company. Hopefully enough for them to denounce Salvamal's experiments."

"What about the others he mentioned?" Pink asked. Texeria fixed her with a quizzical look, so she added, "The ones Gabriel said were docile enough to follow orders."

Texeria frowned. "I must have been retrieving the wolf-type during that part. It doesn't change the plan, though. If anything, it gives us even more reason to act."

"We *could* tell Ashes about this," said Jase, speaking directly to Texeria, which Pink was grateful for. "They might be able to help."

"Please," laughed Sol before Texeria had a chance to reply. "If we join forces with criminals, we might as well lock *ourselves* in Alsing. Besides, how are you going to get in contact with them? If Magicom haven't been able to find August Silvershield after all this time, how on Blake are we?"

"August Silvershield cannot do what Master Wing can," said Texeria quietly. Pink was glad he'd spoken before Jase could respond. Her best friend was emotional; she did not know what he might let slip. She placed a hand on his arm, hoping to send him the correct message. He twitched but made no further sign of acknowledgement. "Magicom would likely call him a liar," continued Texeria. "They cannot discredit Master Wing so, he's a hero of the Spirit Mage Wars, the founder of Wing and the creator of syntaxicite. People would listen to him." Texeria took a deep breath. "Consider this a direct order from an instructor – find Master Wing and tell him all that has happened."

"Wait," came a weak voice. Pink looked over to see Bale climbing gingerly to his feet. Sol made a movement to help, but Bale held out a palm. "I'm fine."

Pink stared at him with the others. *He doesn't look fine!*

Bale, however, met their gazes and said, "I heard all that. I want to go too."

"Absolutely not!" Texeria looked at Bale in disbelief. "You've spent most of the last couple of days being unconscious!"

"Then I'm well rested," said Bale, with an attempt at a smile that looked like more of a grimace.

"He's making a joke. His mind must really be addled," said Jase weakly.

"I need you to return to Wing with me to back up my story," said Texeria.

"You'll just have to do that yourself, Instructor," said Bale. "I doubt it's beyond your abilities." They all stared at him, and he made an impatient noise. "I need to see this through to the end," he told them, his voice taking on a pleading tone. "You weren't there at the mines when we were attacked. I can't just lie in the infirmary while you bring those responsible to light. Please, let me be part of this."

"I think we should let him," said Pink, not taking her eyes from Bale. He fixed her with a grateful look.

"The other instructors are going to love this," muttered Texeria.

***

While they were preparing to leave, Texeria seemed to be thinking about something. Eventually, he called over to Pink and chucked her a bag of coins. "It will be quicker to take the train, and at least once you're aboard, Bale can rest," he said to them. "I'll send for your horses. Take what you need and travel to Poulsen Station. It's not far from here." He paused. "A quiet word, Pink, if you don't mind."

The others looked over curiously as her mentor led her a little further into the trees until they were out of sight and, more importantly, Pink guessed, earshot.

"There is one last thing you should know," he told her. "You've all assumed that Master Wing is the reason I'm at Highstone Hill. Even Gabriel thought the master had sent me to spy on him. But that is not the case. I have not spoken to Articulas Wing in a number of years." He paused, looking solemn. "The one who sent me was August."

Pink's eyes widened. "You're a member of Ashes?"

"Certainly not. I refused all August's requests to join his suicidal little band. But I attended Wing with your brother – we were very good friends." The instructor smiled as if recalling a fond memory. "He used to call me Felix after the sidekick from *Jarian the Dragon Hunter*. Anyway, we went our separate ways after Wing. He had his rebellion; I took on the less clandestine role of an illusionist. However, after Magicom discovered who he was, he thought it only a matter of time before they targeted his old Wing friends. He suggested I would be safer here but admitted he also hoped I would serve as extra protection if Magicom ever found out your identity, especially with Master Wing absent. I agreed, but he was the one who got in contact with the master, who in turn informed Wing of my coming."

Pink felt a tinge of irritation towards August. *Things would have been much easier if he had just told me.*

"Why are you sending me away then?" she asked. "Not that I'm complaining, but you won't be able to keep an eye on me if I'm in Holding and you're at Wing."

"You have proven yourself to be capable," answered Texeria, "and even if it vexes August, I've made the decision as a Wing instructor. Besides, I had to come here for my own safety. Your brother cannot order me to do anything." He turned to go but swivelled around to face her again. "There's one more thing, which I'm sure you've already worked out. Phantex's execution is surely a trap for August. Phantex is my friend as well, and I have sent what little help I can to August, but I hope you, and Jase, for that matter, heed my advice about not seeking August out. There's nothing you can do to help." He turned around once more. "Oh, and for the Trinity's sake, if Bale collapses, make sure you find a healer quickly."

Apparently satisfied, Texeria weaved his way back through the trees to the others. After a moment's pause, in which she attempted to digest everything she'd just learned, Pink followed, returning to where the others waited.

Texeria had mounted his horse and, with his hands on the reins, gave them a final look. "Good luck," he said, grinning as if nothing of importance had happened that morning. Then he took off, the sound of trotting hooves soon fading, leaving them alone in the woods.

"Well," she said at last as the others turned to face her. "Let's go find Master Wing."

CHAPTER TWENTY-THREE

On foot, Pink, Jase, Sol and Bale trudged south through the wilderness – a journey made harder not only by the lack of horses or even a footpath but by the near-death ordeal they had suffered, a mental exhaustion every bit as wearisome as their physical one.

Gabriel is dead. Pink kept replaying the words in her mind as if that would make them more real. Only hours ago, she'd known him as the Assistant Master of Wing – a bit stiff perhaps, but a fair and just man whom so many respected. But it had all been an act, a way to further his work, as he had called it, transfusing manabeast blood into humans, creating something that was neither and ruining the lives of innocent people in the bargain. Then snuffing them out when they were of no more use to him.

And now he's dead. The assistant master of Wing was a traitor, and now he's dead.

She looked to Bale then. He wore a determined look and had refused all offers of rest, but she could hear his heavy breathing and see the beads of sweat forming on his forehead. She turned her attention to Jase. While she still had the map stored safely in her pack, he'd lived in the Poulsen area all his life and knew the general direction of the station, making him the best choice to take the lead. He seemed to have recovered from his earlier strange mood, even helping to apply a bandage to the wound at the back of her head before they'd set off. Since then, however, he'd been as silent as the rest of them. *Perhaps all he needs is time to deal with what happened*. She glanced at Sol, who was walking by her side, eyes downcast. *Perhaps we all do.*

Eventually, Jase found them a footpath, and it wasn't long before it divided into two, a wooden signpost pointing southwest to 'Poulsen' and south to 'Poulsen Station.' With the sun on their backs, they marched on for a little while longer, still in silence, until they reached the latter.

Poulsen Station was a concrete platform built above a track that ran east, with only a small brick building connected to it. Bridleways ran in all directions, and wildflowers dominated, the fragrant smell of the flowers and the tweeting of nearby birds creating a rather idyllic spot.

Pink bought their tickets from the stationmaster – who was sitting behind a square opening built into the brickwork – with some of the coins Instructor Texeria had given her. He spoke only to let them know the next train to Holding would arrive within the hour. They made their way onto the empty, concrete platform, Jase and Bale sitting on a wooden bench they found there and looking at one another.

"So, are we going to talk about what happened?" asked Pink quietly. Bale and Jase looked up, but neither seemed to find anything to say. Sol, standing to one side with his arms crossed, didn't have any such problem.

"What part of our assistant master trying to murder us all did you want to discuss?"

"Along with those Magicom soldiers," said Jase heatedly.

"This isn't going to be one of those conversations," said Pink sternly. Jase looked abashed, but Sol didn't bother trying to hide his frustration. Pink spoke directly to him. "Gabriel has been experimenting on people and manabeasts, ultimately costing them their lives. He has done this *under* the direction of Magicom. Those are the facts. I know you're as disgusted as the rest of us, Sol. What we're doing is directly moving against Magicom, so if you want to leave and return to Wing, now is probably the time."

Sol looked up slowly, but the tension in his face seemed to fade a little. "I still believe those high up in the company likely knew nothing about the experiments and will be just as shocked as we are, but perhaps Master Wing can help expose those involved. Tell me, how do you plan on finding him?"

He still can't admit it, but pushing him any further isn't going to help. She ignored the fluttering feeling in her tummy that seemed to have something to do with Sol staying, but couldn't ignore the way the others were staring at her, as if they were waiting for something. *They think I know. They probably think that's why Instructor Texeria took me to one side.*

"We'll have to ask around, of course," said Pink, the disappointment in their faces confirming her suspicions. *I can't discuss that Keat Texeria was at Wing under August's direction in front of Bale and Sol.* The idea still seemed strange to her anyway. "If he's recently returned to Holding, someone must know where he is."

Silence fell again and remained until the train arrived. It appeared first as a shape and plume of smoke in the distance before the chugging of its chimney and the iambic sound of its wheels marked its arrival at Poulsen Station. It halted at the platform with a screeching of brakes, *'Iron Horse'* printed in golden letters on the locomotive's deep green paint. To Pink, who had only been on a train a couple of times before, the majestic sight was a welcome distraction from her exhaustion. They stepped into the first of the two carriages, which was separated into compartments joined by a small corridor, and quickly found an empty one.

The dust rose in the air as they fell down on the plush seats, evident through the light that streamed through the windows. As the train took off again, Sol, who'd sat a little apart from them near the door to the corridor, closed his eyes. Jase took a window seat, seeming content to watch the hills and fields of the wilderness shoot by. After a moment, Pink did the same, her thoughts soon drifting to Instructor Texeria. Would the other instructors believe Gabriel had been working for Magicom? Without Bale, it was going to take a lot of convincing.

Time passed, and eventually, Bale, who had been sitting next to her, got up and exited the compartment. She could see him through the glass pane of the compartment's door, staring out of the window on the train's other side. She watched him for a moment before stepping out after him and closing the door softly behind.

"How are you holding up?" she asked, coming to stand beside him.

He said nothing for a few moments, seemingly content to stare out of the window, and then – "August Silvershield is your brother."

The statement was so unexpected that Pink turned and stared at him in shock before she could help herself. He didn't turn, but a small smile played on his features as if that was all the confirmation he needed.

"I don't suppose there's any point in denying it, is there?" she asked, at which he shook his head. "How long have you known?"

"For certain? Only now. I've suspected for a while, though, ever since that day you saw his likeness in the Salted Pig. The poster clearly upset you, so I guessed you knew the man on it. It made me wonder *how* you knew him, I suppose. Gabriel asking about you reminded me." Bale paused. "I guess this means your name's not Arrancove, but Silvershield."

"Arrancove was my mother's family name." She turned back, so she was facing the window again. "Are you going to tell anyone?"

"Your secret's safe with me."

Pink supposed she should be grateful, but it was hard. Bale seemed trustworthy, yet having another person know her secret felt as if she was putting August at further risk. *Still, better Bale than Sol.*

"I assume that once we've found Master Wing, you'll be staying in Holding for your brother?" asked Bale. "The execution is scheduled for tomorrow."

Pink furrowed her brow. The thought *had* been at the back of her mind ever since they'd seen Phantex Mason's poster. It didn't matter that the execution might be a trap for August. He would still spring it. He would not leave a friend to die for him; it went against his very nature. He would be in Holding, of that she was sure – he might even be there already. He would believe he could outmanoeuvre Magicom, but … she wasn't so sure. This wasn't another quick steal-and-run from a clinic – he would be up against hundreds of soldiers, maybe thousands, all waiting for him to make his move. The thought wasn't just concerning; it was terrifying. Especially now she'd seen what the company were truly capable of. *And I need to make him aware of Magicom's experiments – if he continues this crusade against Magicom, he needs to know what he's up against. I know Instructor Texeria warned me against getting involved, but this is a decision I can make for myself.*

Bale nodded to himself as if her silence was all he needed. "I won't be joining you." He hesitated. "Like I said before, I want to see this through, but my loyalty's not to you nor any of your … relatives. Once we've completed Instructor Texeria's directive … I'm out."

Pink smiled at that. "I wouldn't expect anything else, Bale."

Bale nodded without looking at her before something seemed to draw his attention. "We're here," he said.

Pink followed his gaze out of the window. The train was moving through a slight curve in the tracks, allowing them to spot the mammoth stone walls of Holding, at least five times the height of Poulsen's. Within moments they had travelled through a small tunnel, and then there was no more countryside but an urban mass of brick houses and roads filled with people, carts and horses. Some of the brickwork even had advertisements for some product or other, 'Mrs Madsen's All-Remedy Cure' and 'Bumblestone's Health Elixir' among them.

The train rose uphill, continuing its journey along a raised track so that Pink could see the slate roofs and chimneys of the houses below. Before long, the familiar screeching noise of the brakes sounded, and the *Iron Horse* slowed and stopped its momentum alongside Holding Station with a final chug. Jase and Sol joined them silently, and together they departed the train, following the other passengers to the exit of the station, a small archway with two Magicom soldiers standing either side of it.

"I'd forgotten Magicom were Holding's City Watch," said Jase, walking up to Pink's side.

"They're probably on the lookout for Ashes members entering the city," murmured Pink, aware Sol was in earshot and choosing her words carefully. "Try not to appear so put out to see them, Jase. They're going to get suspicious otherwise."

They managed to pass through the archway with little more than glares, soon finding themselves on a road that led downhill towards a cluster of houses, the maze of streets visible from their high position, and a nearby tavern aptly called the Station. Its name was written on a sign in bold letters above an illustration depicting a locomotive similar to the *Iron Horse.*

"Why don't we start our enquiries there?" Pink said to the others while the other passengers continued downhill around them. They nodded their acquiescence and together made for the building.

It was still late afternoon, so Pink wasn't surprised to see the tavern relatively quiet. There were only a few occupants in the dimly lit common room, sitting around circular tables and speaking in muffled voices. It was about half the size of the Salted Pig, with oil lamps jutting from brick walls and the smell and haze of pipe smoke travelling on the air. Ahead, a young, dark-haired barkeeper was standing behind the counter, eyeing them as they entered.

"Rooms? Drinks?" he asked once they were at the counter. "Rooms are getting filled up pretty quick today, so you'll have to pay upfront, and they're not going to come cheap either."

Pink raised an eyebrow, not caring for his tone. "Yes, I can hardly move for customers," she replied, making a point of looking around.

The barkeeper fixed Pink with a stony stare. "Lots of people *are* looking for a place to stay tonight, missy, because of the execution. I don't know if you've noticed, but we're right by the station." He paused as if to let the sarcasm sink in. "Which means we've been getting a lot of customers who have travelled from outside the city."

Pink was shocked. "People are visiting Holding to see a man die?"

"A man from Ashes. It'll be quite a spectacle, I'm sure. They're going to hang him in Holding Square. Good for business."

Pink knew she shouldn't be surprised, but the idea that people would travel from all around Blake to watch an execution made her sick to her stomach. She remembered the bodies in the coal mines and the blood spraying from Gabriel's neck. Suddenly, she felt light-headed and dizzy and had to grip the counter for support.

"What's wrong with you?" asked the barkeeper, frowning.

She felt a hand on her arm and saw Sol looking at her, his dark eyes full of concern. She took a deep breath and, although the feeling didn't completely pass, managed to compose herself. She gave Sol a nod to show she was okay.

"I assumed that's why you were here," said the barkeeper, eyeing them. "Those uniforms are Wing, aren't they? If you're not here for the execution, why have you come to Holding?"

"We're here because we're looking for someone," said Pink. Sol took his hand from her arm as she stood up again, but she could still sense him watching. "Articulas Wing."

The barkeeper snorted. "Not just anyone, then. I can assure you Articulas Wing isn't staying here."

"Yes, because that's exactly what I meant."

"We just wondered if someone might have heard word of where in Holding he is," said Jase, no doubt before the barkeeper could react to Pink's own sarcasm. "You must hear a lot, being a man of the trade and all. I'm sure you're knowledgeable about all the important matters in Holding, Mr …?"

"Please stop," groaned the barkeeper. "Your attempts at flattery are worse than her rudeness."

"You're really selling those rooms to us," put in Pink.

"No one's spoken about Articulas Wing in months," said the barkeeper, apparently keen to end the conversation now. "Happy? To be frank, I would've thought you'd know more about his whereabouts than I. If he's in Holding, it's the first I've heard of it. And my name's Jed. You can forget the Mr."

"Thank you, Jed, for your … help," said Pink. "That's all we needed. We'll let you know about those rooms."

They left him muttering behind them.

"Good to see you back to your normal self," said Jase as they found themselves back on the street outside.

Pink grinned, but Sol let out a heavy breath. "Yes, that was all very amusing, but what do we do now?"

She looked out to the city. Despite the response they'd received, she was feeling more energised. "We find more taverns and ask more people," she said. "Someone's bound to know where he is. Come on."

Yet they had no luck in the next tavern they found, a little down the road, nor the one after that. Neither establishment knew where Master Wing was or even that he was in Holding. They tried a few more with the same result, leading Pink to wonder if Instructor Texeria had been mistaken about the master's return. By this point, it was well into the evening, and as Pink had enough coin left to get them rooms for the night and supper, they decided they should do that and try again in the morning.

"Remind me why we're back here?" Jase asked as they found themselves walking back through the doors of the

Station, livelier now than it had been earlier. There was even a girl playing the flute in a corner.

"I felt we really hit it off with the barkeeper. There he is now!"

Jed visibly groaned as he saw them approach. "Not you again," he said.

"But you seemed so keen to sell us those rooms!"

"The rooms are still available but have doubled in price," he said with a smirk.

Pink stared at him open-mouthed for a moment before stepping forward to the counter so quickly that Jed stepped back. "Listen here ..." she started, her finger pointed at him.

"Excuse me," said a voice from behind them. "I don't mean to interrupt, but perhaps we could have a word?"

Pink turned slowly to find a middle-aged man standing behind them. He'd been sitting alone in a corner as they'd entered the tavern, but she hadn't paid him more than a passing glance. He was tall and bald, with skin the colour of onyx and a broad frame wrapped in a black cloak, which was held tight to his chest by a golden brooch. His coal-black eyes fixed on Pink with intensity, but when he spoke, his voice was soft. "You know who I am, don't you, Sara?"

She nodded. She had never met him but had heard him described many times. "Master Wing," she breathed.

Jase gasped while Bale and Sol came closer.

Jed even exclaimed, "You never told me that!"

Articulas Wing smiled at their reactions. "About that word?"

"Yes, of course," Pink managed.

Master Wing strode past her with a flash of his cloak. "My good barman," he said as the barkeeper stood gaping at them. "Perhaps you could be so kind as to arrange a couple of rooms for my mages here, one right away so we can talk in private, and dinner for the evening." He stacked a couple of silver dragon coins on the counter. "I will take the rooms at the normal rate."

Jed flushed. "I was never actually going to charge them extra. I was only teasing …" He seemed to falter under Master Wing's stare. "Yes, right away, sir."

"Gentlemen," said Master Wing, turning to the other three, "I wish to speak with Sara alone. You can have her back when I'm finished. Is that acceptable?"

He spoke as if asking a question, but Pink thought it sounded more like a command. Jase and Bale murmured their agreement right away. Sol looked unhappy, but Pink held his gaze until he nodded.

"Excellent! Sara, we have much to discuss and little time to do it. Let's get to it, shall we?"

CHAPTER TWENTY-FOUR

Jed sent one of the serving girls to show Pink and Master Wing to the room. She led them up several flights of steps to a door near the back of the building, unlocked it, and then practically fled after handing Master Wing the key. Pink watched her scamper back down the hallway, amused. *Jed must have told her who he was.* Inside, there were a few beds, a carpet sitting on the wooden floorboards, and a basin, but not much else. Master Wing walked up to the small square window and looked outside while Pink sat down on the edge of one of the beds.

"Not one of Holding's finest, perhaps," he said, "but I'm sure people of your age find common rooms an enjoyable experience, so maybe you won't have such a bad time."

"M … Master Wing?" Pink asked. He turned, causing his shadow, made by one of the wall's oil lamps, to stretch across the room. "Why are you here? Did you know we were searching for you?"

It was Master Wing's turn to look amused. "You didn't think four Wing mages could ask nearly every tavern in Holding about my whereabouts without it getting back to me, did you? Not while I was in the city myself." His look became serious. "I must be blunt, Sara. While it's fantastic to meet someone from Highstone Hill, and I *am* aware of your unique family situation, I have an awful lot of things to do tonight. I imagine the reason you came looking for me is important, so please let me know what it is. Is this regarding August?"

Pink shook her head, but the question did remind her of something else she wanted to know. "Instructor Texeria thinks you're here for Phantex Mason."

Master Wing bowed his head. "Keat Texeria was always an intelligent boy. I have returned to do what I can."

Pink's heart leapt. Perhaps this meant that August would not need to attempt a rescue mission after all.

Master Wing seemed uncomfortable then as if he could read Pink's thoughts. "It seems unlikely," he admitted, "that I can prevent this execution. Phantex attacked Magicom soldiers with magic. Many were severely injured. Magicom have deemed this proof he is part of Ashes and so an accomplice to every crime August's band have ever committed. Phantex has denied none of this. The government have, unfortunately, already signed his death warrant."

Despite her hopes being dashed, Pink didn't allow her disappointment to show nor interfere with the rest of what she had to say. She still had a directive from her mentor to follow. "We're here about a contract Keat Texeria brought to our attention," she said, and then proceeded to tell him everything – from Magicom's arrival at Wing to their discovery of the missing townsfolk to Gabriel's betrayal and death. Master Wing didn't outwardly react to much of the story, but his eyes narrowed when he heard what Gabriel had done, and by the time she was finished, he was back at the window, fingers rubbing his forehead.

"I'm sorry you all had to go through that, Sara," he

said, turning his head to look at her. He looked back out of the window. "I suppose I'm in need of a new assistant master."

"Is that all you can say?" Pink could not believe his tone – as if all they'd been through was a mild inconvenience. She was conscious he could throw her out of Wing with a word, but too much had happened for her to remain calm. "The experiments you and Gabriel started are directly responsible for people losing their lives!"

"And I take full responsibility for that." He looked very tired then, running a hand down his face and squeezing his eyes shut. "But can you not see the attraction, Sara? Two types of magic exist in this world – the four elements we're able to control and the various magical abilities of manabeasts. One needs arcannen potions to activate and years of training to properly master. The other is instinctive and, in the majority of cases, far more powerful. But what if everyone had access to magic, all the time, without arcannen? What if everyone had the means to protect themselves against manabeasts?"

"Magicm wouldn't exist, for one thing," said Pink.

Articulas Wing started to pace. "I don't think they'd agree. Otherwise, why go ahead with these hybrids, as you called them?" He shook his head. "But this isn't the way. They've gone too far this time. They cannot treat human lives with such disregard."

That last statement resounded with Pink enough for her to put her discontentment to one side. *For now.* "What should we do?" she asked.

He stopped pacing and looked at her then as if he had forgotten she was there. "I'm terribly sorry, Sara. I've got carried away. I will try to investigate further and bring Magicom's experiments to light – they cannot do things with impunity while there is a government around. I fear they will try to find a way to continue, though, and that is worrisome." He frowned. "In the meantime, you must return to Wing with your friends and help the instructors. With your knowledge, you'll be able to keep a lookout for anything like this closer to Highstone Hill. It would give me great comfort to know that while I'm not there, you are. You have all proved yourselves to be great assets to Wing."

Pink looked down. Despite Master Wing's complimentary words, she knew what this was. *A dismissal.*

"It is not safe for you here in Holding," said Articulas Wing, as if guessing her thoughts. "If Rox Salvamal learns of mages who know of Gabriel's research, he will make you disappear, and that is a danger if Miriam Shawgrave has returned to him. Now that Gabriel is no longer at Wing, you should be safe there with your fellow mages and instructors. Besides, you have the added danger of being August's sister, which must remain a secret now more than ever. That's why I'm speaking to you alone, away from your friends. First thing tomorrow morning, you need to return to Highstone Hill." Pink continued to remain silent. "You must trust me on this," he added, watching her closely.

"Very well," she said, deciding at once she would do nothing of the sort.

But that seemed good enough for Master Wing. He headed to the door and put his hand on the knob before turning once more. "Sara, I believe this all to be related – Gabriel, these experiments, Ashes. The reason Magicom have taken these steps is because of the threat August and his companions pose to them. If Ashes gain too much momentum, Magicom may have a large-scale uprising on their hands. That is why General Salvamal is doing all he can to get to August – including, I'm sure, infiltrating

Wing. Keep yourself safe; don't give him another route to your brother."

With a final nod, he turned the handle and left the room.

***

Now that Master Wing was actively doing something about Gabriel and Magicom's experiments, Pink could, if not entirely, forget about the matter – too much had happened for that – at least put it to one side and think about how she would get to Holding Square the following day. It was true that if Magicom found out she was August's sister, she would be at risk, but while she was under no illusions about how much help she could actually offer him, she would not leave the city while he was in danger. Of course, she didn't say any of this to the others as she returned to the common room. They had seen Master Wing leave, but he'd offered no more than a few words of farewell, so, excluding the parts that connected her to August, she passed on everything they'd spoken about.

"Why couldn't Master Wing have told this to all of us?" asked Sol almost as soon as she'd finished.

"He didn't say," replied Pink quickly. Sol frowned but said nothing and thankfully seemed to forget about it as their supper was brought over, which wasn't surprising considering they hadn't eaten since that morning. They wolfed down their food – the standard tavern affair of beef stew and seasoned vegetables – and, before long, were contentedly sipping mugs of cider as the common room became busier and noisier. It felt good, for once, not to be in any immediate danger, and as time went by, the others seemed to relax into their chairs a little more.

Pink struggled to do the same – knowing that she would be heading to Holding Square the following day prevented her from feeling at ease. Nevertheless, she tried to spend the evening conversing with them all, which was a good distraction, finding she spent the most time talking to Sol, discussing battle tactics and different magic uses. Eventually, Bale excused himself to retire for the night. *A good thing, too,* Pink thought. Out of them all, he needed the most rest. It made her think about retiring herself – if she went to bed now, she could get up early and leave before having to answer any unwanted questions. The thought had barely completed when Jase shuffled up next to her. Sol had gone to the counter to get another drink.

"You and Sol seem to be getting on well." There was something in the way he said those words that sent warning bells off in Pink's mind, a sort of inflexion that gave her the feeling more was being unsaid than said.

"He's been a good friend to us, despite our differences," replied Pink slowly. "Why do you bring it up, Jase?"

"Oh, I don't know. Just wondered if you've thought about the consequences of befriending a future Magicom soldier."

Pink did not care for the way this conversation was going. "I can tell you don't approve."

"Would August?" asked Jase slyly.

"Don't say his name," hissed Pink, glancing around the common room. Thankfully, no one was near enough to hear. "Not here, not now. Not with the danger he could be in tomorrow."

"I suppose you're going to be at Holding Square for the execution?"

It seemed he had worked it out after all. She watched him, trying to warn him against saying anything else with her eyes. It didn't work, of course – all it caused Jase to do was titter impatiently.

"And what did Master Wing think about that?"

"He doesn't want me to, of course, but I'm going anyway. I have to be there in case August needs me."

"Pink, we were almost killed outside those coal mines *and* at the dukesbane site! We've witnessed the results of experiments that would get us killed if Magicom found out how much we knew. How many more risks do we have to take?"

"*You* don't have to risk anything!" she said, her temper rising. "And do I need to remind you that you were the one who persuaded me to go to the coal mines in the first place? You and Sol. But I don't remember asking you to come with me tomorrow. Go back to Wing in the morning. The others will be."

"I'm sure Sol will go to Holding Square if you ask him," he sneered. "You obviously have a connection."

"What is your problem with Sol?"

"He's the enemy!"

"The enemy? Jase, do you hear what you're saying? We're all Wing mages!"

But Jase ignored this. "He might as well be in Magicom's forces already," he muttered.

Pink had had enough. There was obviously no getting through to Jase while he was in this mood, and she was fed up with him speaking like he knew better than her. "I think I'll go to bed," she said, standing up.

She was moving away and disappearing into the common room crowd before he could reply, pushing past people who got in her way. She'd only gone a few paces before she realised she was shaking. *How did that happen? Jase and I have never argued before.*

She made her way up the stairs until she found the

floor her room was on. Pink had kept the one that she and Master Wing had spoken in earlier, and the others had their own opposite. She dropped to the bed and exhaled deeply, trying to calm herself. Why was it that Jase thought he could judge her relationship with Sol? They were just friends, and even if they weren't, it was no business of Jase's. Was he jealous about the amount of time they were spending together? There were things she could talk about with Sol that she couldn't with Jase. Didn't he get that? At heart, she and Sol both took being mages seriously. Jase just didn't have the same mindset.

A knock at the door interrupted her thoughts. Thinking it was Jase coming to make peace, she jumped off the bed and opened it at once. She was surprised to find Sol standing there.

"Pink, what is it?" he asked her, concern mirrored in his eyes. "You disappeared without saying anything, and Jase was wearing such a sour expression I thought it best not to ask."

She shook her head. "It's nothing. Really."

"I've been worried about you," Sol said, a businesslike tone coming into his voice. "You looked as if you might faint earlier, and that was a nasty bump you took at the dukesbane site. I have a medical kit in my pack. Let me grab it – then I think we should redress the wound."

Pink rolled her eyes but grinned. "If you think that's necessary, Healer Draeon."

He grinned back and went to the other room to fetch what he needed. He returned quickly and took a position behind her on the bed, taking off the bandage carefully and wiping the wound with a cloth he'd wet in the basin.

"I never thought I'd meet anyone with pink hair," he said as he gently dabbed it. "Do you ever consider dyeing it another colour?"

"I believe in staying true to who I am. What about you?"

"Me?" He sounded surprised.

"Don't you ever fancy dyeing your hair pink?"

There was a pause and then a chuckle as she felt him applying the new bandage. "It's all done," he said, sounding satisfied.

"Those instructors and mages in the coal mines," Pink said once he was finished, "those townsfolk. Do you think we'll ever stop seeing them, Sol?"

He came to sit beside her, so close they were almost touching. "I think this is the life we've chosen," he said at last. She turned to him, raising her eyebrows. His eyes met her own, and there was a sadness in them. "No," he said quietly. "I don't think we'll ever forget."

She smiled at him. "I bet you're regretting ever taking part in Mayor Sharp's contract."

He shrugged. "I don't think I had a choice. Instructor May was very insistent. He's asked me many questions about it since. I've started to wonder if Gabriel put him up to it so he could try to keep an eye on what Instructor Texeria was up to."

"So you're a spy then," she said, giving him a playful shove.

He said nothing for a moment, then placed a hand on her thigh, leaned in and kissed her softly on the lips. Pink moved her head back for a moment, surprised. *What kind of answer is that?* Something in the back of her mind screamed that this was a mistake, that nothing could ever happen with Sol – not while August was her brother and Sol had ambitions of joining Magicom. But some part of her realised she'd wanted this. Then he was kissing her again, and all resistance fled from her mind.

CHAPTER TWENTY-FIVE

We're fortunate to have Rush, August thought as she and Sapphire brushed the fallen leaves away from the forest floor, revealing the wooden trapdoor below. Without her, they would have had to find some other way to sneak into Holding, and the chances of doing that, with every Magicom soldier in the city on the lookout for him, would have been considerably lower.

Through the gaps in the densely populated forest, they could now see the walls of the city and even the turrets of its castle, complete with newly erected Magicom blimps. It seemed Salvamal had been keen to get them airborne again. Not that it mattered to August – that message had already been sent. Holding was only a couple of miles away, and as long as the tunnel was fairly direct, they would be inside the walls within the hour.

"You sure this is still safe?" asked Taurus, to one side with the horses, arms crossed.

"No," replied Rush, swivelling her head to look at him. "But we're going to go anyway, aren't we, big man?"

Taurus' reply was a grunt, and August distinctly thought he heard a mumble along the lines of 'being buried alive.' He tried not to smile as he joined his friend.

"We'll have to untie the horses and let them roam," August said. "It would be convenient if we returned to this spot later with Phantex in tow, but I don't think we can rely on that. If we don't return, it would be cruel to leave the animals tied up."

Another grunt.

"Take only what you need," said August as Rush and Sapphire came over. They moved to their respective mounts and untied their packs from the saddles. August deposited most of the food they'd taken from his uncle's house on the ground but kept a few packets of dried fruit and his waterskin inside his cloak, along with several vials of arcannen. They were going to be clunky, but he had no doubt they'd be distributed before the day was out. The folded bits of square paper sat in his pocket as well, vital as they were to his plan. Once they were ready, they released the horses and moved to the trapdoor, Taurus and Rush heaving it open between them.

"To think of all the things that have been smuggled into this city." Rush grinned as the four of them looked into the depths below. All they could see was a metal ladder disappearing into the earth. "And now we're trying to smuggle a person out."

"The sooner we do it, the better," replied August grimly, the usual excitement he felt going against Magicom offset by fear for his friend's life. He wouldn't let Phantex die. Salvamal thought he had the upper hand, but he wouldn't expect the surprise August had in store for him.

August led their descent down the ladder and into the darkness below.

***

Pink woke tangled in Sol's arms. She took a moment to steel herself, reluctant to give up the heat and comfort of having him so close. *I'm sorry, Sol, but this is something I need to do on my own.* Very carefully, she untangled herself and slipped from the bed, putting on her uniform before creeping from the room. Outside, she created a quick flame in the palm of her hand, making certain her magic was still operational. She'd taken her last arcannen potion almost twenty-four hours previously, so she wouldn't have much more than a couple of hours of magic left. She'd just extinguished it when the door opposite opened, and Bale stepped out, still looking out of place in his cotton infirmary clothing.

His movements slowed as he caught sight of her before he nodded in understanding. "It seems we're both trying to sneak out."

Pink didn't think he was referencing the fact that Sol was still in her room but blushed anyway. *Or maybe he did. He must've realised that Sol never returned to their room last night.* "The execution is at midday," she told him, hoping he hadn't noticed, "but if Jed's right and lots of people have come to witness the hanging, I want to make sure I'm as near as I can be."

He looked at her closely. "Pink, are you sure this is wise? I can see why you're planning to do this on your own, but how much difference can you actually make? Wouldn't it be better to return to Highstone Hill, like Master Wing suggested?"

"If August ends up in Magicom's hands, this may be the last time I ever see my brother. I would never forgive myself if I didn't do everything I could to help."

Bale nodded, and she knew he wouldn't try to convince her any further. *I do like that about him – neither Jase nor Sol would have been so accepting.* It was her turn to look at him closely now. He had dark circles under his eyes, and his complexion was still more pallid than usual, but he looked better than the previous day. *At any rate, he no longer looks as if he might collapse at any moment.*

"See you back at Wing," she said, with a smile more confident than she felt. Bale gave her a look that suggested he wasn't sure how likely that was before turning on his heel and making his way down the hallway. She waited until he was gone and made to follow before realising the door was still slightly ajar. She felt a quick moment of panic, but when she peered back into the room, Sol's sleeping form hadn't moved, which meant their conversation hadn't woken him. She closed the door softly. *Thank the Trinity for that – whatever last night was, Sol can't find out about my connection to Ashes.*

Back in the common room, she found Jed taking chairs off tables. "Hey, could you do me a favour?" she asked him. He took his time meeting her gaze. "When the two upstairs come down looking for me, could you tell them … tell them that I had something to do, and I'll meet them back at Highstone Hill?"

Jed looked at her incredulously. "Now I'm your messenger?"

"It's an important message," she said, and then, thinking quickly, added, "It involves Master Wing. He wouldn't be happy if they didn't receive it."

Jed paled. "Fine," he said, turning his back on her and getting back to work. She allowed herself an amused half-smile.

They had done a considerable amount of walking in Holding the previous day, and many landmarks were signposted, so Pink had a general idea of where she was going. The majority of the city was still sleeping, so she saw very few people walking or riding the cobblestoned streets as she headed in the direction of the square. When she was a good mile or so away from the Station, she passed by a vendor and bought a beef sandwich for her breakfast, washing it down with a mug of tea. It was chilly, but the warm food made her feel better inside. *And who knows when I'll next eat?*

As her feet wandered, so did her mind. She was trying to stay focused on scenarios for later, but the kiss with Sol dominated her thoughts. *Kisses,* she thought, *there were more than one.* She felt bad about the fact that he would wake to find her gone and worried he would think she cared little for him – too little to even tell him what she was doing, despite the message he would get from Jed. And there was Jase too. She'd never had the chance to make up with him.

I can do that when I'm back at Wing, she thought resolutely, *and deal with what happened with Sol … somehow.* Eventually, she reached a street with an open iron gate at its end, in between stone walls about five feet high. Built into one of them was a golden plaque that read 'Holding Square'. Already, on the quadrilateral field that gave the square its name, she could see and hear the beginnings of a crowd.

Before she entered, she had a sudden feeling that someone was behind her, watching. She turned, but the street was empty. Inwardly shrugging, she turned back to face the square, focusing her mind. *It's almost time – please, August, don't do anything stupid.*

You're one to talk, a treacherous part of her mind whispered back.

***

Crowds were increasing in the area around the east gate of Holding. The dozen or so Magicom soldiers posted there were watching everyone arrive under the stone archway, stating their business to a gatekeeper who sat behind a rectangular gap built into the wall.

One of these people, a careworn middle-aged man with a black hat and bearded face, seemed to take everything in, from the carts and wagons populating the open space near the gate to the surrounding taverns and cafes already starting to fill with customers, evident through their street-side windows. He was sitting on his own wagon, a collection of wooden kegs tied securely in the back with his reins in hand.

Roeden was sitting next to him.

"There's trouble in the city today, lad. You sure this is the best time to be looking for work?"

Roeden saw concern in the eyes of the wagon driver. He wasn't sure why a stranger would feel that way, but the look reminded him of something he was unable to put into words. He thought suddenly, inexplicably, of his father, dead now for many years. How different would their lives have been if he was still around? *Phantex would still be fighting Magicom, I'm sure of it.*

"I have no choice," replied Roeden, having to yell a little. It was noisy, from the creaking of the wagon's wheels to the plethora of voices inside the city. He had fed the trader a story – Roeden was a boy looking for work as a chimney sweep. His mother had once told him that young boys and girls often made extra money for their families by cleaning chimneys, so it seemed the most believable reason for someone his age to be travelling the wilderness alone and one that might win him some sympathy on the road. He had not been disappointed. The trader had been one of the first to come by him and, as they were both heading on the western road to Holding, had offered him a lift to the city. *A good thing, too. I wouldn't have made it to Holding in time otherwise.* It had also given him a chance to get some distance from August's uncle after giving him the slip that morning.

"You could always help me shift this ale," said the tradesman, inclining his head to the back of the wagon. "I have a large order today – it seems the inns and taverns are expecting to do well. Having a young lad to help me with the distribution would earn him a few coins. That way, I can take you back to your village before it gets dark."

"I need work for more than one day," replied Roeden quickly, thinking that sounded like the best excuse. "Shall I get off here?"

The tradesman reined in and glanced around. "As you wish, son." He looked at Roeden with a serious expression. "Now, just promise you won't go wandering the wilderness at night. You're a fine lad to be helping out your family and all, but I'm sure they would want you alive and well more than they would want the coin, no matter how difficult things are. They wouldn't want to find you lying on the road somewhere with your throat ripped out."

"I promise," said Roeden, climbing off the cart. He looked up at the man. "And thank you."

The man reached into his jacket and flipped a bronze wyrm at Roeden, who caught it, surprised. "That should at least get you some food. If you change your mind and need a ride back, I'll be passing back this way a couple of hours before sundown." With a final nod, he shook his reins, and his wagon moved into a stream of others ahead. Roeden watched him go, feeling touched despite himself. He again thought of his family, of Phantex and his mother and Axe, and for the first time, he was truly desperate for them to all be together again. *For that to happen, I need to save Phantex. August isn't the only one with plans …*

The first chance he got, he asked someone for directions to Alsing.

***

"Dele," acknowledged August, clasping the hand of the man who'd just entered the underground room of the Flame, Ashes' Holding hideout. The Flame was located in the Walks, a series of zigzag streets to the south of the city centre. Its hub of eccentric taverns, cafes and shops – not to mention people – made it easier for those who looked a bit different to blend in.

Dele was one such man. His hair was barely concealed by a scruffy-looking woolly hat, and he had a face that reminded August a little of a weasel, complete with a scar running from eyebrow to cheek. He didn't look like somebody you wanted to meet alone at night.

"Silvershield," Dele returned with a slight incline of his head.

This man was not a friend – not like Taurus, Phantex, Rush and Sapphire were. He was more a comrade-in-arms and a useful one at that. There were many in Holding who despised Magicom, and Dele happened to know most of them. What was more, he knew the ones who could be called into action, as proven by the support he'd drummed up for the attack on Holding Castle. Many of these people now probably considered themselves members of Ashes, and August was fine with that, especially since he could use them to help free Phantex, but he wasn't foolish enough to let his location be known to anyone other than those currently in the room. If too many people knew how to find him, Magicom would be able to do the same.

That was where Dele came in.

"I was expecting to hear from you," said Dele, "after I

first saw the poster announcing Phantex's execution. How they believe they have the right to judge a man such as he is pure arrogance, and I know many who are ready to make them burn for it." As if to exemplify his point, he conjured a fireball in his palm.

"Careful now," said Dhanos Rain from one of the several round wooden tables at the back of the room. A middle-aged man with a similar build and look to Taurus, although with less ink and beard, and a darker complexion, he wore a sour expression lit up by the table's candlelight. Taurus, arms crossed and wearing a similar look, sat with him while Rush and Sapphire were at the next table over. "Just because I've called my establishment the Flame doesn't mean I want it going up in them."

"Apologies, Dhanos," said Dele. "Not much has happened since Holding Castle. It's frustrating, you know? We made a difference that night, and I thought Ashes would gather momentum. But things went quiet for a while." He turned to August. "I didn't know where you were or what you were doing."

"I was around," said August, "but I had to be careful. I'm a wanted man now."

Dele snorted. "That's half the fun, isn't it? Come, enough talk – they say you always have a plan, and I've been dying to know how you intend to free Phantex with every Magicom soldier in the city watching."

August grinned. He needed people like Dele in the war against Magicom. There were other, more reliable members of Ashes, like Cyrus Grey and Andros Bellion, but they didn't live in the city, and it was too short notice to bring anyone else in. Phantex was captured, Chadwick was gone. That left himself, Rush, Sapphire, Taurus, Dhanos, Dele, and whoever Dele could muster up. It would have to be enough. With that thought in mind, he told Dele his plan.

***

It took Roeden most of the morning to find Alsing. His plan had been to ask directions from passers-by, but most seemed wary of helping him. It was as if they thought his questions were some sort of trick. Roeden was nothing if not persistent though, and in the end, he managed to gather enough information to find out where the complex was situated.

Roeden found it as it began to drizzle, on a street corner with an iron gate set within its high stone walls, a golden plaque on one side naming the building. Beyond, there appeared to be a courtyard of some sort, but Roeden would have to get through the gate before he could see anything else. A quick scan of the area revealed Magicom soldiers standing atop a platform on the wall above the gate. They were deep in conversation and weren't watching the street below.

Roeden crossed the street and waited against the brick wall of a house on the other side, not wanting to be caught staring at the structure. He thought about what to do next. He would have to get in through the gate somehow, but how could he do that unless he called to the soldiers above? And, once he got their attention, what reason could he give for wanting to come inside? *Think, Roeden. If you're going to beat August to freeing Phantex, you've got to think like he does. Better, in fact.* He would have to use what was in the square paper, of course, but even if he did, how was he going to get in through the gate? Still reasoning through this, he almost missed a couple of soldiers marching along the street – that was until they called to those above.

It was now or never. He unravelled the piece of paper that held the black powder and, after a quick look to confirm the residential street was empty, began to apply it – just as the hinges of the gate creaked open. He smudged the grainy substance onto his forehead, face and chest, watching parts of his body below disappear. He quickly worked his way down to his feet, back up to the top of his head, around to his back and his heels, and within moments he'd become a shimmering but transparent figure. He was beyond the amazement he'd first experienced when he had rubbed some on his fingers in the wilderness and watched them disappear – he regretted how much he'd wasted working out that if he applied it on various parts of his body, the invisibility would connect, like the dot-to-dot activities he used to do when he was younger, but at least it had helped him estimate how long the transparency would last. *This would have worked better at night, but Phantex doesn't have until night.* Taking a deep breath, he made his way quickly to the open gate, following the two soldiers inside.

The gate was closing just as he made it into the courtyard. He put his back to the wall on the inner side, his satisfaction fading as he saw what was ahead. Row upon row of grey-uniformed soldiers stood in the centre of the courtyard, at least four dozen strong, as if they were about to march into battle. *Thank the Trinity I'm almost completely invisible!* He chewed his lip thoughtfully. *They must be preparing for Holding Square.*

Ahead and behind the soldiers, he could now see the brick walls of the prison, with a sturdy-looking metal door at its centre and a guard in front of it. Barred windows rose all the way up to the slanted roof and spread across the rectangular building. The complex entrance was perhaps two hundred yards from the gate, and the two new arrivals were walking in that direction between the rows of soldiers.

Roeden pushed himself off the wall, deciding his best chance of not getting caught was to go around the rows of soldiers, away from their line of sight. He darted across the courtyard and towards where the wall rose to his left, trying to make as little noise as possible before continuing on alongside it. He returned to the centre of the courtyard when he was behind the units, timing his run so he could get to the entrance just after the two soldiers he was following.

Then one of them paused and started to turn.

Roeden ducked. It was the only thing he could think to do. If the soldier had been looking directly at him, he would have noticed the shimmering, and even if he hadn't seen Roeden, he would've known someone or something was there. But by leaving his line of sight, Roeden was able to get ahead of the two soldiers while in a crouch and through the door they had just opened, finding himself in a tiny anteroom with a desk where he managed to hide in a little alcove to one side. He placed a hand over his mouth and prayed they wouldn't hear him breathe while his heart hammered in his chest.

"Something wrong?" one of the soldiers asked as they followed him inside.

"I thought I heard something, but … it's nothing."

"Ahh … are you gentlemen here for the Ashes man?"

The voice that spoke this time belonged to an elderly gentleman who was sitting behind the desk, scribbling something with a steel nib. Roeden could see now that the anteroom connected to two corridors. One had a line of yellow painted on its wall, the other green. What these meant, Roeden hadn't a clue.

"Yes, Warden. We're here to sedate and escort him to

Holding Square."

Roeden didn't know what 'sedate' meant but knew he had to get ahead of these soldiers. But how would he know where Phantex was if he went on ahead?

Then Roeden saw – to his horror – parts of him reappearing. If he looked down, he could now see bits and pieces of his chest and legs. Soon he would be visible to anyone looking his way! *I thought it would last longer than this.* Then he realised. *The rain!* He glanced up – the soldiers were making their way along the corridor with the yellow line, and the warden had gone back to his scribing.

There was nothing for it. Roeden crept out of the alcove and towards the same corridor as the two men, heart thumping in his chest. With every step, he expected to hear an exclamation from the warden. But luck was on his side – the elderly gentleman had obviously not looked back up. *A good thing, too,* Roeden thought as he looked down at his hands. The black powder had entirely run its course.

Roeden knew that all the soldiers had to do was look behind to spot him, despite how dimly the oil lamps lit the corridor, so he kept his distance as he followed, relying on the sound of their voices and the yellow line on its side to guide his way until eventually, they arrived at a concrete staircase descending below.

He waited a moment and then followed the men down, finding himself in another corridor with a draught and a musty smell, dominated by cells built into either side of the stone walls and separated by metal bars. Torches lit the way ahead, and as he moved forward, Roeden could see the majority of cells were empty, although he did pass one with a man who watched Roeden with haunted eyes. Much to Roeden's relief, the man remained silent. Roeden hadn't heard the soldiers for a few moments, but now their voices sounded again, muffled but clearly inside one of the cells ahead, its metal door swung open into the corridor. There were concrete pillars between each cell, and Roeden stopped against one of these, feeling the cold surface against his back as he tilted his head forward to listen.

"That should do it," said one. "Let's grab our lunch, then return for the prisoner. The general's not requiring him just yet."

Roeden scrambled inside a nearby open cell, making himself as small as he could in a darkened corner where the torchlight didn't quite reach. He heard the sound of a cell door being closed and then locked before the soldiers' footsteps travelled through the corridor and back up the steps. As soon as Roeden could no longer hear any sound of their movement, he took himself to the next cell.

Phantex was inside. He was unconscious, lying on the ground, but Roeden could see from the rise and fall of his chest he was breathing. The sudden joy at seeing his brother was quickly negated by the dried blood and bruises he saw on his face. Roeden gripped the cold steel of the bars so hard that his palms turned red. *They'll pay for this!*

His anger fueling his courage, Roeden took the container of arcannen from his pocket and examined the black liquid inside. *I'm going to need magic to free Phantex,* he thought, trying to calm himself. They both would – Roeden wasn't afraid of a fight, but Phantex was the mage, and if it came to it, they would need his experience. Roeden would drink half and save the other for his brother. He uncorked the top and drank the right amount carefully.

Ugh, that's disgusting!

Instantly, he sensed the world around him like never

before. He could feel the moisture in the building, and the earth underneath the ground, almost as if he was touching them. He could feel something else in the room, something he knew he could spark with a flick of his hand. And the air. It was everywhere. All he had to do was reach out and take it. It was overwhelming. He could feel these abilities like cords, each as different as the lines that had coloured the prison's corridors.

It feels so … amazing!

On any other day, at any other time, he would have stayed there for longer and marvelled at this new sensation. But he needed to free his brother, and that took precedence. He looked at the cell door. It was locked. He thought about blasting it with fire but at once set that aside. He didn't want to burn Phantex alive. He would blast the door with wind magic, he decided, and see if that took it off the hinges. He held his right arm out, pointing his palm towards the door.

It was easier to draw the air from around him than he imagined. It was almost as if his palm was simultaneously pulling and repelling it until it became a swirling ball of air, visible through the dirt it brought. After a few moments, Roeden decided he'd drawn enough but then realised he didn't know how to stop the process. A sudden feeling of panic rose in him, and he could think of nothing else to do but push the air forward. The air shot from him, but the force pushed him backwards, causing the majority of the magic to shoot from his flailing hand and strike the ceiling.

Fragments of stone exploded downward, showering him. The noise echoed through the corridor. Roeden lay there, dazed. Then he heard shouts coming from the distance. He made his way to his feet, frantically drawing the air again and aiming it at the door, but again the force was too much, and although he didn't fall onto his back this time, he was pushed against the wall behind as the magic shot sideways, making ripples in the air. *I need to draw more! Those soldiers are on their way. I need to defend myself!*

He'd barely completed the thought when the soldiers appeared at the end of the corridor and spotted him.

For the first time, Roeden wondered if he'd made a mistake.

CHAPTER TWENTY-SIX

This is it, thought Rox Salvamal, observing the masses congregating before him.

This is finally it. The culmination of my efforts. The final act that will draw Silvershield out into the open. He can't allow his man to die here, in front of all these people, knowing he did nothing to prevent it. Salvamal looked to one side of the wooden platform that had been set up, where Commander Maynard and his unit stood, their masked faces drawing no shortage of curious glances from the crowd. *Whatever Ashes attempt, they won't be ready for them.*

Holding Square was buzzing with noise, its grassy ground filling with people, the steady drizzle unlikely to prevent a full capacity. Salvamal spotted Linus Atkins standing to one side among a delegation of government officials, their heads bent together in discussion. His eyes travelled over the rest of the crowd, lingering on those he could see wearing syntaxicite, wondering if any were members of Ashes. He didn't dwell on it for long. Silvershield was the only one he really wanted, and even *he* wasn't foolish enough to be waiting in plain sight.

The syntaxicite did make him think of someone else, though. The Master of Wing: Articulas Wing. To think the man had had the gall to try to prevent Phantex Mason's execution. Not that it mattered – his attempts at drumming up support had largely been unsuccessful. But one thing did bother Salvamal – how had Articulas Wing known about the hybrids? Had someone from Wing found out what they were about and passed it on to the Master? Or was Miriam Shawgrave responsible? Word had come back to him about the bodies found at the dukesbane site, but hers hadn't been among them. He shook his head. It mattered little. The experiments were over – soon, men and women from the army would be volunteering to take part in the program.

It had been a shame about Gabriel. His knowledge would've been a huge asset, but they'd found his body with the others, decimated with manabeast wounds, which was itself a mystery. How had a manabeast got into the building in the first place? The main door had shown signs of being blasted with magic, but the one leading into the basement, apparently, had not.

"Excuse me, General?" Salvamal was distracted from his musings by a plain, skinny-looking man holding a small pad of paper in one hand and a pencil in the other. He arched his eyebrows. "I'm Chadwick Chase from *Severity News* – I was told you wanted a reporter present?"

Ah, yes, for the masses. "All I want you to do is your job – that is, write and publish everything that happens here today," Salvamal said, ordering the man like one of his soldiers. "*Severity News* will need to make the consequences of stealing from Magicom clear."

There was uncertainty in the reporter's eyes. "And these soldiers, General? Why are they wearing masks? Why are their eyes … that colour?"

"I will talk about that at another time," said Salvamal, already distracted by the excited murmur beginning to rise from the crowd, where some were pointing at something behind him. He turned to find the steam vans arriving, being driven into the square from one of the many entrances via an area cordoned off with rope, smoke chugging from their funnels. Salvamal didn't think Ashes would be foolish enough to try to break into Alsing, but the route to Holding Square was another matter. He had therefore provided the armoured vehicles and soldiers to ensure that Phantex Mason, who was being carried from one of the now-stationary vehicles, would arrive at his execution as planned. Sedating Mason had been another of his ideas – any rescue attempt en route would be made considerably harder by an unresponsive rescuee.

Mason was coming round by the time he was brought to the platform, a glazed look in his eyes as he took in everything in front of him. There had been a hush on his arrival, but as he was chained to a wooden pole, and made to stand on his own two feet, some of the crowd started jeering and throwing insults. Unsmiling, Salvamal moved away from the reporter and dipped his head close to Mason's.

"Ready for your big day?"

Phantex Mason looked up, hatred etched into the lines of his face. "Go to damnation," he managed.

Salvamal smiled but was distracted from saying anything else by the arrival of Rael Rookevelt, who signalled him to move away from Mason's earshot. "What is it, Lieutenant?"

Rookevelt's look was grim. "Someone tried to free him from Alsing."

That did surprise Salvamal. "Ashes?"

"No – at least we don't think so. A boy. On his own. We believe it was his brother, the one who went missing. They have the same look. But the thing is this, General …" Rookevelt got in close, so nobody else could hear, especially the reporter, who seemed to be watching them with interest. "The boy managed to get all the way to Mason's cell before he was apprehended. We have no idea how he wasn't spotted going in – the grounds were filled with our soldiers. He's rather a small lad, but it seems impossible that nobody would've seen him."

"Well, obviously they didn't," responded Salvamal, dismissing Rookevelt's anxiety. He didn't know what the lieutenant was getting at; it was clear to him that the Alsing guards had been lax in their duties. He would see them punished later. "Having the younger brother means we have another bargaining tool to use against Ashes," he continued, more to himself than Rookevelt. "But once I have Silvershield, we'll let him go. He's too young to hang."

"I don't like it," said Rookevelt, surveying the crowd. "They use strange tactics, these Ashes members – they're hard to predict. It makes you wonder what they'll do next."

Oh, that's where you're wrong, Lieutenant, thought Salvamal as Rookevelt and the reporter took their places towards the back of the stage, as far away from the hybrids as they could, although Rookevelt watched them, frowning. *Silvershield is easy to predict. If he wasn't, there would be no need for this spectacle.* Salvamal once again cast his eyes over the rabble, which now overflowed the square and spilt onto the streets that ran around it. There were even people watching from the windows and balconies of their overlooking houses. Most of Holding and a great deal of Blake seemed to be in attendance.

Where are you hiding, Silvershield?

"Ladies and gentlemen," he boomed with a raise of his hand, feeling the satisfaction of the hush that followed. "You should all by now be aware of today's purpose. The man who stands behind me, Phantex Mason, has aided and abetted the group known as Ashes in the theft of arcannen and resisted arrest by trying to fatally wound my soldiers. Magicom, who are humble servants of the government—"

"WRONG!"

Salvamal turned, disbelievingly, to where Phantex Mason was tied, his head against the pole, but his chin lifted.

"The government pander to Magicom," Phantex shouted, his voice hoarse. "They should be ashamed of letting you do whatever you like. But don't forget to list Magicom's ventures as well as my own, General. The hoarding of arcannen and using it as a means to control Blake. The corruption, kidnappings, assaults and worse. And you dare speak of crimes to me?"

"The usual rhetoric of Ashes," responded Salvamal, turning back to the crowd. Some were jeering at these words, but others – it was impossible to see whom – were shouting in agreement. He'd let Mason speak, as his hanging would only serve to show what happened to these people. *No doubt he's been preparing for this in his cell.* "Lies spun by August Silvershield …"

"MY FATHER WAS KILLED IN ONE OF YOUR MINES!" shouted Mason suddenly. "KILLED MINING YOUR PRECIOUS ARCANNEN!"

The shouting and jeering from the crowd were rising. Salvamal could see his soldiers breaking up scuffles towards the back. He was losing control – there was only one thing that would bring back the crowd's undivided attention.

"Be ready," he called to Maynard, who nodded to show he understood. Salvamal frowned. Was there an excited glint in those eyes? Dismissing the thought, Salvamal moved back to where the prisoner stood.

"I believe those count as your final words," he said to Mason. The look he received back was devoid of any fear, only pure loathing. Salvamal felt a grudging respect. Most people in this situation would be pleading for their lives by now. He inclined his head at the two soldiers who'd brought Mason onto the platform. They untied him and led him to the front of the gallows, over a trapdoor, before placing the noose over his head and around his neck. The crowd quieted. They had finally realised, it seemed, what was about to happen. But where was Silvershield?

Then two things happened at once. The rope attached to the noose split in two as if it had been cut clean through, and the soldiers who had attached it were blown back with such force they were flung over the back of the wooden structure.

Salvamal readied his own wind magic, snarling and looking around. *Where are you, Silvershield? I've got you now; there are too many of us for you to escape.* Many of those inside Holding Square were showing signs of panic, shouting and crying out as they, like Salvamal and his soldiers, tried to work out where the magic was coming from. There seemed to be more skirmishes within the crowd itself, causing further confusion. Then wind magic struck the platform from seemingly everywhere at once – most of it directed at the hybrids. There was an explosion of noise as splintered wood showered the air. Salvamal, Rookevelt and the reporter created air shields, but the hybrids were either unable or unwilling to create their own, and a few of them went down.

The others turned to the crowd, their expressions impossible to see behind the masks, but their intent unmistakable as they moved forward as one and pushed out their arms.

"Wait, stop!" yelled Salvamal as he realised what they

were about to do. But it was too late. They shot energy beams, striking all those ahead of them – civilians, government officials, even Salvamal's own soldiers who'd gone into the masses to try to find out what was happening. Screams filled the air amidst the smoke and smell of burning. People fled in all directions.

Some in the crowd tried to fight back with their own magic. A few of the advancing masked soldiers went down, but not many stayed there. The hybrids shot beam after beam at anyone ahead of them as they advanced into the panicked crowd, ignoring Salvamal's continued commands to fall back. Salvamal saw, to his horror, one of the government officials struck, his body smoking as it hit the ground.

By now, there was so much smoke and dust it was becoming hard to even see the crowd. Salvamal was so transfixed on trying to rein in the hybrids that he almost missed the shimmer of a figure moving onto the stage. He glanced back to see it helping Mason to his feet, trying to move him off the platform.

Something from earlier played in Salvamal's mind. *How did that boy sneak into Alsing without being seen?* "Ashes are here!" he yelled, shouting at Rookevelt and the unmasked soldiers nearer to him. "They're invisible somehow – stop them!"

He roared with irritation at the perplexed looks he received. Drawing his sword and creating a fireball, he spun and shot it at Mason's would-be rescuer. The figure, who was now becoming visible enough to show the black beard and inked arms of a large man, looked round in surprise just as the fireball deflected away from him, exploding behind the platform.

"What!" Salvamal spun to the source of the intercepting wind magic. When he saw where it'd come from, he breathed out the name, almost like a curse itself. "*Silvershield.*"

The leader of Ashes was calmly making his way onto the platform, becoming more solid himself with each step, the black syntaxicite he wore a harsh parody of Magicom's grey. "What have you done, Salvamal?" he asked without preamble, disgust etched on his features. "What are they?"

Salvamal didn't need to ask who Silvershield was talking about, but the look on his enemy's face made him hate the man more than he'd thought possible. "They are the result of your actions," he replied, drawing another fireball into his hand. "They are the future of Magicom."

He shot his hand forward, but Silvershield was quicker, sending him backwards with a burst of air that crashed him into the pole and sent the sword flying from his hand. He looked up, dazed and in pain, to see amongst the smoke, burning and carnage the figure of August Silvershield.

And then the man he hated was gone.

***

Because she'd been to the side of the platform, away from the main bulk of the crowd, Pink hadn't needed to flee from the masked soldiers attacking everyone in their path. As soon as she'd seen the energy beams, she'd known what they were, and Gabriel's words from the dukesbane site had flooded back to her as she'd watched in horror. *Docile enough to follow orders … even if he was wrong about that docile part, this is what he meant!* Many tried to escape in her direction, meaning by the time she saw Dwight Taurus appear, it was more by accident than design, as she'd been clinging to the foundations of the platform to prevent herself from being cast adrift in a sea of charging bodies.

She saw August arrive himself, confront Rox Salvamal, and then merge into the smoke and crowd.

"August!" she cried, thinking he'd never hear her over the noise.

But he did. He turned around sharply, spotted her and sped to where she was, pushing past the bodies in order to get there.

When he reached her, he pulled her down at the side of the platform so they could not be seen. "Sara, what are you doing here?" he hissed, glancing around as he spoke.

"August, listen to me," she said quickly. "Those soldiers, the ones with the masks, they're experiments of Salvamal's and Assistant Master Gabriel's. They've been given manabeast blood."

August shot her a disbelieving look. When he could see she was serious, that shock turned to disgust. "I thought the magic was manabeast," he said, "but it seemed too … unreal." He shook his head.

"Pink!"

Pink swivelled her head to see, to her amazement, Jase and Bale running towards her from the area behind the stage.

"Pink, you're safe! That's great! We were so worried," said Jase as he and Bale knelt down with her and August. Although she was looking away from her brother, she could feel him tense. Jase didn't seem to notice. "I'm sorry about the … you know … words we had."

"I am too," she responded, hugging him. She hugged Bale as well, which he returned awkwardly. *What is he doing here? I thought he'd already left.*

"We don't have time for this," said August, bringing her attention back. He looked keenly at her. "Sara – do you trust your friends?"

"Yes … August, they already know who you are. If

they were going to turn you in, they would have done so already." *That question would have been harder if Sol had been here. Where is he, anyway?*

"In that case, take them to a place called the Flame in the Walks," replied August. "We can talk there. I have a feeling being in the city will soon be unsafe, but there's an underground passage from its cellar you can take to get out of it."

"What about you?"

He grinned as he pulled out a small square packet from his pocket. "Don't worry – I always have a plan." He emptied its contents – which Pink recognised at once – into the palm of his hand and proceeded to rub it on his face, neck and arms. As the smudges began to connect, August himself faded until he was a vague, transparent outline of a person.

"Keat Texeria," she whispered.

"Once this is all over, he and I will be having words." August's voice came from the shape where he had been. "Now get out of here. I'll meet you at the Flame."

He stood up, and his shimmering figure vanished into the crowd.

CHAPTER TWENTY-SEVEN

"You need to leave the city," said August.

Pink faced down her brother in the underground room of the Flame, Jase and Bale at her side. The room was like a distorted version of the main tavern upstairs, but with the illumination of candlelight instead of oil lamps. Kegs of beer, shelves of wine bottles and couches lined the walls, which were made from red brick that looked like it would crumble at the slightest touch. With the wooden trapdoor that sat in one corner of the room, leading to the tunnel out of the city, Pink understood why it was an ideal hideout. Dwight Taurus, whom Pink had met on a couple of occasions, stood behind August with his considerably large arms crossed while Dhanos Rain, a man almost as large, introduced by August as the tavern's proprietor, watched anxiously on from the side. The only other person in the room was Phantex Mason, who lay on one of the couches, covered in blankets and apparently asleep.

"I'm going with you," she replied.

August huffed. "We don't have time for this. The others are out there, mobilizing the people against Magicom. Those hybrids were just the catalyst we needed. I *need* to be with them. I can't do that and worry about you at the same time."

"And what about my fears?" said Pink, getting angry

now. "Am I supposed to leave when you're putting yourself at such risk? If Magicom arrest you, this could be the last time we ever see each other. Besides, I'm a qualified mage. The others are free to take your tunnels, but I'm staying."

"I'm sticking with you, Pink," said Jase from her side in a shaky voice.

"Me too," said Bale.

August's dark eyes flashed. Jase wilted at her side, but she held August's gaze. "Don't look at me like that, August. It won't work. We're not going anywhere."

Taurus placed his hand on August's shoulder. Despite the severity of the situation, something seemed to twitch beneath his beard. "This is doing us no good," he said in his deep voice. "We need to be out there, and Sara's not going to back down." He came forward, looking at her now. "How about this for a compromise? Sara, going out into the city isn't a good idea. Even if you changed your clothing, you're still a Wing mage, and if you were caught fighting Magicom, you could cause massive problems for Highstone Hill. There are already rumours Salvamal wants to take over Wing. Stay here until things run their course. We'll be coming and going, so you'll know what's going on."

Pink's initial reaction was to protest, but Taurus' words rang too true. She sat down and crossed her arms. "Fine. But I'm not leaving the city until you do, August. So when you're ready, we can take the tunnels together."

August threw up his hands, but when he looked back, his features had softened. He pulled something from his cloak and offered it to her. In his palm sat a bit of paper folded into a square. "It's the last of the black powder," he said as she took it, "but I don't think it's going to be particularly useful to me today. The crowds will do a better job of keeping me hidden. No one who knows about this location will give it up, but in an emergency, I'd feel better knowing you had it."

He turned to leave. "August," she said. He turned back. "Try to make sure no one innocent gets hurt."

He looked surprised but gave her a nod before he and Taurus ascended the stairwell while she put the paper somewhere safe within her syntaxicite.

"Are you sure you both want to stay?" she said as Jase and Bale joined her at one of the tables. "I know there's no getting rid of you, Jase. But, Bale, didn't you already leave?"

Bale looked like he'd hoped that particular topic wouldn't come up. "Ah … yes, well, I thought out of, you know, friendship's sake, I should come back."

"We're friends now?" pushed Pink. "Not just Wing comrades?"

"You came for me in the mines, you and Jase and Sol. I won't forget it."

She was lost for words, so she contented herself by smiling at him. He gave her a small one back.

"Speaking of Sol," said Pink, fighting to keep her voice neutral, "where is he?"

Bale shrugged, looking relieved at the change of conversation. "I didn't see him when I returned to the inn." He gave Jase a questioning look.

"I was in the common room when Bale came in," said Jase. "Bale told me he knew about August and that we should follow you. I didn't think it a good idea to get Sol from your room. I assume he still doesn't know about August?"

"He doesn't know," said Pink, blushing at Jase's use of 'your room' and feeling a sinking feeling in the pit of her stomach. *So, Sol's all alone and doesn't know what the rest of us are doing. He must be confused ... and annoyed. Once everything is over, I'll make it up to him … somehow.*

She felt someone's eyes on her. Dhanos had left the room, but looking over to the couch, she saw Phantex Mason watching, his head tilted their way and his eyes open. "I'll be back in a moment," she said to the other two. She stood up and wandered to him, kneeling down. Only then did she see the extent of his injuries.

"Not a pretty sight, am I?" he said, noting her reaction. His voice was barely a croak.

She wondered how many of the cuts on his face would scar and felt sick. She pushed that feeling down and smiled. "Not really, but I've seen worse."

He smiled back.

"Can I get you anything?" she asked. "Do you need some water, or …?"

"What I need is arcannen, but in my current state, I'd be more hindrance than help to the others." He turned his head, looking at her a bit more closely. "I heard all of that. August is wrong not to take you. He needs as many people watching his back as possible, and you seem more than up for the task."

"He'll always see me as his little sister."

"Is that so surprising? So many people lost their parents to the Spirit Mage Wars, and their siblings are all they have left. If you went the same way as them and Ashe, I don't think August would forgive himself. Even though I disagree with him, I understand somewhat. I have a younger brother."

"So, you would let him fight?"

Phantex chuckled - an action that sounded painful for him. "Not at all, but you're a bit older than he is. And much more mature. Thankfully, he's safe at the moment. Taurus told me your uncle is looking after him."

"Then he'll be fine." She placed a hand on his arm. "I hope you're reunited with him, and soon."

Phantex turned his head, so he was facing the ceiling and closed his eyes. "The sooner this is all over, the better."

***

Rox Salvamal watched from the parapets of Holding Castle as the city raged below, a swarm of citizens shouting and screaming at the castle walls, his soldiers keeping them at bay with metal shields and the occasional blast of wind magic. The troubles might have started in Holding Square, but they'd spread from the heart of Holding like a disease, culminating at Magicom's stronghold and, from what he'd heard, every clinic in the city. Fires burned in the distance, filling the skyline with smoke and ash.

Despite the madness of the city, he would not lose his head; he would remain in control, even if inside, his rage for Ashes and August Silvershield burned like the fires themselves. And the people – they would learn there were consequences for their actions.

"You wanted to see me, General?"

Linus Atkins was walking the parapet, escorted by two of Salvamal's soldiers, his bronze arm reflecting the nearby torchlight, a long black woollen cloak reaching the top of his boots.

Salvamal nodded. "Thank you, soldiers. That will be all."

"Are you sure they're yours this time?" asked Atkins, watching them leave. For a brief moment, Salvamal wondered how much it would really matter if he threw Linus Atkins from the parapet onto the hard stone below.

Atkins seemed to know what he was thinking. Salvamal could tell from his arrogant face as it turned back to him. "Have you sent out for reinforcements?" Salvamal asked the official, fighting to keep his voice calm.

"Riders and birds have been dispatched. The city guard from Doscadia have been requested, as well as those from nearby towns. We've also asked Wing for help."

"Wing?" snarled Salvamal. "Are you trying to help us or Ashes?"

"Silvershield training at Wing doesn't mean Highstone Hill are on the side of Ashes. They have a large number of qualified mages; it would be foolish not to request them. Articulas Wing has already agreed and assures me they will help to bring peace to the city." Atkins stopped. "Remember, General, it is the government that has the final say on these matters."

For now. "I don't suppose you've had any word on where August Silvershield is?"

"They say he's like a ghost," said Atkins, turning to look over the parapets as if he was hoping to catch a glimpse of the Ashes leader below. "Appearing where the action is thickest and then disappearing just as quickly. I imagine your soldiers are having difficulty locating him."

"You sound as if you're in awe of him. That reverence won't last. He can't avoid my soldiers all night, and when he's caught, we'll execute him along with the other members of Ashes. The only question we now have to answer is how to punish the citizens of Holding for these riots."

Linus Atkins drummed his fingers on the stone wall. "You realise this has happened because those masked soldiers of yours attacked the crowd, General? What are they anyway? How, by the Trinity, can they use manabeast magic?"

Atkins asked the question as if it was neither here nor there to him, but Salvamal could tell by his sudden stillness that he desperately wanted to know the answer. Perhaps it was the only reason he'd risked coming through the crowd below to have this audience, even if Salvamal had afforded him the luxury and protection of one of his steam vans. Salvamal smiled. "It's something I've been working on for a while alongside Magicom's Technological Department and … interested third parties. I admit they weren't as ready as I thought; I can understand how people may have felt the need to defend themselves at Holding Square, but these riots that all happened afterwards. Law and order have broken down."

"You don't understand, Rox." Atkins was shaking his head now. "You talk about what happened as if it were some training exercise. People have lost their lives because of those soldiers. Including a government official."

Salvamal's patience was wearing thin. "More people are going to lose their lives, *Linus* unless this stops. Tomorrow, arcannen supply in the city will be suspended for a month. Perhaps you've forgotten, but there's a law against citizens using fire magic inside towns and cities, and my soldiers are constantly having to put out the flames alongside keeping the people at bay. If the people don't have magic, they cannot use it. I will require the government's support with this."

"And what about the people who rely on magic for protection or for their livelihoods? What of them?"

"That is the consequence of these riots. Will I have the government's support, or do I need to put someone in your place?"

The narrowing of Atkins' eyes showed Salvamal that his threat had hit its mark. "The government will support Magicom tomorrow," Atkins said in an emotionless voice.

"You are excused then, Mr Atkins."

The outrage in Atkins' eyes was clear to see this time. He gave a curt nod, which was more a jerk of his head than anything else, then stormed away, his long cloak billowing in his wake.

After he'd left, Salvamal's thoughts drifted to his hybrids and to the question that had plagued his mind most of the evening – why had they suddenly failed to follow orders? Wasn't the dukesbane compound supposed to keep them manageable? Whatever it was, the Technological Department would have to work around the clock to fix it. For now, they'd been rounded up and commanded to remain out of sight. At least they had followed *that* order.

Had he made a mistake using them so soon? He shook his head. Such thoughts were pointless. His primary aim was to make Magicom's army the strongest, not just in Blake but in the whole of the Six Isles. He would have to learn from what had happened and move on. He took a flask out of his pocket and drank deeply, appreciating the feeling of the brandy as it burned his throat. He had to deal with Silvershield. Tonight. If he didn't, the board might end up putting someone in *his* place.

Could he use the Mason boy? He'd expected another rescue attempt, but Silvershield was clearly in the midst of these riots and seemed uninterested in Alsing. Salvamal frowned – was it possible that Silvershield *hadn't* sent the boy to rescue his brother and so didn't know of his capture? Or had he simply accepted there was nothing he could do about it? Salvamal wasn't keen, with everything else going on, for the people or government to find out he was holding a child prisoner. But if it came down to it, he would have to send out word to ensure Silvershield found out. *Perhaps Silvershield might even trade himself.*

"Sir!"

Salvamal turned to find one of his soldiers hurrying to his position, wide-eyed and flushed. She handed him a note.

"What is this?" he asked, opening it.

"From Lieutenant Rookevelt, sir. He said it was urgent."

When Salvamal read what was inside, a surge of triumph rose in him. *Finally … I have you, Silvershield!*

"Ready me a steam van," he told his soldier, barely able to conceal his glee.

***

The noise from the city was muffled, but the fact they could hear it at all from underground told Pink how loud it must have been on the surface. Hundreds were apparently in conflict with Magicom soldiers at a nearby clinic, and every time an explosion resounded, it felt as if the very building shook.

"What are they trying to do, bring the clinic down?" asked Jase.

"That's exactly what they're trying to do," replied Dhanos Rain, looking up at the ceiling.

It had been hours since August and Taurus had left. Dhanos had found Bale some new clothes, and Pink thought he looked far less fragile in the trousers, shirt and cloak he was now wearing, the latter wrapped around him as he slept near Phantex on one of the couches. Pink had almost forgotten he'd been Gabriel's captive the day before; she supposed it was hardly surprising he needed more rest.

Dhanos offered to get them some food, which they gratefully accepted, leaving them alone with the two sleeping figures.

"I want to talk about … how I acted last night," said Jase unexpectedly once he had gone.

Pink started. "What – Jase, it's fine. We don't need to …"

"Please, I need you to hear this," said Jase, holding out his hands. "It's just … after Gabriel, and everything else that happened to us, I … I wasn't handling things very well."

"I've struggled as well, Jase," she said kindly, "we all have." *Is that why … Sol happened?* She shook her head; she wasn't going to reason through *that* with Jase.

Jase, thankfully, didn't seem to notice her sudden realisation. "I know it's been hard on everyone. But what I'm trying to say is … I realised that it wasn't you that I was unhappy with, or even Sol for that matter … it was myself. Sometimes I just feel so … useless." Jase took a deep shuddering breath, a wetness in his eyes appearing as he looked down. "You, Bale and Sol could have easily handled this contract without me."

"That's not true," said Pink, more firmly this time. "How would we have got Bale out of the mines if you hadn't been there?"

But Jase didn't look back up. Knowing nothing she would say would change his mind now that it had been made up, Pink contented herself with putting her hand over his. After a moment, he put his other hand on top, and there they stayed for a while, in silence.

Eventually, Dhanos rejoined them with the food. Seemingly grateful to have company, he asked them all sorts of questions about their lives as mages. Jase, perking up, answered most, which Pink was grateful for. She was too preoccupied thinking about what was going on in the city, and Sol, to contribute much herself.

As the hours passed, members of Ashes came in and out. When they appeared, they would relay information about where the attacks were the thickest or the rumoured location of the masked soldiers. One of those who came back frequently was a woman named Rush. Seemingly delighted to find out August had a sister, she was keen to converse with Pink especially, and so was the one they got most of the information from. The blue-haired Sapphire, who was often at her side, was far less talkative.

It was several hours after they'd arrived that Rush and Sapphire returned again, looking sweaty and dirty but happy.

"We've taken the nearest clinic," said Rush as they took clinking arcannen vials out from their cloak pockets and deposited them on one of the tables. "I have a feeling we'll need these in the coming weeks," she added with a grin.

"Where are you going next?" asked Dhanos.

"The Central Clinic. I heard August's there, leading the charge."

About an hour later, August came back himself. He was with Dwight Taurus and a scruffy-looking man called Dele. August stopped at the foot of the stairs while the other two proceeded further into the room, Dele to the table filled with arcannen, where Dhanos was sorting the potions into a wooden box, and Taurus to the back to check on Phantex.

"We took out the Central Clinic, but not before Magicom removed their arcannen via one of those steam vans," said August, taking off his hooded cloak. His hair looked matted with ash, and one side of his face was covered with dried-up blood, probably the result of the gash on his cheekbone. "Most of those protesting are at Holding Castle, but those who are serious are at the clinics. Bringing them all down would be a big blow to Magicom."

"What will people do for arcannen?" Pink asked.

August looked uncomfortable. "I've thought of that, but taking out the clinics has to take precedence. People can still protect themselves if they head into the wilderness. The weapon shops will do good business tomorrow."

From above, Pink heard the sound of the door opening again. August, who had turned in an almost lazy manner, suddenly tensed and drew a fireball into his hand.

"Who are you?" he demanded.

Pink couldn't see who it was but heard footsteps. Feeling a knot in her stomach, she got to her feet with Jase and a now-awake Bale beside her. Together they waited with their eyes on the stairwell.

"So you're all still here," Sol said as he reached its bottom. Pink, who had been ready to summon her own magic, dropped her hand to her side, her eyes widening. There seemed to be a mixture of emotions on Sol's face, but she could tell that none were good.

"Is this another of your friends, Sara?" said August, looking him over. Sol had acquired a cloak from somewhere, but his Wing uniform could still be seen underneath. August hadn't relinquished his fireball.

"Yes, but …" She stared at Sol. "How did you know we were here?"

"I know about everything," said Sol. He seemed agitated now, shuffling and running his hand up and down his arm. "I know this is an Ashes lair." He looked at August, and his face was full of contempt. "I know you're August Silvershield."

August's eyes narrowed.

Sol's eyes moved to Pink, and only a little of the

contempt faded. "I know you're his sister. I heard you and Bale talking earlier. I couldn't believe it, but when I followed you to the square and saw you three with him, I knew it to be true. I followed you here as well."

That was hours ago. Has he been outside all this time? Pink caught movement out of the corner of her eyes and saw Dele and Dhanos coming forward, fanning out around Sol. Sol's look hardened.

"Sol," Pink said his name gently before things could get out of hand. "I know how you feel about Ashes, but we've been through so much together. We're friends. We need to talk this through before you decide what you do and don't know."

"Friends!" Sol laughed. "Yeah, that's what I thought. Until I realised you had been Ashes all along. By the looks of it, all three of you have. Knowing my feelings, you must have all been laughing behind my back this entire time."

"It wasn't like that, Sol," said Bale quietly. "I only found out yesterday."

But Sol wasn't listening. He ran a hand down his face, looking quite deranged.

"I think Sara's right. You all need to have a talk together," said August, his voice taking on an understanding tone as he extinguished his flame. He waved down Dele and Dhanos, who reluctantly stopped where they were. *He knows what I'm doing.* August moved towards Sol. "You use this room. We'll move upstairs."

As August came closer, Sol bowed his head, and for a second, Pink thought they'd got through to him. But then his hand shot out of his pocket, and there was a flash of silver as he stabbed something into August's arm.

Taurus' wind magic blasted Sol against the wall.

"What is …?" said August, looking down at the syringe Sol had stabbed him with. Wearing a confused expression, he pulled it out before toppling to the ground, trying and failing to use a nearby table to keep him upright.

"August!" Pink ran to him, her heart hammering, panic gripping her like a vice. He'd fallen on his back, already unconscious. She knelt down and shook him.

"Some sort of sedative," Taurus muttered as he joined them, gently lifting August's head and opening his eyelids. He looked sideways at Pink. "He'll be okay." Taurus' eyes found Sol's crumpled form, and there was fury in them. "But we need to leave. Now."

"We can't leave, Taurus!" said Dele. "Not after everything we've achieved tonight!"

"With the amount of damage these riots have done to Magicom, we can count it as a win. You can stay if you want and continue the assault on the clinics, but it's imperative that Magicom don't get their hands on August. Who knows who that boy's told? We need to get August out of the city, and we need to vacate this place." He turned to Dhanos. "Sorry, Rain. I think you'd better close down until things become clearer."

"It's too late," said Sol, grimacing as he straightened his back against the wall. Taurus shot him another hard look. "Do you think I would find out Ashes' location and not ensure those inside were brought to justice? This whole building's surrounded."

Pink's and Taurus' eyes met, and she knew they were both thinking the same thing. *We need to get to the tunnels!* But before either could act, she heard the sound of the door swinging open from above again. Pink joined Taurus in standing over August protectively and readied her magic as the first Magicom soldiers charged into the space, led by a man with short silver hair.

Pink and Taurus conjured air shields as the soldiers shot blasts of air. Out of the corner of her eye, she could see Dele and Dhanos moving into action. Pink turned and opened her mouth to encourage Jase and Bale to head for the trapdoor, but that proved to be a mistake. Something blasted through her defences, sending her flying. The last thing she saw, as her vision clouded, was a blur of grey.

CHAPTER TWENTY-EIGHT

Pink sat on the hard, coverless bed of her cell with her palm turned upwards, attempting to summon her magic.

It was no surprise that she could not. She'd no recollection of her journey to the prison (due to the same reason she now had a painful lump on her forehead, to go with the gash at the back), but it was clear Magicom had either given her antimage, a potion that negated arcannen, or her own arcannen had run out. The lack of magic made her feel empty inside and powerless.

She placed her hands over her face and screamed in frustration.

I should have gone back to Wing and trusted August to look after himself, she thought, fighting back tears. As reckless as August could be, he'd never failed to outmanoeuvre Rox Salvamal and Magicom. That was until she had put herself into the equation. Then again, if not for Sol …

No, I won't think about him!

She bowed her head, wrapping her arms tightly around her midriff. It was cold in the cell, the air drifting in through a square opening in the wall above, where vertical metal bars cut off any chance of escape. Not that she'd be able to anyway. If she stood on the bed, she could see through the opening, and it was clear that her cell was located high up, likely at the very top of the building. Aside from the bed, there was only a toilet and sink. She rose and moved to the latter, turning on the tap. Trickling was probably the most appropriate word to describe the flow of water, but it was enough to (eventually) fill her hands and splash onto her face. As the water dripped back into the basin, she thought of Jase and Bale, who now would suffer the same fate as her. Would Magicom work out they weren't part of Ashes? Would they even care? If it was true that Salvamal wanted to shut down Wing, would the general use them all as an excuse?

A sudden shuffling from the opposite cell broke into these thoughts. She looked over curiously. The corridor between the two was lined with oil lamps, and through the light, she could see a small figure approach its bars.

"Are you okay?" came a child's voice. "I heard you scream, but … I wasn't sure if I should say anything."

Pink frowned. "I'm sorry about that. I thought I was alone." She stepped to her own bars and wrapped her hands around them, feeling the cold steel against her palms. *Magicom are imprisoning children now?* "I'm Pink. What's your name?" she asked kindly.

"Roeden. Wow, you're one of the magic-born! Did your parents name you Pink because of your hair? I saw them bring you in. Why were you arrested?"

Despite everything, Pink allowed herself a small smile. *This one likes to talk.* "Pink started as a nickname, but nearly everyone calls me that now," she replied. "I was arrested because of … association. What about you?"

"I'm in Ashes … or I was, anyway. I left to do things on my own."

Pink smiled again. *Obviously quite an imaginative child.* "And what were you trying to do on your own, Roeden, that resulted in your current predicament?"

"I was trying to free my brother, Phantex. I snuck into Alsing thanks to a special kind of powder that I … that

August gave to me. But when it ran out, I was caught. Do you know what's happened to my brother? They took him before he even knew I was here, and I'm worried about him."

The smile dropped from Pink's face. *Special kind of powder? Phantex?* But hadn't Phantex said his brother was with her uncle? "He was there when Magicom found us. He's likely back in a cell by now. I'm … sorry."

Roeden let out a soft moan. Pink felt a wave of sympathy as she watched him turn and walk to the corner of his cell, where he slumped to the ground.

"Roeden, listen …"

She stopped. She could hear approaching footsteps. Roeden's head turned towards the sound, and Pink took a step back, feeling a tightening in her chest. She knew what was coming; she remembered what Phantex had looked like after spending time in Alsing. The footsteps drew nearer until a figure stopped in front of her cell, a young man in a Magicom uniform whose face was cast in shadow. The figure turned to look at her before putting a key in the lock and opening the cell door. As he took a step inside, his features became clearer.

Sol.

Pink suddenly felt as if her legs might collapse beneath her.

"What are you doing here?" she said, her voice no more than a croak, the mixture of emotions she felt threatening to overwhelm her. She could see Roeden in the background, hands on the bars of his cell again.

"I've come to rescue you." Each word sounded like it had been picked carefully, despite the nervousness in Sol's voice. His eyes were pleading.

She could have asked him a thousand questions. But there was one that felt more important than any other.

"You're the very reason why I'm in here. Why should I trust you?"

"Pink, we don't have time for this. We have to be quick."

"Why are you helping me now?" she demanded, taking a step towards him, anger becoming the prominent emotion. "Wouldn't it have been easier to just, oh, I don't know, *not turn us in*?"

He licked his lips nervously, but when he spoke, it was with more confidence than before. "Look, I didn't know you and the others would be taken. I went to Rael Rookevelt to tell him about Salvamal's experiments and Ashes' location, and he assured me you and the others would be left alone. But they arrested you anyway. Afterwards, Lieutenant Rookevelt said it had been Salvamal's order, and he couldn't do anything about it. And on top of that, I … it's just … I didn't realise until after they took you how I felt. I … look, I've felt so bad …"

Pink couldn't use magic, so she punched him in the face. As hard as she could. Roeden gasped as Sol hit the floor, holding his bleeding nose, looking up at her with a pained expression. One that just made her angrier.

"*You* feel so bad!" she yelled at him. "You don't *look* so bad with your shiny new Magicom uniform! Thanks to you, they have August! Surely you know what they'll do to him!"

"Pink …" It wasn't Sol who spoke this time, but Roeden. Reluctantly, she looked from Sol to Roeden's cell. "I don't know what's going on, but this man *is* rescuing you."

"I know! I'm not going to blow this chance, it's just …" She looked back at Sol, who was cautiously climbing to his feet, watching her as he wiped the blood from his face. "I don't forgive you," she said, forcing her voice to become calmer.

Sol had the nerve to look hurt. "Fair enough. We'll talk about this later, but for now, we'd better leave." He took a deep breath. "Luckily, you've been taken to the political prisoner cells. I don't know why. Perhaps the lieutenant had a say in it. But the advantage for us is there's less security. If we can find a uniform and perhaps a cap to hide your hair, we might be able to walk you right out of here."

"What about him?" she asked, nodding her head towards Roeden.

"Releasing you is one thing, but another prisoner …"

"You will release him," said Pink. "That chain you're carrying has all the keys on it."

Sol must have seen something in her eyes because, after making a noise between impatience and disbelief, he walked back and unlocked the door to Roeden's cell.

"What about Phantex?" Roeden demanded as soon as he'd stepped out into the corridor.

Pink fixed him with what she hoped was a reassuring smile. "I haven't forgotten." She turned to Sol. "Your job is to get Roeden out of here."

Sol was aghast. "I can't pass him off as a soldier! He's about eight!"

"I'm ten!" said Roeden indignantly.

"You won't have to." Pink put a hand in her uniform, where she had the bit of folded paper August had given her. She assumed that she'd been searched for arcannen while she'd been unconscious, so she was thankful the paper hadn't been discovered. "This is Instructor Texeria's powder. Use it to get him out. He's used it before, haven't you, Roeden?"

Roeden nodded.

"Magicom must be on the lookout for that by now," said Sol, eyeing it with distrust.

"Maybe for someone sneaking *into* Alsing, but not for someone going *out*. It's the only way to get Roeden out of the building. I don't know what Magicom plan to do with him, but I won't allow someone so young to get caught up in all this."

"But …"

"You said you felt bad. This is the only way you can make up for what you've done." *I still won't forgive you, though.*

She didn't think he needed to know that part.

"And what do you plan to do?" he asked, suspicion evident in his eyes.

"I'm going to use your set of keys to get the others out. There's not enough powder for more than one person, so we'll lead an assault from within Alsing. With the element of surprise, it might just work. Of course, we'll need arcannen. I assume you have some?"

Sol had the look of someone who knew he was losing control of something. "All Magicom soldiers have a couple of vials within their uniforms."

"I'll take those." She held out her hand, thinking of how many of them there were, as a reluctant-looking Sol passed the potions over. *Me, August, Dhanos, Dele, Jase and Bale.* "We'll have enough for what's needed," she said, unstopping one of the vials and drinking about a third before placing them both in the pocket of her uniform, relief filling her as she felt the arcannen work its way around her body. "You said they're underground? How do I get to them?"

Sol let out a bark of laughter. "Not easily."

She stared at him until he shrugged his shoulders. "There might be a way you can get to them without being caught. Most of the soldiers in the building patrol the corridors where the cells are. However, we're on the fourth floor. If we take the stairwell to the ground floor, there's a route that takes you through the central garden. You'll bypass the cells that way, so you'll have less chance of being seen. What you'll do when you get underground, though …"

"And how do I know where I'm going?"

"Pink … are you sure about this? If you're caught, I won't be able to save you a second time."

She gave him a withering look. "I don't need you to save me. Answer the question."

Sol let out an exaggerated sigh. "There's a yellow line painted on the wall when we get to the ground floor, which leads to the underground cells."

"Fine. We have a plan." She stopped. Roeden was staring at her strangely. "What is it?" she asked, not unkindly.

"Nothing." He merely shook his head. "It's just … you and August are a lot alike."

***

Roeden made sure to keep up with Pink and Sol as they followed the red line that ran along the white-painted walls, their footsteps echoing throughout the corridor until they reached the stairwell at its end. Several flights of stairs later, they found themselves in a square space on the ground floor. Two corridors ran in two directions, one where the red line continued and another where a yellow one started.

Taking a deep breath, Pink clapped Roeden on the shoulder, gave him a reassuring smile, and jogged down the corridor with the yellow line, ignoring Sol completely.

Roeden watched her go, disappointed. He'd have preferred to stay with Pink and help free Phantex and August, but deep down, he knew he'd only get in the way, especially as giving him more arcannen would be a waste – the arcannen he had taken earlier had been negated by a disgusting pale-blue potion forced upon him by a Magicom soldier. He looked to Sol, who was watching Pink leave, his expression one of regret. Sol seemed to notice and turned his attention towards Roeden.

"Well, I suppose you'd better use that powder," he said.

Roeden let out a breath. For the briefest moment, he had thought that Sol might turn him in. He *was* a Magicom soldier, after all.

Sol's grumpiness seemed to vanish as Roeden became invisible. "He would have been useful to have around at the moment," he muttered.

"Who?" Roeden asked.

"Never mind. Come on, let's get this over with."

Sol led Roeden through the other corridor and they made their way through the complex. They never directly ran into any soldiers but twice saw patrols in intersecting corridors. Sol nodded greetings as they passed, and Roeden, despite knowing it wouldn't make a difference, kept his head down. The closest they came to another human was the warden working at the front desk. He glanced up as they passed, but Sol moved his body, so it was in the way of Roeden's shimmering form while his footsteps hid the sound of Roeden's own.

The cold night air hit them as they departed the building. Roeden felt glad it had stopped raining and that there were apparently fewer soldiers than before in the courtyard, the only ones Roeden could see were by the gate or on the walkway above. Roeden guessed the others were out in the city streets. As they neared the gate, Roeden noticed it was open and, on the street side, a man was arguing, occupying the soldiers' attention.

"It's imperative I see General Salvamal tonight!"

"No one in or out, not even reporters, that's the general's orders."

The man continued to argue, only sparing Sol a glance as Sol and Roeden passed through the open gate and onto the street. When they were far enough away, at a point where they could no longer be seen nor heard by the soldiers, Roeden pulled Sol's sleeve and said,

"I need to speak to that man."

"Who? The reporter? Do you know him?"

Roeden nodded. "He might be able to help us. Can you bring him here?"

Roeden thought Sol would say no – he certainly looked like he wanted to. But he gave an exaggerated shrug and walked back to the prison. A couple of minutes later, he returned with the man in tow. As the black powder began to wear away, Roeden could see the man's eyes widening.

"Roeden, you're safe!" Chadwick ran to him and placed his hands on Roeden's shoulders. He wore a look of joy and bewilderment. "The black powder! Did you use that to escape? I've been trying to get into Alsing to get you out!"

Roeden stared up at him. "Didn't seem like that was going well."

"Well, I'm … I'm not the one with the plans. That's August! Speaking of which, is it true Salvamal has him?"

Roeden nodded. "But Pink's going to get him out."

"Pink? Who's that?"

"One of the magic-born. His sister." Roeden quickly recounted everything to Chadwick. "We've got to do something," said Roeden when he'd finished. "Chadwick, we have to help them!"

Chadwick looked over his shoulder in the direction of the prison. "I'm sorry, Roeden, but what can we do? It's nothing short of incredible that you got in *and* out of the prison, even with the help of this man." He spared a quick glance at Sol, who was watching their exchange in obvious confusion. "But I think you've used up your surprises. Even if we could get in, what exactly could the two of us do against all those Magicom soldiers?"

Roeden looked to Sol, eyes imploring.

"I'm sorry," said Sol, answering the unasked question. He wore the same expression of regret as earlier. "I tried to help Pink, but she's made her choice, and I've made mine." He sighed and looked towards the prison. "It's all down to her now."

CHAPTER TWENTY-NINE

Pink followed the yellow line that ran along the walls of Alsing, ignoring both the pain within her skull and the deep exhaustion threatening to overwhelm her. Stopping was out of the question. The only way her brother, friends and the rest of Ashes could escape was if they were released from their cells and supplied with magic, and the only one who could do that was her. Had it been just her and August, breaking out would have been unlikely, but because Magicom had arrested so many of them …

Her mind went to Sol then. Did he really expect she would just forgive him? Even if he had thought he'd struck a deal to ensure her, Jase and Bale's safety, he'd led Magicom to *her* brother, knowing exactly what they would do to him.

I can't think about that right now; I need to focus.

Eventually, she found herself in front of a wooden door with a cast metal sign above, reading 'Garden' in black, bold letters. Pushing through, she found herself in an internal courtyard, breathing in the fresh night air. The grass was neatly cut, and wooden benches sat underneath tall lampposts, orbs of light hanging from their tips. She guessed it was an area where the staff took their breaks and praised her good fortune that none were currently there. Directly in front of her, another door led back into the building, where the yellow line likely continued. *I must be close.* She moved forward, but at that moment, the door opened, and a line of masked Magicom soldiers strode through.

There was nowhere to hide. She froze, and so did they, but then they were encircling her, their yellow eyes luminous and feral. She took a step back.

"I'm on orders from the general," she said, fighting to keep her voice from shaking. *So this is where Salvamal's been keeping them. How much like the townsfolk are they? Can I fool them?* "Don't let me keep you."

For one long moment, they did nothing. Then the one in front, a man with a shock of blond hair, let out a callous laugh.

"Silvershield," he said in a hoarse voice.

He put out his arms, and the others followed. Pink's eyes widened in alarm, and she dived out of the way as a number of energy beams struck where she'd just been, exploding the dirt into the air, the smell of earth and smoke mingling together.

She didn't let herself think. She simply moved – running to the side of the garden and shooting fireballs as she went, her training kicking in as she rolled to avoid more energy beams, regaining her feet quickly and turning to face her attackers. Pink didn't think for a moment she could win, at least not in any conventional sense. She would have to try something drastic to survive long enough to escape, to free August and the others. Making a quick decision, she summoned the earth from underneath their feet, *pulling* it towards her as their arms extended again, causing it to explode upwards.

Earth magic was hard to control, and she stumbled as she released it, the force pulling her forwards. It had been a risk, she could have easily buried herself alive, but it had done the job – with the amount of earth in the air, she could now barely see a few feet in front of her. She used her sleeve to cover her mouth and tried to orientate herself. It was at this point she realised she was in front of a door. Not the one she'd been heading towards, but a smaller one on the side of the courtyard. Her eyes bulged. Had sheer luck brought her to an escape route? She turned the handle and pushed through into the corridor beyond.

She had barely got inside before she ran head-on into someone who grabbed her by the shoulders.

She looked up into the furious eyes of Rox Salvamal.

CHAPTER THIRTY

At swordpoint, Pink was taken to a nearby room and forced to drink a vial of antimage, cutting her off from the elements. Again. The room was long but bare, with oil lamps lining the wall opposite the windows and a carpeted floor. She noticed little else, her mind too fraught with distress to pay attention to such extraneous details.

She should have been more prepared. Of course, others would investigate the commotion coming from outside. But she had not had time to ready her magic before Salvamal had drawn his sword and held it to her neck. The general had been flanked by two soldiers, and they'd been ordered to take over while Salvamal dealt with their masked counterparts, who'd followed Pink into the building. The masked soldiers followed his command to stand down, but Pink had glanced back, and something she saw in their eyes told her Salvamal's control over them was fragile at best.

She squeezed her eyes shut. *I was so close. How are we going to escape now? August …*

It felt as if her heart was being torn to shreds.

Eventually, Rox Salvamal stepped into the room, followed by five of his masked soldiers. Pink wasn't sure what was more horrifying, the bestial behaviour of the Poulsen townsfolk or these eerie but intelligent syntaxicite-clad soldiers. Salvamal, barely offering her more than a glance, looked at one of the masked soldiers and nodded at Pink. If Salvamal recognised her as one of the mages he'd met in Katton, he showed no sign of it. The soldier, the man with the shock of blond hair, grabbed her roughly by the arm from the maskless soldiers – who moved quickly away – and held her tightly. He smelled of sweat and dirt.

And then more of the masked soldiers brought August in.

He was unconscious still, his hair plastered against his forehead and his cloak gone. They dragged him by the arms alongside Pink and sat him down, slumped on a chair. Salvamal stood in a position where both siblings faced him.

"August," she whispered. No response. She looked at Salvamal. Never before in her life had she felt such hatred. "You're evil," she spat at the general.

Salvamal didn't bother to reply. He was staring at August, a sneer curling his lip.

"Leave us," Salvamal said to the maskless soldiers, who had gathered together in the centre of the room. They looked at one another in confusion but did as their general asked.

Salvamal raised a hand towards August. Pink cried out, but the general only conjured a ball of water, projecting it onto her brother's face.

"Wake up," the general demanded as August spluttered and coughed, breathing in a lungful of air. "I want you conscious for this."

After a few moments, August looked up at Salvamal, his hair still dripping liquid. There was no fear in his expression – at least, there wasn't until he noticed Pink in the room with him. His eyes met hers and widened.

"I'm not taking any more risks," said Salvamal. August looked back at the general, his expression now one of rage. "You don't have any arcannen left in your body, but if you try to escape any other way, Commander Maynard here will blast a hole in your sister's pretty head." Pink felt pressure against the side of her skull as the man called Maynard placed his palm on her. "Is that understood?"

"Yes," said August at once. Despite the look in his eyes, his tone was one of resignation.

Don't give up, August. How many situations like this have you got out of before? There must be a way.

But she couldn't see it.

"You will be executed," Salvamal said, "right here in this room."

"No!" Pink screamed, trying to struggle from Maynard's grip. But Maynard was strong and held her in place.

"Sara," said August gently. He took his eyes from Salvamal and looked at her, pleading. "Please."

"Good, you understand," said Salvamal with satisfaction. "I have no reason to execute your sister. Nor the other two from Wing. In fact, it would cause problems for me if I did, with Master Wing in the city. But I will if I have to."

"This is the only way now," said August, continuing to look at Pink. He gave her a sad smile. "Despite who he is, what he says is true. Killing you gains them very little. I can accept my death if I know it ensures your life."

"But August …" Pink was sobbing harder than ever. "*No.*" She didn't know what else to say.

"However, your Ashes ringleaders will have to suffer your fate," continued Salvamal. August turned back to Salvamal sharply. "I can't have another uprising. Your followers who weren't in your little hideout will forever be attempting rescues. One by one, those you were arrested with will be brought into this room and quietly disposed of." August stared at Salvamal in horror. He twitched, a movement Salvamal did not miss. "Remember what will happen to Sara here if you try to resist. They might not be as easily controlled as you with the threat to your sister's life; therefore, I suggest you don't tell them. It would be kinder not to, in fact." A strange look came over Salvamal's face. "I didn't want to do this," he said, "but you have forced my hand. That's why you will watch with me and share the responsibility. I will not execute you first and allow you to escape your sins. Only when the deed is done will you be allowed to follow those who blindly followed you."

Salvamal had barely finished speaking when two other masked soldiers entered the room, escorting Dele between them. The hat Dele had been wearing earlier was gone, and his hair was as plastered against his scalp as August's was. Dele looked at August questioningly.

August paled. "Dele," he said, seeming to struggle for words. "I'm so sorry," he whispered at last.

Dele continued to look at him in confusion, even when he was pushed into the centre of the room and forced to kneel. "What's going on?"

"Now," said Salvamal to one of the soldiers holding him.

Pink shut her eyes. She heard a fizzing sound, a cry (she didn't know if it was her, August or Dele) and then a thud. When she opened them, Dele was slumped on the ground, a pool of blood around him. The side of his head was a mess, fingers of smoke rising from it.

August screamed in rage while Pink felt bile rise up in her throat. Making a conscious effort not to be sick, she tried to make eye contact with August, but his eyes were screwed shut. After a moment, Dele's body was dragged from the room, a trail of blood following in its wake.

This isn't happening … this isn't happening …

Minutes later, those who'd taken Dele's body returned with Dwight Taurus in tow. The big man seemed to understand what was happening at once, just from looking at August's bowed form. Taurus took in the number of soldiers in the room with a resigned look. "It's okay, August," he said. Her brother raised his head and looked at Taurus with eyes full of pain. Taurus took another glance around the room. "So, this is how you're keeping August from killing you all," he said, not the slightest bit of fear in his voice. "He could, you know. Manabeast magic or not. Cowards, every last one of you, right until the end." He looked at Salvamal, who was gritting his teeth, his expression contemptuous. "You're the worst of the lot, General. But remember this – there will always be people like us who stop people like you." He got on his knees of his own accord. "Close your eyes, Sara," he said, speaking gently as he turned to her.

It was the dukesbane site all over again, but this time there would be no Keat Texeria to save them. *Why is this happening? How can one man be so evil?* She complied with Taurus' final request, screwing her eyes shut, unable to control her sobs. That was when she felt the hard vials of arcannen in her pocket, the ones she'd demanded from Sol. Was there some way to get one to August? If she moved quickly enough, could she pass him a vial in the confusion? Likely, Maynard would use his magic on her, and that would be the end. But it would be worth the risk. Her life for his – he was prepared to die for her, she could do the same for him. She readied herself to move.

"That's enough," came a new voice.

Pink snapped open her eyes. Entering the room was

the silver-haired Magicom officer who'd led the attack at the Flame, followed by half a dozen soldiers. A man and a woman wearing grey suits entered next, and then …

"Master Wing!" she gasped.

The master, towering over nearly everyone there, gave her a small smile but waved his hands downwards as if warning her to stay quiet.

Salvamal frowned at the officer. "What's the meaning of this, Lieutenant Rookevelt? Why are you with these people?"

Rookevelt held out his hand. One of the new soldiers produced a scroll and handed it to him. "These are orders for your removal, Rox," Rookevelt responded calmly as he unravelled it, and his eyes moved downwards to read the scroll. "The board have decreed they are stripping you of your title due to gross negligence and the unauthorised experimentation on our soldiers. These men and women are no longer under your command."

Salvamal looked like he'd been hit with a brick. "Seize him!" he shouted at the masked soldiers. This caused sudden movement in the room. The soldiers who'd come with Rookevelt pushed their arms out, and the two well-dressed individuals took a step back. Among the newcomers, Master Wing alone seemed unmoved.

Pink looked at the masked soldiers to see what they would do. It was impossible to read their expressions, but they did not follow Salvamal's orders. In fact, was it her imagination, or did Maynard now hold her in a loosened grip?

"They understand, I think, that it's over for you," said Rookevelt. "You have done a good job on them. They follow Magicom orders, and you are no longer Magicom."

"You have overreached yourself, Rox," said the well-dressed man. As he stepped forward, Pink noticed he had an arm made from bronze. "Did you think the government would stand for the death of one of their own?"

"The government stands for what Magicom tells it to stand for," sneered Salvamal. "You will all pay for this."

"Magicom no longer wants any part in this," said the lady in a velvety-smooth voice. Pink glanced at August, but he was staring at the woman. She'd never seen him look so relieved. "You have risked everything on their behalf, burned too many bridges in your attempt to get to August Silvershield."

Salvamal screamed and threw out his arms. Whom he was planning to strike, Pink didn't find out. Salvamal was blasted from every direction with wind magic before he had a chance to use any magic of his own.

***

What happened next was a blur to Pink. Rox Salvamal, now unconscious, was removed from the room, along with Dwight Taurus, while the masked soldiers were ordered out. Master Wing remained, speaking in hushed voices with the three he'd arrived with, but Pink didn't take any of it in. She had moved at once to August, ignoring the soreness in her arm where Maynard had held her and knelt beside him. All he could seem to do was stare at the bloodstained carpet where Dele had been lying until she took his hand and squeezed. Only then did he break out of the trance and squeeze back, giving her a small smile.

Eventually, Master Wing dragged two chairs towards them, one for Pink and one for himself. As she took a seat, she noticed that, aside from two Magicom soldiers standing guard at the door, only the three of them remained.

"It's been a while, Master," August said, speaking for the first time.

Master Wing's look was sardonic as he took his own seat, wrapping his cloak more tightly around himself. Pink noticed his eyes shift to the guards at the door. "August, the next couple of hours are going to be vital," he said in a low voice.

"What will happen now Salvamal's gone?" Pink asked.

"Nothing fatal if we play things right," said Master Wing. Sudden hope rose in Pink. She spun her head to look at August, but he hadn't reacted. He just continued to stare at the Master. "Strangely, Rox Salvamal has given you both a lifeline," Master Wing continued. "These hybrid soldiers … the Magicom board weren't prepared for the backlash they've caused and are now trying to distance themselves from them."

"And how do you know this?" August asked.

"I've been to see them – along with Linus Atkins, Verity Ravenscar and Rael Rookevelt."

"You've always been good at politics," said August. Pink knitted her brow. She could detect a hint of contempt in August's voice.

"Think of them as peace talks," said Master Wing, who seemed to have noticed the same thing. "I didn't mentor you to see you die in this room, August."

"When we spoke before, it sounded like you couldn't do much to help August," said Pink quietly.

Master Wing let out a long breath. "When we spoke before, Sara, Salvamal hadn't let loose his masked soldiers on the people of Holding, nor had a government official been killed. And, thanks to the information you gave me about Gabriel's involvement, I was able to locate someone who was hiding in the city, someone involved in the original experiments."

Pink's mind worked quickly. "Miriam Shawgrave!"

"She confessed to everything she'd done under Salvamal's orders in front of Atkins and Ravenscar. I think that, along with Rael Rookevelt speaking out against him, made Magicom's board realise they had to cut ties with their general. As for these riots, they've been left with two choices: crush their opposition or soothe tensions. Which will cost them less, both in terms of coin and resources?"

"Based on the fact I'm still in this room, talking to you, they want something from me, don't they, Master?" said August.

"They want Ashes gone. But they don't know how many of you may still be roaming free. They realised that if they execute you, another could stand in your place and use your death as a rallying call to increase their numbers. At least, this is what I've told them might happen. Ravenscar suggested that if you can be made to recall your remaining members and use your status to call for an end to the riots in exchange for your freedom, further damage might be avoided. This is something Salvamal would never have accepted, but the board think differently." He took a deep breath. "As an added measure, they want you to sign a contract that confirms you will do these things and that you will not, from this point on, steal arcannen from Magicom clinics. They know you could break this contract once you're out of the city, but as you would have already helped them to achieve their goal, they're happy to take this risk."

"So basically, Magicom want to give the impression we're working together?"

Master Wing's look softened. "I'm sorry, August. But it's the only way."

"And what if I refuse?"

"Look at the situation. Magicom have you, your followers and your sister all within the walls of Alsing. You have no magic. There's only so much I can do for you. The only way you and those you love get out of here is if you sign this contract."

"August, please," said Pink.

August said nothing.

Master Wing continued to stare at him. "You do her memory no harm by surviving to fight another day."

"It looks like I have no choice," said August, at last, bitterly. "But I want Sara and her friends allowed out first. They're not part of Ashes, nor are they adults. Make Magicom agree to *that*, Master."

Master Wing nodded, looking relieved. "I'll see what I can do."

"Master Wing," said Pink, an idea coming to her. She nodded to a table where a water jug and glasses lay. "Can you pour August some water?"

Master Wing looked surprised but complied.

"What are you doing?" muttered August.

"I'll take it," said Pink, accepting the glass from Master Wing. "Master … if you could stay standing there a moment," she added quietly. *Thank the Trinity for the size of his shoulders.* "And … um … perhaps close your eyes."

She pulled out the arcannen vial from within her uniform, uncorked it and poured its contents into the water, which August, eyes wide, took and drank hurriedly. She replaced the vial, and August handed back the glass to Master Wing, who looked a mixture between exasperated and amused.

"Just in case there are any complications," said Pink.

***

The sky was lightening, hues of purple and blue signalling the coming dawn, when August and his companions were let out of Alsing.

Hair lank and face bloodied, August fought to keep his head held high as he trudged the length of the courtyard with his companions, enclosed by Magicom soldiers who matched their steps, Rael Rookevelt at their point.

Taurus walked at his side while Dhanos supported Phantex from a little further back. In his mind, the ghost of Dele walked with them, an invisible reminder of Magicom's crimes. Salvamal might have ordered Dele's murder, but the former general was just a byproduct of a corrupt organisation, and August would never forget it. He glanced behind at Master Wing, strolling with Verity Ravenscar and Linus Atkins outside the ring of soldiers, towering over everyone. Despite August's unease with the agreement that he had been forced into, the master had tried to protect them, and for that, he was grateful. Still, he would wait until they were all safely out of the city before he believed Magicom would let him and the others go.

"Phantex!"

August frowned. *I recognise that voice. Surely … it can't be …?* He looked ahead and saw, to his amazement, Roeden run from the open gates of Alsing towards them. Even more amazingly, he spotted Chadwick waiting anxiously just outside, standing with Sara and her friends.

The Magicom soldiers stopped and tensed as Roeden neared, but Rookevelt made a downward movement with his hand. Roeden broke into the group and ran into Phantex, hugging him tightly.

August allowed himself a small smile before moving forward to Rookevelt. "I want to speak to my sister privately," he said.

Rookevelt gave him a sideways glance and nodded.

"I wish you had left the city straight away like I asked you," said August as she entered the courtyard and gave him a hug. Her friends followed her. They all looked dead on their feet. August nodded at Chadwick, whose returning smile seemed just a bit forced. August didn't know what he was doing there but guessed it had something to do with Roeden.

"I'm not one of your followers to order around," replied Sara simply. "What happened?"

"I signed their contract."

"So … no more Ashes?"

"This is temporary," said August, careful to keep his voice low, for there were guards standing at the gates. "It was the only way I could keep everyone safe." He took a deep breath. "I will keep my word – I will no longer steal from the clinics. But I will never stop until Magicom are brought to justice. There are, however, other ways to deal with them." He briefly glanced at Verity Ravenscar and Linus Atkins. "And they've already begun."

"A steam van should be arriving shortly," came Rookevelt's curt voice as he joined them. "Are you ready?"

"What's going to happen with these masked soldiers?" Sara asked Rookevelt.

Rookevelt looked surprised at the question. "They are Magicom. Our Technological Department will deal with them. If there's any way to … reverse what was done, then that's what we'll do." He must have noticed August's sceptical reaction because he added, "Don't think I do not value the lives of those men and women, Silvershield. They're the very reason why I helped convince the board that Salvamal needed to be removed."

"So you've won," came a sneering voice. August

turned to see Rox Salvamal being led out of Alsing, a soldier holding his arm from either side.

"This was never about us, Salvamal," replied August as the former general stopped before him, and Rookevelt moved away to speak to one of the guards. Salvamal's weapon had been taken, and August guessed he'd been given antimage. He was no longer a threat. "This was about putting an end to an organisation that for too long has done what it likes, committed countless atrocities, and remained protected by the power it held by controlling arcannen."

"You think Magicom are finished?" snarled Salvamal. "You think the board weren't aware of my actions? Already, they're protecting themselves by using me as a shield. Where do you think I'm going now? No doubt they'll make me sign a contract like the one you've obviously been given, ensuring I take all the blame. Eventually, though, someone will take my place and continue the work I started."

"Goodbye, Salvamal," said August, turning away, unwilling to look at his pitiful state any longer. It did not bring him the satisfaction he'd thought it would.

"Goodbye, Silvershield."

"August!" Sara suddenly cried in warning. Salvamal had momentarily broken free of his guards and pulled a sword from one, lunging at August with the blade pointed.

It was Jase, of all people, who reacted quickest. While August was still staring, he barrelled into the former general, knocking him off course. Salvamal, screaming in rage, grabbed Sara's friend by the collar and threw him into his guards before lunging at August again. But this time August was ready. Summoning water and freezing it to ice, with one hand, he caught Salvamal's arm, and with the other, he thrust the jagged crystal he'd formed into the former general's chest.

Salvamal staggered back, his eyes a mixture of shock and rage as he tumbled backwards, blood pooling from around the protruding shard in his chest. Then there was chaos. Magicom soldiers were running towards them from their position in the courtyard, Taurus was shouting, and Rookevelt was calling for a medic. *Salvamal was no longer a threat? I was wrong … so wrong.* August met Sara's widened eyes. *What's going to happen now?*

He looked down at the former general, ready to curse him, but Salvamal's eyes were open and unseeing.

CHAPTER THIRTY-ONE

MAGICOM SAVES CITY

Reported by Chadwick Chase

The city of Holding is still reeling from scenes at week's end where civil unrest, led by the group known as Ashes, caused unprecedented damage to its infrastructure and injury to its citizens. Magicom, whose soldiers were able to bring order back to the city, have today offered to help the Blakian Government with the cost of repairs, despite the damage done to their clinics. "We hope this gesture of goodwill will help remind the people of Holding that where there is strife, Magicom – as its city watch – will respond with law and order," said Rael Rookevelt, 48. The lieutenant is widely reported to be in the running for the company's vacant military general position following Rox Salvamal's tragic death during the riots. Meanwhile, the whereabouts of August Silvershield, infamous leader of Ashes, remain unknown.

Pink finished reading the front page of *Severity News* and handed it to Jase, not able to stomach any more of the story, which ran on for several pages. She sighed, trying instead to bask in the warmth of the day and admire the view from atop Highstone Hill. After how it had almost all been taken away, she felt as if she should appreciate the simplicity of the rolling hills and clear, blue sky.

"What do you think?" asked Bale. He and Jase were both watching her keenly from either side of the bench they were sitting on.

"What do I think? I think Magicom have done their usual job of controlling the narrative. But it doesn't tell us anything about August. He could be missing because Magicom kept their word and allowed him to leave the city, or …"

She didn't need to say more. Jase and Bale had both heard her fears enough over the last couple of days.

Despite Salvamal's death, the fragile truce that Ashes, the government and Magicom had established in Holding had remained intact, and August had called back the few remaining members of Ashes, doing his part in talking to and calming the crowds. Pink wondered if Salvamal's death had actually done Magicom a favour. *It's easier to blame everything on a dead man.* But, following Master Wing's orders, the three of them had returned to Highstone Hill whilst this was still going on, and she had heard nothing since. Surely August would have sent a letter to let her know he was safe? She had received one from Roeden, letting her know he had arrived in Sermouth safely with his family. His mother had also written a few lines expressing her gratitude, the memory of which made Pink smile, despite her current anxiety. She had only known Roeden briefly, but she had liked him. She was glad he was safe.

"That reporter, Chadwick, was with Roeden that night." Bale looked thoughtful. "Yet this article is very pro-Magicom."

"He was clearly helping Roeden," said Jase. "I think things are more complicated than that."

Like with Sol. The thought came at once, unbidden, like many she'd had about him over the last couple of days. She'd been training her mind not to think of him – or at least trying to; it was difficult when the majority of Highstone Hill was talking about Magicom paying off his training so he could join their ranks. She supposed she shouldn't be surprised; such a thing had never happened before.

She'd seen him one last time after he'd freed her and Roeden. He'd been one of the soldiers who'd escorted August and the others from Alsing. They had locked eyes, but she'd turned away and hadn't looked back in his direction. He had made his choice, and she had made hers.

Her thoughts were interrupted by the door of East House opening and Victorian calling them in. They stepped inside, finding the sitting room empty aside from the orange-haired instructor. Pink half-expected to find her lounging in the armchair, like when she and Jase had gone to see her a million years ago, but Victorian stood waiting for them with her hands behind her back, fully dressed in her Wing uniform.

"Instructor Dex," greeted Pink.

Victorian smiled, creases appearing at her eyes. "Still refusing to call me Victorian, I see. You'll never change, Pink. How are you all? Perola discharged you this morning, didn't he?"

"Healer Perola insisted on keeping us there for two whole days," said Pink, "but we're fine."

"He *is* a rather neurotic man." Victorian's eyes twinkled. She waved her hand towards the sofa. "I have a message from Master Wing," she said once they had sat. "He wishes you all the best, and he's … very sorry for everything that happened."

"Did he say anything about August?" Despite blurting out the question, Pink no longer had the capacity to feel embarrassed with Victorian. Her concern for August's wellbeing didn't allow for anything else.

Victorian's look was sympathetic. "I'm afraid not."

Pink, who had been hoping Victorian had sent for them because she had news of August, sank into the sofa.

"I'm sure he's fine, Pink," said Jase. He placed a hand on her arm. "If Magicom had done something to him, I think they'd proclaim it far and wide."

"Salvamal might have," said Pink bitterly, "but perhaps Magicom's board decided a quieter approach would be best."

"I won't tell you not to fear the worst," said Victorian, drawing her attention back, "but from what you told me when you first returned, it seems like your brother has allies in the city. I suspect they would ensure Magicom kept their word."

Pink nodded, and Victorian continued to watch her. "You know, it's still strange to me that August Silvershield is your brother. I remember him from my days as a newly-qualified mage – he and Keat Texeria were always together. And I remember Ashe as well. Ashes … I suppose it all makes sense now."

Pink nodded but didn't say anything. She did notice, however, that Victorian looked as if she wanted to say something more.

"What is it?" asked Pink.

"There was something else in Master Wing's letter.

He's … made me the new assistant master."

"That's amazing!" Pink offered Victorian a smile. "Congratulations!"

Victorian smiled in return, and Bale and Jase spoke their own words of congratulations. "I'm not the most experienced of the instructors," said Victorian, "so I have to admit it came as a bit of a surprise."

"I can't pretend to know Master Wing's reasons," said Bale, "but after Gabriel, I imagine he wanted someone he could trust. After you came to our aid at the coal mines … he knows you'd do anything for Wing trainees and mages."

Victorian appeared speechless while Pink and Jase stared at Bale.

"You're getting more talkative," said Jase weakly.

"Which means Instructor Texeria can continue to mentor you for your three years of service," said Victorian, finding her voice again.

"Instructor Texeria's still at Wing?" said Pink, surprised and momentarily forgetting her anxiousness. "I thought he'd left. He hasn't been to see us."

"He's been cooped up in that storage room for the last couple of days." Victorian looked suddenly worried. "You don't think he minds that we locked him up until we could verify his story? When he came back with news of Gabriel's death …"

"I don't think he minds," said Pink. "He was prepared for it when he left us. He's probably got some new project. I suppose that's why he hasn't visited." She looked at Victorian. "Are you happy for him to continue being my mentor? I mean, I know you requested me …"

"I think it would be foolish for you to change now. Especially after all you've been through together. I can still support you as assistant master."

"Thank you, Assistant Master Dex … Victorian … truly." Pink stood up, and Jase and Bale followed. "Anyway, I think if Instructor Texeria won't come to us, we'll go to him."

Victorian inclined her head, and Pink led the others into the attached corridor and familiar space of the storage room. It was barer than it had been. There were still piles of crates, but the armadillo-types' glass cage was empty, and the wolf-type's gone. Keat Texeria was there, though. He was perched over at his desk, looking at something under the lens of a magnifying glass that had been set up on a stand.

"Instructor," said Pink.

Texeria turned and smiled. "It's about time," he drawled as he rose.

"Didn't fancy visiting us in the infirmary?" asked Pink shrewdly. "Thought you were going to get accused of something again?"

"That's all in the past," he said with a wave of his hand. "I knew you were all safe. I haven't visited because I have a surprise for you. And we wanted you to be rested first. We knew you would come here when you were ready."

"Sounds like an excuse," muttered Jase.

But Bale had noticed what Pink had. "We?" he asked. "Who do you mean?" He thought for a moment. "Ratchette?"

But someone else came to Pink's mind. *By the Trinity, I'm going to kill him.*

Footsteps resounded from somewhere in the room before August appeared from behind one row of crates, grinning. He was dressed in his usual black syntaxicite and cloak, looking much cleaner and healthier than the last time she'd seen him.

"Hello, Sara," he said.

ABOUT THE AUTHOR

Adam Joseph was born in Brighton in 1987. In 2023, he published *Magicom*, his debut novel. He currently lives in Exeter and works as a primary school teacher.

For writing news and updates please join my free newsletter, found at:
www.adamjosephauthor.com

Printed in Poland
by Amazon Fulfillment
Poland Sp. z o.o., Wrocław
23 April 2023

02e0af64-62df-4293-bb11-27629b68a12fR01